THE CURVY GIRLS CLUB

Michele Gorman is the Number One Best-Selling author of *The Expat Diaries* series and *Bella Summer Takes a Chance*. She has also written upmarket commercial fiction under the pen name Jamie Scott.

Born and raised in the US, Michele has lived in London for sixteen years. You can find out more about Michele by following her on twitter, Facebook, Pinterest, Goodreads, or by reading her blog or website. Do chat with her on twitter or facebook – she's always looking for an excuse to procrastinate!

MICHELE GORMAN

The Curvy Girls Club

AVON

This novel is entirely a work of fiction.
The names, characters and incidents portrayed in it are
the work of the author's imagination. Any resemblance to
actual persons, living or dead, events or localities is
entirely coincidental.

AVON

A division of HarperCollins*Publishers*
77–85 Fulham Palace Road,
London W6 8JB

www.harpercollins.co.uk

A Paperback Original 2015
2

A catalogue record for this book is
available from the British Library

ISBN-13: 978-0-00-758562-5

Set in Sabon LT Std by Palimpsest Book Production Limited,
Falkirk, Stirlingshire

Printed and bound in Great Britain by
Clays Ltd, St Ives plc

MIX
Paper from
responsible sources
FSC® C007454

FSC™ is a non-profit international organisation established to promote
the responsible management of the world's forests. Products carrying the
FSC label are independently certified to assure consumers that they come
from forests that are managed to meet the social, economic and
ecological needs of present and future generations,
and other controlled sources.

Find out more about HarperCollins and the environment at
www.harpercollins.co.uk/green

ACKNOWLEDGEMENTS

Thanks to my Mom, whose conversation years ago sparked the idea for this book, and to my fantastic agent Caroline, who continues to believe in me, keeps me on track and answers my emails even when I know they're annoying. I'm also enormously grateful to my editor Lydia, who launched my debut with Penguin and has brought me into the Avon family, and to all my author pals in real life and on Facebook and Twitter who continue to be such a source of support and laughter. I'd like to give especially big bouncy kisses to the Notting Hill Press gang – you are wonderful – and last but certainly not least to my husband Andrew, who is wonderful beyond words.

For all women of every shape and size. There's so much more to us than meets the eye.

CHAPTER ONE

Pixie rejoined our little group, muttering as she shot dirty looks at Pam, our Slimming Zone consultant and weekly bearer of bad news.

'I've had it,' she said. 'Do you know how much weight I've lost in the last four years? Do you? I worked it out over Christmas. Seventy-six pounds. That's two hundred and sixty *thousand* calories I haven't enjoyed,' she continued, saving us calculating that depressing equation. 'And do you know how much weight I've gained back?' Her hazel eyes glinted.

Glances bounced between Ellie and Jane and me. I wouldn't answer that question if water-boarded.

'All but seven pounds. It's taken me years to lose what I could have flushed down the loo with a minor bout of dysentery. I'd have been better off drinking the water on holiday in Morocco.'

'You've just hit a wall, that's all,' said Ellie. 'It happens to everyone. You'll feel better next week.'

'It feels like the Great Wall of China, love.' She shook her head. 'Why should next week be any better, or the week after that?'

Ellie was flummoxed by such blasphemy. 'It just will be. You've got to stick with it. Pam says—'

'I know what Pam says, Ellie. I've been coming here for four years. Four years. I've lost seven pounds. I'm sick of it. Why do we keep doing this to ourselves?' She gestured around the room, to the crowd of new faces. Post-Christmas optimists. By Easter they'd be as bitter as Pixie.

'Because we love each other and get to see each other every week here,' said Ellie. 'You're my best friends. Katie and I wouldn't have met you if it wasn't for Slimming Zone.'

We'd joined not long after Pixie did, and I couldn't have been more grateful to have Ellie at my side. I'd looked forward to that first meeting about as much as my family's annual visit to Great Aunt Bernardine, who smelled of cats and liked to explain to me why I was single.

We'd entered the church hall fearing the worst. Would they announce our weight in booming voices tinged with judgement? Would everyone laugh? Was the rest of the group only there to lose those stubborn last five pounds, making us the elephants in the room?

We needn't have worried. Everyone was friendly and supportive. Nobody announced pounds gained, only pounds lost. And as Ellie just pointed out, that's how we met Jane and Pixie. They were already friends, Jane having joined about a year before Pixie. They might seem like opposites but Slimming Zone had brought them together, as it had us all.

I scanned the packed hall, thinking about Pixie's question. 'We *could* be anywhere together,' I said.

'But we have fun here,' Ellie said.

'No we don't,' Pixie scoffed. 'We have fun at dinner after we leave here.'

'I like these meetings,' Jane said, staring at the growing pile of knitting in her lap. 'I feel like they help me. And we're . . . amongst friends here.'

2

'I'm with Jane,' Ellie said. 'I feel better for coming.'

'And it has worked for you, Ellie.' As her flatmate, work colleague and best friend I knew how hard she tried. She was only twenty-five, with all the lovely elasticity that brings, so hers was puppy fat rather than the established fat of us older dogs. She'd lost a fair amount of weight but still saw no beauty in her size sixteen frame.

'I love you girls,' I said. 'But Pixie's right. Our friendship is built mostly around how many Maltesers we've eaten.'

Being overweight does tend to preoccupy one. Like having a hangnail, it's always there to irritate you. Sometimes it's painful but usually it's just tedious.

'I think we need more than this.'

'I gained a pound,' said Jane at the next meeting. 'And I've eaten nothing but Special K for a week.' She glared at her thighs. 'My wee stinks of wheat.'

Jane was no stranger to unpleasant side effects. When she was on the cabbage soup diet none of us could be in the car with her unless the windows were down.

'That's not healthy, Jane,' I said.

'Neither is being two stone overweight,' she snapped back. 'I don't know what I'm doing wrong.'

Ellie bounded over to Jane for a hug. She reminded me of a half-grown sheepdog when she moved, with her blondish-brown flyaway curls that always found their way over her eyes. She was just as friendly and gawky and I often had the urge to pet her.

'How much Special K are you eating?' she gently enquired.

Jane shrugged her off. 'So shoot me, I get hungry! Those serving sizes are for children.' Tears sprang to her eyes.

'Oh Jane, I didn't mean to upset you. I only asked. Maybe something a bit more well-balanced than cereal might work better?'

'It's just till I get started,' she said. She always said that.

Dieting was an extreme sport for Jane – the more outrageous, the bigger the potential payoff. There wasn't a fad, plan, pill or potion that she hadn't tried since having her children, but nothing shifted the baby weight. Those babies were now nine and seven. Her house was full of photos of her pre-child days, when she wore wispy dresses and wasn't afraid of shorts. Her friendly, heart-shaped face beamed at the camera, wide blue eyes sparkling and long, thick blonde hair cascading over her shoulders. She didn't pose for the camera any more.

'But those adverts!' she said as she pressed her double chin with the back of her hand. She hated that chin. Last year she spent hours making kissy fish faces in a bid to tone it. Pixie threatened to demonstrate her Kegel exercises if she didn't stop doing it with us in public. 'They couldn't run the adverts if they weren't true. Trading Standards wouldn't let them. Would they?'

Our expressions answered her.

'I knew it. Poxy adverts.'

'It's not the adverts,' Pixie said. 'It's just human nature. If we stuck to exactly what they told us to eat we'd lose weight. We'd also lose the will to live.' She shook her head. 'A woman can't live on no-fat, no-fun food alone . . . which is why I've made a decision. Ladies, this is my last meeting.'

'No!' Jane and Ellie said together.

'You can't quit!' Jane said.

Pixie shrugged. 'Of course I can. I'm sick to death of letting my entire life revolve around every calorie I put into my gob. I told you last week it wasn't worth it for me.' She crossed her arms. There was no budging her when she did that. 'I say bollocks to weekly weigh-ins.'

'But what about us?' Ellie's voice hitched in her throat.

'You could always quit too. Then we can do something fun together instead.'

'I'm not ready to quit,' said Jane.

'Me neither,' Ellie said.

Was I ready to quit? As veteran slimmers on the scale of World War soldiers, we'd all seen several tours of duty. Heads of state should lay wreaths before the scales each November to honour our bravery in fighting the 100 Pounds War. I was battle-hardened.

But as I thought about what Pixie had said I realised I was finally ready to resign my commission.

'She's right,' I said. 'I'd rather spend the evening with you doing something fun than be judged by the calories I've eaten. But there's no reason you couldn't do both for a while if that makes you feel better. Let's plan something in addition to Slimming Zone.'

'I'm in!' Jane said, her hands flying over her knitting. 'What shall we do?'

In London, the options were endless. Film, theatre, comedy, music? A night stuffing fivers down male strippers' G-strings? No, none of us was rich. They'd have to settle for pound coins.

'I've been dying to see *Thriller Live*,' Ellie finally said.

'I thought you were going with Thomas?' I asked.

She reddened. 'I thought he was going to surprise me with tickets a few weeks ago, but he hasn't yet.' She smiled, no doubt thinking about lovely Thomas. They'd snogged at our company Christmas party and, unusually, didn't spend the next month avoiding each other in the kitchen.

'I wouldn't wait around for him,' Pixie said. 'Why don't you book them?'

'Well, if we want to go together,' she said, 'then let's book tickets for us.'

Pixie grinned. 'We'll have a girls' night out. Jane, could Andy watch my two on the night as well?'

'Of course, I'm sure he won't mind.'

'Thanks, love. It's bad enough that Trevor's got to mind them tonight.'

Ellie, Jane and I bounced our usual looks between us. Trevor was a waste of space. Unfortunately he was wasting space in Pixie's house, as the father of her children.

'Are things any better at home?' Ellie asked as we collected our coats and bags.

Pixie nodded at first, then shook her head. 'Darts have started again so he's out after tea most nights.' She sighed. 'A point to the temple is probably too much to hope for.' We smiled at her lame joke, recognising the honesty in it. 'At least by the time he gets home, the children and I are in bed.'

They'd had separate bedrooms for years on account of Pixie's sleep apnoea. Trevor claimed to need a good night's sleep since he worked. Given how sporadic that work was, he should have been okay with sporadic sleep as well.

Pixie had a new plan to leave him at least twice a year. Her list of reasons was endless, and totally justified. Not that he physically abused her. She'd knock his teeth out if he laid a finger on her or the children. But his constant complaints and insults were a slow form of torture.

The problem was, since she hadn't worked in years, she was a bit stuck. So she stayed with him, hoping things would get better. As her friends, we added our hopes to hers.

CHAPTER TWO

Ellie and I splurged on takeaway sushi on our way home from the meeting. Eating tiny bits of fish and rice made us feel virtuous on a par with the Buddha. Which justified the ice cream we bought for dessert. Life was a balancing act, after all.

Ellie got the good wine glasses from the kitchen and threw herself beside me on the ancient sofa. Mum and Dad had brought it from home when I bought the flat. Lucky for me, as I was so skint by the end of the process that even Ikea was out of my reach.

I loved our sofa. It was old and worn but its scarlet velvet cushions held countless memories. It was where I was sitting when Mum announced she'd been appointed headmistress of her school. I threw myself on it when opening my university acceptance letter. And it was where I first had sex . . . a detail I'd skipped when reminiscing with my parents on moving day.

How I'd loved Rory McAdams, ever since Year Nine when he offered to help me with maths. He wasn't the most popular boy, or the sportiest or smartest or funniest. He was a bit on the short side, and failed to grow the peach fuzz that our classmates managed. But he was incredibly nice, and he became one of my only friends at school.

It would be generous to say that I went through an awkward phase at school. It was more like a pariah phase. I slowly outgrew it at uni, away from the bullies who'd tormented me, but it was a slow process and I never did gain a big group of friends. Since meeting Ellie, Jane and Pixie, I hadn't felt I needed any more.

But Rory wasn't put off by my leper-like status at school. We became such good mates that our parents started referring to us in the plural. We were Katie-and-Rory. Naturally this convinced me that we were as good as going out, in a non-kissing, non-hand-holding, one-sided way.

But while I pined for my friend, he pined for a tall girl on the hockey team who didn't know he was alive. Sometimes I wondered if anyone got to go out with the person they liked.

One night, just before leaving sixth form, we went to the pub. We'd both had too much cider and before I knew what was happening, Rory kissed me. Or I kissed him. The details were fuzzy but the fact was, we kissed. I was snogging the boy I loved. We left the pub holding hands, and he kissed me again when we got to my door.

Mum and Dad didn't usually leave me alone overnight but as I was now eighteen (I reminded them of this every chance I got), they'd taken a rare trip without me to visit my cat-wee auntie. When I invited Rory inside I knew exactly what I was doing and wasn't at all nervous about having sex for the first time. I was, however, self-conscious, aware that my body wasn't slim like the girls in the magazines. I was probably around the same size as Ellie is now, with the same puppy fat coating my five-foot-five frame. Rory switched the light on. I switched it off. He laughed and said I was being silly, but left us in the dark.

The sex mostly involved fumbling with the condom he optimistically carried in his wallet for Miss Jolly Hockeysticks. We both tried to hide our surprise that he was using it with me. The velvet cushions weren't great for traction and we slid to the floor more than once.

My head was too full of our new relationship to sleep after kissing Rory good-bye. By morning my imagination had us nearly engaged. Unfortunately Rory's sleep hadn't been disturbed by similar fantasies, and when he said he wanted to talk the next day, I knew he wouldn't be proposing. I managed to hide my dismay when he apologised for taking advantage of me, and he managed to hide most of his awkwardness. I was his best girl mate, he said, and a right laugh, and he didn't want to lose me as a friend. I pretended not to mind and we did stay friends as we went off to university. I saw him in London a few years ago and finally told him of the torch I'd carried all those years. He swore he'd had no idea of my feelings. He was, of course, just being kind. He'd have had to be blind not to notice. Infatuation isn't a subtle emotion.

Now, at thirty, I wasn't yet consigned to spinsterhood, despite Great Aunt Bernardine's theories. But I had to be realistic as I looked in the mirror. Sure, my face was okay. A teacher once even likened me to Elizabeth Taylor (presumably in her early years), probably because we had the same colour eyes and dark wavy hair. My nose and lips were about the right size and I wasn't too spotty. But not everyone wanted to go out with a woman who carried the equivalent of a seven-year-old under her dress.

'I feel ill,' Ellie said, chucking the spoon into her empty bowl with satisfaction. 'I can't believe we ate the whole thing.'

'It was light ice cream,' I pointed out, patting my own tummy. 'And we did only have sushi.'

'We should definitely go for a walk.'

'Are you sure? It's kind of cold out there.'

'Shivering burns calories.' She went for her trainers. 'Come on. Get off your arse.'

I made a face, which she ignored. Ellie was one of those annoying women who enjoyed exercise. She had a gym membership that she actually used, whereas I spent thirty quid a month to feel guilty that my gym shoes sat in the wardrobe most of the time.

Ellie's phone rang just as I locked our front door. 'It's Thomas,' she said. 'Hi, Thomas. I'm fine, thank you. Katie and I are just going for a walk. Can I call you back in about an hour?'

'An hour?' I mouthed. She nodded sadistically as she hung up. 'Will lovely Thomas survive that long without you?'

'He'll manage.' She scrunched her face up in a smile.

'He really is lovely, isn't he?'

'I think he is. I know it's early days—'

'Not such early days, Ell, when you consider that you've known him, non-biblically, for years. You'd have a pretty good idea by now if he was a knob.'

'Who'd have thought I'd get together with someone from work?' she said. 'At the Christmas party no less?'

'You're a walking cliché.' I stuck my arm over her shoulder and hugged. 'In the best possible way. I really am so happy for you.' Ellie was the kind of woman you wanted nice things to happen to.

'Mmm, I suppose,' she said, glancing sideways.

'Ellie, I've warned you. Don't overthink things. You know how he feels about you. He's told you. And he shows it all the time. You've got to forget about her.'

'That's easy for you to say. Your boyfriend doesn't have a crush on his colleague.'

'Christ, Ellie, he never should have told you. It was a crush. *Was*. All the way back when they were in school together. You've got nothing to worry about. It's not a big deal but you're going to make it one if you keep dwelling.' I stopped, and made her stop too. 'You know I'm right. You've got to relax about this. Don't make problems where there aren't any.'

She nodded. 'I know, but I can't help how I feel. I hate her.'

'You can't hate someone who's never done anything to you. That's silly. She doesn't even know that he liked her, does she? They're just mates.'

'No, but what if she finds out about his feelings and decides she likes him too? Then what'll happen?'

'Well, let's see. Maybe he'll shag her on the desk during his lunch break. And while we're in the world of "maybes", maybe the Queen will abdicate in favour of Prince Charles, and the bee population will recover and Wayne Rooney will grow an afro. All of those things are possible, but are you really going to worry about the possibility that they might happen at some point in the future?'

'I'm not going out with Prince Charles or Wayne Rooney, and I'm allergic to bees.'

'You're being purposely obtuse. Honeybun, lovely Thomas is nuts about you. He's going out with you and you're happy together. If you don't dial up the crazy, that'll continue to be the case. Believe me, I know about crazy.'

'You don't still blame yourself for Alex, do you? Anybody would have misunderstood the situation. That was totally not your fault.'

Maybe not, but my face burned just thinking about the Christmas party.

Everyone had looked forward to it. Our company, Nutritious, always put on a fantastic party whether it was a record year or a terrible one. Ostensibly it started after work at the pub on the corner, but most of us went out for a very long lunch beforehand. By the time I saw Alex sitting alone at the table, it was latish and the room was a bit spinny.

He looked amazing. But then he always looked amazing to me. An unbiased observer might have noted that his shirt was untucked and he was wearing that fixed smile he got when trying to look sober. I'd seen it enough over the years.

It never put me off. He'd have to soil himself unrepentantly to fall in my estimation. And even then I'm sure I'd find an excuse to love him again.

I'd had Rory-like feelings for Alex for years. They started nearly the first time we spoke, a few weeks after Nutritious hired me. When he asked me out to lunch I could barely eat (proof of my feelings if ever there was any). But I sussed pretty quickly that it wasn't a date. As the company's finance director, he was also on the board of directors. They took it in turns to welcome the new recruits with lunch. It was simply the luck of the draw that I got Alex instead of our balding middle-aged CEO.

Alex wasn't balding or middle aged. He was thirty-six (birthday November 4th), from a middle-class family in Surrey (only child), and had a two-bedroom flat in Pimlico where he lived alone (the address of which I knew by heart). To me he was perfection on legs. Tall, but not too tall, with broad shoulders and a narrow waist. His strong jawline suited the stubble he usually wore. He had swoon-making thick dark eyelashes that framed his vivid blue eyes. His skin was sun-kissed even in February thanks to his skiing obsession, and his big straight teeth were practically American. I fanta-sised about getting my hands into his thick, straight, flaxen hair. I'd never tire of looking at him.

So when I noticed him sitting in that booth, alone as the rest of our colleagues danced and drank, naturally I went over to say hello.

He smiled when he saw me, and patted the bench beside him. 'Katie. Katie Katie Katie. Happy Christmas,' he slurred. 'It's not been a bad year, eh, considering? Still a lot of work to do though, tough nuts to crack and all that.'

I laughed, thinking of my problem client, Jenny. 'I *will* get Philips Pharmacy on board next year,' I declared. 'In fact I called Jenny before lunch.' I didn't need to tell him who Jenny was. She was a company legend.

'Hoping for some last-minute Christmas cheer?' he said.

'False hope. She told me not to stuff my face full of mince pies because the extra pounds would be hard to shift come January.' In other words, a typical conversation with Jenny.

'Ouch. Still, at least you know it's not personal. She's never met any of us.' He leaned forward. 'So all you want for Christmas is a deal with Jenny. I wonder what else Father Christmas will put in your stocking this year, eh? Have you been a good girl?'

Was he actually flirting with me? I could barely breathe. Maybe my support pants were too tight. We sat awkwardly facing each other in the booth.

'I've been pretty good,' I said, leaving room for interpretation.

'Oh? Have you been a little bit bad, too?' He leaned closer.

I wasn't sure where he was going with his line of questioning, but tonight, I was going to find out. I took a deep breath and raised the stakes. 'I'm so bad that I'm sometimes very good.'

He smiled. It was a filthy smile, full of the kind of promises I dreamed about. He leaned still closer. He closed his eyes. I closed mine too, leaning in to meet him. Our lips met. His were warm, soft and as perfect as I imagined. We stayed like that for a second, two, three . . . five, six . . . ten. He didn't move. I peeked. His eyes were still closed. Slowly I broke our kiss. He remained motionless. Then, slowly, he leaned forward until his head rested on the edge of the table.

Frantically I looked around to see if anyone had spotted us. But they were too drunk. As was Alex, apparently. He slept peacefully on the table. With humiliation flaming my cheeks, I fled the party. I could only hope he really had been too drunk to remember anything.

CHAPTER THREE

'Do I look okay?' asked Ellie, making a face at her electric blue jersey dress.

'You look lovely. Now please hurry, we're late as it is!' We had less than an hour to get to the theatre to meet Pixie and Jane.

'Don't the leggings look funny with these shoes?'

'How about boots then?'

'Ah, of course!' She rushed off to find her boots.

It was useless trying to rush Ellie when she got like this. She approached dressing like Sir Edmund Hillary approached Everest. I was her Tenzing Norgay, there for critical support.

Eventually we emerged from Piccadilly Circus Tube into a swirling throng of people. Girls in various states of undress despite the frigid January air teetered in shoes that would keep chiropodists in business for years. The boys swaggered with bravado and lager. Excitement coursed through me at the thought of the night ahead.

'There's Pixie and Jane,' Ellie said, quickening her step as we approached the red-brick-fronted theatre on Shaftesbury Avenue. It was mobbed.

'You look pretty!' I said, admiring Pixie's striking eye makeup and sheer lips. I was glad to see her making an effort. She rarely bothered any more.

'Well, it's not every night we get to go out on the town. Will you look at this? It's a proper Saturday night out! I'm *well* excited.'

We joined the buzzing crowd to make our way inside, where the usher directed us to the stalls.

'Wow,' whispered Jane as we walked down the side aisle toward our seats. 'This is grand.'

'I'm glad we're not up there,' Ellie said, nodding to the three ornately painted gold and burgundy balconies above us. 'It looks cramped.'

'I'm not sure this is much better,' I said as I realised where our seats were. It was pretty clear that four large ladies weren't going to be able to squeeze past the theatregoers already in their seats. 'Erm, excuse me,' I said to the couple on the end. 'It might be easier if you . . .'

The older woman took a split second to take in the situation before her eyes slid away and she shifted into the aisle with her husband.

'Oh,' said Pixie behind me, a look of uncertainty flashing across her face.

The next couple realised they'd need to come out into the aisle too. Apologetic murmurs escaped us as we shuffled along. Then, again, we were at an impasse.

'What should we do?' Ellie asked with dismay.

'Should we see if there are seats at the back?' Jane wondered. She hated making a scene.

'At the back?' Pixie said. 'We paid sixty bloody pounds for these tickets! I'm not sitting at the back.'

She was right. Of course she was right. That didn't make the situation any easier.

'I'm really sorry,' I said to the couple who were shuffling along the row towards us. 'Could you possibly ask the people next to you to come out too? And maybe ask them to tell the people next to them? We're seats eleven, twelve, thirteen and fourteen.' In other words, directly in the middle of the blooming row.

I felt my face go hot. Of course everyone around us noticed the commotion. How could they not? Some avoided eye contact. A few whispered. Others smiled in commiseration. Those embarrassed looks of sympathy were the worst.

Perhaps we should have turned at the first hurdle and cut our losses. But how were we to know that the theatre's seats couldn't accommodate a sixteen-stone woman with curves like Pixie's?

She called them her saddlebags, and joked that she liked to keep her weekly food shopping in them. But it was no joke when she lowered herself into her seat.

'Bloody hell, I don't fit!' she whispered. She tried angling in sideways. There just wasn't enough room. Or, to be precise, there was just too much Pixie. 'I'm sorry,' she said. 'I'm going to have to see if they've got another seat at the back. This is going to be too uncomfortable.'

'You can't leave!' Ellie whispered.

'I'm not leaving, love. I'll just find a more comfortable seat.'

'We'll go with you,' Jane said.

'You'll do nothing of the sort, you lovely daft cow,' Pixie smiled, shaking her head. 'There's no need for all of us to go. I'll meet you in the bar at the interval, okay?'

She smiled brightly, but I wasn't fooled. I saw the flush creeping across her cheeks before she turned away.

''Scuse me, love,' she said to the man next to her. 'I hate to disturb you again but I just got a call from George Clooney. He's dying to take me to dinner. That man just will not take no for an answer. 'Fraid I've got to go. Can you maybe ask the others to scoot out again? For George's sake?' That raised

16

a chuckle from the man as he passed the message down the line.

A few minutes later the lights went down and Jackson's best-loved hits washed over us. But I kept thinking about Pixie. I wasn't sure we would see her at the interval. If it had been me I probably would have sneaked away.

But Pixie wasn't about to let a little thing like mortal embarrassment get her down. She was there by the bar during the break, chatting amiably with an old couple wearing matching purple jumpers that made them look Starburst.

'Isn't it fantastic?' she said as we approached. 'Though I couldn't see if he actually looks like Michael. You lot are closer. Does he?'

'Not really,' I said. 'Where are you sitting?'

'Oh, just at the back. One of the box office ladies found me a chair. We just drag it out into the aisle after everyone has sat down. I've got VIP seating . . . Will you stop looking at me like that?'

'Like what, sweetheart?' Jane asked.

'Like I've got terminal cancer and don't know it. Like you feel sorry for me.'

'Sorry!' we all said at once, knowing how that look can undermine a poorly constructed façade.

'Drink?' I said, pulling out my purse.

By the time the bells rang for us to sit again, we'd nearly forgotten the seating difficulties. Pixie had been right – it felt wonderful to be out like normal people instead of confessing our chocolate transgressions to one another.

We were all in high spirits when the theatre doors disgorged us into the cold night. There was no question of us heading for the Tube yet. None of us wanted the evening to end.

The bar we settled on, close to the theatre, was heaving with noisy drinkers.

'So what should we see next?' Pixie shouted when we

found a spot to huddle with our drinks near the men's loos. Every time the door opened, our night was perfumed by the whiff of urinal cake.

'Or do? We could do something next time,' I said. 'Maybe go somewhere nice like Kew Gardens? Or Windsor or Bath on a weekend?'

Ellie nodded. 'I'd love to go to Windsor. Could we do a tour of the palace?'

'I'm not sure in the winter, but we can check,' Jane said. 'As long as we don't go back to that theatre.' I knew that Jane would hold a grudge on Pixie's behalf for a long time. She was a good friend like that.

'There should be a way to know beforehand whether seats will be comfortable,' Ellie said. 'A nice easy rating system like they do with the food in restaurants.'

'Maybe we should make one.'

'No way,' said Pixie, laughing. 'I don't fancy jamming my arse into seats all over London.'

'Okay, so we don't jam our arses into that theatre's seats,' I said. 'We just need to find some that are more accommodating for the larger lady.'

'That would be useful information to have,' Jane said. 'Not just for us – for lots of people.'

'I guess we could ask when we book the tickets,' I said. 'Send someone down from the box office with a measuring tape. Get him to bounce on the seats, assess springiness, see if his knees hit the seat in front.'

Jane wasn't laughing with the rest of us. 'Jane?'

'That's a really good idea,' she said. 'Seriously, why don't we ask these things before we book again? After all, we want to have fun, and it's not fun when one of us has to sit on an office chair at the back.'

This reminder sobered us. 'So we'll ask next time,' said Pixie. 'Cheers, ladies. To us.'

18

'Here's to many more nights like this!' Ellie said. 'With comfortable seats.' We all clinked to that.

Later we walked towards the Tube feeling very merry. I offered to find the next performance with roomy seating and I knew I'd book it as soon as possible. I hadn't felt this good in ages. It was so much better than stepping on the scales every week.

'Hang on,' Ellie said, steering us towards the cash machine. 'I need to get some money for tomorrow morning. It's my turn to buy the office treats.'

Jane was getting her groove on while we waited, singing one of Jackson's hits while she danced in place.

Two young men passing by glanced over. Then one of them started singing, '*I'm fat, you're fat, come on, you know, woo!*' They laughed as they carried on up the road.

'Beat it!' Pixie shouted, catching my eye.

'You don't wanna be starting something!' I said.

'That's all right, it doesn't matter,' Jane said. 'They're out of my life anyway.' But she slouched into her coat with her hands in her pockets and we didn't talk much on the walk to the Tube.

CHAPTER FOUR

I wasn't about to lose momentum with our girls' nights out, and spent most of the next morning between work phone calls googling theatres with roomier seats. I was quickly able to whittle down my list. To my surprise, people did take the time to gripe about their bad experiences online. Unfortunately there was no centralised whingers' repository, which made the process a bit slow.

I kept watch for Cressida. She had a knack for popping up over the cubicle wall like a censorious jack-in-the-box whenever I faffed around. As my boss, I suppose she had the right to do this but given that most people didn't even want to do my job, she should really have been grateful that I was there at all. Calling up strangers with money-saving offers put me just above a Jehovah's Witness in the social acceptability stakes. Sure, I called pharmacies, nutritionists and health food shops, not people in the middle of dinner. But that still meant I got hung up on. A lot.

Even so, I liked my work, though I'd had my doubts when they first hired me. They sent us on a week-long training course to learn the science behind the nutritional supplements we were selling. Men in white lab coats explained everything in mind-numbing detail. Luckily I had a head for mind-numbing detail. It didn't take long to start managing my own client list, but it wasn't always easy. Oversharing clients sometimes admitted to heinous bodily irregularities before I could remind them that I wasn't a trained professional in that sense. Then I spent weeks worrying about their health.

Eventually I got used to being tethered to my desk by the sleek headset that made us all look like Justin Bieber's backup singers. It took some practice to learn to ignore the other sales reps' patter, to concentrate only on my own call. But now it was completely normal. What a funny word that was: normal. It was all a matter of perspective.

I spotted Alex before he reached my desk, and used those few milliseconds to remember I hadn't plucked the chin hair I noticed in the mirror that morning.

'Hiya!' he said, oblivious to my chin. 'Want to try that new Japanese place for lunch?'

'That depends. Are you buying?'

'I'll spring for the green tea if you'll consult on the sushi. I never know what to get besides California rolls.'

'Well, I do know my way around a bento box.' What was I saying? There's no sushi in a bento box.

'One o'clock?'

'Make it twelve-thirty.'

That still gave me enough time to nip to Boots for tweezers.

It wasn't unusual to go to lunch with Alex, which meant I'd had ample opportunity over the past month to feel awkward about the Christmas Kiss. He never let on that he remembered, but he could be cagey like that and I was constantly alert for clues. If we were proper friends I'd have just asked him, but as things stood I didn't want to spook him. It had taken me six years to get to the friendly acquaint-anceship stage with him. Given enough time and luck, we might just become something more exciting one day. I lived in hope.

The restaurant was packed. We wedged onto a cramped table in one corner. The large plate-glass window at the front ran with condensation and the menus were already spotted with soy sauce. The prices were good and if the food was even mediocre, it was the kind of place that'd do a brisk lunchtime trade amidst the sea of sandwich shops in the area.

Alex closed his menu. 'I won't pretend to know what I'm looking at,' he said with a grin that loosened my insides.

'You just asked me here to order for you.'

'I did warn you. And I'm paying you handsomely in tea, don't forget.'

I sighed dramatically. 'I'm not just brains you know. I'm also a pretty face.'

'Of that,' he said, raising his tiny tea cup, 'there's no doubt. Now order quick, I'm starving.'

There seemed to be just one waitress in the restaurant, a gangly young woman with long blonde hair tied haphazardly into a loose bun so that tendrils escaped to frame her pretty face. When I tried to do that I looked like I'd been in bed with 'flu for three days. Finally she approached our table.

'Are you ready to order?' she asked, looking at Alex, who nodded to me.

'Yes, please may we have two orders of spicy tuna roll, one California roll . . .' I stopped talking when I noticed she wasn't looking at me. 'One soft-shell crab roll and one salmon nigiri . . . did you get all that?'

She nodded, finally looking my way before heading for the kitchen.

'Thanks for ordering,' Alex said, oblivious to the waitress's rudeness. 'Everything sounds great.'

'Now you know what to order for next time.'

'Nah, I won't remember,' he said.

'Will I have to come with you every time you want sushi? That might be awkward on a date.' Even as I joked my heart skidded at the thought of Alex on a date. Steady on, girl, I told myself. You'd think I'd be able to look at the man without wanting to lunge over the table. Not even Rory had this much hold over me. And that was at least based on a solid friendship.

I glared at the waitress for the rest of the meal but she remained unaware of my loathing, not even once glancing in my direction. She was all smiles for Alex though. She must have thought he was paying. Or else she had a crush on him. Or . . . as I suspected, I was Invisible Katie.

The worst part about being a fat woman isn't that people look at you with judgement in their eyes. It's that most don't look at you at all. You cease to be a person for whom they need to account. They look over your shoulder, or at the ground in front of you, or they glaze their eyes and look directly through you. It's like being a ghost, but with none of the fun of haunting. That waitress wasn't ignoring me. I was simply inconsequential.

Alex and I went back to the office and straight into our meeting together, as if lunch hadn't just happened.

I made it sound nonchalant, didn't I? *Our meeting together*. Like I had them all the time and hadn't taken nearly an hour to dress this morning.

Our company was always on the lookout for ways to get more work out of us without breaking EU employment law. So instead of just asking, they liked to make it look like overworking was our idea. We'd had personality tests that told us it was okay to be a workaholic. We'd been given motivational tee shirts and posters. There was a weekly prize for Awesomeness. We were on a slippery slope, one group hug away from going on retreats together to chant affirmations and weave everlasting friendship lanyards.

When Alex asked for a volunteer last month to help implement their latest improvement (vision boards stuck with aspirational magazine images to help us reach our goals), I had to fight the urge to shout *Pick me, Pick me* with my hand in the air.

Of course it was a stupid idea. But it was our boss Clive's stupid idea, so everyone had to show willing, at least to his face. *My* face didn't garner the same respect. I was now known as Karma Katie around the office.

In the conference room, I tried to shake off that henchman feeling as I double-checked my notes. Yes, Herr Commandant, everything was carried out as you instructed.

Alex pointed to his steaming cup. 'No coffee for you?' The very idea baffled him.

It smelled delicious. 'I'd love to but I'm off coffee at the moment. My heart's been doing something funny lately.' As I hadn't dropped dead from it I wasn't overly worried about a heart attack. It was more of an unusual rhythm – da-da-da-da-da-da-kerthunk! Sometimes it made me out of breath.

'It's not dangerous, is it? You should get it checked.'

'Oh, I'm sure there's nothing really wrong.' I tried not to get carried away with fantasies of him kneeling at my bedside, holding my hand to declare his love.

He nodded, unaware of the role he was playing in my imagination. 'Let's try to make this quick. I've got another meeting at two.' He rolled his eyes.

This was his way of letting me know that he might be on the board, but he wasn't one of The Establishment. He was far too cool for that. He windsurfed, for goodness sake. Just imagine him emerging from the sea, streaming with water, sun glistening . . .

The vision popped as he opened his notebook to get down to work.

'Yep, agreed,' I said. 'Let's make it a quickie. I mean . . . well, I didn't mean that.' Well done, Katie. Cool as usual. I pushed a thick lock of hair out of my face, accidently sticking myself in the eye as I did so. 'Ouch.'

'Are you all right?' he asked. I waved away his concern, squinting attractively. 'So, tell me then. Have you made your vision board? Are all your darkest desires pasted on cardboard for the universe to fulfil? It only accepts paper requests you know.'

'Every single one is documented for the Fates to act on,' I said. 'I even stuck the Philips Pharmacy logo on there. If I could find a photo of Jenny, I'd add it. Maybe with a lock of hair and a voodoo doll.' Jenny's latest objection was that we tested the products on animals. We didn't, but once she was on a roll it was hard stopping her. 'And I used staples on the really important ones . . . calorie-free cupcakes and world domination.'

'Lofty goals. I'm glad you didn't waste time on trivial things like cancer cures or filthy riches.'

'Without calorie-free cupcakes, what's the point of the rest of it?'

His throaty laugh gave me bedroom visions. 'You always brighten my day, Katie Winterbottom. '

That's me, the day-brightener. If I'd had a quid for every time I'd heard that from someone I fancied, the calorie-free cupcake research fund would be nearly full. I suppose being appreciated for my conversations was all right, if he wasn't going to love me for my body.

'I'm sorry that I wasn't able to make our last meeting,' he said. 'A good mate got us last-minute tickets to the rugby. Promise not to breathe a word of it to the higher-ups. They think my mother needed a ride to her chiropractor.'

I held up my hand in oath.

'Your email was very thorough though. I didn't expect graphics.'

I knew I'd gone overboard when I found myself in the office after eight p.m. trying to animate tiny pencils to march across the presentation.

'You must let me take you out for a drink,' he continued. 'You've saved my arse once again. And I suppose you'll have to save it today too. We need something to show the board. We can't really monitor progress, can we? I mean without violating HR policy. The damn things are probably supposed to be confidential.'

'I suppose I could ask everyone if they've done it. That'd give you something to report back on. Maybe a few people would be willing to show theirs to the board.'

'Would you be willing to show me yours?' he asked.

I'd show him mine right there on the conference table. 'I, erm.'

'That sounded rude, didn't it?' He smiled, not making any effort to correct it. *Did* he mean what he'd said?

Then he laughed a deep, rich chuckle that made my reproductive system wobble with glee.

'Don't you need to get to your next meeting?'

He ran his hand through his gorgeous hair, blowing out his cheeks. 'In my next life please remind me to study architecture or film-making, not finance. Honestly, Katie, I don't know what I did in my past life to deserve this.'

'You must have been very naughty,' I said before I could stop myself. Oh. My. God. I sounded like a MILF from some nineties porn movie. 'Karma, I mean. Bad karma transformed into a career in finance. You should watch yourself or you'll come back as something even worse next time. Maybe an ambulance-chasing solicitor. Har har.'

'My parents are both solicitors,' he said. 'Personal injury.'

'Oh, I didn't mean it! I'm sure they're very nice people and they probably didn't do anything horrible in a previous life to deserve to be solicitors. I mean, it was just—'

'Katie, relax, I was only joking. My parents are doctors. Shall we get on with this?'

I left the meeting in a muddle. He didn't mention anything about the Christmas party. Still no hints that he might remember more than he was letting on. No lovely innuendos. I'd carried a torch for this man for six years, which hadn't dimmed one iota. I must have used extra-long life batteries. It couldn't go on like this.

CHAPTER FIVE

Our overdrafts wouldn't survive sixty-quid theatre tickets for very long, so our girls' nights were interspersed with thriftier options.

'I've never seen so many skinny jeans in one place,' Jane said, shifting in her chair to tuck her legs further beneath the table in the cinema's foyer. 'Have we walked into a Topshop advert?'

'They're hipsters,' Ellie whispered, as if observing them on safari. Maybe she was afraid they'd stampede if spooked. 'They all dress like this in the East End. It looks good on teenagers but I could never wear jeans like that.'

'Oh, but Ellie,' Jane said, 'of course you can, you're only twenty-five! I'm the one who's probably too old to be trendy.'

'You make yourself sound like a granny, Jane,' I said. 'You're only thirty-five. And a young-looking thirty-five at that.'

'She's right,' Pixie said, smoothing her hands over her thighs. 'I'm thirty-five and I'm wearing them. I am! You don't have to be a size zero you know. Skinny just means they fit your body . . . whatever body you've got. I can't stand those baggy ones they always stock in big sizes. They make me look like a postie. My calves aren't too bad. I may as well show them off.'

She did have pretty calves, and slender ankles. She often said her parents had some spinning top mixed in with their Yorkshire heritage. I loved that she could see the good in herself, even when sometimes others didn't.

'I don't know how you do it, Pixie,' Jane said. 'I admire you so much. I can't even let Andy see my wobbly bits, let alone the wider world. I make him turn all the lights out when we're in bed.'

How I wished some of Pixie's confidence would rub off on Jane. 'Doesn't he get cross about that?'

She smiled. 'If he does, he doesn't let on. He's too good a husband.'

Ellie was keen to find our seats, even though we'd already reserved them. I hadn't seen her so excited since the Selfridges shoe sale last year. But then it wasn't every day that her favourite film director offered to do a talk after his film.

There was a collective intake of breath when we saw the huge cushy green velvet armchairs. Pixie made a face. 'They're not big enough . . .'

'Very funny,' I said. It was nap-worthy seating. 'This could be the perfect cinema experience, thank you, Hackney Picturehouse!' I imagined all the cold, rainy weekend afternoons we could spend lounging in cinematic splendour. In seats like that I'd even watch Vin Diesel without too much of a grump.

Within minutes of the opening credits though, I was yearning for Vin. Instead we sat through two hours of bleak inner angst. As if I needed any more of that, after the day I'd had. My mind replayed the afternoon's meeting while the actors wept on-screen. Stupid arthouse film.

* * *

Every month the entire Nutritious sales team met in the big conference room to divvy up new client prospects and report on progress with existing clients. Everybody lied, of course (occupational hazard), but it was important to go through the motions to give our bosses the illusion of control.

As usual, Clive (he of the vision boards) chaired the meeting and, as usual, we played Buzzword Bingo. Trading the cards around each month made sure that everyone got an equal chance over time.

Nobody could sling vacuous office speak like Clive, and he never disappointed. Ellie jumped when he said 'Let's focus on the bottom line, team' and I knew she had my card from last month. *Focus* and *bottom line* in one go. Well played, Ellie.

'All right, last order of business,' he said as I ticked off one of my boxes. Just *touch base* and *game plan* left to win. 'New account visits. We've got sixteen this month. Who can take Camelot in Northampton?'

I raised my hand with lots of others.

'Steve, thanks. Cohens in Leeds?'

Again my hand went up. 'Susan, great. Faith Fitness, also in Leeds? Susan, do you want to take that too? Thanks. Havens Chemist? Matt.'

Each time my hand went up. Each time Clive chose a colleague to take the meeting. By the end of the list, my arm was tired. So was I.

'Right,' said Clive. 'Thank you, ladies and gents. Same time next month. Any questions, just touch base with me.'

'Erm, Clive? Isn't there a client I could take?' I asked, subtly ticking off my *touch base* box.

He smiled his grandfatherly smile. 'I'm sorry, Katie, that's the end of the list. Next time you should volunteer earlier.' Ellie grimaced her support as she took the minutes. She was lucky. As the company secretary and all-round indispensable person, she didn't have to fight for client meetings with the rest of us.

I didn't bother pointing out that my hand was in the air the whole time. I could have danced on the desk and he'd have passed me over. It was a long-standing fact. I was one of their top salespeople on the phone. I never got client meetings.

Once Ellie's moany film ended we had to stay for another twenty minutes while sycophantic fans stroked the director's ego. Even she looked ready for a drink by the time we finally made for the pub down the road.

'You know what I really want?' Ellie asked as we carried our wine to an empty table. 'Cake. I could murder a slice of gooey chocolate gateau.' She licked her lips thinking about it.

'I could eat two slices,' I said. Lately my appetite had been colossal. 'With ice cream.'

'God, don't!' moaned Jane. 'I haven't had anything sweet all week.'

'You're not still on your stinking wee cereal diet?' Pixie said. 'Love, give it up. There's no reason to put yourself through something that clearly doesn't work.' When Ellie protested this rather blunt statement, she said, 'What? Jane has said as much. It's been over a month and she hasn't lost any weight.'

'I gained a pound,' Jane confirmed. 'But I'm going to try something new. Katie, you might know about this too, from work. It's called Alli. Have you heard of it?'

'We don't sell any diet aids.' I made a mental note to ask the science types around at the office about it anyway.

'You take it with meals,' she explained. 'And it keeps your body from absorbing fat. The best part is you can eat whatever you like!'

'It sounds too good to be true,' Ellie said. 'Is it safe?'

'I bought it at Boots, so it must be,' she said. 'This could be the miracle I've been looking for.'

I hated seeing Jane get so excited about the latest fad only to be disappointed.

'Are you finished?' Pixie glared at us. 'Jesus, will you listen to yourselves? We may as well just go to Slimming Zone. It'd be cheaper and we can have the exact same monotonous conversations. Aren't you tired of always thinking about what you ate yesterday, what you can eat today? It's exhausting. I quit Slimming Zone to get away from all that and you're bringing it with you on our nights out.' Her look softened. 'Ladies. We are more than the sum total of our BMIs. Honestly, I'm sick to death of it all. Aren't you?'

Actually I was. And Pixie was right. We had better things to talk about than our waistlines. 'Well, I thought that film was a load of old donkey's bollocks.'

'How can you say that?' Ellie asked. 'It was beautiful.'

'It was boring.'

'That's not fair,' Pixie said. 'Donkey's bollocks aren't boring.'

'Not all films move along at the pace of *Love, Actually*.'

Ellie knew I judged all cinema against the Richard Curtis classics.

I shrugged. 'That storyline was Jurassic. Glaciers move faster.'

'I thought the main guy was hot,' Jane said.

Ellie made a face. 'He didn't look well-bathed.'

'And with that seventies porn moustache?' Pixie laughed. 'But I suppose you also like Tom Selleck and Sam Elliot.'

'Do you also have a thing for seventies porn, Jane?' I asked.

'Bow chicka bow-wow!' Ellie said. 'It's making a comeback you know.'

'Seventies porn?'

She nodded. 'It's vintage now that everybody's waxing off all their body hair. Some men still like a full muff.'

'How do you know that? Does lovely Thomas like a hirsute woman?'

She blushed to her roots. 'I read it in *Cosmo*. And I know where this conversation is going, so don't even bother.'

'Sorry, sweetheart,' said Jane. 'But you're the only one around here with an active sex life. I love Andy but with two children, we're lucky if we remember to kiss good night. I'm afraid you must share with the group.'

But Ellie wouldn't be drawn down that road. 'Jane, something tells me that you're protesting too much. You and Andy are probably still ten times more romantic than the rest of us could hope to be.'

'Infinitely more,' said Pixie. 'Speaking for myself.'

Jane had one of those relationships that inspired envy in both singletons, the smugly wed and, as Pixie just proved, the extremely disgruntled. Andy was practically an urban legend, a type often discussed but never seen in real dating life: intelligent, funny, sexy and kind. His equanimity was legendary, but then Jane was just as warm and supportive. Whenever she talked about how she and Andy met, she grinned like a lunatic. It seemed a match made in heaven.

It had actually been a match made in Ibiza, sweaty and knee-deep in foam. Jane was there for her cousin's hen weekend. Andy was there hoping to snog hens. They danced into each other in the early hours of Sunday morning and by the time they kissed at the airport that night they knew their good-byes would be hellos within the week back in London.

Holiday romances rarely work out, but Andy and Jane weren't your normal twenty-three year olds. Only two years into her fledgling BBC career, Jane had already bought her own flat. She had a pension and knew exactly what she wanted in life. Unlike most of her friends, whose views on procreation were ambivalent at best, Jane wanted a big, noisy, happy family like the one she came from.

Andy's future was no less clear, and just as clearly focused on having a family. He was an IT programmer, weekend rugby player, and the friend that everyone trusted with their spare keys. Within a month, he had Jane's keys too, and she had his. They were deliriously in love with each other and tried their best not to be smug about it. They spent the next two summers taking most of their holiday to go to music festivals and on Jane's twenty-fifth birthday, they married in a small summer ceremony in Jane's hometown. Her birthday party cum wedding reception was a huge BBQ in a muddy Suffolk field. Jane wore wellies with her dress. Her wedding photos, which she kept all over the house, looked like they were ordered straight from beautifulbohemianweddings.com.

Children were always part of their plan and they didn't waste time. Andy knew Jane would be the most perfect mother, and told her constantly how excited he was to see her holding their very own baby one day.

Unfortunately though, nature wasn't taking direction from Andy. As the months passed and her periods remained regular, Jane started to suspect something was wrong.

Of course, being Jane, she read every book, article and blog she could find. There had to be a way to fix what was clearly broken. She'd always been fit. She ate healthily, took her vitamins, avoided preservatives and mercury-laden tuna. Was she *too* healthy? Maybe the body functioned best in the middle of the range rather than at the extremes.

Everyone around her seemed to be getting pregnant. Even the teenage daughter of the corner shop owner was knocked up, the stupid girl, and her cousin, the hen weekend raver, was already pregnant with her second child.

At first Jane loved seeing her cousin, but as the months passed it got harder to smile convincingly when she held her cousin's tiny baby. With every sniff of that delicious little head, Jane felt more despondent, and surer that her insides weren't functioning like everyone else's. She didn't tell Andy about her fears. She wasn't about to blow his illusion of her perfection so early in their marriage. So she kept it to herself, and it festered.

Andy was the first to bring up the 'I' word.

'But we're young,' Jane said, panicking to hear her biggest fear from Andy's lips. 'We can't be infertile.'

'I'm sure we're not,' he said, smoothing the hair from her face. 'There's probably a very simple explanation.' His IT-programming brain knew there must be an answer for this run-time error. 'Maybe we should just get checked out to make sure everything's okay. If you like, I can make appointments for us.'

Dear Andy was willing to wank in a cup for the love of his life. But Jane kept putting off the appointments, and hoping, until finally Andy confronted her.

All her fear tumbled out in a wave that threatened to wash away what they had together. But Andy wouldn't let it. He held on, anchoring them both, and convinced Jane to go for tests with him.

CHAPTER SIX

'You've lost two pounds. Well done, Katie,' gushed Pam the next week at Slimming Zone as she updated my chart. Pam was a gusher, which made her the perfect slimming coach. She acted like we'd found a cure for PMT every time we dropped a bit of weight.

The last time I'd lost two pounds was when Jane made us do the Caveman Diet. It was no compensation for the eggy burps. Thankfully, womankind then left the caves and evolved to discover baked goods.

I grinned at my friends. Ellie pulled a face. Sore gainer.

'That's fantastic,' Jane said when I joined them. 'How did you do that?'

'I've no idea,' I said. 'I didn't do anything unusual. Ellie, you know I had at least two do-over days last week.' I wasn't gloating too much. Two pounds is a drop in the sea when you're a woman of larger proportions.

Besides, I was starting to see Pixie's point. If we spent as much time and effort actually losing weight as we did talking and thinking about it, we'd all be size eights. I'd never noticed how much our conversations revolved around weight. It was just a normal part of my life with my friends.

But something had begun to shift in my head over the past month. Each time we went out together, I found myself becoming less conscious of my size. For those few hours I forgot I was Fat Katie. I was simply a normal woman having fun with her best friends.

But as we *were* at the meeting to talk about weight, I couldn't begrudge Jane her congratulations when Pam announced that she'd dropped three pounds, even if her methods were suspect. She'd been pill-popping her way to weight loss.

'Do you know I can actually imagine getting back to my goal weight?' she said. 'Two and a half stone to go. I can do this. Alli, I love you!'

'But isn't it making you poo all the time?' I asked, knowing the answer. 'I wouldn't be as unconditionally in love with something that made me incontinent.'

'And it's not just the frequent poos, is it?' Ellie raised her eyebrow. 'I looked it up too. It sounds like there can be some other nasty shocks. Jane? Would you like to tell everyone what's really been happening?'

That got my full attention.

Jane's peaches-and-cream complexion reddened. 'Well, you really do need to eat a low-fat diet or there are problems. The warnings are all over the instructions. So it's no magic pill to make up for going overboard. In fact, it's the opposite. You definitely *shouldn't* take them when you've eaten too much fat. I didn't believe that, until it happened . . .' She shook her head. 'I shat my pants. I thought it was just wind. It was more.'

'Oh god, that's disgusting!'

'Did you *shart*?'

Her shoulders shook as she covered her face. 'I sharted!' she said through her fingers. 'Thank god I was at home so I could shower and change.' She lowered her voice. 'The pills keep you from absorbing fat. If it doesn't get absorbed, it's got to go somewhere. That means the poos are more . . . juicy than normal. A bit greasy.'

'Jane, are you sure about this?' I said. 'Slippery bowel movements can't be worth the weight loss.'

'I think they are,' she said quietly. When I saw her expression I let the topic drop.

Rob hurried into the meeting, shrugging his coat off as he headed for Pam. His face lit up when he saw us at the back. 'I'll be right with you,' he said, loping to the scales for his reckoning.

I wasn't sure why Rob came to the meetings. He was one of those men well-suited to his size – big and comfortingly solid. He always wore jeans that flattered his long athletic legs and favoured band tee shirts with linen jackets, and Converse trainers or those brown leather bowling shoes. Because of his height he had the look of a gentle bear. A friendly, handsome, gentle bear.

'You're the talk of the meeting, you know,' he said as he flung himself into a chair with all the grace of a walrus on land. 'Rumour has it you've started some kind of club.'

'Oh, but it's not a club,' Jane said. 'It's just us. We've been going out together lately. We went to an improvisational acting class last night!'

As she told Rob about it I found myself grinning madly. When Jane suggested the evening taster class, I'd cringed at the thought. And acting in front of my best friends? My feelings on the subject flip-flopped between excitement and dread.

'If we're made to roll around on the floor and get in touch with our inner child, I'll meet you at the pub around the corner when you're done,' Pixie had said as we'd made our way down the primary school's corridor, where crayoned artwork decorated the walls. We passed the children's Ikea-bright blue and yellow lockers and found our classroom.

There were around a dozen women already there. The desks and chairs had been pushed into the corners and a woman of about fifty stood in the centre of the room. She was wearing a leotard. I moved between Pixie and the door.

'It's not exercise, is it?' Jane whispered, scrutinising the woman's hand-knitted legwarmers. 'Because I haven't got the right clothes.'

'I haven't got the right frame of mind,' Pixie added.

'Let's see if it's weird. If it is we'll make an excuse and leave. Agreed?' Everyone nodded.

Despite her penchant for *Glee*-inspired attire, the instructor, Alexandra, wasn't at all weird. Within minutes we all wanted to be her friend. She explained what we'd be doing, with a huge disclaimer about not being able to make us award-winning actors in a single evening. Everyone laughed at the very idea. Few serious actors began their careers at an adult learning evening in the local primary school.

'Okay, we'll start with a few warm-ups,' said Alexandra, sparking Pixie's suspicion once again. 'Everyone please make a circle. This is called The Shakes, and it's meant to help with any performance anxiety we may feel. I'll explain as we go.'

Alexandra slowly looked at her hand, which began to twitch. She raised it in front of her, where her fingers started to spasm more regularly. The spasms became shudders, then judders until finally her fingers were toodloo-ing, giving her a very enthusiastic jazz hand.

'Now, I'm going to look at someone and throw them my shakes. When they catch them, their fingers will also start to shake like mine. Then the shakes will move from their fingers to another part of their body, any part. They'll look at someone else and that person will catch the new shakes.' She jerked her head and looked straight at Ellie.

'Oh, already? Well, all right then, I'll try.' She quivered admirably before throwing a bobble head at me.

I caught it, and my head began a side to side movement to rival that nodding dog off the Churchill advert. Then I let the shakes settle into my shoulders. I could feel the backs of my arms jiggle, and my boobs began to bounce despite wearing a support bra that could shore up a landslide. Back and forth my shoulders went, as my arms went out by my sides, palms facing forward. Then my shoulders shook in smaller and smaller movements as my breasts began a dangerously pendulous sway. I looked at Pixie.

'You are joking, love.'

I shrugged, briefly throwing myself off my rhythm.

'All right,' she said. 'I'm sorry for everyone who has to watch this.' With that she began to shimmy. By the end of the exercise everyone was definitely warmed up, if out of breath. The night flew by as we played Pinocchio – 'awakening' each body part from our foreheads to our toes – and something called Freeze, where we actually got to act a bit. By the end of the evening it was safe to say that none of us was destined for the stage, but my sides ached from laughing (and my boobs hurt).

'So we just meet once or twice a week to do something fun,' I explained when Jane finished recounting the night.

'That sounds like a club to me,' Rob said.

Ellie laughed. 'A club of four. We don't exactly need to hire out the O2 for our annual conference.'

'So it's very exclusive,' he said amiably.

'I suppose not,' Jane said. 'We haven't really discussed whether more people could come along . . .?'

'The more the merrier,' I said. 'Depending on what we're doing.'

'I agree,' said Ellie. 'But we'd want to check with Pixie too, in case she'd rather stick to just us four.'

Rob smiled at her apologetic look. 'Where is Pixie?'

'She quit.'

He considered this for a moment. 'Good for her. She hasn't seemed happy here for a while. Make sure it's okay with Pixie and if everyone agrees then I'm sure the others would love to join you. The rumour mill has been grinding. They think you've been out on champagne-soaked excursions. Amanda said she heard you went to Monaco.'

'Ha! We've gone to Hackney,' I said. 'It sounds like we've got a lot to live up to.'

Rob suddenly looked bashful. 'If it's not an all-girls' club, maybe I could come along too?'

'It's not a club!'

'I suppose it could be a club though,' Ellie said. 'Would you want to come out with us, Rob?' I could see her eyes asking us if that was all right.

'Fine with me,' I said.

'Me too,' said Jane. 'Rob, I'd love for you to join us.'

'Then we just need to see if Pixie objects.'

CHAPTER SEVEN

Pixie didn't object. In fact she thought it was a marvellous idea to welcome everyone. Which was how we found ourselves dancing salsa with two dozen other Slimming Zone friends in the back room of my local pub the following Sunday afternoon.

The pub landlord was more than happy for us to work up a thirst in his otherwise dead pub, and there were plenty of out-of-work salsa instructors in London to choose from. I explained that what we lacked in fitness we'd make up for in enthusiasm, and everyone pitched in five quid to pay Ricco the Snake-Hipped Wonder.

'I haven't laughed that hard since Trevor did a headstand in the lounge on a piece of Lego.' Pixie laughed again at the thought. 'Pure comedy genius, though he obviously didn't see the humour.'

Pixie didn't often talk about Trevor without swearing. 'You sounded almost fond of Trevor when you said that.'

'Did I? It must be the wine. Although he has been rather fond of me lately.' She rolled her eyes. 'He's become a randy old git. It's all I can do to keep out of his reach.'

'Well, you are in separate bedrooms,' I pointed out. 'Can't you just lock your door?'

She smiled at me. 'Dear, innocent Katie, so much to learn. The trick to a happy marriage is—'

'But you don't have a happy marriage,' Jane said.

'The trick to a marriage, then, is to make the man think he's getting what he wants, when in actual fact, you're getting what you want.'

'Oh really?' I said. 'And how are you making him think he's having sex with you?' This ought to be good.

'I'm making him think I *want* to have sex with him. It's nearly as good. He's usually so pissed when he comes home that if I can stall him, he forgets what he's after. Then I tell him in the morning, just before he has to leave for work, when the children are still at home, that I went into his room but he was asleep. That way he can't try for a quickie.'

She looked very pleased with herself.

'How long do you think you can keep that up?' Ellie asked.

'Hopefully until I hit menopause. Oh, thanks, love,' she said to Rob as he set our drinks down. 'Ellie, I've got to say, you were busting some moves in there. It's like there's sangria in your blood.'

Ellie stopped fanning herself with her beer mat. 'You are joking!'

Pixie nodded that yes, she was joking. 'Love, you've got *dos* left feet.'

'How would you know? You were too busy staring at the instructor's crotch to notice anybody's feet.'

She shrugged. 'Didn't he look like he had a nice chorizo?'

'Please stop,' Jane said. 'You'll put me off my drink.'

'The thought of chorizo probably makes you want to poo.' Pixie poked her side at around intestine-level.

'Not as much as the thought of you and that man's chorizo,' she said.

Amanda, one of the Slimming Zone veterans, sidled up to the table. 'Katie, please say we can do this again! I feel . . . wonderful. Really, that was the most fun I've had in ages.' Her round face glowed with exertion and happiness. 'It doesn't have to be dancing again. It can be anything, really, just count me in, okay? I've got to dash to pick up the children. Thanks again for including me. See you next week at the meeting!'

I recognised the feeling that swelled in me, though it wasn't a common one. We'd pulled off a great event, if I did say so myself. Inside I was glowing with pride.

Amanda's words were echoed by the others as they said their good-byes and rushed off for the rest of their Sunday afternoons.

'I'd say your club is a success,' said Rob.

'It's not a club!' Jane and Ellie said together.

'Maybe it could be though?' I mused. 'Why not? I mean, if we want others to join us anyway, then why not make it a club?'

'That sounds very formal,' Pixie said.

'Well, I guess there'd be some organising to do, but I could do that . . . of course, we could all do it too.'

'You did such a great job with this,' Ellie said. 'I'm happy to go along with whatever you plan. Unless you want me to help?'

'Only if you want to,' I said, realising how quickly the conversation was descending into ridiculously polite territory. 'I could look into something for the next night out and we can decide who wants to plan after that.'

'We could set up a Facebook page to tell the others,' Jane said. 'At the meeting next week we'd just need to tell them to like the page.'

'What about people who don't use Facebook?' Rob asked, raising his hand. For an IT programmer he was remarkably unconnected in cyberspace. Even I used Facebook and my computer skills peaked before Jedward could drive.

'We could make a simple website,' he proposed. 'We could even do one on Blogger. It's free.'

'When you say *we*,' I began.

'I mean me,' he said. 'Don't worry. I wouldn't make you step out of your comfort zone. I know you only use your computer to read celebrity gossip. I can knock up a website at work in just a few minutes. I'd be happy to.'

'It would be good, right, to make it official?' Jane said. 'I *have* felt like I've been part of something these past few months. Like we're stronger together when we go out.'

'I feel normal,' said Pixie quietly. 'For the first time in years I'm not the freak with the elastic waistband. We're all the freaks with the elastic waistbands. There's safety in numbers.'

'Exactly.' Ellie nodded, her hair flying over her eyes. 'I don't feel self-conscious. Just . . . normal. That feels so good.'

'That's because we *are* the norm here,' Pixie said. 'Actually we're the norm out there too. You've seen the news; most people are overweight. It just doesn't seem like it, looking around. Maybe it's time to be loud and proud.'

'The Loud and Proud Club,' Rob said, raising his glass. 'You'll need a name for the website.'

'The Loud and Proud Club sounds like a gay band,' Pixie said. 'What about the Loud Proud Social Club? Then you know what we are.'

'Now it sounds like a gay social club,' I said.

'The Big Girls Social Club?' Jane proposed.

Ooh, I liked that very much.

'What about big boys?' Rob said. 'Don't be sexist.'

'But you're like a girl,' Ellie said.

'Thank you for emasculating me.'

'I just mean that you're a friend, like us girls,' she clarified. 'What about the Big Boned Social Club?'

'God, no,' Pixie winced. 'That's what people call you when they think they're being nice. It makes me think of women shot-putters. Besides, not everyone who's fat is big-boned. Some of us are just curvy.'

'The Curvy Girls Club?' Jane proposed.

A tremor of enthusiasm coursed through me. The Curvy Girls Club. That was it. 'I love it!'

'Me too!'

'But it's not just for women, right?' Ellie asked, glancing quickly at Rob.

'No way, everyone is welcome,' Jane said. 'That's the whole point.'

'Do we need to account for that in the title, then?' I asked.

Pixie laughed. 'Katie, you're in sales. Since when are you worried about a little thing like accuracy?' She thought for a moment. 'We can put a little asterisk in the title and add a disclaimer in tiny writing at the bottom, like they do with payday loans and volumising mascara.'

'Problem solved then,' I said. 'We're the Wonga of social clubs. Rob, you'll join us, right?'

He grinned. 'Sure. Only I probably won't tell people I'm a member of the Curvy Girls Club. Maybe the CGC. That sounds much manlier.'

Jane lifted her drink. 'To the Curvy Girls Club.'

'Asterisk . . . and men!' said Rob.

We all raised our glasses to our new club. I hadn't been so excited since my Rory days, and this didn't even involve the potential for sex.

My friends placed great trust in me and once we were officially a club, the planning seemed doubly important. Besides, Rob made good on his threat and created a website that would feature our nights out. Plus, everyone who'd gone to the salsa lesson wanted to know what was next. So no pressure then.

Luckily I talked on the phone for a living, so nobody noticed the dozens of calls I made to help figure out whether events and venues would be suitable for our members. It took a lot longer than I imagined but by the end of the week we'd added half a dozen events to the website and Facebook page.

Funny how quickly perspectives can change. It was probably a similar feeling to that experienced by the newly engaged or pregnant, who suddenly notice things like bridal shops and stretch-mark creams for the first time. Those were still off my radar but every theatre marquee, restaurant review and band poster sparked my interest. I went to bed each night thinking about possible events. And I awoke every morning with excitement gently fizzing in my tummy.

CHAPTER EIGHT

The next few weeks flew by in a whirlwind of activity. One minute we were dancing salsa with friends, the next we were organising nights out for more than fifty people, and getting bollocked for not doing enough. Speaking for myself, anyway.

'I did try to book,' said the woman with her arms crossed over her ample bosom as we waited for Pam to start the Slimming Zone meeting. She was acting like I'd purposely kept her from seeing *Jersey Boys* with us. 'I got an error message saying that it was sold out.'

I could tell from the consternation lining her over-tanned face that she wasn't going to let it go. I tried again. 'I'm really sorry. We've been getting a lot of interest in the theatre. If you try booking a bit earlier next time . . .'

'I know some people are bringing their friends. That's why there wasn't room for me. That's not right when I'm a member here.'

'I'm sorry,' I said again. 'But the events aren't just for Slimming Zone members. In fact we don't have members. They're for anyone who wants to come.'

Her sense of entitlement really pissed me off. The Curvy

Girls Club was ours. She was lucky we'd opened it up to other people at all.

I looked across the room at Jane and Ellie as they laughed with a group of women who'd come with us to Kew Gardens last weekend. Jane was awkwardly accepting a compliment on the club's behalf. So how did I end up as head of the Complaints Department?

'Excuse me a minute,' I said to the whinger, cutting her off mid-indignation. 'I think Jane wants a word with me.'

'Fiona was just telling us about a Thames river cruise,' she said when I approached. 'Some of the boats have Dixieland jazz bands. Doesn't that sound fun?' I hadn't seen Jane so animated in a long time. She'd even abandoned her needles and yarn for this conversation.

I nodded, already thinking about the questions I'd ask the organisers – how big are the life jackets? Are there many steps? Will people be helped onto/off the boat? I could make a few calls tomorrow morning before my review.

Finally Pam rapped her hand on the table, dragging our attention away from boats and bands. 'I know everyone is excited, but can we please start the meeting? Who'd like to come up and pop on the scales?'

A few of the women made their way to the front. Ellie and I hung about at the back as usual.

'Jane, I figured you'd run up there tonight,' I said when she made no move. 'Aren't you curious to know how much you've crapped out this week?'

She shook her head. 'I know the answer. It's zero pounds. I stopped the pills.'

'Good!' Ellie and I said together.

'You don't need them. Tell her, Rob,' Ellie said as he joined us.

'Tell her what?' He shrugged out of his heavy wool coat.

'Tell Jane she doesn't need diet pills.'

'But I do need them,' she said. 'I just can't stand the side effects any more. I'll think of something else. What?' she demanded when I rolled my eyes.

I did love her but sometimes I wanted to shake her. 'Why don't you try changing your mind set instead of your waist-line? That seems healthier to me.'

'What should I do, Katie? Tell me, please. Should I just give up and grow into a huge blob that Andy will eventually have to winch out of bed?'

'God, you can be dramatic sometimes. You know you *could* stop starving yourself and going on these crazy diets without turning into a blob. You eat healthily most of the time. You do exercise. I just think we should all stop beating ourselves up because we're not models.'

'Katie's right,' said Ellie. 'I've been thinking about what Pixie said. If I'm honest I'm tired of always worrying about my weight. These last couple of months have . . . I don't know, they've made me see things a little differently.'

'Me too,' I said. 'Isn't it more important to be happy with ourselves than to constantly think we should be doing better? Every time I promise myself to *do better*, eat less, cut carbs, exercise more, that's saying that I'm not good enough as I am. I don't want to do that to myself any more.'

'So you're just going to give up, slob out and embrace your inner fattie?' Jane asked, jutting out her chin. 'That's irresponsible. You have to take responsibility for your size, Katie . . . it's lazy.'

Her judgement hurt. It wasn't a surprising message – I'd heard it my whole life in one form or another, often as friendly advice, sometimes as a hostile declaration – but it still hurt. As if I hadn't sadly wondered myself how it had come to this. A pound here, an extra few inches there. Over the years, gradual changes became the new norm. Who amongst us hadn't grabbed handfuls of tummy just to feel its squidgy bulk? Or shimmied naked in the mirror to watch the seismic shifts happening below her waistline? I just didn't want to let that define me any more.

'I'm not saying I'm going to totally slob out, Jane. I'm just saying that while we may not be perfect, none of us is getting bigger, right? We packed these pounds on years ago, and we're still punishing ourselves for them. You wouldn't still blame Andy or the children for something they did years ago, would you?'

'Of course not,' Jane said.

'Then why do you keep blaming yourself? We do eat a balanced diet and exercise and do all the things we're supposed to. Our lifestyles are healthy now. We should respect ourselves as much as we do other people.'

The fight left Jane. 'I do try.'

Ellie hugged her. 'I know you do. But cutting three and a half thousand calories out of our diets just to lose a pound is *hard*! Katie is right. We need to stop beating ourselves up for what we aren't doing and be happy with what we are.'

I drew myself up in my chair. 'I'm quitting Slimming Zone. I joined to learn how to be healthier and to find support. Well, now I know how to be healthy, and you give me all the support I could ever want. And lately when we're out together, I have so much fun that I don't even think about my weight. I feel . . . well, not pretty, exactly. But normal. I don't need to come to these meetings any more . . . and if you think about it, you might realise that you don't either.'

I watched their faces for a reaction. Jane was the first to speak. 'I can't promise that I'll ever love my fat, but I'm willing to try.' Her hands reached for her knitting. 'On one condition. The Curvy Girls Club has to continue. I've been happier these last few months than I have been for years.'

'Me too,' Ellie said. 'And I do think we're ready to go it alone. Together, I mean, but not here. What do you think, Jane?'

She smiled. 'Well, it'll be no fun coming here without you lot. And what Katie says is true . . . so yes, I'm ready. Besides, it's not like we don't all have scales at home.'

'You're missing the point a bit though, Jane,' I said. 'We've got to learn to be happy as we are instead of constantly worrying about how we'd like to be. That's what I'm going to do from now on.'

Rob grinned at me. 'Promise?'

'I promise,' I said. 'What about you? Want to quit with us?'

He shrugged. 'I only come here for the women anyway. And I think it's safe to say that the club will keep going, Jane, at least if demand is any factor. Take a guess at how many unique views you've had on the website and blog.'

We all shrugged. I had no idea what a good number might be.

'You're averaging nearly three hundred a week.'

'What does that mean?'

'It means you'd better get some more events lined up. Your club is starting to get very popular.'

Two years earlier, when Nutritious pared back the whole company's hours to four days a week, there was very little silver lining in that ominous thundercloud. But the company needed to save a lot of money or we wouldn't have had any chance of keeping our jobs, and in the middle of a recession nobody felt much like arguing above a disgruntled whisper.

It didn't actually have much of an impact on us salespeople, since most of our pay cheques came from commissions. So we just squeezed a bit more work into the remaining four days to keep the clients happy, and once again the company got more work out of us for less money.

Ellie survived a month of *Jeremy Kyle* before getting herself work at the café around the corner on her day off. She preferred getting paid to serve the down-and-outs to watching them for free on TV. Besides, she didn't have sales commissions like the rest of us, so the cut in hours hurt.

I shared neither her urge to work nor her aversion to daytime telly, which, as the club business accelerated, was turning out to be a good thing. I started splitting my Tuesdays between the equally important tasks of napping, watching old films and club business. Invariably, though, I still had to make some calls from the office.

I'd just hung up with the river cruise people when Alex appeared beside my desk. 'I've got something for you. Want to grab a coffee before my next meeting?'

Of course I did. Despite all my unsubtle hints, we hadn't been to lunch again. Still, there was no doubt we were on more familiar terrain now.

'I'll need some caffeine,' I said. 'I've got my appraisal this afternoon.'

I was willing to make an exception to my no-caffeine rule to get me through that meeting.

When it came to my comfort and enjoyment, reviews were on par with smear tests. True, no tears had been shed during them in the entire six years I'd worked at Nutritious. Yet no matter how hard I worked, I'd never been more than Adequate. Five grades to choose from and my boss always put me in the middle. What kind of motivation was that? Adequate was a nice way of saying *meh*. It was so-so, a verbal shrug. They claimed it meant I was doing everything I was supposed to. It meant they had no complaints. Was it any wonder I always walked away with a sense of disappointment?

But today I was going to make my stand (not my normal modus operandi). I knew I was better than adequate. I just had to grow the meatballs to tell Cressida why.

Alex made me wait until our steaming takeaway cups were

in hand before pulling a small white envelope from his jacket pocket.

Inside were two tickets for the orchestra at the weekend. 'Wow, thank you!'

'You mentioned that you like classical music, and there were some extra tickets going, so I thought . . .' He grinned, watching my expression.

'I'd love to, thanks!' I nearly dropped my coffee as I lunged to hug him. It was an unusual feeling, and, being honest, slightly awkward. 'I had no idea you liked the symphony. You never said.' I added that to the list of his perfect man credentials.

'That's because I can't stand it. I'd lose the will to live halfway through the performance. I thought you and Ellie could go. Like I said, we've got the extra tickets so someone may as well use them.'

Then this wasn't a date. It was a nice gesture from a work colleague. 'Well, thanks very much, I'm sure she'd love to. Really, this is very kind of you.' I kept my voice bright to hide the disappointment that suddenly hit me.

How much longer was I prepared to let this stupid crush go on? Snap out of it, Katie. Perhaps it was time to heed six years of evidence that he's not into you.

I'd got some perspective again by the time we reached the office. Alex had, after all, remembered that I liked classical music. And he had thought to give me the tickets. Those were the actions of a friend. So he wasn't interested in me romantically. I could live with that. I *had* lived with that for over half a decade. And we were friends, of a sort. No, I wouldn't call him to discuss weekend plans (although this was mainly because I didn't have his phone number, not because I exercised any restraint), but we were friendly. It was time I let that be enough.

The office kitchen was abuzz an hour later when I went

in to microwave my cooling coffee. A large dark chocolate cake sat on the table. Next to it was an envelope, scrawled with the invitation to *Help yourselves you greedy sods*. A few people had hacked into it, revealing layers of chocolate sponge held together with creamy cocoa icing. My mouth watered.

'That looks delicious!' I said to my colleagues. 'Have you tried any?'

Mark and Matt both nodded.

'I'm having seconds!' said Stacy, our HR bod. Everyone called her Racy Stacy behind her back, thanks to her talent for seducing most of the men in the office. She stuck her finger into the slice she'd just cut, licking the icing off while Mark and Matt tried to calm their erections. 'Mmm, I could swallow the whole thing.'

I had no doubt about that.

'Are you having any?' she asked me.

'Oh, no thanks. I've got my cappuccino here.' I waved my unsatisfying-by-comparison drink, determined to practise what I preached since quitting Slimming Zone. 'That's my treat for the day.' Moderate Katie, that was me.

'You're doing it right,' she said. 'My cousin lost thirty pounds just by cutting out carbs. They're really bad for you.' She forked in another bite.

'Exercise helps too,' said Matt. 'I can eat anything as long as I run. You should try running, Katie.'

'Swimming is better,' Mark said. 'There's less strain on the joints, so anyone can do it, regardless of their siz— fitness.'

I smiled politely while my colleagues debated the best ways to slim me down, while shovelling in more cake. The fact that I hadn't asked for their advice never occurred to them.

CHAPTER NINE

I tried to calm my nerves as I walked towards the conference room, where Cressida waited with my employee file. She was an okay manager (some might say Adequate), and generally a nice lady.

'Hey, all right?' she said, smiling through the bright red lipstick she always wore. She was a fit woman of a certain age who'd been with Nutritious since it was founded twenty years ago. She was always impeccably presented. Her makeup never wore off, her hair stayed where it was supposed to and her chin didn't sport the stubborn hairs the rest of us worried about when the sun shone.

'How was the meeting yesterday?' Cressida asked.

Our company liked to keep us abreast of the latest ways to legally harass people. Everyone else had gone to the sales techniques meeting.

'Tuesday is my day off, remember?'

'Oh, that's right,' she said vaguely. 'I've been so tied up with reviews that I've been a total scatterbrain. So, you know the drill by now.' I nodded. 'We talk about how you've done these past six months . . . but first, there's something else.'

I waited.

'As you know, the company has been doing everything it can to get through the downturn. Unfortunately our revenues have still fallen off, so we have to make some adjustments. I'm sure you can appreciate that these decisions aren't easy, and I wish I was able to give you better news, but Katie, we need to ask you to go down to three days a week. But that does mean that you can have Fridays off!'

She said this like she'd just given me a free holiday, not an unpaid one. I did a quick calculation to see if I could live on three days a week. I could, just about.

'Is this permanent?'

'Hopefully not!' Cressida said, sounding relieved that I hadn't burst into tears. 'We'll assess in a few months and if business has improved, we'll look to bring people back on board.'

Sure they would. That's what they said after cutting our hours last time.

'After all, productivity will be affected with the reduced hours, so we don't want to make these cuts,' she continued. 'Don't worry about that though, we'll adjust your objectives accordingly. Do you have any questions?'

'Yes, one. Does this affect all the staff like last time?'

She shook her head. 'Luckily we didn't have to be that drastic, so we're only forced to make some cuts.'

In that case, actually I had two questions. 'Why me?'

'It's nothing personal, Katie. We looked at everyone and had to make some difficult decisions. Now, if there are no more questions we can move on to your appraisal.'

She waited to see if I'd object further. There wasn't any point. Asking more questions, or complaining about the decision, wouldn't change her mind.

'How many others have lost a day?'

'Around twenty.'

That made me feel better. Misery did love a bit of company.

'Is Ellie one of them?'

'I can't discuss other employees with you. But no, she's not.'

I nodded, happy for her at least.

'I've no more questions.'

'All right then, let's continue,' she said, clearly relieved to be back on solid ground. 'How do you feel you've done these past six months?

In the few moments before I answered I tried to calm my racing thoughts. In the lead was *My Mortgage Payment*, who always ran well in difficult conditions. Following closely behind came *Why Me?*, looking like a strong contender for the prize. But then on the inside rail, *Day Off* was making up ground, and *Could Be Worse* began passing the field on the outside. It was going to be a tight race.

All right, Katie, old girl, enough daydreaming (nightmaring), concentrate on the question. Now's your chance. Ignore the fact that you've just lost a day. You can do this; remember you've got the meatballs. Mmm, meatballs. My tummy rumbled.

'I've done well.'

Cressida's face remained impassive.

'I think I have. I mean, I've done everything you've asked me to.'

'You have.' She nodded, speaking slowly. 'Your performance is as good as it was last time round.'

'No!'

She jumped in her chair.

'I mean, it's better than last time. Look.' I pointed to my last appraisal. 'See here? My goal was to renew five client contracts. I renewed six. And here, I signed up two new accounts.'

'How's Jenny?' she asked.

I cringed at the thought of my nemesis. 'No change,' I admitted.

58

Most people just put the phone down on me when they didn't want to listen to my spiel. And they didn't take my calls when I tried again. Not Jenny. She always took my call. They usually went something like this:

Her (in her nasally Australian accent): Go ahead, I've got five minutes. What are you going to tell me that I haven't heard before?

Invariably I rose to the bait, launching into the features and claims about our newest products. I always listened to our weekly product briefings with Jenny in mind, optimistic that one day I'd win her over.

Her, after listening in silence: And you claim this works? It sounds like another one of your gimmicks.

I'd explain that they weren't *my* gimmicks, that we had an entire team of scientists who developed the products. Then I'd point to all the studies that proved their efficacy. Our company armed us well like that.

Her: You fund those studies. Of course they're going to give you the results you want.

We didn't fund the studies, I'd explain (every time). They were independent studies.

Her, changing tack: People today are just lazy. They're happy to stuff pills down their gob instead of addressing the underlying issues.

Me, breathing deeply through my gob: Our products are for people who need some help staying healthy.

Her: Lazy people. Would you use this product?

Me: Yes.

Her: Then you're one of the ones I'm talking about. Why would I buy from you? Clearly your company is only interested in shortcuts. Maintaining health is a lifelong process, not a quick fix.

At which point the conversation would veer off into a philosophical debate about the psychology of our culture today.

That's the part I rather enjoyed, and the reason I wouldn't give her up when Cressida asked if I wanted to take her off my list.

'Jenny aside,' Cressida said. 'You've done very well with your prospects, though you haven't quite met your client meeting target, have you?'

'But I'm never allowed out to see clients. Clive doesn't give me the new clients and you never approve travel expenses.'

'It's tough right now. Finance checks every expense.' She looked sad to have to tell me this. 'You know we have to look at each request based on the cost-benefit of the meeting. If one salesperson can see several clients in the same area, we have to do that. It's a cost-efficiency decision.'

It wasn't, but I needed to stay on-point. 'Then why am I being penalised for not meeting that target?'

'You're not penalised. Not at all. I've still given you Adequate on your client meetings, even though you haven't hit the target.'

'But it counts as a negative when I point out where I've exceeded the target.'

Cressida sighed. 'Katie. Your overall grade is based on your aggregate performance.' She spoke as if to a dim-witted child. 'In order to exceed expectations you mustn't be behind in any of your goals. I've really given you a very good review, considering . . .' She shifted in her chair. The mood changed suddenly. 'There is just one thing we need to discuss.'

I got the feeling I was about to find out why I'd been the lucky winner of another day off.

'Our records show that you've been using company resources for your own personal use.'

I racked my brains for something to say. 'I, I might have taken a pen home, accidentally.'

'I'm not talking about pens.' She fished in her folder. 'Your telephone records show a lot of personal calls.' Dozens of phone numbers were circled in purple pen. They never used red pen these days, since the consultants came in last year and declared it to be a shouty colour. 'These aren't clients, and they're not on the cold-call lists. Are you making personal calls from work? I don't mean the odd call home to check your messages. This looks like much more. '

It was a rhetorical question. The evidence sat on the table between us. Is ignorance a valid self-defence? Your honour, it never occurred to me that these were crimes. Everyone made personal calls on company time. Like everyone took pens home (I had a stationery cupboard in my handbag).

'I'm really sorry, Cressida, and I'm very embarrassed about this. I didn't think it was a problem. And I didn't realise I'd made quite so many calls. Of course I won't do it again.' Though I wasn't sure how I was going to keep that promise. I'd have to find someone else to make the club calls on the days I worked. Maybe Pixie could do it. She was at home, though with her children and husband there, it wasn't a very conducive work environment. Maybe Rob.

Cressida smiled. 'It's fine. I just had to mention it, as your boss, that's all. Really, don't worry about it. It's definitely not a big deal.'

'Did it factor into your decision to cut my hours?'

'No, not at all!'

I exhaled with relief. 'I feel really foolish.'

'Please don't. You're right, everybody does it. It just got flagged up because there was a pattern. You know how the company likes its exception reports. Seriously, don't think any more about it. Have you got any more questions about your review before we set your goals for the next six months?'

I shook my head, feeling stupid for trying to argue my way out of the Adequate box. She took my final review from her folder and slid it over the table.

Needs Improvement. My face burned. 'But I thought you said it was no big deal?' I whispered.

'Oh, it's not, believe me. We just had to put you there since the reports were flagged up. HR policy. But in reality it's not an issue as long as you don't turn up on any more reports. Your performance has been fine. Now, shall we talk about your goals?'

She talked through the rest of the review, but I wasn't paying much attention. I Needed Improvement.

Alex's email was waiting for me when I returned to my desk.

You okay?

Did you know about the cut in hours?

Yes, I'm sorry. I couldn't say anything until everyone was told. It's a companywide decision. Hopefully it won't mean a big cut in income as long as you keep up with your commissions. Seriously though, are you okay?

I guess so, thanks. I'm trying to see it as a positive – I get an extra day off!

That's my girl. It'll be fine, you'll see.

As I typed smiley faces in response, something occurred to me. Were those sympathetic symphony tickets he gave me, to cushion the blow?

CHAPTER TEN

Whether they were pity tickets or not, Ellie and I enjoyed the symphony tremendously. By the time the last note faded away I wasn't thinking about my change in circumstances at all.

But of course, being told you've been singled out for partial redundancy does prey on the mind, so after the concert I obsessed about it all weekend. Dress it up any way you like, it hurt to know I'd been singled out. Cressida had said it wasn't because I Needed Improvement, but if not that, then why?

Alex was at my desk when I got into work on Monday. He whisked me away to the coffee shop, his face creased with concern as we sipped our steaming drinks.

'Will you fight it?' he asked.

I shook my head. I'd spent the weekend figuring out what I wanted, and how I might get it. When I told Alex, he smiled.

'You're a very sharp woman,' he said, touching my hand as my tummy cartwheeled.

Back at the office I put on my game face and told Cressida that if they insisted on taking work away from me, then I wanted my days off to be Thursday and Friday. Given that

I was the one being underemployed, I reasoned, she should accommodate my wishes. Plus, it would be easier to find part-time work when I didn't have to split my days. At the mention of another job, Cressida flinched and easily acquiesced. I was glad she felt guilty. She bloody well should, having given me the Judas kiss.

Not that I had any plans to get a part-time job. Ellie worked through my budget with her Worst Case Scenario hat on and I'd still have just enough money with the pay cut. Besides, I had a better idea about what to do on those days. So I called our first official Curvy Girls Club meeting.

A smattering of the regulars sat at stools along the bar in our local, while most of the booths were colonised by the trendsters who'd moved into the area in the past few years. As a quasi-local (four years in the neighbourhood), of course I pretended to commiserate with the pub landlord's rants about the Uniqlo-clad newbies ruining the character of the place. But given that the estate at the end of my road was raided weekly and the strip club on the corner had to install blue lights outside to keep the addicts from shooting up on the property, I welcomed the fact that our new neighbours raised my property value and didn't usually carry concealed weapons. And if the owner saw fit to use some of his windfall to replace the burgundy paisley carpet that still stank years after the last fag was puffed in there, all the better.

'I have news,' I said as Ellie and I returned to the booth with everyone's drinks. 'I'm down to three days a week at Nutritious. They've cut my hours again.'

'Oh no, that's terrible!' Jane's hands paused over her knitting. 'Both of you?'

Ellie shook her head.

'Bastards.' That was Pixie.

'Well, it's not completely bad news,' I said, hoping that

was true. 'Looking on the bright side, it'll free me up to do other things . . . like maybe work more on the Curvy Girls Club?'

'Well of course, sweetheart, you can, but can you afford not to work that day? I mean not getting paid for doing it. I know doing the organising is a lot of work.'

'Well, that's the thing. Maybe I could get paid for doing it.' I took a deep breath. 'I've been thinking and it *is* a lot of work to put the events together. So maybe it's reasonable to charge a small booking fee – just a few quid to cover overheads. Rob designed the website and is running it for free. If we had a bit of money coming in then we could afford to pay for the time everyone puts into the club.'

I watched my friends' faces as they mulled this over. A little smile played around Ellie's lips. She already knew of my proposal, of course. I'd told her as soon as I'd thought of it.

'Then it would be a business?' Jane asked, sounding uncertain.

'Do we want it to be a business?' asked Pixie.

I shook my head. 'I don't, not really. But it does seem to be getting more popular, and I'm excited about where it could go. It's been so fun, but I also feel like it's important. I suppose we could just plan events as and when we've got time . . . It's just that we've started something now. I really want to keep it going.'

'Me too,' Pixie said. 'These past few months have been great. Every time we go out I feel like I find a little piece of myself again. I can't remember when I was so chuffed with my life. Sometimes I even forget about that bloody man at home. That's worth more than a couple of quid to me.'

We laughed at her statement, but I recognised the sad honesty in it. 'Is he still trying to get into your knickers?'

She nodded. 'I don't know what's gotten into him lately. He's bloody keen for someone who constantly tells me how fat and ugly I am. Last night he called me a . . . and I quote, a "shit-filled pig". He was angry that we ate tea without him. As if I'd starve myself or the children just because he's two hours late back from the pub. But he's a walking contradiction. One minute he's saying things like that, pointing out the fat rolls on my tummy or jiggling the backs of my arms, and the next he's pointing his erection at me and telling me how much he loves me.'

'Pixie, you can't let him do that to you!' Ellie said. 'I mean making you feel bad about your weight, not the other thing.'

'He's not hurting me.'

'Maybe not physically,' I said. 'But mentally he is. Ellie's right. You can't let him do that.'

She sighed. 'I pick my battles, love. He'd never dare lay a hand on me or the children. Believe me, that would be going too far.' She chuckled. 'And now I think I've got a way to keep him from laying anything on me . . .' Her eyes glinted as she dug her mobile phone from her bag and scrolled through a few screens. 'Look what I've just bought!'

'Oh my god,' Jane said, as we all looked at the photo. 'Are *you* planning to wear that?'

'I got three of them. They arrived in the post today. I'm going to try one tonight. Sexy, eh?' She grinned wickedly.

Pixie seemed to be suggesting wearing a puke-green, thick terrycloth onesie around the house as birth control. The one she showed us had a hood and feet and zipped up the front. She was right. I didn't imagine Trevor would unzip that unless she was going into cardiac arrest.

'I hope it works,' Ellie said. 'But you really should think about leaving, Pixie.'

'I do, every waking moment, love, but I'd need to find work or the children and I won't be able to live. Right, thank you for depressing me.'

'Sorry!' we all said.

66

She smiled. 'That's all right. I know you're just watching out for me. Now, where were we, before you convinced me to share my fashion advice with you?'

Pixie often snapped shut as quickly as she opened up, so I wasn't surprised to hear her change the subject.

'Charging for events,' I said. 'I did the maths. If we'd charged two quid for each event we've had so far, we'd have over six hundred quid now.'

'That *is* interesting,' Pixie said. 'It actually could be a business if we wanted it to be.'

'Assuming people will pay,' Jane said.

'Assuming people will pay,' echoed Pixie. 'We could also expand the events.'

'That's what we're saying, sweetheart.'

'No, I mean we could expand the *range* of events we host. They don't all have to be things we want to do ourselves. If it's an official club now, and a business, shouldn't we think of things that will be popular even though they may not be our cup of tea?'

I nodded. 'Like what?'

She thought for a moment. 'What about speed-dating?'

My face told her my thoughts on that.

'Why not? A lot of the people coming are single. They might like it. We could call it something fun, like Find a Chubby Hubby.'

'Wasn't that a brand of ice cream?' Jane wondered.

'Right. Copyright issues. How about Fat Friends?' she proposed. 'I don't know, something fun.'

I definitely *didn't* like that idea. 'That was a TV programme . . . besides, there's nothing fun about Fat Friends. It's insulting.'

'Oh, get off your high horse. We're fat. We're friends. It does what it says on the tin.'

'All right,' Ellie said. 'We don't have to decide right now.

The important thing is that we agree we'll charge a fee, right? So we can grow the Curvy Girls Club. The sky's the limit, ladies.'

Everyone nodded and I felt like I'd just watched our child take her first step. How had this become so important to me? Sappy Katie.

We'd just sat down to dinner a week later at Pixie's favourite pizza place when Jane dropped her bombshell on us.

'I can't wait any longer,' she said. 'Look!' She yanked a copy of the *Evening Standard* from her cavernous bag, dragging out most of her knitting in the process.

London's 'biggest' social club?
There's a new kid on the block in London's entertainment industry, and it's not for everyone. A group of fed-up slimmers have come together to launch the Curvy Girls Club, an entertainment resource for the larger lady.

The long article went on to describe how we'd started and some of the events we'd done so far.

'Ooh look, we're named!' Ellie wriggled. 'I had no idea we were going to get into the newspaper!' She said it like our names had appeared written in the night sky. 'And Katie, you're quoted!'

I pulled the paper closer.

'I hope you don't mind, sweetheart. They wanted a quote and I remembered what you said at Slimming Zone. It seemed perfect so . . .'

I read the line twice. *The point is to learn to be happy the way we are, says co-founder Katie Winterbottom, instead of constantly worrying about how we'd like to look.*

'You sly bugger,' said Pixie. 'How did you do this?'

Jane blushed. 'I hope you don't mind. It happened by

accident, really. One of the mums at Abigail's school writes for them, and one afternoon last month we got talking when we dropped the children off. Actually I was surprised she spoke to me. She's part of the immaculate crowd who drive up in their huge sparkling clean SUVs, looking like they've just come from the salon. They don't usually talk to me, just stare like I'm something they've accidently stepped in. They probably go off to their gyms afterwards to perfect their already perfect bodies. Meanwhile I turn up in the same tracksuit from the day before, with no makeup and dirty hair, shove the children out the door and go home to eat the remains of their breakfast. Plus all the biscuits I can find in the house. It's depressing. If we had the money I'd hire a nanny just to do the school runs.'

Ellie squeezed Jane's hand.

'Oh, it's all right, sweetheart. I'm not the only slummy mummy at the school gates. It just feels like that sometimes. So anyway, I'd accidentally boxed her car in and instead of just telling me to move, she mentioned that her daughter loves Abigail and it went from there, really. When she mentioned her work I thought I had nothing to lose by telling her what we were doing. She loved the idea and pitched it to her editor. So then we did a telephone interview about the club. She told me not to get my hopes up, so I didn't mention anything, but then it came out tonight.'

'I wonder if anyone went on the website to have a look.'

'Call Rob!' Pixie and Ellie said at once.

'Okay, okay.' My hand was already on my phone. 'Though it's dinnertime. I'll text him in case he's eating.' I tapped the short message about the article and pressed send.

'We could try getting into other papers,' I said. 'If the *Evening Standard* were interested then maybe the other local papers will be too.'

'The *Evening Standard* isn't local,' Ellie said. 'It's national!'

'No, Ellie, it's London's local paper.'

She shook her head. 'It's not national? I just assumed.'

'Spoken like a true southerner,' said Pixie. 'No, my love, it's just for London. Katie's right though, we could try other locals like the *Ham & High*.'

'And maybe the nationals would be interested too,' said Ellie. 'Imagine getting into *The Times* or *The Guardian*. Jane, do you think it's possible?'

She nodded. 'It's possible, but probably more likely for the local papers. I'd be happy to write a short PR piece and send it round to the editors. I can get contact details from work.'

'Then it's official,' I teased. 'You're our head of PR.' With Jane's connections at Channel 4, where she worked as a programme developer, I couldn't think of a better candidate.

It was funny how we'd slipped naturally into the roles that suited us – Rob on the website, me organising the events and now Jane handling the PR. Pixie and Ellie didn't have as much free time as we did – Trevor resented any time Pixie wasn't slavishly looking after him or the children, and Ellie's time was tied up between her second job and lovely Thomas – but they came to most of the events and had become the de facto hosts.

'Sure, I'm happy to be our publicist,' Jane said, looking chuffed with her new role.

'This is all starting to become official now, isn't it?' Ellie said. 'I mean, the Curvy Girls Club is a going concern.'

'Do we need to formalise anything?' I asked. 'Now that we're charging a fee, do we need to register somewhere, or tell HMRC?'

Pixie shrugged. 'We're not exactly Philip Green yet.'

'No, but we should probably set up something simple,' Jane said. 'When my brother started his business he did have to register with HMRC, even though he wasn't making any money at first. I can ask him about it. We'd probably just need to nominate ourselves as directors and file some paperwork.'

'Does that mean we get to be on the board of directors?' Ellie's eyes shone. 'And have a president and everything?'

'I nominate Katie for president,' Pixie said. 'After all, you're doing most of the work, love.'

'I second it,' said Jane and Ellie at the same time. 'All in favour?'

'Aye!'

My phone pinged with a text just as the waitress set the results of our first executive decisions before us. (I chose the cheese-less seafood pizza.)

Website is going nuts, Rob's text read. *As Chief Brody once said, You're gonna need a bigger boat. Let's talk about upping the bandwidth. Off work tmrw, let's meet.*

I showed everyone the text. 'I guess that means the article has worked,' I said, grinning. 'Maybe it's time to think about an official launch.'

CHAPTER ELEVEN

It was after eleven the next morning by the time I met Rob.
He'd suggested an address in Hackney that I had to use my
iPhone to find. Not that I felt particularly comfortable waving
it around in the desolate neighbourhood.

Come through the red door under the arches, he'd said.
Yeah right. That was how sadistic horror films started.
Tentatively I knocked, ready to spring into the road if
necessary.

'Hello!' Rob said, looking at his watch. 'Is everything
okay?'

'I'm really sorry I'm late. I didn't sleep well again last
night.' I stifled a yawn, which sparked him off.

'Come inside,' he said, throwing open the big metal door.
'I got you a coffee but you probably want to heat it up.'

It took me a second for my brain to register what my eyes
were seeing. 'What the heck is this place?'

'It could be your bigger boat,' he said.

'Hmm?'

'Technically it's my cousin's studio, but it's huge and he
only uses a little bit. He said we can use it for meetings
whenever we want.'

We were in a damp, strip-lit space with a very unusual décor. I stared at the seven-foot-high grizzly bear wearing a jaunty bowler hat.

'That's Pete,' he said, making introductions.

'And your cousin does what exactly?'

'Taxidermy. I'd have thought that was obvious. Should we warm up your coffee? Come on, I'll show you around.'

I followed Rob to the makeshift kitchen as he explained about his cousin, David. He liked to work at night, he said, so we'd probably never see him. David's clients usually picked up their newly stuffed pets quickly but every so often they'd fail to return for their dearly departed. Which explained the menagerie around the place. A rather angry-looking Pekingese wearing a tiara stood guard on one of the desks.

I shifted a tiny mouse orchestra to the side with my now-too-hot coffee cup.

'I didn't expect you to have a cousin who stuffed animals for a living.' Rob looked warm-blooded, for one thing, with thick brown, lively looking hair and sparkly blue eyes. 'Don't you find all this a bit ghoulish?'

He laughed. 'I'm used to it. You should see my cousin. He looks like Marilyn Manson. But he's a nice guy and I thought this might work as an office space for the club. As you can see there are loads of desks and David is fine with us being here. He just asks that we replace the teabags if we use them.'

I couldn't argue with a bargain like that. 'Well thanks, I think it's great. And I suppose I'll get used to the dead animals eventually. Lucky none of us is vegetarian.' Still, I didn't think Ellie would be crazy about this place.

I stifled another yawn as we brainstormed PR ideas for the club's official launch in a few weeks. It would soon be six months since we went to see Thriller together.

'Fireworks?' Rob suggested.

'Mmm. Maybe with something else. It needs to be big,

something that'll draw in new clients from the whole of London.'

'Unlimited free doughnuts? We'd have a stampede on our hands. Or maybe a concert?'

'We don't have any money,' I said. 'We could serve day-old doughnuts or maybe get some Morris dancers for free.' I shook my head. 'But we need to think big.'

'With no money.'

'Right.'

We stared at each other, willing inspiration to come.

'We might need to spend *some* money,' he said eventually. 'You've got the chance to grow the club into something huge. The website had nearly seven hundred unique visitors this week.'

'You're talking IT again. I don't speak that language.'

He laughed. 'It's the number of actual people that went on your site. Seven hundred, all looking at the events. Do you want me to send you weekly stats?'

'Only if you translate them first.'

'Don't worry, I won't blind you with science. I can text you the number of unique visitors and the number of people who've signed up for events each week.'

'How many people signed up this week?'

He held up his finger, took out his phone and started texting.

My phone pinged.

196 signups, 700 unique views. Next update in a week. Rob

'You couldn't just tell me?'

'If this is a business, we should follow protocol.'

'What does protocol say about more coffee?'

'I'd need to check the handbook but I think it says we should have lunch if we're going to go to the wine tasting at three. I'm pretty sure that section was amended after what you told me about last time.'

I knew I shouldn't have told him the details about the club's first wine tasting last month, when I'd made the mistake of not eating beforehand. The hotel's sommelier, a dapper Frenchman with handlebar moustaches, had poured me a glass of bubbly when I arrived. I'd felt very Continental, swanning around the grand rooms to check on the arrangements. But planning events for the club was a little trickier than doing it for ladies-who-lunched. London socialites demanded low-GI food or a certain brand of bottled water. Our clients needed wide doorways (for the occasional mobility scooter) and sturdy chairs. We didn't want anyone crashing to the ground amidst the splinters of Louis XVI furniture.

The hotel had followed our instructions to the letter – sturdy banqueting chairs surrounded the enormous polished wood table. Armless and indestructible, they were the overweight person's friend.

So there hadn't been much to do in the hour before the guests arrived except flirt with the sommelier, whose accent was pant-strippingly sexy. By the time everyone turned up we'd finished most of the first bottle.

I fell off my chair some time around the Loire Valley Chenin Blancs. I'd hardly felt the bump on my head when I hit the table. One minute I was eye-to-eye with thirty people. The next I was giggling on the floor. It hadn't been my finest hour.

Rob and I made our way to the wine tasting after a stomach-lining lunch. It felt like a typically dreary January morning. Which would be fine except that it was mid-May. The dank, stained arches and industrial rubbish bins blocking the narrow pavement felt better suited to Dickensian London than East London.

Rob and I saw the problem as soon as he held the restaurant door open for me.

'We're all ready for you,' said the manager, gesturing to the long table in the middle of the narrow restaurant.

'Thank you,' I said, preparing my diplomatic approach. 'There's just one thing. There'll be eighteen of us.'

He looked at the table, bobbing his fingers as he counted. 'Yes, eighteen, that's right. We've arranged enough chairs.'

Well done on being able to count to eighteen. 'It's just that they're a little close together. Could you add a couple more tables to the end?'

'I don't see how I could.' He looked around the room as if he couldn't imagine where he might find another table in a restaurant full of them. 'It's a very small restaurant.'

'Yes, but we're not very small people. I'm sure you can see the issue.'

'There should be enough room.' His manner turned chilly. For someone whose restaurant wasn't usually open between lunch and dinner, who didn't even have to pay any chefs or waiters, and who was pocketing our wine tasting fees as pure profit, he could have toned down the attitude.

'Fine, then I'll show you what I mean,' I said. 'Rob, please sit here.' He did as he was told. I sat beside him, scooching my chair close to his. 'Now,' I said to the manager. 'Why don't you sit beside us?'

Being no mere slip of a man himself, his position at the table put him halfway between two place settings. 'Do you see our problem? We're the curvy girls . . . and boys club. We need a bit more room. I'm really sorry about that. We did mention it in our emails.'

He reluctantly hauled over two more tables, clearly put out that we really did live up to our name.

Everyone arrived within half an hour. A few were Slimming Zone regulars, and felt like old friends. A few others, like Arthur, were regulars and felt like pains in the neck.

'Katie! This should be a fun afternoon. Although it would

have been better perhaps to concentrate on the lesser known French regions. But never mind. You did the best you could. Shall I sit here next to you?'

This was Arthur's idea of a compliment. He could make me cry when he wanted to be mean.

'Thanks, Arthur. And I'd love for you to be next to me, really, but I thought you might like to sit next to, erm,' I looked quickly at my list, 'Jade. You remember her from the book club meeting?' I felt bad (momentarily) about inflicting him on a perfectly nice woman like Jade, but I'd put a lovely man on her other side. One hand giveth, the other taketh away.

Despite what Arthur said, the wine tasting proved almost incidental to the afternoon. I'd noticed this over the past months and at first it bothered me. I lost sleep over the plans I concocted. They bloody well should appreciate them. It took some time for me to realise that they did appreciate them, very much.

Sometimes being fat was isolating and sometimes isolated people got fat. It didn't matter which was chicken and which was egg. The end result was that for some of our members, these outings were their social life. They were just as happy to taste wine in the company of others as they were to watch a film or listen to music in the company of others. People naturally focused on the curvy part of our name, but it was a *social* club at the end of the day.

I sneaked a glimpse at Jade. She didn't look too angry about Arthur. In fact, she looked . . .

'Rob. Are you noticing what I'm noticing?'

Rob was staring down the table. He smiled, then quietly started a passable Barry White rendition.

Everyone was talking to, nay, flirting with their neighbour. 'Is it the wine? What have we started?'

'I'm not sure,' he said. 'But this might be the highest-rated event yet. Did you have a method in your seating plan?'

'Of course not. I threw it together on the Tube ride over to you this morning based on who I knew.'

I had noticed that more than the usual number of men had signed up for today. Maybe the high male quotient was making everyone randy. Even Arthur was talking to the woman opposite him, and she seemed to be answering of her own free will.

While it was nice to see everyone getting along, it reminded me of an uncomfortable development. 'Pixie thinks we should start a dating business,' I told Rob as the wine guy poured us another red.

'Remember,' said the wine guy, who looked about eleven. 'Swirl, swish, spit!' He demonstrated. Everyone at the table defiantly swallowed. He didn't know his audience at all.

'She's mentioned it a few times,' I said quietly. 'And again last week.'

He nodded. 'I can see the sense in it. We've got men, we've got women. They might like that kind of thing. Well, just look around. Maybe we should think about launching that for the anniversary.'

'No way. She wants to call it Fat Friends.' I whispered, rolling my eyes. A couple of specialist dating websites had popped up in the past few years. I wasn't one to judge if someone got off on fireman uniforms or wearing nappies. But my gut told me that running a dating business for our clientele risked stigmatising them further. That's the last thing they needed. 'We've got to come up with a better idea than that. There must be something better we can do for the anniversary.'

'What's this?' Amanda asked, overhearing us.

'Oh, we're trying to think of ideas for our anniversary,' I said.

'You and Rob are together? I had no idea, congratulations!'

'Oh no, we're not—'

'We're not a couple,' Rob said smoothly.

'What a shame. You'd make a lovely couple.'

'I think so, but Katie won't hear of it,' he said as I reddened further. He grinned to let me know he wasn't being serious. 'We've got too many cultural differences. She's a McVitie's fan and I'm loyal to the Garibaldi. It would never work. We've managed to bridge the biscuit divide in friendship though. No, we were talking about an event to officially launch the Curvy Girls Club. Any thoughts?'

Luckily the conversation turned to the launch and my face slowly returned to its normal colour. It wasn't strictly true that I didn't want to go out with Rob. He was such a lovely man. Who wouldn't want to? I'd definitely had fantasies about us strolling together hand in hand along the South Bank, or being wrapped up in his big arms in front of the telly on a Friday night. But things weren't that simple. We were working together for one thing. We were mates for another. And I couldn't stop thinking about Alex. Nail in the coffin. Not exactly a recipe for happily ever after.

'You should plaster yourselves on billboards across the country,' the man next to Amanda said, eying her appreciatively. We didn't need a dating website. We should just run more wine tastings.

'Nah,' said the man to my right. 'Nobody pays attention to billboards unless there's something really eye-catching on it.' Eyebrows all along the table shot into the air as he realised what he'd just said. 'I don't mean you're not eye-catching! You're lovely, really! I just meant that people would stop and stare if they saw something out of the ordinary. Though you wouldn't want them stopping and staring on the M4. Imagine. Pileups across the country from staring at four naked women!'

'Who said anything about naked?' Rob asked as the man reddened again. He was on a foot-in-mouth hot streak.

'Well, that would certainly be eye-catching,' I said, showing I had no hard feelings about the man picturing my arse above the motorway.

'Like that programme on Channel 4, *How to Look Good Naked*. I love that one,' said Amanda as she glanced at the wine bottle a bit further down the table. Her afternoon suitor obliged, topping up her glass. This was less of a wine tasting than an approved drinkathon. 'Though those women don't have anything to worry about. A few extra pounds around their middle and they think it's the end of the world. They should feature us instead. We'd give Gok Wan a run for his money!'

As we continued to chat, my tummy started fizzing. I had an idea. An incredible idea. An incredible long-shot of an idea that, if it worked, could literally give us all the exposure we ever dreamed of.

CHAPTER TWELVE

'I'm really sorry to make you all meet me at such short notice,' I said as Jane returned to the table with more sugar packets for our coffees. 'And for being so cagey on the phone. I just can't wait till next week to tell you, and I think we should talk about it all together.'

'You're scaring me,' Pixie said. 'Is everything all right, love? Are you ill?' She grasped my hand as the lunchtime horde milled around us.

'Oh, no, no nothing like that. This is good news. At least I think it is. Maybe great news, in fact.'

Jane searched my face for signs of brave mendacity. Then, satisfied that the risk of crisis was behind us, she resumed her knitting.

'What are you making?' Ellie asked her, touching the soft blue yarn.

'Hats.'

'It's May,' Pixie pointed out. 'Are you that pessimistic about summer?'

Jane smiled. She didn't even look at her stitches when she knitted. She was completely at peace lap-deep in yarn. She'd knit her own shoes if she found a waterproof stitch.

Pixie shook her head. 'You take all the fun out of gift-giving when you make them in front of us.'

'That's not true! I love my jumper.' Ellie smoothed the front of the delicate Fair Isle Jane made for her birthday last year. 'Anyway, Katie, sorry, we interrupted. What's your news?'

'Well, I have an idea for our launch. What if we were able to do that show, *How to Look Good Naked*?'

Pixie was the first to speak. 'You are bloody joking, right? You mean the one where they plaster your arse on the side of a building and invite strangers to talk about it? Thanks, but no thanks, love.'

'I'd die of embarrassment,' Ellie said. She started to redden just thinking about it.

'But Ellie, you of all people! You're beautiful. And you'd get to meet Gok Wan . . .'

That made her stop and think. Ellie loved celebrities. She once saw Rupert Everett in a Costa Coffee. When he left she snatched the half-eaten muffin from his tray. It's in a box frame in her bedroom.

But then she shook her head. Not even the allure of celebrity would sway her.

'And you know it's all tastefully done,' I continued. 'Ellie, I'm not proposing that you be the one to do it, but wouldn't the publicity be amazing?' I could hardly contain my excitement yesterday, and actually dragged Rob away before we'd finished our wine to tell him about my scheme. He loved it. Of course he did. He didn't have to get his kit off on national television.

'I couldn't,' Jane said quietly. 'Maybe before I had the children, when I was thin.' She looked so sad. 'But not now.'

I'd known Jane for many months before she told me about their fertility problems. I knew the memories still made her uncomfortable.

82

The doctors had run a series of fertility tests on them both to try to figure out why they weren't populating their nursery as planned. Jane hardly believed her doctor when he told her all the results were normal. She'd spent so long blaming her uterus that she'd worn a rut deep into her self-confidence. Her body's acquittal was hard to accept.

Andy's diagnosis wasn't as good. He had lazy sperm, said the doctor. Most of the little fellas just couldn't muster the enthusiasm for the long swim. 'I'm so sorry,' Andy kept saying to his wife. 'All this time you've been thinking that it was you, when it's been my fault. Don't worry, though, I'll do whatever it takes to get them moving.'

'Maybe they need some dance music,' Jane had joked.

What they needed was a good wash. So after Andy spent some more time in a private room with a stack of magazines and a cup, the doctors spun his spunk to weed out the dozy ones. Those that were left were probably a bit dizzy, so the doctors helped them along their route with a giant turkey baster. It wasn't the romantic candle-lit conception Jane had dreamed of but after a few tries, she was pregnant.

Sometimes she wondered if it was possible to be too happy. Every morning when she woke with Andy's hand on her tummy or his sleeping face next to hers, she let a few joyous tears leak into her pillow. A religious person would have said she was blessed. Jane said she was lucky.

She was also terrified. The fear gripped her as tightly as her happiness did. What if she did something to lose the baby? Just the pain of thinking about the possibility was almost too much to bear. She knew she'd never forgive herself if it actually happened. And she wouldn't blame Andy if he didn't forgive her either.

It seemed that everything she loved to eat could harm a foetus – sushi, stinky cheeses, rare steaks, smoked salmon, pâté and eggs benedict. Within weeks of seeing the little plus sign on the wee-soaked stick, she knew more than some biologists about listeria, salmonella and toxoplasmosis. One ill-advised mouthful and the little life could be extinguished.

'You need to relax, Jane,' Andy had said. 'You're making yourself sick with worry. Everything will be fine.'

That was easy for him to say. It wasn't his sole responsibility to carry their child.

Jane knew she was being over-cautious, but it was such a small price to pay for a few months. She'd have put herself on complete bed rest if she hadn't had to go to work every day. So she did the next best thing. She made the most comfortable, least exertive environment she could for the little foetus.

Jane bloomed, quite literally, as she carried her first child to term. That was perfectly normal, she thought. Everyone had some baby weight to lose after a pregnancy. She'd just have to work a little harder than some. The important thing was to give the baby the best possible start in life.

And that's exactly what Jane did. When Matthew was born, hale and hearty at just over eight pounds, Jane thought she'd explode with love for that child. She wanted to spend the rest of her life holding him in her arms. Actually, she wanted to gobble him up and keep him safe inside her until he was of pensionable age.

Unfortunately, all that mooning over Matthew meant that Jane's physique remained buried under the baby weight. At first she was too besotted with her first-born to care very much but as he started to walk, then toddle and then run, it became clear that her fitness wasn't what it once was. She wheezed up the stairs and puffed even when she walked on level ground. The pregnancy clothes she continued to wear were starting to look a bit tired. Though, thanks to them, she did still sometimes get a seat on the rush-hour Tube.

But no sooner had she started to think seriously about

shedding the pounds when Andy's sperm got their groove on. She fell pregnant again, this time without any help from the doctors. So the diet flew out the window while she concentrated on bringing their daughter into the world.

Throughout the whole period Andy couldn't have been more wonderful, but he was worried. His father had died young of a heart attack, and he wanted to grow very old with Jane. 'Darling, why don't we start walking together? We could take Matthew in the pram and walk around the park when we get home from work.'

'We can't take Matthew out at night, in the dark!' she laughed.

'Well then, I could watch him if you wanted to go for a walk.'

She stared at Andy. 'Why would I do that?'

Naturally he looked uncomfortable. 'Well, you have mentioned wanting to drop a few pounds. I just thought . . . this could help,' he finished lamely.

'You think I'm fat?' Jane knew she was just picking a fight. *She* knew she was fat. It could hardly have escaped Andy's notice.

'No, darling! I think you're perfect. But you've mentioned several times . . . Never mind. Come here.' He gathered her into his arms and tried to push his worry aside. 'The important thing is for you and the baby to be healthy.'

That conversation stuck with Jane. She told us about it when we first met at Slimming Zone.

So I knew exactly what she meant about not wanting anyone to look at her. At first I couldn't imagine strangers staring at my puckered thighs and undulating tummy. Then I started to wonder: why not? What, exactly, was it about strangers looking at me that made me so uncomfortable? After all, I went out in public every day, didn't I? People watched me eat my lunch, sit on the Tube, go up the stairs on the bus. I knew that some judged me as deficient, lacking the self-control, the motivation, the determination not to be fat. Yet still I went out.

Then I pictured that judgement multiplied across the country. Me, Katie Winterbottom, available for scorn in living rooms across the land. They wouldn't even need to leave their sofas to do it.

I thought about the women I'd seen on the show. It couldn't have been easy for them either, and yet they did it. Their reasons were probably as varied as their bodies were. But the end result seemed to be the same. They showed the rest of us that beauty comes in all shapes and sizes. And they seemed happier with themselves.

Did I need to be happier with myself? Was that why I was willing to bare all for the cameras? I hadn't realised it until the club came along, but yes, I needed a mind makeover as much as anything Gok could dream up. I wore my skin comfortably when I was out with my friends, and I wanted to feel that way all the time. Hell, I'd been quoted as saying as much in the *Evening Standard*, so it must be true.

'I've been thinking,' I said, instead of contemplating my potentially damaged psyche. 'What if we tie in the *How to Look Good Naked* part with some kind of makeover segment for curvy people? It could be a real feel-good programme. Everyone would love that, right?'

Jane nodded. Being a television executive, I knew she'd see the possibilities. 'I could check to see what they've got planned,' she said. 'We might be able to pitch something for Love Your Body month.'

Only Jane would know such a thing existed. 'I love it! Could we really pitch something, do you think?'

'I don't see why not. It's not my side of the programming but I can find out who to talk to. The worst they can do is say no. You haven't answered the question though, sweetheart. Are *you* willing to go on the show and strip for the cause?'

'I am,' I said with more conviction than I felt. 'What do you think? Is this a good idea? It probably wouldn't be in time for the anniversary but in a way it's so much better, don't you think? And would you consider doing the makeover part if I do the naked part?'

'I do feel like we'll need to offer them a bit more to cement the proposal,' Jane said, clearly happy to be on familiar (clothed) ground. 'There'd need to be least two of us for them to consider commissioning something, and we'd have to go to them with the idea fully formed. How it would work, what we'd need in terms of staff, format, length, intended audience, differentiation.'

'Jane,' I said. 'Can we work together on a pitch? I could come to your house on Friday afternoon.' If I didn't combust from excitement first. 'Then you wouldn't have to worry about getting someone to mind the children.'

If we pulled this off . . . it was such a long-shot but if we could . . . wow.

Jane laughed. 'Oh, Katie, it's kind of you to offer but sometimes it's really clear you live a blissfully child-free existence. I promise you, as a parent you'd jump at any excuse to get out of the house.'

'Bring them round to mine,' offered Pixie. 'Trevor's on a job down in Kent all week. He won't be back until teatime, so the house will be peaceful. We'll do some baking and the girls can practise their dance routines.'

We grinned at each other. We knew we had a whopper of an idea for getting the Curvy Girls Club all the publicity it could hope to have. We just needed to convince one of the biggest television stations in the country to spend the time and money making the programme. And I'd just need to stand naked in front of a nation. I didn't even like getting out of the pool in my swimsuit. As Ellie and I rushed back to work, I practised holding in my tummy.

Perversely, the more success the Curvy Girls Club enjoyed, the more worried I became about my job. It always made me nervous when things seemed to be going really well. Cressida had said my review was no big deal, but what if I got fired? I had to get myself out of that Needs Improvement box. And fast.

'Ellie, have you got a minute?' I asked as she ended her call.

'Sure, is everything okay?' Her forehead creased with concern.

'Oh yes. I just need a quick word. In the conference room?'

I hadn't told her about my review. I know I should have. We were best friends after all. If we could talk about period cramps and nipple hair, we ought to be able to talk about this. But I was too embarrassed. She was always Superior and I knew she'd feel terrible for me. I didn't want her above-adequate pity.

She listened as I told her all about my meeting with Cressida. A few times she interrupted to ask if I was okay.

'I've got to get out of that box,' I told her. 'And I think I've figured out a way. If I can get meetings with clients where nobody else has them, then Cressida has to let me go, right? There'll be nobody else who can do it. Will you help me?'

'Of course. What do you want me to do?'

'I need you to get the whole client list from lovely Thomas, with their office addresses. He sends out all the marketing materials to them. He could probably print it off in about two minutes . . . but he can't tell anyone what I'm doing.'

She suddenly looked upset.

'Oh, it's not against company policy or anything like that,'

I rushed to assure her. 'Thomas won't get into trouble, I promise. I wouldn't do anything to jeopardise your relationship! I'm already planning my speech for your wedding.'

At that, she burst into messy snot-bubble tears.

'What's the matter? Ellie, what's wrong?' I reached for her hand. 'Talk to me, honey.'

'I've ruined my relationship,' she announced. 'It's over between Thomas and me. I was going to tell you at home tonight but it couldn't w-w-w-waiiiitt!'

I peered at Ellie. Much as I hated to see her upset, we had been down this road before. 'Are you sure? Is it really over, or just in-your-head over? Have you actually broken up? Out loud?' One had to ask these things with Ellie. She ran about six miles ahead of any given situation.

'It's as good as over. I talked to him about Colleen this morning.'

Ah yes, Colleen, Thomas's colleague and one-time crush. 'When you say *talked*?'

'All right, I shouted. But he deserved it!' She started crying again. 'They've been out together, Katie. They've been out and he didn't tell me.'

'Well, they are friends, Ellie. Friends do go out sometimes. Where did they go? Was it a romantic dinner? Dancing into the night? A weekend away?'

'Don't make fun of my heartbreak. They went to Pizza Express.'

'Did they . . .' Gasp. 'Share a pizza?! Oh, Ellie, why do you do this to yourself? So they went out for a meal. That's not a big deal.'

'First it's pizza, Katie. Then it's a cosy French bistro with candles and those accordion players who sell roses, then who knows what? The important thing is, he didn't tell me about it. I had to find out myself.'

'What do you mean you had to find out yourself?'

Her eyes slid away. 'I might have checked the calendar on his iPhone.'

'Ellie, you didn't!'

'Well, he should have a password if he doesn't want people seeing it! Besides, I knew he wasn't telling me something. What was I supposed to do?'

'Oh, I don't know. How about trusting your boyfriend instead of hacking into his phone?' I sighed. 'All right. So what did you say to him? Did you accuse him of sharing his mozzarella with another woman?'

'No, of course not. I asked him what he did last night.'

'And?'

'And he told me.'

'That jerk, how could he? So you teed off on him?'

'I wouldn't say I – yes, I did.' She looked contrite. Finally. 'He should have told me beforehand.'

Awkwardly, I put my arm around her. Conference rooms weren't configured for comforting friends. She sank into me. 'Ellie, honey, I'm sure he didn't think to tell you because he wasn't doing anything wrong. How did he react?'

'He was confused. He apologised and asked if we could talk tonight.'

'You will talk to him, won't you? Believe me, if I thought you had anything to worry about I'd tell you. I'll always take your side over a boyfriend's. But, from an objective, outsider's perspective, I don't think you have anything to worry about. Talk to him tonight. Okay?'

She promised she would and we got ready to leave for the day. I'd kill to have just one of the chances at love that she seemed so intent on throwing away.

CHAPTER THIRTEEN

Ellie was trying to torture me. She'd talked to Thomas days ago but wouldn't tell me a thing unless I went with her to the gym. I'd tried prising information out of her over lunch, on our coffee breaks, every chance I got. She wouldn't budge. She was an exercise extortionist.

I knew I'd cave in to her demands. I wasn't against exercise *per se*. I just didn't like it to seem like exercise. Walking on Hampstead Heath or along the Thames towards Hampton Court Palace was delightful. There were interesting things to see, excellent conversations to be had, and glasses of wine to enjoy at the end. Working out in a gym was like eating a bar of chocolate with the wrapper still on. Technically the same chocolate but quite a different experience.

Plus, it was bad enough as a fit person trying to survive a treadmill session or hyperactive aerobics instructor. It was completely disheartening trying to do it as an overweight one. Imagine jogging. Then strap five sacks of potatoes into a rucksack. Not so much fun now, is it?

That's why I admired Ellie's devotion to fitness. I knew it wasn't easy for her and yet she still did it.

We were halfway through the much-begrudged spin class

when our instructor yelled at me for the hundredth time. He'd taken to calling my name every five seconds in an attempt to encourage me. He was just pissing me off.

'Come on, Katie,' he said again, his thighs straining against Lycra. 'We're on the hill now. Are you joining us?'

'No, thanks,' I said, pedalling on the lightest setting on the bike. 'I'm taking the A road around the hill. It's flat down here. You go on though, I'll meet you on the other side. Maybe we can stop for an ice cream.'

Ellie shot me a dirty look from beneath her mop, which had gone completely mental between the heat and constant standing up, sitting down, standing up, sitting down. She made me tired just watching her.

'You could try,' she panted.

'I didn't agree to try. I agreed to come with you. Are you going to make me wait until after class to find out how your talk went?'

'Yes, because I can't . . . talk right now . . . and because I know . . . you'd leave as soon as I told you.'

I tried to look offended, but she was right. I'd be in the café with a strawberry smoothie five seconds after she finished her story.

The class ended with the instructor telling us that we were uh-maaz-ing and deserved a nice dinner. It was finally something we agreed on.

'So tell me everything,' I said when we got to the café. 'It must have gone well or you wouldn't have spent every night this week at his place.'

Her smile was full of joy. And sex. There was a lot of sex in that smile.

'Sun Tzu says to keep your friends close and your enemies closer.'

'I see. And are you sleeping with the enemy?'

She blushed. 'None of your business.'

'I'll take that as a yes then. So things are better?'

'It's complicated.'

'It's really not, Ellie.' I was always torn when she said things like this. We'd been here before. Of course I wanted to support her but sometimes she needed protecting from herself. She wrecked her last relationship with unfounded suspicions. We did tell her that a man writing a woman's name in his diary wasn't conclusive proof of an affair. We also told her that she really ought not to be looking at his diary, but that advice clearly hadn't stuck either. Her jealousy could be all-consuming. I wasn't about to let it consume her relationship with Thomas when he might very well be The One. 'Did you tell him how you felt? Do you feel better now?'

'I'd feel better if they weren't friends. But they are, and that doesn't seem likely to change. You should hear him talk about her. Like she's Beyoncé and Jesus all wrapped in one.'

I tried to conjure that mental image.

'And of course I didn't tell him. He'd think I was insane. As it was I had to convince him I hadn't lost my mind the other day when I shouted at him.'

'Did you . . .?'

'Blamed it on PMT, yes. I know you're right, Katie. I just get a little crazy sometimes because I like him so much. This feels like it might be it, you know? The real thing. I'm petrified it's all going to turn out to be a big mistake. What if this whole relationship is just a misunderstanding and he doesn't really like me at all?'

'As in, oh I'm terribly sorry. I meant to pour you a coffee and accidentally had sex with you for several months?'

'Well, not when you put it like that. But I may have misinterpreted his intentions, longer-term. If I did then he'll feel terrible for leading me on and I'll want to curl up and die. I mean, look at him. He's perfect. And look at me.' She made a face at her reflection in the wall of mirrors. Why did gyms think we wanted three-hundred-and-sixty degree reminders of why we were there?

'He is not perfect! And believe me, I'll be here to point out every single flaw, physical, mental and emotional, if he ever hurts you. But I don't think he will.'

'At what point do I get to actually enjoy this without being terrified it's going to end?'

'I don't know, honeybun, I wish I did.'

Ellie and I parted with the question hanging between us. Was anyone actually comfortable in their relationship when they were in love? Or did they sleep with one eye open, alert to the possibility that fate would snatch away their happiness? Like I had any idea. Unrequited love had its own problems.

'Hey, I was just going to phone in case you'd forgotten,' Jane said when I arrived at our new offices. Rob had had keys cut for us all, and his cousin, taxidermy David, really was fine with us using the space as often as we liked. So far we hadn't met our benevolent landlord, possibly because he avoided daylight (and garlic, I suspected).

'Why are you all red?' Jane asked. 'Are you having an allergic reaction?'

'I've come from the gym.'

The look on her face almost made the sweaty humiliation in workout gear worthwhile.

'It was under duress.'

'You do look like you've lost more weight,' she said suspiciously.

As it happened, I had. Ellie made me step on the scale twice at the gym, just to be sure. Six pounds altogether, and I had no idea how. I'd never had a dainty appetite (*quelle surprise*) but I'd been ravenous lately. Maybe my metabolism was speeding up. Maybe that's why my heart raced all the time.

'Oh no,' I lied, not wanting to make Jane feel bad. 'I don't think so. In fact I'm starving.' That part was true. I dove into my bag for the open packet of Snack a Jacks there.

'You don't know starving until you've been fasting,' she said, sweeping her lustrous blonde locks up off her face and deftly twisting them into a bun. 'Day two. I can eat two hundred more calories today. Woo hoo. But my colleague swears it works. She's lost over a stone.'

'But Jane, at what cost? It can't be good to starve yourself. You promised no more crazy diets.'

'It's not a crazy diet. It's a different way of eating. It's medically proven to work. And it's safe. We agreed to eat healthily and try not to worry about our weight. I'm following orders.' She smiled. 'I'm working on the not worrying part, but this way of eating retrains your body to crave healthy food instead of junk and speeds up your metabolism by, well, I can't remember all the details.'

'That's because you're starving your brain. Have you got enough energy to work on the pitch? If I put the pen in your hand, could you scratch out a few words?'

She moved the mouse orchestra aside and even managed a smile in her depleted state. 'I've been thinking a lot about the idea and I really do think Channel 4 might go for it if it's pitched correctly. That means hitting the right angle, and I think we're on to something with Love Your Body month. The fact that we're the Curvy Girls Club is almost incidental, although not for us, obviously. If we can pitch it on a huge scale it'll make them sit up and take notice. The important thing is the message. You can be beautiful at any shape or size. It's not about being thin. It's about showing off what you've got.'

Jane saw no irony in saying this as she anticipated her next two hundred calories . . .

'You're right,' I said. 'The pitch has to be huge. Ideally

95

we'd all be involved. I know you don't want to get naked for the cameras. That's fine. But would you do the makeover part? Whether you like it or not, you're a minor celebrity.'

'I am not!'

'You were on telly for years, and you are a bit famous. So if you were on the programme, it'd add to our likelihood of getting it commissioned. Right?'

She stared at me. 'You're right. I dread the very idea. Oh god. Being on camera again.' She shook her head.

'You make yourself sound like a grotesque monster.'

'Not a monster, Katie, but I don't like what I see in the mirror. And before you tell me I'm beautiful, you lovely *lovely* friend, it doesn't matter what you see. Andy tells me I'm beautiful every day. It doesn't matter. It's what I see that matters.'

'You need to be on the programme, Jane.' I didn't elaborate on my reasons. Let her think it was for the good of the Curvy Girls Club.

We sat quietly together, surrounded by David's taxidermied animals. Pete the bear seemed to approve of our idea but the angry Pekingese didn't look so sure.

My phone pinged. *770 unique views, 211 signups. Next update in a week. Rob*

That translated into another four hundred quid into the club account. I showed Jane, and explained about unique views. 'Almost eight hundred people went on the website last week because there's finally somewhere for them to feel included. Think how many more people would love to have that chance, if they knew about it.'

'All right. I'll do it,' she finally said. 'Let's write the pitch with us as definite participants. We should pitch it as *The Great British Makeover*. They can run makeover segments in London, Manchester, Edinburgh, Cardiff, all the big cities in the UK. We could even suggest using volunteers for the styling if they're concerned about budget. I'm sure if they offered the right publicity to everyone they'd be able to source them. It would get huge viewership between the live event and the catch-ups on More4. Plus they'd get highlighted on their website. They might even do a separate references page so people could have contact details for their area handy.' She nodded happily. 'Yes, I can see the producers getting very excited about this.'

'I'm excited about it!' I said. Watching Jane so animated about the idea, I could almost forget the demons she fought every time she looked in the mirror. There had to be a way to help her. I knew just how hard the past decade had been.

CHAPTER FOURTEEN

Jane's crazy diets started long before we met, soon after her daughter Abigail was born. By that time, Jane had said many times, she couldn't imagine ever seeing a flat tummy again. It seemed like an impossibly long road. Part of the problem was that after years of roominess, her body was quite used to the larger accommodation. It wasn't giving up that extra space easily.

Besides, Jane was absurdly happy with her life, and sorting out her expanding waistline just wasn't at the top of her priority list. Enjoying her expanding family was.

Now more than five years into her BBC career and co-presenting a well-loved morning breakfast show, she couldn't take off much time when Abigail was born. Since her show was broadcast live in the early mornings, Andy handled the children's waking up routine, but she was back in her warm kitchen with her babies by nine a.m. Then Andy went off to develop IT systems for his company's clients across London. Between the children and preparing for the next morning's show, the days flowed smoothly into one another.

After having Abigail, Jane even started loosening her grip

on the children. She still wanted to seal them into a bubble, safely away from the world, and wouldn't dream of leaving the house without a month's supply of anti-bacterial wipes. But Andy's gentle persuasion eventually convinced her that children were actually quite tough little creatures who needed lots of outside play and friends. Even when that meant catching colds and scraping knees.

So Jane's life was pretty great when the show's producers called her in for a meeting just before Abigail's six-month birthday.

'We just wanted to talk about the show, Jane,' said Karen, the executive producer who'd recruited her. 'As you know, when we ran our focus groups a few years back, everyone absolutely loved you.'

Jane glowed with pleasure. Her on-air job wasn't quite as important as her work as a mum, but it was a very close second. She was constantly grateful that she got to do both.

'It's just that ratings have been flat for the past several months,' Karen continued. 'So we need to look at every aspect of the show.'

'Am I doing something wrong?' Jane asked.

'No no, not at all! Like I said, you've tested well with viewers in the past . . . Jane, this isn't an easy thing to say, and it's nothing personal at all. But you know that we're presenting a certain image on the show. Of course we understand that you've had a baby, and we hope you're getting back on track now. If there's anything we can do to help, just let us know, okay?'

Jane thanked her producers and left the meeting on shaking legs. Her weight, up till then the only cloud on her horizon, had just grown more menacing.

She knew her dress size shouldn't matter. She was an excellent presenter, warm and friendly enough to put her guests at ease while not shying away from probing questions (as long as they were entertaining, as per the show's brief). And the audience liked her.

But Karen's message was loud and clear. Jane needed to lose weight or risk losing her job. She couldn't wait to whinge to Andy about it. The injustice!

'They can't tell you that,' he said, perfectly affronted on his wife's behalf, just as she knew he'd be. 'It's one thing if you wanted to lose weight, but they can't force you, or threaten you if you don't.'

'But I do want to lose weight! That's the irony. They're suggesting that I do what I've been saying I would for years. I guess I'll really have to try now.' She stared at the gooey slab of brie that they'd been sharing before they started cooking dinner together.

'I'll support you in any way I possibly can,' Andy said, putting his arms around her. 'Just tell me what to do and I'll do it. We'll do it together.'

Jane smiled into his shoulder. Andy was one in a million.

'If you lost fifty pounds you'd blow away, sweetheart. No, it's up to me to do this.'

But Jane had already tried shedding the weight by watching what she ate. Knowing that that hadn't worked meant more drastic action was needed. Luckily there were as many insane diets as there were desperate slimmers.

Whenever Ellie, Pixie and I chastised her about her latest fad diet, Jane reminded us of that period, and all the diets she'd tried. She was trying to demonstrate how relatively far she'd come from the crazy old days. But she just reminded us how despondent she must have been, because it took desperation to drink cider vinegar as an appetite suppressant or eat cotton wool to feel full. Jane had done both. She'd also spent a few happy weeks on the cookie diet, until she realised she wasn't supposed to eat regular cookies. After tearing through a few dozen packets of chocolate digestives, she had to drink cider vinegar again to lose the extra dough around her middle.

It was a common pattern. She'd shift a few pounds on some nutty diet, only to gain it all back when she ate normally again. After more than a year of trying, she'd lost and gained back her baby weight several times over.

And it was having consequences for her marriage, but by the time she noticed how fed up Andy was getting with her moods yo-yoing along with her weight, he'd been pissed off for months. Things came to a head one night just after they'd put the children to bed.

'Do you want a glass of wine?' Andy asked.

'You know I can't have wine on my diet!'

'Well, I'm sorry, Jane. I can't keep up with what you can and can't have these days. Do you mind if I have a glass?' He knew that sometimes she needed to feel the solidarity of him being miserable too.

'Do what you want.'

'I *want* to have a relaxing evening, but it looks like that's not going to happen,' he muttered.

'If you're so unhappy, why don't you just go somewhere else then? You don't have to be around me if it pains you so much.'

'Don't be daft, Jane. For better or worse, we're in this together.' He slumped in the chair across the room.

Jane sensed something that made her insides freeze. 'Andy? What is it? Something's wrong, I can tell.'

Instead of laughing off her question like she'd hoped, he just stared at her. 'It's nothing.'

'Tell me. Andy. Tell me.' It was hard to utter those words. She couldn't unhear whatever he was about to say.

'It's just that lately things have been . . . I don't know. I guess I've been less happy lately. I love you, Jane, but you've been so obsessed with your diets. It hasn't been fun.'

101

'Marriage isn't always fun.'

'I know. I know that. I guess I didn't realise that it was affecting me.'

'Do you think I enjoy starving myself?' She laughed bitterly. 'It's not all about you, you know.'

He nodded. 'I know . . . Jane, I need to tell you about something. I don't know what to think about it. I don't want to hurt you. That's why I'm telling you now.'

Jane hardly let him finish the sentence. 'Are you having an affair?'

'No, Jane, no. It's not an affair. I promise.'

'But it's something.'

He nodded. 'Lately, I've found myself attracted to someone.'

She held her breath as his words punched her in the solar plexus. 'Who is she?'

'You don't know her. She's another programmer who started about a year ago. Nothing has happened between us, Jane, I swear, I haven't cheated. But I can't keep the fact that I've been attracted to her from you. We've always been completely honest with each other, and I can't keep things from you now. Jane? Please say something. Anything. I can't stand it when you just stare at me like that.'

'What should I say, Andy? That it's okay for you to lust after another woman? Or maybe that you should follow your penis wherever it takes you? I'm sorry, but I can't do that. You may not have cheated, but you've broken my trust. I'm sorry that I'm so disgusting that I've driven you into someone else's arms.'

Andy protested, of course, but no matter what he said, and he said quite a lot as they talked into the early hours, Jane knew that their marriage was in serious jeopardy.

So many thoughts and emotions hit Jane when Andy told her he fancied his colleague that soon she wasn't sure which ones were new and which were repeats. She knew one thing though. She had to fix things.

Andy was no less distraught. He might have relieved the guilt he'd dragged around for months, but that was overwhelmed by the impact his confession had on Jane. He'd truly believed it was the right thing to do, but Jane said she wasn't so sure.

'If he knew he'd never act on it then what was the point of telling me?' she'd fumed when she'd recalled it over drinks one night about a year after we all met. 'Honesty in the relationship, blah blah blah. To me, it smacked of selfishness. He may have felt better, but I didn't. I couldn't stop thinking about her, and imagining how perfect she must be. I was miserable thinking about them together every day. Even though he promised he was completely ignoring her, just knowing they were in the same office drove me mad. He'd made everything worse.'

Andy knew he had to fix what he'd broken. No matter how often he told Jane that she had nothing to worry about, knowing how he'd felt about his colleague was eating her up. He couldn't ask the woman to quit. It wasn't her fault he'd lusted after her or told Jane about it. And with a family to support he couldn't leave his job either. So he tried the next best thing.

'I've asked for a transfer,' he'd announced one night. 'Jane, I can't stand seeing you like this, and knowing it's because of me. I've been so stupid, and I'll spend the rest of my life apologising for that. But we need to be able to move forward and if that means me taking another job, then it's worth it for us to be happy again.'

A smile slowly crept across Jane's face. 'You're doing that for me?'

He nodded. 'For us. There's just one thing. The only open position is in Bristol.'

'Bristol!'

'I know. I wish there was something in another London office, but there just isn't right now. Hopefully it won't be for more than a year; then I can apply for a transfer back to London, to another office.' He took Jane's hands. 'I know it's not ideal but I hope it will make you happy again. I'll be able to leave early on Friday afternoons so I can be home by dinner.'

It took Jane a minute to understand what he was saying. 'Of course we're coming with you.'

'I can't ask you to leave your job, Jane. Fucking things up between us was bad enough.'

'But you can't think that being apart five days a week is going to help.' Jane felt even more panicky at that idea.

'Won't my being in Bristol make you feel better?'

'No!' Tears sprang to Jane's eyes. Why couldn't she just be an adult about this? Married people probably had crushes all the time. If she hadn't fallen to pieces over it, her husband wouldn't be proposing to move away. 'Andy, I'd do anything to get over how I feel and get our life back the way it was. But I can't, and banishing you to Bristol doesn't sound like the answer. We're coming with you. I can see about taking a year off, but if they won't let me then that's fine too. I'll find something else, either in Bristol or when we come back to London. I just want us to make a new start. Together. Now don't start crying, you silly man,' she said as he hiccupped back his tears. 'One of us bawling is bad enough. When do we go?'

'We can go as soon as you want to. I love you so much, Jane.'

'I know,' she said. 'And I love you too.' She felt lighter than she had in months.

Her producer, Karen, seemed more relieved than sad to see her go. She met her replacement a few weeks before she left, and helped transition her into the role. She was no bigger than a size six.

Then they moved to Bristol, and things were good. They settled in quickly and thought the smaller city suited them. Andy's colleagues were friendly and he sometimes went out with them for a quick drink after work. He made sure they were all men.

As the children weren't yet in school though, it didn't take long for Jane to grow lonely. But at least, she reasoned, she wasn't tempted off her diet by invitations for afternoon tea or lunches or dinners. Because there weren't any invitations.

Not that dieting in Bristol was any easier than it was in London, and it was about this time that she first tried the pills. It wouldn't be the last.

CHAPTER FIFTEEN

Jane sent *The Great British Makeover* pitch off to her contacts, and we waited. Days went by, then two weeks. I did my best to get some perspective. Fat chance of that. I got excited when Ben & Jerry's came out with a new flavour. I had no chance of remaining calm about this. I knew it was a long-shot, and yet I couldn't keep my breath from hitching in my throat whenever a text pinged. You'd think I was seventeen again, waiting to hear from Rory.

And then finally, a text from Jane. *Are you free to talk?*

I called her straight back. 'Is it good news?!'

'You can't even imagine,' she said. 'Remember you asked me to send PR out to the news outlets and such? I sent emails off to loads of editors at the nationals, and all the relevant TV programmes. And one just emailed back.'

So it wasn't about Channel 4. It took me a moment to digest what she'd said. Nationals? As in newspapers?

'Who?' If it was the *Telegraph* my parents were going to have strokes. When Granddad's death announcement got in there they told everyone, including the neighbours and the man who sometimes fixed Dad's work van.

'It's from the producer of *On the Couch*.'

'THE *On the Couch*? As in the national television programme?' I was a huge fan of the current affairs chat show, along with most of the rest of the country. 'But how are they going to feature the press release on telly?'

She hesitated. 'They're not featuring the press release. They've invited you on to the show.'

'WHAT?! Why me?' My heart began hammering in my chest.

Again she hesitated, making me wish we were face-to-face. 'It's standard procedure in PR to say we're available for interviews.'

'Uh huh. So how did *we* become me? Can't you do it?'

'No way,' she said. 'My days in front of the camera are over.'

Her tone made me feel guilty for suggesting it.

Jane didn't go back to the BBC when she and Andy came back from Bristol. Instead she went to work for Channel 4. She said she was happy in her job behind the cameras instead of in front of them and it did let her work flexible hours mostly from home. But I had the feeling that if she was a size ten again, she'd have different career aspirations.

'Besides,' Jane continued. 'It makes sense for you to do it, since you're really our leader. You've been the driving force from the start. Just think about the exposure for the club.'

All I could think of was my own exposure. The very thought made me feel ill. 'Can't we draw straws or something?'

'Sweetheart, you do remember that we've got a pitch out to Channel 4 in which you've agreed to be naked on national television. At least you'll have your clothes on for this.'

I couldn't argue with her logic. 'Can I think about it?'

'Of course, but I need to know in the next hour. They want you on for tomorrow.'

Oh god oh god oh god.

* * *

My trousers were too tight. I was about to go on live telly looking like an overstuffed sausage. My glands stained ever-widening rings under the arms of my silk blouse. I bet Mila Kunis didn't have crises like these.

At least my face wasn't beading up. The makeup artist had applied some kind of sealant. Dad had used a similar filler on the lounge walls when he helped me repaint my flat last year. I'd got a leak in the kitchen within a week. Dad promised they were unrelated events, but I wasn't so sure. Did that mean my sweat would pop out elsewhere in a few minutes? Was I about to fill my shoes with perspiration?

The Green Room was small, stifling and not green. Boxy red faux-leather chairs lined the white walls on three sides. A battered blonde-wood coffee table was ringed with scars from hot tea cups, placed there by the nervous guests who'd gone before. It was about as calming as my GP's waiting room. I shifted in my chair, eliciting a faux-leathery fart from the cushion. Lovely. My arse was sweating.

The door flew open. 'We're ready for you,' announced the painfully thin young intern who spoke as if her words were missing a deadline. Her jaw clenched every few seconds as she scanned her notes. 'We've just gone to break. Are you ready?' She eyed the half-eaten doughnut in my hand. 'You've got a bit of, er . . .' She pointed to my lip.

I quickly wiped away the sticky glaze. 'Oh no,' I said, staring at the bright streak on my hand. 'I'm so sorry. I forgot about the lipstick. I don't usually wear it.' They'd lacquered me in orangey-pink. I looked like I was smiling through raw salmon fillets.

The girl sighed, her jaw working overtime. 'That's all right. Nadia,' she barked into the hallway. 'We need you in here now!'

The makeup artist smiled as she approached with her brushes. 'No worries, pet, it'll just take a second to fix.'

'Walk while you work, please,' said the intern. 'We've got less than two minutes.'

'Don't be daft. I'll fix it when she sits. Are you ready for national telly?' she asked me.

I nodded, feeling faint as I followed them into the studio, where Nadia repainted my lipstick, telling me again how unusually dark blue my eyes were. I heard that a lot from strangers who were stuck for compliments below the neckline.

The hot lights blazed overhead as I tried to keep my armpits under cover. There was an odds-on chance that my tummy was about to reintroduce the doughnut to a live television audience.

The women of *On the Couch* smiled warmly in greeting, and I relaxed a tiny bit. They weren't there to make a fool of me, I told myself. It was a friendly chat, not Jeremy Paxman on *Newsnight*.

'Ready?' Lorraine asked as she waved the hovering intern away.

Friendly chat or not, I was *not* ready.

The presenters' demeanours changed as the audience began to clap. Lorraine flashed her perfect Hollywood-by-way-of-Manchester smile straight into the camera. 'We're back with our next guest, and she's one I've been dying to talk to. Please welcome the co-founder of the Curvy Girls Club, Katie Winterbottom!' She waited for the applause to subside. 'Katie, we are so excited to have you on the programme today. Your club is single-handedly striking a blow for all of us with expanding waistlines. With two-thirds of us now curvy, how does it feel to be the spokesperson for a nation?'

Four pairs of eyes were on me. I tried not to think of the other one-point-four million watching from home.

'It feels weird, actually,' I said with a wavering voice. 'I never expected this to happen. We started with just four of us at the back of a slimming class.'

Lorraine nodded for me to continue the story.

'It was my friend Pixie's idea,' I said, avoiding eye contact with the camera and, by extension, the rest of the UK. 'We just wanted something to look forward to every week. Something other than the slimming meetings, because they can get a little disheartening after a while.'

As I told the women how the Curvy Girls Club was born I started to relax. I always did when thinking about it. In fact it more than relaxed me. It sustained me.

By the time I finished telling Lorraine about the fateful night we saw *Thriller*, the cameras and audience no longer seemed as intimidating. I was even starting to enjoy myself.

'We wanted to do the same fun things that everyone else does. But we have to be realistic. Sometimes there are limitations for the waistband-challenged. It seemed like a good idea to keep those in mind as we made our plans. That way nobody feels self-conscious or embarrassed. We have gone to the theatre again, but we choose venues with roomier seats. We always make sure there'll be no ugly surprises.'

'So you vet the events to make sure they're appropriate,' said Lorraine.

'That's right. At first we just did it for ourselves and a few people who wanted to come along, but it's really taken off in the last six months, so we've had to scale up as the demand has increased. We charge a small administrative fee to cover our overheads.'

'You aren't still working at your job, are you?' asked Ruby, the grand dame of the *Couch* ladies. I was in the midst of chat-show royalty!

'Oh yes, still working. I'm a sales rep for Nutritious. I work there three days a week.'

'They must be thrilled to have you to represent them.'

'Erm, yes, I guess they are.' That was a lie, but I wasn't about to gripe about them on national telly. 'The other two days I work for the club as the events coordinator. We all work according to how much time we can devote to it. Pixie, Jane and Ellie are all on the board of directors with me.'

'How wonderful to do something you're so passionate about,' Lorraine said. 'And to be a role model for other curvy people out there. Thank you so much, Katie, for spending time with us on the couch today.' When the clapping died down she turned to camera. 'Stay with us after the break, when we'll continue the discussion of this weighty issue.'

The presenters relaxed again and I knew we were off-air. The intern swooped in to lead me from the set.

'Thanks, Katie,' said Lorraine. 'That was great.' She turned to the intern. 'Please make sure Katie gets some lunch.' She fixed her with a stern look. 'And try eating something yourself. You look like a famine victim.'

I chuckled at that. Even in the midst of my panic earlier in the Green Room, when I'd looked at the intern all I could think was that she needed a sandwich.

By the time I got to the office I was a legend in my own imagination. Get me, on national TV! My phone had chirped steadily with congratulations texts. Honestly, it was easy to see how film stars got swollen egos. I was one chat show away from demanding green M&Ms and bathing in Evian. When the intern asked whether I wanted to be driven to work, I felt like a proper star.

Of course I wasn't a star. I was just the only one daft enough to agree to be on TV. Besides, stars didn't get driven to work. Being stars *was* their work. I could be ridiculous sometimes.

Rob phoned to say that the website was going nuts with hits. Even our less popular events – those with no prospect of food or drinks – were selling out. One-point-four million people had watched me talk about the Curvy Girls Club.

111

I soon realised that none of them worked in my office. My colleagues hadn't the faintest idea where I'd been all morning. There, I was just regular old Katie, the fat girl in sales. I was a little deflated as I tucked my hair behind my ears, put on my headset and plugged into my computer. Well, what did I expect? That the world would change because I'd spent five minutes on TV? Really, Katie, get over yourself. You didn't cure cancer.

Suddenly a giant bouquet of pink and orange gerberas rose above my cubicle divider. As I stood up, Pixie, Jane and Ellie popped up behind it, whisper-shouting *Surprise!* We were in an open-plan office, after all, where everyone was on the phone.

Pixie rushed around the partition wall to hug me. 'We are so proud of you, love, congratulations!'

'You were brilliant!' said Jane, throwing her arms around Pixie and me. 'That was fantastic, sweetheart. Honestly, that was good television.'

'You should know,' I said. 'I can't believe you came all the way over here to see me. You're the best friends ever.'

'Tell me everything!' Ellie said, hugging me. 'God, your hair is lacquered.' She patted my wavy dark Elnett helmet. 'Were you nervous? Did you get to see Peter Andre? What shade of Tango is he? Did he talk to you?!'

'He went on before me,' I said. 'So I only saw him for a few minutes while we waited in the Green Room. And he's now mahogany.'

She swooned a bit at this delicious titbit. 'Did you remember to tell them how many unique views we've had?'

Rob had texted me the stats that morning. *817 unique views, 233 signups. Break a leg! Rob :-)*

'Oh no, I'm sorry, I was so nervous that I forgot. Next time you do the telly, okay? You could meet people like Peter Andre.'

She seemed to consider this sweetener, then shook her head, her mop whipping around her face. 'No way, it's not worth it. I'd die in front of the cameras. You're the face of the Curvy Girls Club, Katie.'

As Ellie went back to her desk and Jane and Pixie went off to collect their children, her words rang in my ears. I tried not to crave green M&Ms and Evian baths, but I admit it was going to my head, a bit.

CHAPTER SIXTEEN

My job had a way of bringing me down to earth, and it did so with a bump the next day, as I had to train the new crop of office newbies. This was part of the company's more(work)-for-less(money) ethos. Wouldn't it be *fun*, they enthused, to *help each other*?

I stood in front of eight young faces, awkwardly working through a baffling PowerPoint presentation cobbled together by one of the board members. When I got to a page of diagrams that weren't even recognisable to me after working there for six years, I gave up.

'Listen,' I told my charges, some of whom snapped awake. 'You're going to be salespeople. Why don't we talk about that instead of . . .' I tried not to make a face. 'This.'

Their relief was evident. I remembered being in their shoes. They were fresh out of college or uni. They'd just been through the scientific training week. Now they needed to know that their job wasn't as terrifying as they imagined it to be.

'I've got an idea. You've all had the scripts, right?' We worked to rigorously planned scripts. We had to. Salespeople teetered on a tightrope between truth and fiction. Tying up our words kept us from going 'rogue' with the products, ensuring the company got revenue, not lawsuits. 'Okay. Break into pairs and we'll role play. Client and Nutritious rep.'

'It sounds like corporate porn,' said one young man near the front. He had the dimples and cheeky smile of a natural salesman.

I laughed. 'That would make for a very boring wank.' Oops, possibly shouldn't have said wank to my new colleague. 'Right, one of you is the client, the other is the rep. Clients, don't make it easy for the rep, but keep it realistic. How would you honestly answer if cold-called like this? We'll switch around roles in a little bit.'

I walked between the groups, making suggestions as I listened to each conversation. They soon got the hang of it and within an hour everyone was pitching like seasoned liars.

'Excellent, very good,' I said just as the clock struck time-to-go-home. 'We're finished. Does anyone have any questions?'

A willowy young woman at the front raised her hand. 'Given that we're in the business of selling health products, are there any rules, or guidelines, really, about how we should look? Not that I plan to get fat or anything!'

The boy with the cheeky smile sniggered and I felt the flush creep up my face. My smile froze in position. A few of the others stopped looking at me.

The girl said, 'No, I didn't mean . . . I wasn't talking about—'

I cut her off. 'There are no formal guidelines beyond our dress code,' I said smoothly. 'You'll find that in your induction manual. Now, if there are no more questions, we can go. Good luck on the phones tomorrow.'

Eight new hires watched the embarrassed girl lumber from the conference room.

I couldn't stop my heart from racing, even after sitting

on the bench in the square next to our building. It was a tiny oasis of green where I often sat to clear my mind of the phone jabber. Tucked behind a line of evergreens, I was separated from the commuters shuffling along the pavement.

I put my hand on my chest, feeling my heart pound. Da-da-da-da-da-da- kerthunk! Maybe it wasn't the caffeine, but thoughtless remarks from size eight women. One little comment and suddenly I was no longer Katie Winterbottom, competent salesperson. I was Cakey Katie, the ten-year-old child being teased in the playground. Of course kids were cruel little buggers. I just wished adults would think before they spoke. How many people bled from the cut of a sharp tongue?

Unsteadily I made my way back inside to the loo for a quick makeup triage. I actually felt a bit dizzy as I tried to steady my hand. I hoped I wasn't coming down with something because there was no way I was going to miss my dinner reservation.

When I arrived, Rob was already in the restaurant's reception room with around a dozen other Curvy Girls Club members.

'Hi! Are you excited? I'm excited!' I said as I kissed his cheek, inhaling his citrusy aftershave. I thought of Rob whenever I smelled lemons.

'I'm excited, I'm excited!' He jumped up and down flapping his hands.

'Is that supposed to be me?'

'What's the matter? Not enough height on the leaps?'

'Well, excuse me for looking forward to tonight.' How could I not be enthused about eating a mysterious dinner in a pitch-black restaurant?

'I love your excitement. It reminds me of my parents' dog when I visit. Sometimes she even wees on the floor.'

116

'Lucky for you I've just been to the loo.' The room looked like any normal bar – black-clad staff, black-topped bar, wooden floors and large windows facing out onto Clerkenwell Green. Next door the pub was busy with after-work punters crowding the pavement to enjoy the mild evening.

'This was an inspired suggestion, if I do say so myself,' Rob said. 'I'm looking forward to seeing what happens next. No pun intended. Do the lights go out in here? Or do we go through to another room?'

I shrugged, delighting in the element of surprise. 'I can't wait!'

'Don't get your hopes up too much, Katie. I don't know if this will top the £2.65 you won at bingo last week. Nights like that are priceless.'

'They are not priceless. They're worth exactly £2.65.'

'You can't diss bingo. Potential for riches aside, the beautiful décor—'

'You see beauty in strip lighting and 1970s panelling?'

'Glamorous women?'

I grasped the backs of my arms. 'Now I know where the expression bingo wings came from. Most of us could fly across the channel without setting foot in an airport.'

'Handsome men?'

'Did you see one with his own hair or teeth?'

'Excuse me,' he said, pointing to himself. 'I'll have you know this is all me.' He flashed me a grin. I'd never thought to ask him if he'd had braces. He had a beautiful smile.

'Present company excluded,' I acknowledged. 'As wonderful as it was to spend the night in bingo splendour, I have a feeling this is more my cup of tea.'

'Because nobody can see you?'

I looked up sharply. 'What makes you say that?'

'Uh, because we're going to be eating in the dark? Are you okay?' He frowned.

117

'Oh, fine. I'm fine. Just getting hungry, that's all. Is everybody here?'

'Katie, what's—'

'I'll just go see if they're ready for us.' I hurried away before he could ask me again what was wrong.

I was being silly. Oversensitive from the training meeting, that was all. Or else my heart jitters were making me irritable.

I flagged down the manager to let him know we'd all arrived. Back on safe ground. That was better. He gathered us all into a scrum to hand out menus, neatly solving the first mystery of the night. At least we wouldn't have to point at our menus in the pitch black. Not that choosing our dishes was any more illuminating. There were just four cryptic options: fish, meat, vegetarian and Chef's Surprise. If the surprise was the chef groping me in the dark, I'd have a few suggestions for their comment card.

A current of excitement ran through the group as the waiters began to assemble us, amidst much nervous giggling.

The blind waiters were probably perfectly at home navigating a room in the dark. After all, they worked in that world twenty-four hours a day. We, however, would break limbs without guidance. We stood in groups of four or five, one behind the other, with our hand on the shoulder in front. Our waiter led us through one curtain, into semi-darkness, and then through another.

It was absolutely pitch black. I felt my eyes widen as my head swivelled, searching for any point of reference. I could hear people in conversation ahead of us. I didn't want to let go of Rob's shoulder.

But soon the waiter led him away to the table. I stood still, feeling suddenly exposed. I knew this was a safe experience. Yet I started to feel a little panicky that someone was right in front of me. I felt my heart quicken again. I didn't like it.

118

'Come this way,' the waiter then said quietly. He put my hand on his shoulder again and we walked a few steps. He placed my hand on the back of a chair. 'The chair is pulled out. You can sit.'

I did, immediately reaching out to feel the place in front of me. Plate, napkin, cutlery, small tumbler.

'Thank you,' I told my invisible guide.

'I'm glad you're next to me,' said Rob. He sounded very close to my side. In fact all of the voices sounded closer, clearer than I was used to. Maybe because there was no background noise to muffle them.

'Okay, this is officially a weird experience,' I said. 'How will we find our food on the plate? We'll have to stick our hands in everything.' I hadn't really believed it would be completely dark in there.

'All part of the fun,' he said. I could hear the smile in his voice beneath his gentle Yorkshire accent. It was easy to picture his face. 'Are you having wine?'

'Oh no, I ordered red. I'm going to come out of here looking like I've murdered someone.'

'Nah, don't worry. The food you're going to spill down your front will camouflage any wine stains.'

'Thanks very much for your confidence in my ability to feed myself.'

'I'm just playing the odds.'

Even though I knew the restaurant was full of people, it seemed as if we were alone in our little conversational bubble. We could say anything. It might be the same sense of anonymity that made people overshare on the internet. Thanks to Facebook I knew the sexual, dietary and bathroom habits of virtual strangers. Complete with photos, sometimes.

The waiter returned to tell us our drinks had arrived. He poured the wine (so he said – I had to trust him on that) and said if we wanted more, it was to my right. I found my tumbler and put it to my lips.

'It smells of fruit, berries maybe,' I said. 'But it tastes peppery.'

'You're a wine wank, Katie, but I like you anyway.'

I smiled for him though he couldn't see.

The noise level rose as our little group introduced themselves. Often people came to these things with friends, but some also came on their own. I always worried about that, but a certain ethos had already built up around the club. Everyone was looked after so that nobody was left alone to stand around like a lemon. I guess that's what happens when a bunch of people who are used to feeling like outsiders get together.

'You know something, Katie? You've got a very nice voice,' said Rob. 'All these years together and I never noticed.'

'Thanks. And I never noticed how much I rely on people's facial expressions when they talk. Isn't it funny not to have any visual clues to go by? In here it doesn't even matter what anyone looks like.' That makeup I'd reapplied earlier was a complete waste of time.

'It's a perfect world then,' he said.

'What do you mean?'

'We don't have to think about what we look like. We can be happy just the way we are. You said it in the *Evening Standard*, remember? Did you mean it?'

'Yes, definitely. I want to be happy with myself, not worry that I'm not perfect. Life is too short.'

Just imagine living in a world where looks didn't matter. Would it be a better or worse place? My instinct said better. It'd be dead easy for anyone with an appealing personality to find dates. But then . . . the only way we'd know if we were physically attracted to someone would be to touch them. That seemed a bit forward. *Oops, ever so sorry, but now that we've had a good grope around I find I don't fancy you at all.* It was one thing never to have a chance with a man. Nobody wanted to be rejected after being felt up.

'I admire your attitude,' he said. 'More people should think like that.'

I didn't point out that I'd said I *wanted* to be happy with myself, not that I actually was yet. But I was working on it.

'Do you think they can see us?' Rob asked.

'They? Who? Are you hearing the voices in your head again?' I asked. 'Flashing back to 'Nam?'

'The managers, or a security person at least. You'd think they'd have to be able to see us for health and safety reasons. Night-vision cameras maybe. Otherwise we could get up to who knows what kind of nefarious activities. The cloak of darkness masks everything. Mwah ha ha ha ha!'

'Is that your hand on my knee?' I joked.

'Who says it's my hand?'

My unladylike guffaw bounced off the walls. 'I feel freer in the dark.'

'Me too. We could be sitting here in our pants and nobody would know. I could pick my nose, or make gurny faces.'

I stuck my tongue out as far as I could, just to prove his point.

'. . . Or I could, for example, lean in, like this.'

I could feel the heat of his body as he moved closer. I knew his face was inches from mine.

'And then what would you do?' I whispered.

'I'd kiss you.'

His lips met mine, soft and warm. He kissed, and I kissed back. His hand found my cheek, his fingertips stroking my jaw. I wanted to grab his face with both hands. Wow. That was unexpected.

He broke away. 'This dining in the dark lark is great, isn't it? I'm definitely writing a five-star review for this place.'

'Me too. Two thumbs up.' I wanted more kissing. In the darkness, I wasn't able to tell him that without saying the words. 'Rob? What's this all about?'

He was quiet so long I wondered if he'd gone to the loo.

'It's simple, really,' he finally said. 'I like you. I've liked you for years. I know that makes me a pathetically slow mover. After joking about it the other day, the time just seemed right to tell you that.'

I felt a hand on my shoulder. 'Here's your starter, from the Chef's Surprise menu,' said the waiter. Oh, right. I wasn't just there for the kissing. 'Your cutlery is beside your plate. Do you need anything else?'

Some time to think would be nice. I shook my head, then remembered he couldn't see me, and thanked him.

'Are you going to say anything?' Rob asked when the waiter had left. At least, I thought he'd left. He might have been standing behind me, waiting to hear how this turned out.

I wasn't sure what to say to Rob. We were mates. Yet I had thought of Rob *in that way* before. Boyfriend fantasies that popped up every so often. The hand-in-hand walks, the cuddles on the sofa. If I was honest with myself, I did want more with him.

'Thank you?' I said.

He laughed. 'You're welcome. I'm glad your manners haven't completely left you. But I meant are you going to say anything about what I said.'

'I'm not sure what to say. I mean, I'm not sure. This is rather sudden.'

'Not for me, it isn't. But I know what you mean. It's come out of the blue. Or the black, in this case. I don't want to pressure you into anything. You know how I feel. You can make up your own mind. Have you tried your food yet?'

'No. Have you?'

'Uh uh. On three?'

Ah, blessed distraction. Gingerly I edged my finger along my plate until I felt something cold and smooth. 'They wouldn't feed us anything gross, right?'

'It is the surprise menu. It might be Michelin star. It could be turd. Ready?'

I forked a bit into my mouth. Pâté, maybe. That was the consistency. Could also be turd. Tasty turd, if it was.

'It tastes like—'

'Shh, don't tell me.' He gently touched my leg. I tingled. 'I'm enjoying having to rely only on my senses. We'll compare notes later.'

As I munched through my Michelin star turd, I made myself think of something other than Rob's kiss. At least for a few seconds. We'd been friends for nearly four years. We'd seen each other at least weekly for the past few months. He'd had hundreds of chances to kiss me before now. But he waited until we couldn't see each other.

Did he kiss me because he couldn't see me? I thought again about a world where looks weren't a factor. No more paparazzi, for one thing. In fact the whole gossip magazine industry would probably implode. With no stories about celebrities losing the baby weight or having facelifts, how would they fill their pages? They might actually have to talk about Angelina Jolie's charity work or Ryan Gosling's acting.

And just think what might happen to our psyches. Would people who were now judged and found wanting all feel better about themselves? Possibly. But wouldn't it have the opposite effect on those whose confidence was founded on their appearance? I wasn't sure that trading one set of hurt feelings for another was the answer.

Of course I couldn't concentrate on my main course. Rob's declaration was the first I'd heard in years. Scratch that. It was the first proper grown-up declaration I'd ever heard. I couldn't really count Rory's slurry *Wanna get outta here?*

when we were eighteen. Did I? Wanna get outta here, so to speak?

Alex popped into my head. He had a bad habit of doing that. Damn him and his perfection. It wasn't healthy to hold such a torch for someone who didn't know I was alive. Just a silly crush. A silly, six-year crush. I was not about to pass up the only opportunity I'd had for a date since . . . Oh god, I couldn't bear to think how long it had been.

'Rob? Let's get a drink after this. We can compare notes.'

Yes, let's call it comparing notes. I couldn't very well say *and kiss each other's faces off*, could I?

CHAPTER SEVENTEEN

Rob and I *compared notes* after dinner. They were very good notes, full of tenderness and cheeky fun. We compared them in the bar where we went after our meal, and again when he walked me to my door. I didn't ask him inside, and he didn't try his luck. Whatever this was, it wasn't like that.

Of course I was in a complete muddle over what this might mean for Rob and me. Were we just two friends snogging in the dark to pass the time between courses? Could this be a fling, or a torrid affair, or even the start of a lifelong relationship? I wasn't sure. More importantly, I wasn't quite sure what I wanted it to be.

It certainly didn't look like any relationship I'd ever seen. Man declares feelings. Woman says all right then. Relationship commences based on friendship and mutual attraction. Surely that couldn't really exist. What about the drama, the uncertainty, the complications? Look at Ellie. Look at Pixie. Look at every rom-com and *Jeremy Kyle* episode ever aired. Reality didn't work like that.

Besides, I couldn't simply transfer my devotion from one person to another like I was changing over a handbag. Six years of feelings for Alex had built up. *Six years*. Lots of married people had shorter relationships. And he'd been extra-attentive since my review. He was emailing most days – just friendly notes to see how I was. This was definitely a step forward.

Oh, of course it was probably still hopeless, but I was on safe ground with Alex. I got all the tummy-tickling excitement with none of the confidence-crushing anxiety. It was the perfect fake relationship. Insane, yes, but it was my constant.

How ironic that before we kissed, Rob would have been on my Grand Council of Man-Woe Advisors. He always gave excellent advice. Now that I knew his feelings, remembering how I'd prattled on about Alex made me feel like an arse. That couldn't have been nice for him, although he must have known there was nothing to worry about. Alex was about as likely to want to date me as I was to want to do exercise. Maybe the time had come to face that.

But I just wasn't ready. Not yet. So I pretended nothing had happened in the dark, and in the pub and at my front door. We were comfortably friends again, at least on the surface. He didn't mention anything when we hosted events together, and I tried to forget that I had quite liked snogging him.

A week later, I woke early on the morning of my first client meetings. I say I woke, though I didn't feel as if I'd actually slept. My new best friend, insomnia, ganged up with excitement to make me bleary-eyed. After lovely Thomas made good Ellie's promise to hand over the client lists, I'd taken my proposal straight to Cressida. She promised to look into it. At first she tried the usual *Somebody else can do these meetings* line. Sorry, I told her sweetly, nobody else had clients within twenty miles. Plus, they were important clients whose renewals were coming up. At that point she knew she'd been out-manoeuvred. I was under no illusions though. I might have found a way around her objections this time, but it was a one-off.

When she first hired me she made much of the fact that salespeople got to visit clients. She meant *other* salespeople. It took me a couple of years of wishing my colleagues luck as they went out to exercise their expense accounts to realise that it was my figure, stupid. Sure, clients liked me on the phone. I was an authority on nutritional supplements. As far as they knew I was the poster child for healthy lifestyles. Cressida wasn't about to let me waddle in and burst their bubble.

As I got close to the Tube entrance nearest to our flat, my heart sank. The gates were down. A mob of angry commuters stood waiting to enter. I had a non-changeable ticket from King's Cross in forty-five minutes and they decide to close *this* station *now*?

'Excuse me,' I said to one of the commuters as she huffed and fumed. 'Do you know what's happening?'

'Of course bloody not! They just shut the gates and won't let anybody in. I've got a meeting in thirty minutes.' She checked her watch again. She was definitely one of those obsessive lift button pushers. 'Just bloody great,' she said as fat raindrops began spattering the ground. I stepped away, in case of Tube rage.

'Excuse me.' I tried a slender young man who stood with his face in his paper, oblivious to the intensifying deluge. 'Do you know why they've closed the station?'

'Electrical failure, apparently,' he said, not looking up.

'Did they say how long till it reopens?'

He shrugged.

I'd definitely miss my train unless I did something fast. The next closest station was a twenty-five-minute walk away. In my pinchy shoes I'd end up in tears with bleeding feet halfway there. And the station might not even be open.

I had about ten minutes to spare. I could wait but what if the station was closed longer? This felt like one of those pivotal decisions. There seemed to be a lot of those lately.

Dammit, I was *not* going to give up my one chance to visit clients. I pushed my way back through the crowd and hurried to the kerb to flag down a black cab.

The taxi crept along in the rush-hour traffic, giving me palpitations all the way to the station. By the time I found my platform, the train was boarding. I ran to the first open carriage with my heart clanging in my chest. Extra girth aside, I'd always been healthy. My joints didn't ache and I usually managed to avoid the worst of the winter colds. So my heart pounding like an unbalanced spin cycle was Not Normal. I spent the entire journey trying to remember the symptoms of a heart attack.

Things had calmed down a bit, cardiovascularly, by the time I reached the client's offices so I no longer felt the urgent need to dial 999. Then the whole day became a blur of meetings and taxis and sheeting rain and I forgot all about it. The clients were all nice and by the time I limped back to the train station on blistered feet, I was tired but triumphant.

My mobile trilled just as the train pulled away from the platform. 'Hi, Rob!'

'Hey, Katie. I just wondered how your meetings went today. Did you get my text this morning? I wanted to wish you good luck. I'd have called earlier but was afraid I'd disturb you. Though I'm sure you had your phone off anyway.'

Right. Turn phone off, so mates ringing in the middle of meetings didn't make you look like the amateur you were. Note for next time.

'God, I don't think I could do this every day,' I told him. 'It's too exhausting!' I recounted the stressful journey to King's Cross. 'But the meetings themselves went really well.

128

One client as good as promised to renew her contract, so I've got something pretty concrete to tell my boss.'

'That's great, well done! I'm sure it was ace to meet everyone, and put faces to names. Do you want to tell me all about it over a celebratory drink? I'm buying.'

'No, I can't tonight, I'm meeting the girls. Can we go out another night?'

'Are you just saying that, or would you really like to go out?'

'I'd really like to go out with you.' And I meant it. 'I need to see the girls tonight. Can we please go out another night?'

'Of course we can. I'll plan something nice for us in the next couple of days. And Katie, I'm really glad everything went well for you today. You deserve a lot of success.'

'Thanks, Rob. You're very sweet.' And not just sweet. Hot too. My mind went back to the night we kissed. 'I'm looking forward to our date. See you soon.'

Through the rest of the train journey back to London, my tummy told me just how much I looked forward to seeing him soon. Maybe I wasn't in Rory-love just yet, or Alex-lust, but my feelings for him were definitely not platonic.

Rob's text pinged to my phone just as I got to the restaurant to meet everyone. I smiled. Date plans already?

Forgot to tell you, it read. *833 uniques, 253 signups last week. We could use some more events. Rob x*

No date yet, but still I grinned as I went inside. Great client meetings, the prospect of Rob's kisses, another great week for the club *and* a night out with my best friends? My life felt pretty good just then.

'Ooh, aren't you a fancy thing!' Pixie said when she saw my outfit. I generally favoured empire waist dresses or flared trousers with roomy tunics. My interview suit made very rare appearances. 'C'mon, love, give us a spin.'

I did, adjusting my skirt again. It had inched its way back-to-front all day long and was going in the charity box pile as soon as I got home.

Pixie's eyes narrowed as she stared at me. 'Come here,' she said, making a grab for my suit jacket. 'Look at you, skin and bones!' she announced as she pulled it against my tummy.

That was poetic licence if ever I'd heard it, but I had to admit that my clothes were more voluminous than normal. 'Don't be ridiculous,' I said. 'I might have lost a few pounds.'

But I was lying. I knew exactly how much weight I'd lost. Fourteen pounds. On top of the six I lost before. That was seriously meaningful weight! Excitement stirred. Wasn't twenty pounds equal to four dress sizes? That meant that the Holy Grail – Topshop – was within my grasp.

Pixie was the first to break the increasingly uncomfortable silence. 'How the bloody hell did you do that?'

I shook my head, feeling my friends' eyes boring into me. 'I have absolutely no idea, honestly. I haven't done anything differently. Ellie, you've seen me. I'm not doing anything. I feel like I'm eating more than usual.'

I couldn't account for it. Lately I woke every morning with my stomach grumbling for breakfast, and the defiant little organ never seemed to be satisfied.

'Katie, if you've not meant to lose that kind of weight, you need to see a doctor,' Jane said gently. 'I've fasted for three weeks and lost three pounds.' She shook her head. 'I'll try not to be jealous of you. I just feel like if I could drop some weight my life would be perfect. I feel guilty even saying that.'

'That's because no matter what you see in the mirror, you're going to listen to what's inside your head. If the fat girl is still in there she'll drown out everything else, unless you figure out a way to get her to shut up.'

I was trying my best to silence Fat Katie, but I knew how Jane felt. It wasn't easy. I might be pleased with what I saw in the mirror, but it only took one snub from a stranger, or a colleague's comment, to give her voice again. Mostly she stayed quiet though, muffled by the club.

'Come off it, Katie,' Pixie said. 'It's easy to ignore the fat girl when you're not fat any more. Apparently you've miraculously got a Get Out Of Jail free card.'

'Pixie, I don't know why this is happening and you're acting like you don't believe me.'

'Of course we believe you,' Ellie said. 'We're just worried. I hadn't noticed you'd lost so much weight. You always wear baggy clothes. Now that Pixie pulled your top back though, I can see it. Maybe Jane's right. You should just check with your GP. Have you been feeling unwell?'

I glanced between their faces. Concern. Concern. Disbelief and concern (that was Pixie). What if I did need to see a doctor? There I was thinking about summer fashions when there might be something seriously wrong with me. I felt fine, generally, except for the constant hunger. And the fact that I wasn't sleeping, though that could be related to my demanding tummy. And my racing heart was . . . just joyful anticipation of my next meal? Even I didn't believe that.

Then I remembered my grandmother. She got really skinny about a year before she died. Mum and Dad took her to the doctor, who knew pretty quickly what was wrong. Granny asked not to know the details. She wanted to live her life as normally as possible. The cancer had spread everywhere anyway. They weren't even sure where it had started.

She was seventy-two when she died.

I was only thirty and I had my whole life in front of me. At least I thought I had.

CHAPTER EIGHTEEN

I rang my GP the next morning but he couldn't see me for a few days. Over much wine at dinner my friends had convinced me not to worry too much. I was probably just the luckiest slimmer in the western world. By the time I woke for work the next morning, I nearly believed them.

'Here, I've made breakfast,' said Ellie when I got to the kitchen for my coffee. She was wielding a spatula with remarkable ease for someone who rarely cooked. 'Scrambled eggs and toast and bacon and beans.'

'What's all this?'

'We got through a lot of wine last night. You must be hungover too.'

'This isn't because you're worried about me?'

'What? No!' she said.

I'd be a rich woman if I played poker against her. 'Ellie, it's okay. You don't have to force-feed me. I promise I'm not anorexic.'

She set the spatula down. 'I'm sorry. I'm being stupid. And I can't even cook!'

I scrutinised my plate, unable to disagree with her. 'Here,' I said. 'Give me your rashers and I'll pop them in the microwave to finish cooking. You'll give us both food poisoning.'

As I set the microwave my mobile started buzzing on the table, sending my mind racing towards Rob. Maybe he was calling to ask me out tonight. He'd want to be sure I had enough warning to know what to wear.

'It's Jane,' Ellie announced, handing me the phone.

'Katie,' she said. 'I'm sorry to ring so early but I've just heard from the Channel 4 producer. She can fit us in this morning if you can make a meeting at ten.'

'Oh, well I'll have to call Cressida and tell her I'll be late into work. But yes, of course I can! Does this mean the producer liked the pitch?' I caught Ellie's eye.

'She loved it! I've got to dash to get the children to school first. I'll text you the address.'

Ellie was doing her excited puppy dance by the time I hung up. 'Yayyy!' she shouted just as the microwave pinged.

I was in a complete tizzy by the time we got to Channel 4's offices. How could I be calm at a time like this? Behind the four-storey-high glass façade sat the people who could give the Curvy Girls Club a sparkling future. We entered the busy atrium to check in with reception. When Jane showed her pass the woman behind the desk sent us straight upstairs. We were in!

A slender middle-aged woman was on the phone when we arrived at her open door. If the décor was an indication of this woman's mind then she was a mess. The room was crowded with red packing crates full of handbags and shoes. Papers were piled on every surface and scattered across the floor. Carefully we picked our way through the chaos to the chairs she'd pointed to in front of her desk.

'So sorry about the mess,' she said when she hung up. 'Samples. We get them constantly. Anyway, I'm Rea Benton, one of the executive producers. You're Jane, yes?' She shook Jane's hand warmly. 'I used to love watching you!'

Jane blushed and graciously thanked her.

'So you must be Katie. Pleasure to meet you. Thanks so much for coming in at such short notice. I'm off on holiday tomorrow but wanted to get the ball rolling on this.' She scanned a piece of paper. 'We love your idea. *The Great British Makeover* is right up our street, and the Curvy Girls Club angle is perfect. Katie, I caught up with your segment on *On The Couch*. Excellent. You're exactly the kind of girl Gok would love to work with.'

Gok Wan would love me! I felt faint. 'Thank you.'

'So you'd like to commission it?' Jane asked.

'Oh yes, definitely. You two would be on the show, right? What about the others? There are four of you, I understand.'

'I'm afraid the other two are camera shy,' Jane explained. 'Is that a problem?'

'No . . . as long as you're confirmed as definite, then we can start sketching out the segment to see what we'll need. We'd look to air it in late September, and filming would start in late August. We can confirm exact dates later. You haven't got any plans to be out of the country for an extended period, have you?'

We shook our heads. I only recently got to go to Southend-on-Sea for the day.

'Good. So, I'll just get a few snapshots of you both so everyone knows who they're working with. And we'll need to take some measurements.' She held up a tape measure. 'Katie, can you please stand up over here?'

I stood by the window as directed, feeling very self-conscious as she snapped away with her digital camera. And this was with my clothes *on*. My tummy lurched at the thought of what lay ahead.

She took my measurements – I tried not to flinch as she committed those irrefutable facts to the public record. Then she snapped Jane.

'Perfect. So, no dramatic changes please, between now and when we film. The stylists will plan your looks based on these photos and stats. I'll have contracts sent out to you to sign. Is email okay?'

Within five minutes we were back in Channel 4's lobby with our heads spinning.

'So that's it?' I asked Jane. 'We've got it?' It seemed like there should be a more formal *Ta-da!* when something this big happened.

Jane grinned. 'Yes, sweetheart, that's it. We've got it. It's times like this that I'm so glad I work in television!'

'Do you ever miss it, Jane? Being a presenter, I mean. You were so good. You seemed so natural.'

She shrugged. 'Oh, I made my peace with giving it up long ago. At the time, moving to Bristol with Andy and the children was the most important thing for me. I've never regretted that for a moment. I don't think there's anything that could pull us apart now. Not many people can say that, so it was worth it a hundred times over. A job will always be a job for me, but my family and my happiness are everything. And to be honest, when we came back to London I didn't have the stomach to try for another presenting job. I hadn't lost any weight, and knowing how my producer felt about that made looking for another position seem ridiculous. Besides, I've enjoyed being on the development side. If I wasn't, we might not have had the chance to meet Rea today. I'll forward the contract as soon as she sends it to me, okay? It'll be pretty standard, just to make sure you can't sue them if you don't like the show.'

'You mean in case the camera makes me look fat?'

She laughed. 'Exactly. Do you remember how to get back to the Tube? I'll stay and do some work here. Thanks again for making the meeting. And Katie? This is really huge.'

Those words rang in my ears all the way back to the office.

There wasn't a soul on the floor when I got to my desk. Odd. Cressida hadn't mentioned an away day when I phoned earlier and it was too early for lunch.

Just as I was plugging into my computer, my colleagues emerged from the big conference room at the far end of the office. When I caught the look on Ellie's face I grabbed my handbag.

'What's going on?' I asked as we got in the lift.

'Not till we're outside,' she said, giving me an attack of the worries all the way to the ground floor. I told her about the Channel 4 meeting, but she was too distracted to be properly excited. My anxiety stepped up a notch.

We went across the road to our usual café. The barista didn't need to ask for our orders. Two skinny caffè macchiatos appeared.

'This is bad,' she said.

I knew she wasn't talking about her macchiato.

'The company's still having serious problems. They wouldn't give us the details, naturally, but it was easy to read between the lines. We're not making enough money. Cressida blamed all the internet supplement companies. Our clients think they can get them cheaper online.'

'It's probably true.'

'It's definitely true, which makes it disastrous for our business. And for our chances of keeping our jobs.' She flinched when she said this. 'Sorry! I know you've been dealing with this for a while now. But it sounds like it's going to get a lot worse.'

'Did they mention redundancies?'

'No. They definitely *didn't* mention redundancies. Which is why I suspect they're coming.' She blew out her cheeks. 'That would be very bad for me. I haven't exactly been sticking to my savings plan.'

I looked at her in surprise. 'You have a savings plan?'

She nodded. 'I plan to save one day.'

'Almost everything I had saved went into the flat. It's not as if I have a redundancy fund.' Dad always pestered me about having six months' living expenses in the bank, just in case. I had about six weeks' worth, if I lived on tinned soup and didn't take the Tube.

'I wouldn't worry if I were you,' I said. 'You're the only one who knows how to keep the office running. Clive can't live without you.' Me, on the other hand . . . I looked at my coffee. 'Maybe we should drink the free stuff from the machine from now on.'

Losing my job hadn't factored into my thinking. I vaguely remembered the bank mentioning something about redundancy insurance when I got my mortgage. I'd waived it away. Me? Redundancy? The chances of that happening were as slim as . . .

'I also found out that Thomas and Colleen are having lunch together next week. Bad news comes in threes, right? What's next?'

. . . As slim as Ellie calming down about Thomas and Colleen, probably. 'Have you been hacking his phone again?'

'Of course not. He mentioned it just now, in the meeting.'

'And you think it's a double-bluff? He's using lunch to cover for the fact that he wants to butter Colleen's baps?'

'I wish you wouldn't be so flippant about my love life. I need your support, not your jokes.'

Chastened, I said, 'I'm sorry. I just don't want you to get upset over nothing. What will it take to make you feel better? Shall we follow them around to make sure they're not up to anything?'

I stopped smiling when I caught her expression. 'Oh, Ellie, no. You're not seriously thinking about it. Do you realise that that will officially tip you into stalker territory?'

'Not if you come with me. Then it's just two friends having lunch who just happen to turn up in the same place where one friend's boyfriend may or may not be flirting with his colleague.'

'But what if he sees us?'

'Then we're just two friends having lunch who just happen to turn up in the same place where one's boyfriend—'

'. . . may or may not be flirting with his colleague. Got it. Do we need disguises?'

'No, but you'd better practise your innocent-looking face, just in case.' She looked at her watch. 'We should get back and make some money. Otherwise we may be serving this coffee one day instead of drinking it.'

'For the customers' sake, I hope not.' We made our way back to try to keep our company afloat.

CHAPTER NINETEEN

Just thinking about our first speed-dating event was making me go all stabby.

At least *I* wasn't the one speed-dating. I had quite enough to obsess over between my non-relationships with Rob and Alex. And I definitely didn't begrudge anyone finding love in three minutes. I just didn't want the Curvy Girls Club to go down that slippery slope.

Judging by her smile, Pixie felt none of my angst. She was already there when I arrived at the bar.

'Here's your badge, love,' she said, pasting the label to my left breast. 'Are your boobs shrinking too?' she accused.

'Thanks for feeling me up, and no, they are not.' They were, a bit, but I wasn't about to give her that kind of satisfaction. 'I've got the doctor's appointment at the end of the week.'

'Good. You know I don't want anything bad to happen to you.'

'As long as I don't lose weight.'

'So shoot me.' She shrugged. 'It's just not fair.'

'What is this?' I asked, looking closely at my badge. 'I thought we agreed. We aren't calling it Fat Friends.'

'Did we? I must have forgotten.' She turned away to label the two women who'd just arrived.

She absolutely had not forgotten. I was seething as I went to check on arrangements. It wasn't the first time Pixie and I had disagreed on things. It also wasn't the first time she'd done whatever she wanted. In some ways I admired her bullheadedness. Just not when it clashed with my own.

The bar was dimly lit (always good when meeting potential dates) and spacious (also good for mingling afterwards) with a nice long bar (to ensure spirits remained high). We had a very good turnout. It just remained to be seen whether the night would end in tears.

It wasn't just my gut telling me that Fat Friends was a bad idea. There was hard science to prove it. Not long after Pixie first brought up the idea, I'd read an article about how differently men and women see themselves. Some clever Danes found that while overweight men were convinced they were perfect (I'm paraphrasing), they mentally added weight to their wives and girlfriends. On the flip side, women didn't need any encouragement to see themselves as fat – they added pounds to their view of themselves with no help from anyone else. So what did you get when you put a bunch of chubby people in the same room? Flabby fellas rejecting women for having the very same jiggles, and a load of women feeling like gigundo monsters as a result.

But Pixie wouldn't take no for an answer. That's why we were labelling plump singles for romance in three-minute intervals.

As we got everyone settled in their places I tried to look objectively at the event. All right, fine. It was well-attended. Nearly eighty people had signed up. And they did look like they were up for a laugh. I imagined myself coming to one of these events. Yes, it would be fun. If I'd met someone like Rob here, I'd definitely consider the night a success. And

Alex? I'd probably make a fool of myself lunging over the table at him . . . if history was anything to go by.

There was no doubt that these kinds of events were money-makers. With almost no expenses the £15 fee was nearly pure profit. I just couldn't shake the feeling that it wouldn't end well.

'Nice turnout,' I admitted to Pixie as I set the three-minute timer.

She smiled. 'I told you it was a good idea. Even though in ten years they'll probably hate the sight of each other.'

'We probably won't use your quotes in the marketing. And you never know. Lots of people are still in love after a decade.'

'You say that, love, but it's the luck of the draw. There's no way to tell at the beginning. Himself and I were so in love at first it was sickening. We couldn't fart without the other thinking it smelt of roses. When he proposed I nearly passed out I was so happy. Everybody was. My family loved him. My friends loved him. I'd never met such a clever, funny, friendly, happy man.' She laughed. 'I can see the question on your face. What the hell happened to him then?' She shrugged, and continued her story as I dinged the bell every three minutes. The fact that she was talking about him at all told me how bad things must be.

Trevor had always liked a drink. He was happiest being the life of the party. The problem was, he wasn't very happy away from the party. And he didn't see why he *should* be away from it just because he was a husband. Not that Pixie wanted to stop him then. Those were the honeymoon years. They went out nearly every night with their friends, just as they had when they were first dating. But then the late nights started wearing Pixie down. She was tired all the time. Even one drink made her feel ill. She quickly sussed out the problem, but she worried about telling Trevor. With his building business still waiting to take off, even the few quid she earned as a dinner lady would be missed if she stopped working.

Eventually she had to tell him. Her excuses had worn thin and she was starting to show. She made him a nice dinner, lit the candles, poured him a drink, and told him he was going to be a father.

'I thought you were on the pill?' he asked. It wasn't the reaction she'd hoped for. For a split second she thought about making a joke about his manly sperm, but his expression stopped her. She was on the pill, she said, but she may have missed a day or two.

'You did this on purpose!' he shouted. 'You know I'm just getting the business going. We agreed to wait a few years before you had any brats.'

His words stung her. 'It's your brat too,' she said quietly.

'I don't want it. Get rid of it.'

'No fecking way, Trevor! How dare you even say that to me? If you don't want our baby, fine. I'll raise it myself.'

By the time the baby was born they were barely speaking. He hated everything about her pregnancy. As if the stretch marks and sore nipples and weight gain had been pleasant for her. He went to the pub every night as usual, but without her. The honeymoon was well and truly over.

'Why didn't you leave him then?' I asked gently.

'I was all talk, love. I still loved him, and I had a little baby to look after. How was I going to support her? What would I do with her while I worked? Tuck her in the warming tray whilst I dished up the children's school dinners? My parents are up in Manchester. They didn't have the money to have me back at home, with a granddaughter to look after as well. And Trevor did love Kaitlin. He does love her. He softened a little after she was born. It was even good sometimes. Our friends started having children and

142

our social life shifted a bit. More dinner parties, fewer knees-ups at the pub. So it wasn't all terrible.'

But it wasn't all good, either, she said. Trevor had made little jokes about her weight when she was pregnant. But when she failed to shed the pounds afterwards, his jokes turned overtly hostile.

'I'd always been plump,' she said. 'And Trevor liked me having a bit of extra meat on my bones. *I* liked me with curves. I've never fancied being one of those scaffolding board women. So it wasn't like I ballooned from a size ten, but I did balloon. Like someone stuck an air hose up my leg. And if you're told you're fat and ugly often enough, I don't care who you are, you start to believe it. Every time I looked in the mirror I saw what Trevor saw. You'd think that would have kicked me up the arse to do something about it, but I didn't have the energy. Then I fell pregnant again. This time Trevor was happier about it. He'd started the business with his partner and they were doing okay. Even though the drink was becoming a problem, we were better. When Connor was born, Trevor was absolutely over the moon.'

Trevor fell in love with his son and Pixie wondered if things might turn out all right after all. For a year or so they felt like a proper family. Money was tight with only Trevor working but everyone needed builders. Pixie loved being a mother and her children adored her. They didn't mind her squidgy tummy or her saddlebags. In their eyes, Pixie was the most beautiful woman on the planet.

Unfortunately Trevor's eyes were elsewhere.

'He blamed me when I found out about the slapper he was banging at his job. If I'd been a *proper wife* he wouldn't have strayed. I just wasn't appealing to him with the extra weight. So I showed him. I gained three stone.'

'You were depressed,' I said.

Yes, low-level depression, her GP said. He offered medication, but given that weight gain was a possible side effect, that didn't seem like the answer. Nothing seemed like an answer, until she found Slimming Zone.

'So I'm still fat but at least I don't feel so alone,' she said. 'I'm even starting to like myself again.'

'And clearly, so is Trevor,' I said. 'Or has your furry onesie finally put him off?'

'I wish. No, he's still after me most nights. He's getting desperate for another baby.'

'I'm surprised. He doesn't seem overly keen on the ones he has.' Pixie had often mentioned Trevor's indifference to her children. That hurt her at least as much as his taunts and insults.

'Ah, Katie, that's why he wants another one. He thinks I've poisoned the children against him. He says I've ruined them. He wants another one that he can make in his own image.' She closed her eyes. 'I shudder at the thought.'

What an egotistical, selfish, horrible man. 'Definitely go on the pill, Pixie. You cannot have another child with him.'

'I know that, but I can't go on the pill. You only have to look at me and I'm up the duff. He knows that. If we had sex and I didn't get pregnant he'd know I was preventing it. I've got to avoid him until I can get out. And I can't let him find out what I'm doing.'

She didn't say what she was probably thinking. She didn't need to. She was afraid he'd hurt her if he realised what she was doing.

'I really am going to leave the bastard this time, Katie. Want to hear how I'm going to do it?'

As she outlined her plan I felt elated and sick in turns. She was right. She'd finally figured out a realistic strategy. To do it she needed to work for the club. Unfortunately that meant expanding it with the launch of Fat Friends. And I couldn't let that happen.

CHAPTER TWENTY

'This place is a circus!' I said to Rob the next night, pointing to Royal Albert Hall's *Cirque du Soleil* banners. It had been a spectacular walk from the Tube at Hyde Park Corner. In response to a rare sunny day, the park was heaving with after-work picnickers, cyclists, joggers and lazy layabouts. Leafy plane trees, oaks and chestnuts stood out against the brilliant blue sky as we wandered along the edge of the park. Further along, the mosaicked and gilded Albert Memorial was blindingly beautiful in the early evening sun. It was, at least for the moment, finally summer.

'You know what?' Rob said as he shoved me playfully on the shoulder. 'I'd have bet a thousand quid you'd say that.'

'Am I that cheesily predictable?' I shoved him back but he didn't move much.

'I just know you well,' he said, not answering the question, I noticed.

'How on earth did you get tickets? It's been sold out for months.' We'd looked at *Cirque du Soleil* as a possible club event but we'd have had to sell our kidneys to score tickets. I hoped Rob wouldn't now need dialysis.

'I've got friends in high places,' he said, guiding me

through the door. His hand on the small of my back made me shiver.

Our seats were right down on the floor, in the third row. As people streamed in around us, the looks on their faces reflected the same open-mouthed awe at the spectacle. A few skimpy rope ladders snaked their way to the high ceiling. Poles and wires were tantalisingly braced from the floor, hinting at the acrobatics ahead. It sounded as if hundreds of birds were in the rafters, which were bathed in deep blue light. Spotlights shone randomly every few minutes. Then I realised they were shining into the audience. Close to us.

'Rob! This isn't an audience participation event, is it?'

He grinned and patted my leg. Pleasant tingles turned to nervous ones.

There were clowns prowling about. I had an uncomfortable relationship with clowns, thanks to a birthday party that went wrong as a child. One, dressed as a jester in a long-beaked bird mask, came closer to us. I did my best to look like a bad sport. 'If he tries to make me do anything,' I whispered to Rob, 'promise you won't let him, okay?'

'And you're going on national telly in a few months to bare it all?'

'This is different!'

'Okay, don't worry. I won't let them take you away.' He reached over and grabbed my hand. I clung to it. They'd have to knock me out to make me let go.

Luckily the bird-man had younger prey in mind. He chose a boy of about ten, who was soon surrounded by the clowns. As people laughed and cheered, the boy was hoisted onto the clown's shoulders. He looked like he was having a fabulous time, the little show-off. I spent the last few minutes before the show started avoiding eye contact with anyone who looked like they might haul me on stage. It was worse than having front row seats at a comedy club.

Then the lights changed and a pot-bellied stooped figure dressed in a scarlet frock coat marched down one of the side aisles. Behind him came about a dozen men and women dressed in white – the band. '*Alegria!*' he shouted into the vast space. Accordions, basses and drums added to the suddenly surreal feeling. It wasn't a show. It was an experience.

By the time the hauntingly beautiful white-clad lady stepped gracefully on to the circular stage, I was prepared for anything to happen. Was she a bug? She had antennae. Her dress was part ballerina tutu and part bird cage. Despite her white curls she was quite young. Then she opened her mouth to sing and I was surprised once again. Her growly, twenty-a-day voice washed over us. Tears sprang to my eyes. It was magical.

Rob searched my face. 'I knew you'd love it,' he whispered, taking my hand again. We stayed like that for most of the show. His hand was warm, enveloping and comfortable. Many times he stroked my thumb with his. When I peeked at him, he was completely lost in the feats of the acrobats, trapeze artists and contortionists. He had that rare ability to be *present*, whether watching a film or a show, playing football or talking to a friend. I'd often admired that about him.

I jumped to my feet at the end of the show, clapping till my palms were numb. I couldn't imagine a cast more deserving of a standing ovation.

'That was . . . oh my god, that was amazing!' I beamed at Rob. 'Thank you so much for taking me, although . . . you probably should have ended the date with this, not started it. How on earth will we top it?'

His mouth flew open in mock-affront. 'Katie, as a gentleman I am shocked, *shocked* I tell you, to hear you hint so obviously at *sexual relations*. Really, what do you take me for?'

'For the record, I wasn't implying that any activity later would be less than deserving of a standing ovation.'

'So long as we're clear on that. Come on.' He took my hand again. 'We've got dinner reservations.'

'Where?'

'Don't be so nosy. You'll see when we get there.'

We took the Tube into Covent Garden where the streets were packed. The warm day gave everyone the urge to grab the nearest pint of beer or glass of rosé and run into the street. Eventually we stopped in front of a restaurant.

It was more suited to a country village than London's streets. I half-expected it to be filled with muddy-booted ramblers and shaggy dogs sleeping by the hearth. A riot of pink, red and blue flowers overflowed the enormous pots and hanging baskets. Flowering trees, palms and bay trees stood guard.

'After you, Katie.' He held open the door.

There were no wellies or fleabitten mutts inside. If I had to find the opposite of a gentle countryside pub, this would be it. It was the world's campest decorator's wet dream. Rousing opera music boomed around the huge restaurant, which was swathed in gold. Gold lamé, rich purple and red brocades were draped over the tables. Strings of pearls hung from the chandeliers. Stone buddhas, Tiffany lamps and ornate crosses decorated the walls and ceiling. It was *Arabian Nights* meets the props room at the Royal Opera house.

The waitress led us to a small table tucked into an alcove. Carmen could have sung her famous aria on the balcony above us.

'I feel like I'm backstage at the opera,' I said to Rob as he sat beside me on the bench.

'I never pictured you as an opera groupie,' he said. 'Did you flash your well-developed vocal chords as a teenager and scream at the stage door for Carrera's autograph?'

'I do love me a bit of tenor.'

'They're the real role models for the Curvy Girls Club you know. Nobody expects a skinny soprano.'

'It's all a matter of perspective.'

'And expectations,' he said. 'Five hundred years ago being thin was a sign of poverty.'

'Then I'm rich,' I said.

'Getting poorer by the day though.'

I blushed. Now that there was a bit less of me to clothe I'd resorted to the back of my wardrobe for my date outfit. Excavating through the last decade unearthed as many memories as frocks. Every billowing dress and stretchy waistband told the story of a girl who wanted to look better than she did. I'd had fun in some of those outfits, days and nights of laughter and even sometimes a little bit of lust. At times I forgot the body I wore. But there was always that moment before going out when I had to check myself in the mirror. No tucking in, sucking in, thrusting or adjusting was going to turn this duck into a swan. Only a lot fewer breadcrumbs could do that.

Shaking out the pale yellow and red cinch-waisted, circle-skirted dress rekindled the night I wore it to impress Rory. The closest I got to him noticing was when his friend said I looked nice and he nodded. When you're young, you take what you can get. Tonight I hoped for a better reception.

As if reading my mind, Rob said, 'You look lovely tonight. That dress really suits you.'

'Thank you. Now that I'm not such a heifer I've got more options. It feels *so good* not to be dragging around so much fat.' I grinned. 'I really do love this new me.'

'I like the old you.'

'Oh please, this is so much better. I mean, I know I'm no Kate Moss, and never will be, but at least some of the bulk is gone. I'm swimming in some of my old clothes now. Luckily

I've still got some even older clothes. I haven't worn this one in years . . . not that you aren't worth a new dress!' I rushed to clarify. 'But you moved fast on the date scheduling.'

'I didn't want to miss my window, in case I only had a couple of days till you changed your mind.'

I laughed. 'Well, when you only give me two days' notice, you get the best dress from the back of my wardrobe. I'm glad it's still pretty.'

'You'd be pretty without it.'

'Mister Chandler!'

'I didn't mean . . . well, actually, hell, yes, that's exactly what I meant.' He laughed. 'You look exceptionally hot tonight.'

'You're drunk.'

'I'm serious, Katie. Curves are sexy. Look at Marilyn Monroe.'

I examined my tummy, rising in a soft mound beneath the snug waist of the dress. Marilyn's lap didn't make you want to lie on it to have a nap.

'If you say so. But I could still have curves and be thin.'

'You could.' He shrugged. 'I'm just saying that it's the curves that are attractive.'

'You're biased because you're . . . my friend.'

'Your chubby friend, you mean. Maybe. But I wasn't always fat you know, and I've always enjoyed curves.'

'You are not fat!' I loved Rob's physique – his big broad chest and beefy arms were made for snuggling. He was quite fit, actually, thanks to his local five-a-side football team and lido in the park. He just loved to eat. Who didn't?

'That's not what my last girlfriend said.'

His face slid into sadness, which naturally made me want to throttle the bitch.

'I'm sorry. She was mistaken,' I said instead, practising for a role in the diplomatic services. 'Was that why she broke up with you?'

150

'I broke up with her. On our six-month anniversary.'

He clearly wanted to talk about it. The story came rushing out. They were set up at a mutual friend's wedding, sat next to each other, asked to pose in photos and dance together. By the end of the reception the meddling bride got her wish. They snogged in the cloakroom and traded phone numbers.

At first Rob thought he'd met the perfect girl. Bright, funny and very pretty (the bitch – my words, not his), they were steadily moving towards a serious relationship when they planned their first holiday abroad. Rob wanted something active – trekking or sailing or just going from place to place by bus in a foreign land. She wanted a beach holiday and since she was the one with the vagina, she won (my words again).

At first, he said, he noticed a jokey comment here and there. 'Mind the splash' when he went in the pool, or 'Of course he does' when asked about second helpings. He laughed it off. They were solid, comfortable, and moving in the right direction. But by the end of their holiday he could no longer ignore her jibes.

'Do you think I'm fat?' he asked her at dinner on their last night.

'Not fat . . . just portly.'

'Is that a problem?'

She smiled and took his hand. 'Not really. Especially since you're so active. All you need to do is work out a little more and cut down on the portions and you'll be perfect in no time.' She leaned across to kiss him.

'I don't want to be perfect. I want to be me.'

'A more perfect version of you would be great.'

'Is this version of me so bad?'

'Not *so* bad.'

They continued to go out for a few months after that, but the relationship was doomed. She wanted someone with ripped abs and perfect pecs. He wanted to be happy and comfortable as he was. Her constant comments wouldn't allow that to happen.

'Just because a person doesn't look perfect doesn't mean they're less, somehow. Ultimately she didn't understand that. So I broke up with her when we went away for our anniversary.'

'But it must have bothered you since you went to Slimming Zone. Nobody volunteers to be weighed in front of a room full of people unless they want to lose weight.'

'Part of me wanted to know if it would make a difference. I don't mean with her; that was over. But I wouldn't say no to a perfect body like your friend Alex.'

'You wouldn't get any argument from me either!' I laughed.

He looked at me sharply, then spooned in another mouthful of chocolate mousse. 'Last bite?'

'Thanks!' Nobody needed to offer chocolate mousse twice. 'So that was your last big romance?'

'I've gone out with a few women since then, but nothing serious. I'm not really a dating kind of guy. There's no way I'd sign up for Guardian Soulmates or speed-dating.'

'I have thought about it,' I said. I didn't tell him that I'd imagined what it would be like to meet him there. 'It was kind of sad the other night. One of the women said she felt even worse afterwards. I knew that would happen.'

It wasn't fair to burden Rob on our very first official date, but I had to talk to someone about it. I gave him the highlights of the night, ending with Pixie declaring it a storming success despite the woman's feelings.

'It's a bad idea, and one we shouldn't be involved in.'

'But no event is going to be perfect,' he reasonably pointed out. 'Were there more happy people than unhappy ones at the end?'

I admitted there probably were.

'Then it was a success. You've got to look at the evidence. It's very lucrative. It's well-attended. And most people enjoyed it. I'm sorry, Katie, but there's no basis for rejecting it for that reason.'

I didn't like the way our date was turning out. Rob was supposed to wine me, dine me and agree with me.

'Can we talk about something else? Fat Friends would be terrible for our image. We'll be seen as exploiting vulnerable people. I don't want to be associated with anything like that.'

Rob considered this. Then he said, 'You don't want the club to be associated with it, or *you* don't want to be associated with it?'

'It's the same thing.'

'No, it's not the same thing. One answer comes from your business head and the other comes from your ego. If you don't separate the two, you might not do what's best for the club. Just . . . please don't let your own vanity run away with you, okay? Hey,' he said, noticing my expression. 'I didn't mean to upset you. Personally I'll always back you. I hope you know that.'

I nodded, pushing Fat Friends from my mind as he gently guided me to him. His kiss was as electric as it had been the first time around. Before the waiters could clear the plates we were making a spectacle of ourselves in the restaurant. Rob was a stellar kisser and I was getting used to the idea that this might be more than a passing fling.

CHAPTER TWENTY-ONE

I felt ill the next morning. Not only was my head pounding from all the wine I drank with Rob, but by the time I reached my GP's office, I'd diagnosed myself. The news wasn't good. It was definitely either a tapeworm or cancer. Or lupus, though I'd only thought of that on the Tube and wasn't exactly sure what it was. It sounded like a prime cause of unexplained weight loss though.

My GP and I hadn't always seen eye-to-eye. It wasn't that he was a bad doctor. He listened to my ailments and made sensible suggestions. He kept up-to-date with medical advances, stocked pretty good magazines in his waiting room and had warm hands. But he was also keen to try out all the latest diagnostic kit, and that's where our opinions diverged. When he came at me with callipers, I nearly kicked him in the shin.

'It's to test your body fat,' he'd explained. 'It's not just your weight that's important. Don't you want to know your body fat percentage too?'

I did not. I was perfectly happy to have my blood pressure checked (it was absolutely normal). I was even prepared to let him painfully draw blood for a cholesterol test (nice and low for the bad kind and high for the good stuff). But to use a tool to pinch my fat was a step too far. As if I didn't do it anyway in the mirror every day without the help of a calibrated instrument.

So we'd enjoyed an uneasy truce, my GP and me, as long as he didn't manhandle any flabby bits. I got straight down to business when he called me into his office. 'I've lost weight.'

'Good for you, Miss Winterbottom.' He considered me over his bifocals. If he wasn't a doctor he'd have made an excellent nutty professor, on looks alone. He was probably around sixty, tall and lanky, with a fondness for corduroys and those thick button-up jumpers worn by granddads and landed gentry.

'Thank you, doctor, but I haven't done it on purpose.'

'Why don't you pop on the scales?'

He was always telling me to pop something. Pop on the scales, pop my top off, pop my feet in the stirrups. As if being weighed, stripped to the waist or laid out with legs akimbo was more enjoyable thanks to the catchy phrase.

I popped, he weighed, then checked his records. 'Yes, you have lost quite a bit of weight. Twenty-three pounds. I can see you haven't been on any medication. Any dieting? Have you changed your exercise regime significantly?'

I loved that he thought I had an exercise regime. 'No, and I'm really worried.'

'Well, don't worry just yet,' he said. 'There are a lot of reasons why you might lose weight.'

'Do you think it might be cancer?' I could feel my eyes prick with tears. Poor Granny. She must have been terrified when Mum took her to the doctor. No wonder she didn't want to know the results.

He shook his head. 'No, I doubt very much that it's cancer. You're young, you don't smoke and you're not predisposed to any hereditary cancers. I'm sure there's a very simple explanation. We just need to find it.'

'But my granny had lung cancer!'

He consulted his screen. 'You said she was a heavy smoker and wasn't diagnosed until her seventies. I don't think you need to worry. Let's chat a bit and then I'll take some blood for tests. Okay?'

Shakily, I agreed. I was a young non-smoker with good genes. Of course I didn't have cancer. The question was: what did I have?

I was no closer to an answer at the end of the consultation. Doctor Tight Lips wouldn't indulge my hypochondria one bit. He kept saying 'Let's just see what the tests say.' Some bedside manner that was.

I very much wanted to talk to Rob. How had we functioned before we could text to prompt phone calls? Oh that's right, we phoned landlines and hung up.

Just been to the doctor, I texted. *I've lost 23lbs, woo hoo! Could be the start of a whole new me – roll on Thin Katie! K xo*

Something stopped me from telling him the reason I was at the GP's in the first place. I guess I wanted him to call because he'd had a lovely night too, not because he was worried. And why shouldn't I brag a bit about the weight loss? Twenty-three pounds without even trying. As long as I didn't have a life-threatening disease to thank, surely that could only be good news.

Rob's text back was short and sweet. *Congratulations. xx* I waited in case he'd accidentally sent the text before finishing it, but nothing followed. He didn't call.

I saw the Post-it when I got to my desk in the late morning. Shockingly pink, it was stuck to the top of the pile of new product brochures I was supposed to read.

Katie, I need you. Alex

I looked around. Was it a joke? Alex had never left a note on my desk before. Surely he'd email if he needed something. I turned to my colleague.

'Was Alex here?'

'Yeah, about half an hour ago.'

I hurried to his office. Excitement and nerves vied for the privilege of churning up my tummy.

'Alex? What's up?'

'Ah, Katie, close the door please.' My heart hammered in my chest (also nothing to worry about, my doctor claimed). 'Listen, I need a favour please.' I nodded. 'Will you mentor Smith?'

'Sure . . . Who's Smith?'

'The new hire in sales. I believe you trained him a few weeks ago. Young guy? Dark hair?'

Ah yes, the sniggerer from the training session. Delightful chap.

'I remember him,' I said carefully. 'Isn't there someone else? I mean someone else for me to mentor. I'm happy to do it, but maybe another of the new hires? What about the girl who started with him? You know, the skinny one?'

'I'm afraid she's already taken.' He ran his hand through his hair, making it stand on end. 'I was supposed to assign him last week but with all the meetings lately, I completely forgot. I'm his corporate *buddy*' (he made ditto fingers) 'and of course everyone else's *buddies* already assigned their mentors. So I'm stuck, and I've got the meeting with Clive in thirty minutes. Can you do it? Please? I'd owe you big-time.'

'What do I have to do?'

'It's easy. You'll just let him shadow you in your job, teach him the ropes, take him on some client visits. In fact, you could take him to see Jenny. Show him what it's really like in the trenches.'

157

As if I'd ever inflict Jenny on him. Or anyone, for that matter. She tore strips off me over the phone. She'd eat a new hire alive.

'Do you want me to mentor him or get him to hand in his resignation? I don't know, Alex. I've got a lot on at the moment.'

'C'mon, it'll be fun.'

'It doesn't sound like much fun.' But I knew I'd do it, just because Alex was the one asking.

'No, you're right, it's a pain in the arse and you'll probably hate it. Which is why I insist you let me take you out for drinks. I won't take no for an answer.'

As if I'd reject an offer like that. *Although*, a little voice whispered. Rob's kisses were less than twenty-four hours old. *On the other hand*, we'd only kissed. And Alex wasn't exactly proposing to whisk me away for a dirty weekend. We'd simply be two colleagues going for drinks.

'I suppose it's the least you can do for me,' I said.

'There's a lot more I could do, but HR might object.' He grinned as I imagined all the things HR might object to. Then I thought about Rob and felt properly guilty. And *then* I remembered my lunchtime plans, which made Rob disappear and gave me a whole new set of reasons to worry about HR.

CHAPTER TWENTY-TWO

'Ready?' said Ellie when I stopped by her desk. She was putting on lipstick and trying to get her hair to lie down flat. As if successfully stalking her boyfriend depended on perfect lips.

'If I said no, would you let me get sandwiches from Pret instead of following Thomas and Colleen? I think that's a much healthier option, don't you?'

She shook her head, her hair already flying away. 'That's what you're wearing?' She stared at my top, her hands jammed on her hips.

I thought my loose red tunic and black wide-legged trousers looked rather fetching. Especially given how hard it was to wear my usual clothes these days. I'd taken to safety-pinning some of my trousers. It was thrilling not to feel my waistband pinching but things were getting serious, sartorially speaking.

'Did you expect a moustache and a hat?' I said.

'I mean that top. It's a bit conspicuous.'

'Ellie, we're following your boyfriend at lunchtime, not stealing the Hope Diamond. I'm sure I'm not the only person in a red top in Central London today. It *is* summertime.'

She knew I wasn't going to change, so she let it go. 'Let's go wait in the park till they come out. They'll have to pass us.'

'Where are they going for lunch?'

She shrugged. 'I don't know, do I? That's why we're following them.'

'I thought you knew.'

'Well, I would have if you'd let me look in his diary.'

Suddenly our little jaunt, where we happened to turn up in the same sandwich shop as lovely Thomas, had turned sinister.

'Are you saying that we actually have to follow them? As in hiding behind pillars? This is crazy, you know.'

'You said you'd do it. Come on or we'll miss them.' She strode toward the lift without looking back.

Ellie wasn't one for changing her mind once she got her teeth into an idea. I tried very hard to put myself in her shoes (and her top, since she objected to mine). Would I be as stalky in the same situation? Probably. I didn't even need a boyfriend to do it. I cringed at the memory of last year's Operation Alex. It seemed like a reasonable plan. If I happened to be in the same places as him, naturally he couldn't fail to notice how compatible we were. Granted, our compatibility involved mostly pubs where I knew he liked to drink. Even I wasn't mad enough to check his diary and turn up to his football matches. He might believe I liked the same pubs but it would be a stretch to claim a passion for watching amateur footie in the park across town from me.

The little square next to our building was already busy with the smokers who'd been banned from the pavements in front of their offices. I wasn't a fan of smoking but did sometimes feel bad for them. They were already treated like lepers. It was only a matter of time before they'd be forced to wear bells around their necks in public and be branded with a scarlet S over their lungs.

'There they are!' I whispered, catching a glimpse of Colleen's bright blue mac. I could see why Ellie worried about her. This wasn't a woman who worried about puckery trousers or bra strap indentations. She was, I noted, also very touchy-feely, and when the touchee was your boyfriend, naturally you'd be a bit concerned.

We moved to follow them at a safe distance as they headed for the Tube. 'Have you got money on your Oyster card?' Ellie whispered.

My need to top up could scupper the mission.

'I'm not sure.'

I held my breath as I tapped my card against the turnstile. Beep beep beep. Of course there wasn't enough money on it. 'Go ahead, I'll catch up,' I told her as she hurried through.

I ran to the pay point and jammed a note into the machine. Come on, come on. I couldn't lose sight of Ellie. With two Tube lines to choose from, each going in two directions, I didn't fancy my chances of finding them.

I bolted through the turnstile, grateful for shoes I could run in. As I pounded down the escalator I realised I was too late. They'd either gone on the Central Line or one level deeper to the Piccadilly Line. Which had better lunch options?

I had no idea, so since the Central Line required running down fewer stairs, I took the lazy option. East or west? God, I hated pressure-cooker decisions. West was closest. Laziness won out again. I could hear the train pulling into the platform as I got to the bottom of the stairs.

The platform was heaving, as one would expect at lunchtime. They packed into the carriages, office workers and noisy groups of tourists, until the platform was nearly empty. Then I saw her.

Three carriages away, Ellie spotted me too. Get on the train, she gestured, then pointed further up the carriages.

I hopped through the closing doors, sweaty, agitated and

getting hungry. If this was spying then James Bond could keep his job. Slowly I excused my way through the packed carriage to the doors at the end. *Danger, risk of death if used while train is moving*. The wind whipped through the carriage as I opened the door. 'Sorry!' I yelled to the startled passengers.

The things I did for my friends.

When I got to Ellie, her eagle eyes were trained on lovely Thomas and Colleen in the next carriage. 'We'll just hop off when they do,' she said as the train slowed for the next station. 'Look, there they go!'

Now that there were so many people around, and our chances of getting caught were slimmer, I started to have a bit more fun.

'This'll be easy,' I said. 'If we're caught we'll say we were shopping. I actually do need to pick up a few things. If we've got time we could stop in Selfridges. Or is that a bit far from here? I guess it's at the other end. Maybe John Lewis instead? That's not too . . . What's the matter?' I'd been so preoccupied with our shopping alibi that I'd lost sight of Thomas.

'I don't believe it. They've gone in there.' She pointed to a sex shop.

'No. Ellie, they can't have.'

'I'm telling you, I just saw them go in. I feel ill. I don't need to see any more. Let's go.' She turned back towards the Tube station.

'No way,' I said desperately. 'You must be wrong. We'll stay. You'll see. They won't come out of there. Look. There's a suit shop just next door. That's probably where they went. Thomas just needs some new clothes, that's all. Didn't you say he wanted to change his style? I'm sure that's where he is. Shall we walk by? You'll see.'

Meekly she followed me. I willed Thomas to be in the shop getting his inseam measured or perusing the summer wools.

But he wasn't buying Italian suits. The shop, we could see, was empty.

'It doesn't prove anything,' I said. 'You can go if you want. I'm staying because I'm sure they're not in a sex shop. Go ahead, go on. I'll prove it to you.'

'No, I'll wait with you.'

I knew she'd stay. Ellie led with her heart. She wanted to believe there was a logical explanation as much as I did. Plus, I knew she hated it when I called her bluff.

Nearly fifteen minutes went by and my tummy was rumbling like a concrete mixer when Thomas and Colleen emerged from the sex shop. He carried a bag. She had her arm looped through his. They were laughing. I stared at Ellie, not knowing what to say.

'Let's go,' she said. 'I've seen enough.'

I put my arm around her and we walked slowly amongst the lunchtime throng. They were oblivious to the breaking heart in their midst.

She wasn't ready to talk until we finished work. I had no idea what to say to her anyway. I couldn't pretend everything was okay. Whatever Thomas had bought in that shop proved that things were far from okay.

As I knew she would, Ellie had worked through every possible scenario. I'd watched her carefully over the desks all afternoon, ready to spring into action at the first sign of tears. I could see the emotions playing across her face – confusion, hurt, anger. At one point I swore she argued with herself. *Blah blah blah blah. Oh yeah? Well what about blah blah blah? Good point. And another thing* . . . But she didn't cry. I think she was too shocked for that.

'I'm not going to say anything to him,' she declared as we hurried to catch the Tube home.

I stopped walking, much to the surprise of the commuters walking closely behind.

'You're not going to say *anything*?' I'd never seen Ellie practise such restraint. I suspected a trap.

She shook her head. 'No. I'm tired of rushing to conclusions. You're right. What do we know, really? Only that he went with his friend into a shop. That's all. It might have been her bag. Hell, maybe it was his, I don't know. We haven't been seeing each other that long. How do I know he doesn't have some kind of fetish for wearing feather boas or zebra-striped mankinis when I'm not around?'

I should have been happy that she was finally seeing reason, only it wasn't reason at all. It was denial.

'I never said you should ignore this, Ellie. I was all for giving him the benefit of the doubt when you were clearly behaving insanely. But I have to say that if my boyfriend came out of a sex shop with a woman, I'd have a problem with it.'

Tears finally filled her eyes. She sat on the bus stop bench.

'I'm frightened, Katie. If I confront him and there's an innocent explanation, he may very well break up with me for following him. And he'd be justified after the last time I went nuts on him. He'd know I snooped on his phone. He'd know I'm insane. Nobody wants a crazy girlfriend.'

I felt terrible for so flippantly calling her crazy. Sometimes I could be a real dick.

'I understand. So you're just going to wait and see what happens? I guess that's okay as long as you *do* talk to him at some point. It's one thing if it's all a big misunderstanding, but you don't deserve to be treated badly. We'll monitor the situation.'

'What are you now, a UN observer?'

'I've always looked nice in blue hats. They match my eyes.'

CHAPTER TWENTY-THREE

I nearly fell off my chair a week later when Alex's email pinged into my box. The two little words I'd waited six years to hear. 'Drinks tonight?' I went straight to Ellie but she was on the phone. It took all my restraint not to disconnect her call.

'Lunch,' I mouthed while she said her good-byes.

Of course Ellie knew about my Alex-infatuation. I'd been a smitten fool for as long as she'd known me. What she *didn't* know anything about was my date with Rob.

She wriggled as I told her about the email, and our recent more-flirty-than-usual conversations.

'I can't believe it!' she squealed. 'And you look so pretty today too. Just think – that'll be your first-date outfit.'

I examined my royal blue empire waist dress, which definitely flattered my figure. It had been years since I'd been able to say that. Incurable disease or not, I had a waist.

'You're jumping ahead, Ellie. It's not a date. He offered to take me for drinks to say thanks for some work I've done for him. It might be nothing.'

'Are you trying to convince me, or you?'

I grinned. 'Me. You know what I'm like when I get nervous. I'll make a complete tit of myself if I get overexcited.' She nodded, no doubt thinking about her cousin. She'd been very sweet to set me up with him after we met at her dad's birthday party. It wasn't her fault that he mistook the purpose of our meeting. I should have read the signals when he formally shook my hand at the bar. Instead I deluded myself that since Ellie had a bit of German on one side, he was just respecting his culture. I also should have noted that he asked a lot of questions about my job. It began to sound like an interview and any normal person would have put two and two together. But not me. I ploughed on, flirting, answering his questions with double-entendres, inching closer on the sofa we shared in the busy bar. When he said he thought there was something he could do for me, and I answered . . . ugh, I still shudder. I *growled* that I just bet there was. It honestly never occurred to me that as a recruitment consultant he was only there to offer me career advice. Ellie had to tell him I was on pain medication that day.

'There is one thing,' I said as Ellie ate her superfood salad. It was best to just come straight out with it, right? 'Rob.'

'Rob?'

I nodded. 'We've been on a few dates. Well, one, technically. We snogged. A lot. It's nothing serious, but it does . . .'

. . . It does what? Exactly what had Rob's kisses meant? I'd be damned if I knew. He'd been completely silent on the subject for two weeks, as if he'd come down with amnesia. I didn't get it. We saw each other at the club events as usual, and my flirtation bordered on sexual harassment. I'd even bought some new clothes that, if I did say so myself, made the most of my emerging figure. And I *had* to say so myself since he didn't even seem to notice. I fished so often for compliments that he finally asked me to stop.

'Does it matter about Rob?' I asked Ellie.

She considered my question. 'That depends on how you feel. Do you like him?'

166

'Of course I like him, or I wouldn't have kissed him. He's a good friend, a nice, fun, handsome man.'

'But?'

But Rob had obviously done some kind of secret arithmetic and factored himself out of the equation. It didn't matter if I still wanted to work the sums together.

'But this is Alex. *Alex*,' I said to Ellie instead. 'It's a different thing altogether.'

'Would you kiss Alex if you got the chance? Given what's happened with Rob?'

'I don't think I need to worry about that,' I said. But I was worrying, a little, and not just about what might happen with Alex.

I must have done something to make Rob go off me in a single night. If I had any guts I'd ask him. Imagine that conversation. *Hey Rob, tell me. Was it my kissing that put you off, or maybe my conversation? Was it because I didn't laugh at your favourite knock-knock joke? Come on, Rob, you can be honest with me. I can (sniff) take it.*

I might never recover from knowing the answer. I knew I wouldn't ask.

Ellie's comment dragged me back to our lunch. 'Colleen has been calling Thomas at home,' she said. 'He's taken at least two calls while I was with him.' She confessed this like it was her fault.

'When you say you were with him, what exactly do you mean?' If he answered his phone while they were in bed together I was going to punch him in the nose myself. 'What did he say?'

'I have no idea. I saw her name come up on his screen just before he snatched the phone and went off to the other room where I couldn't hear him.' She shook her head. 'He didn't say anything about the calls afterwards. You know what the weirdest thing is? He's not acting weird. He's just as loving and attentive as always. Wouldn't he be distant if he was having an affair? Isn't that a sign? And he hasn't gone the other way either. He's not being overly affectionate. And he doesn't go MIA. I can always reach him on his phone. Sex is the same, no more, no less and no new tricks. It just doesn't make any sense.'

'Ellie, have you been googling again? You know we've talked about that.' For my own good she'd made me triple-promise not to google my racing heart and weight loss. I should have remembered to extract the same promise from her after we followed Thomas to the sex shop. Bad friend.

She nodded. '*Cosmo*'s Eleven Signs of a Cheating Man . . . I know I have to talk to him, if only to put my mind at ease. I can't continue like this, feeling terrible all the time. I'm going to talk to him this week.'

I grabbed her hand and squeezed. How could I blame her for trying to find out if she was overreacting? I'd do exactly the same thing in her shoes. The question was whether Thomas deserved the suspicion.

Alex and I emailed back and forth all afternoon, which did my productivity no favours. I accidentally disconnected two client calls before giving up and pretending to work on admin for the rest of the day. I wish it was excitement that made me so inept, but it was nerves. I'd felt exactly the same way when taking my exams, knowing I only had one chance to make the grade. I was afraid I hadn't prepared well enough for tonight's paper.

We walked together to a pub around the corner. It wasn't our local – everyone from the office went to the one up the road. Alex was, of course, completely cool. I stayed mute to minimise the risk of idiocy before we'd even had a drink.

A crowd was already gathered outside. 'Do you mind if we sit inside?' Alex asked. 'I'm too old to stand on the pavement pretending to have fun. And since I quit smoking it kills me whenever someone lights up around me. You don't smoke, do you?'

'Me, smoke? No, filthy habit. Not that you're filthy. I didn't mean that. You're fine. Unfilthy.' Shut up, Katie. 'Yes, let's sit inside. Then we can talk properly. Not that I've got anything serious to talk about. Or secret.' Why couldn't I just stop? 'Just the normal chitchat, really. No big deal.'

Alex went off to the bar wondering what he'd got himself into.

I was going off the rails. I hadn't even wanted Rory as much as I wanted something to happen with Alex. Just as I'd nearly convinced myself that this was a completely hopeless crush, Alex had to completely ruin it by being extra nice. *Of course* that made a girl hope. Plus he looked gorgeous as usual. Normally I was suspicious of men who wore jeans with suit jackets, but Alex carried it off. His broad shoulders and narrow waist were suited to that kind of smart casual contrast. Plus his day-old stubble made him look like someone in music or media, not nutritional supplements.

We squeezed onto the end of a big table by the window, him with a pint of dark ale and me with a large glass of wine.

'Cheers,' I said, raising my glass.

'Thank you, Katie. Officially. You've been a huge help and I really appreciate it.'

So there it was then. This was an official glass of Sauvignon Blanc, not Alex thinking I was cute, or fun or even potential friend material (which I'd accept in the absence of a better offer). Stupid stupid pipe dream.

'That's okay,' I said. 'I'm glad to help out.' Which I was, even with no prospect of fringe benefits. But if this was a work meeting, I had to stay on-topic. The last time I strayed into seduction I ended up kissing a sleeping man. Professional

Katie, engage brain. 'I met with Smith and he's going to come with me on my next client visit. I should be able to arrange something soon.' I hadn't really expected my cunning plan to work but Cressida was happy with my performance and hinted at more meetings in the future. Things certainly did seem to be looking up.

'I'm glad Cressida is finally lightening up on you,' he said. 'You deserve a break after all this time. You're turning into the perfect package.'

My face reddened. His words confirmed what I'd suspected all along: Cressida had taken issue less with my competence than with my control pants.

The shallow cow.

Of course now that there was less of me to take issue with, my career was looking up. And as unfair as that was on the old Katie, this new Katie quite liked the way things were heading.

'So you've got your own work gimp now,' Alex continued, leaning back after an obviously satisfying sip. 'Ah, I remember my first intern like it was yesterday. Stop looking at me like that, Katie. What do you take me for?'

Rampant sex god. 'I'm not looking at you any way.' I totally was.

'What I meant was, you've got your own personal gopher. What will you make him do for you?'

'Smith has to do whatever I want?' I said, relieved to be back on non-sexual ground. 'I had no idea there were such perks to being a *buddy*. How exciting. Let's see. Well, naturally I'll start with fetching. He can fetch my dry cleaning and lunch. And afternoon coffee.'

'Do you have a car? He could wash that for you.'

'No, but I suppose he could wash my bicycle.'

'Do you have a bike? I always pictured you as more of a taxi girl. Do you ride it much?'

I wasn't even sure I still had it. Dad had probably cleared out the garden shed in the last decade.

'Sometimes,' I lied. 'Do you have a bike?'

'Yeah, I love it. It's a pain in the arse riding in the city though. I usually take the train out to Windsor or Sussex or up around the Chilterns on weekends. There are some lovely pubs there.'

'So you cycle between pubs? I like your motivation.'

'Restaurants too. I do get some hills in while I'm there. If you ever want to come along just say the word.'

I nearly exploded at the thought of Alex cycling ahead of me in Lycra. We'd been safely on work topics just a minute ago. How had we leaped to sweating in skin-tight clothing?

'I'd just hold you up.'

'Speaking of which, another drink?'

I was surprised by my empty glass. 'I'd better slow down. Just a small glass this time, please.'

'That's absolutely out of the question. I'm getting you drunk tonight.' He took my glass and went back to the bar. I had a bad (by which I meant very good) feeling about the night ahead.

Our conversation flowed as easily as the alcohol and in the next few hours I saw the Alex who wasn't the finance director for Nutritious. We had things in common. Not exercise, mind you, but other things like music and cinema and places we'd both been on holiday.

When I told him all about the Curvy Girls Club, he said, 'What you're doing is amazing, and it sounds like it's important to a lot of people. I so admire people with passions like yours.'

I was lost in his gaze, and his praise. It was still hard to believe what we'd achieved in less than six months. Nearly three hundred people attended our events each week and they usually sold out. I was working from breakfast to supper on my days away from Nutritious just to find enough experiences to add to the website. And I was even drawing a small salary for my time.

But more important than the money was the fact that I was so happy in this new normal. Being with the members was a bit like being in the darkened restaurant. Size didn't matter. And that was immensely freeing. I'd turned a corner, and started to feel that good in the 'real' world. I didn't want to go back to my old neighbourhood ever again.

The night galloped along until suddenly Alex and I found ourselves in uncharted territory. 'Have you got a boyfriend, Katie?' he asked, slightly slurry.

I shook my head.

'How can that be? You're smart, funny, fun, pretty . . . and if you don't mind my saying, getting sexier by the day.'

I wanted to pretend I hadn't heard, just to make him repeat himself. Suddenly the room felt a bit warm. Could it be that instead of seeing Katie from sales who always made him laugh, Alex had suddenly realised that I might be more than just a funny face?

'Ah, you're just being kind.'

'No, I'm not really. I tell it like it is. You're different lately. In a nice way . . . you're not going to haul me in front of HR now, are you?'

'That depends on what you're proposing.' I smiled. I might have even batted my eyelashes. Well, don't blame me. He started it.

'I'm proposing to see you again, if you'd like that. Dinner?'

I don't know what made me say the next words. 'Fishing off the company pier, Alex? It's not smart to date employees you know.'

Ugh. Why hadn't I just said yes?

'Give it a few months,' he said. 'If we don't turn things around, we may not be employees any more. Problem solved.' He realised what he'd said. 'That's not for public dissemination, by the way. Top secret. Promise?'

I promised, feeling suddenly much more sober at the prospect of unemployment.

When we left the pub, he didn't reach for my hand or throw a friendly arm over my shoulder, and I showed admirable restraint by not launching myself at his front. If I moved too fast I might send him scampering off into the night. Be cool, Katie.

We said good-bye inside the Tube station, him going southbound and me going north. He lingered as everyone around us rushed for the last trains. But he didn't try to kiss me.

'See you tomorrow,' he said instead.

'Thanks so much for tonight, it was really fun.' It really was.

'It was definitely fun,' he said, grasping my hand and squeezing once before turning to his platform.

As my train made its way to Wood Green, Rob popped into my head. He'd been absent all evening, crowded out by Alex. He journeyed with me towards home, not admonishing or challenging me. He just let me know he was there.

He'd still be awake. I was tempted to call him when I got home. No. That was just the guilt talking. But guilt over what, exactly? Nothing had happened between me and Alex.

CHAPTER TWENTY-FOUR

What was it with the men in my life? Alex didn't once mention dinner the following week. There wasn't even the slightest hint that we'd gone for drinks. If I hadn't had the hangover to prove it, I'd have thought it was just a dream. I was starting to give up any hope of a dinner date. It was the Christmas party all over again. Mental note: must try for proposition when Alex isn't legless.

And given that Rob would probably never ask me out either, it was unfair for *him* to be stuck in my mind, gently reminding me of our kisses. Honestly, some men had no follow-through, and a terrible sense of timing.

At least my GP was reliable. He called on Friday to say my test results were ready. Was it any wonder, what with all the impatience building up, that I was tempted to grab my handbag and sprint for his surgery? But I didn't. The sniff of redundancies at Nutritious meant I took the latest appointment in the day. Then I obsessed until it was time to leave.

Rob texted just as I was checking in with the nurse.

Just got your message. Good luck. I hope you get some answers. xo

Thanks, I'm cacking myself. I hope it's not bad news. xx

Don't worry, it won't be. Call me when you're done okay? xo

Normally I'd have taken the time to analyse the number and frequency of his text kisses, but my nerves were shot. Despite promising Ellie I wouldn't google, I'd amassed a laundry list of potential diseases. By the time I got to the surgery I was finding it hard to breathe.

'Hello, Miss Winterbottom,' my doctor said. 'Please sit down.'

Sitting down couldn't be good. I braced myself.

'How are you feeling? Any better?'

Surely he could hear my heart shuddering in my chest. 'No, no better. My heart is still racing. I'm still tired. And do you see this?' I pointed to my eye. 'I've now got a tic.' I'd been winking at people all week. Something was seriously wrong.

'We've got the test results back and I can put your mind at rest. As I thought, it's not cancer. You've got an overactive thyroid. It's called hyperthyroidism and can cause a number of the symptoms you're experiencing. We've done two blood tests to check your TSH and thyroxine levels. A low reading on TSH and/or high reading on thyroxine indicates the condition. In your case, both a low TSH and high thyroxine means hyperthyroidism.'

'Is it curable?'

'There are treatments to get you functioning normally again. We can discuss the options once we know what's causing it.'

'Is this dangerous to have?'

'Not if it's treated properly and managed. I'll just need to pop you up on the table to check your thyroid.'

More popping. 'Where is my thyroid?'

'In the front of your neck.'

Excellent, no stirrups then. I climbed on the table and let the doctor thump my neck.

175

'There's no enlargement of the thyroid,' he said, feeling around. 'Which would be a sign of Graves' Disease. So that's good. But I can feel one nodule. This is very unlikely to be malignant, but we'll want to check. I can schedule you in for a biopsy.'

'A biopsy?' But he just said it wasn't cancer.

'It's a fine-needle aspiration procedure. That means we anesthetise the area and use a very small needle to extract cells from the nodule. Don't worry, it's not painful.'

Easy for him to say when it wasn't his neck being stuck with a needle. 'But you said it wasn't cancer.'

'It isn't cancer. It's an overactive thyroid.'

I couldn't help feeling he was splitting hairs. 'But that might be caused by a malignant nodule? Doesn't malignant mean cancer?'

'It's very rare for thyroid nodules to be malignant. We're just checking to be sure. Please don't worry, Miss Winterbottom. We'll schedule you in for the procedure as soon as possible.'

'Why do you have to schedule me as soon as possible? Because you're afraid it's spreading?'

'Noo. Because you've come to me with uncomfortable symptoms and I'd like to alleviate them as soon as possible.' His bushy eyebrows bounced up and down to emphasise his point.

'All right then, assuming it's not cancer, what's the treatment?'

'There are various medications we can try. The specialist will talk with you about specific treatment when all the test results are finished.' He updated his notes on the computer and the printer whirred into life. 'Here's your referral for the specialist. I'll schedule you for the fine-needle aspiration.' I noticed he'd stopped calling it a biopsy. 'You should get a letter within a week with the appointment. All right?'

Aside from possible thyroid cancer, yes, I suppose I was all right.

I called Rob on the walk back to the Tube. 'I've got to

have a biopsy.' Just saying the word brought tears bubbling to the surface.

'Why a biopsy?! Do they think it's cancer?'

Finally, a sensible reaction from someone. 'Thank you! A biopsy means it could be cancer, right? The doctor made it sound like it was no big deal.' I recounted our conversation which, as I repeated it, did make me sound a smidge less rational than when I first challenged the doctor's words.

'Well, it doesn't sound like he's concerned, Katie. So try not to worry. They should see you quickly and then you can take the medication to get it sorted. How are you feeling about it?'

I loved that he asked me that. 'I guess I'm okay. There's no use worrying until I know there's something to worry about. And on the plus side, I've lost more weight, so that's some compensation. I'm glad I know what it is, at least, if not the cause. And that there's a treatment. I'm sorry, I've got to go. I'm just about to catch the Tube home. Can I call you later? I'm meeting the girls at the office, so maybe after that?'

'Sure you can. And Katie? Don't worry. Everything will be fine.'

I was nearly home before I realised he hadn't offered to meet me.

I should have felt the change in the air when I entered our flat. Hell, I should have felt it from the Tube. Ellie was home already. Thomas was with her. They were glaring at each other on the sofa, dribbling negative karma all over my favourite piece of furniture.

'What's up?' Feigning ignorance might cut the custard-thick tension.

'Ellie's just been telling me about the field trip you two took to Oxford Street the other day.'

Uh oh. How much did he know?

'Oh? Yes, it's nice to be outside at lunchtime. Bit of fresh air . . .'

'It's okay, Katie,' Ellie said. 'He knows we followed them.' She turned to Thomas, her face red. 'You can be as angry as you like. Okay, maybe I shouldn't have done it, but in this case, the ends justified the means. Otherwise I wouldn't have known you were visiting sex shops with Colleen now, would I?' She crossed her arms, daring him to deny it.

I probably should have left them alone, but this was too good to miss. Besides, Ellie might need backup. That's what friends were for. Eavesdropping and backup.

'Anything else?' Thomas asked. His normally open, friendly face remained impassive.

'Well, yes, as we're on the subject,' said Ellie. 'Your secret phone calls from Colleen. Care to explain those?'

Normally jovial and eager-to-please, it was easy to forget that my best friend had a titanium core. She probably let people tread on her a bit too often but she did come out swinging when it was important. Clearly this was important.

'Well . . . first of all they weren't secret, since I answered my phone in front of you.'

He had a point there.

'And second, are you sure you want to know what we've been talking about?' A smile played around his mouth.

And I thought I knew this man. How could he be so cruel, daring Ellie to listen to his lover's patter?! He wasn't lovely Thomas at all.

Ellie looked like she was regretting the whole conversation. 'Thomas, I'm not going to let you make me feel bad. I can do that for myself. I think you should leave.'

'Not until I tell you what Colleen and I have been doing,' he said.

'Thomas!' I said. 'Stop being horrible. You heard Ellie. You should go now.'

'I'm not leaving.' He tried to take Ellie's hand. She snatched it back. 'Ellie, I'm sorry I've kept secrets from you. And I'm very, very sorry that that's made you feel bad.'

'Well, of course it's made her feel bad!' I blurted. 'Surely you knew it would. Honestly, Thomas, you're being a real knob.'

Thomas smiled again. Did he not understand the seriousness of this situation?

'I don't mean to be a real knob.' He grabbed for Ellie's hand again. This time she let him take it. 'I mean to be romantic. Ellie. I wanted to take you away somewhere as a surprise. I asked Colleen to help because she's my best female mate and I figured she'd know what you might like. Hence the trip to the shop. Which was unbelievably uncomfortable, by the way, but I hope you'll like what I found. I'm so sorry that you thought it was something else. I really just wanted this weekend to be a total surprise.' He turned to me. 'I'm sorry, Katie. I'd have told you but . . .'

I tried to look offended that he thought I couldn't keep a secret. Of course he was right.

'Ellie, I planned to tell you on Friday afternoon. It's all booked.'

'You're not having an affair with Colleen?' Ellie asked. 'Really?'

'How could I, when I love you so much? I love you, Ellie.'

A little sound escaped Ellie. 'You . . . love me?'

He smiled. 'More than I ever thought I could love someone. You're remarkable, tremendous. I love you very much.'

She launched herself into his arms. 'I love you too!' Within minutes the sofa was having flashbacks to Rory and me.

Happy as I was for them, it *was* getting a bit uncomfortable. 'Ehem, I'm really sorry, Ellie, but we've got to go.

We've got the meeting, remember? Normally I'd say you could skip it, but it's an important one tonight. I'm really sorry, Thomas.'

'That's okay,' Thomas said, not looking the least bit put out that I'd interrupted his big moment. He was lovely Thomas again. 'This was sprung on Ellie. I'll see you after, right?' he asked. I assumed he wasn't talking to me as I shuffled Ellie out the door.

We were late as we hurried to the offices, but had a valid excuse. The aerodynamics of Ellie's enormous grin slowed us down.

She talked about Thomas all the way there, punctuating her commentary with declarations of love every few minutes. As I listened happily I realised how much she'd been holding back. But now that she knew the water was completely safe, she plunged in over her head. I gave them a year before they walked down the aisle.

'Nice of you to join us, ladies,' said Pixie as we let ourselves in.

I could see that Rob's cousin had been busy again. Our menagerie was much expanded. We played spot-the-difference every time we came into the offices, looking for furred or feathered evidence of David's latest taxidermic efforts.

'Do you think he's actually selling these any more, or just scouring the roadside for things to stuff?' Ellie examined the skinny black and white cat on her desk. It was sitting primly, working a Liza Minnelli vibe in a tiny top hat.

'Maybe Rob should have a word with him?' Jane said. 'They are starting to cramp the space.'

'And some of them are pongy,' Pixie said. 'I'm all for the creative arts, but I draw the line there. That bear probably has fleas.'

'Fleas don't live on dead things,' I pointed out. 'No blood

to suck. I don't really think we should rock the boat at this point since we can't afford to move anywhere else. Maybe once we're making some more money.'

'Speaking of which,' said Pixie. 'We should start.' She winced as she tried to shift her chair around to the other side of the desk.

'Pixie? Are you all right?'

She stared at us for a second before answering. 'I'm fine, love. Just pulled a muscle, that's all.'

We knew she was lying. Pixie couldn't pull a muscle because Pixie didn't exert herself.

'A pulled muscle, eh?' I said. 'How did you do that?'

'Oh, well, I tripped over the chair in the lounge. You know, the big green one. Trevor and I were rowing and I wasn't paying attention to where I was going. Stupid, really.'

'Pixie. What really happened?' Ellie asked.

She flushed, and sighed loudly. 'Trevor's getting worse. He's picking fights every night. I'm not even sure how this one started. His dinner was a bit cold or something. He went off on his usual tirade about how lazy and stupid I am. How he works all the time . . . ha, if he worked all the time I wouldn't have to choose between new school uniforms or paying the Sky bill. The children's uniforms aren't even blue any more, and poor Connor's trousers hardly reach his ankles. Not that Trevor cares about that . . . I think he's drinking after work now. He denies it but I can smell it on him.'

'Did he hit you?' I asked. There was no reason to beat around the bush about beating.

'No.' She looked from one doubtful face to another. 'I promise you, he didn't. We were arguing in the lounge. It was getting quite heated, even for us. And when I turned to check on the children, he grabbed my arm and spun me around. That's when I fell over the back of the chair.'

'You fell, or he pushed you?'

'I fell. I think I fell. It happened so fast that I didn't even have time to put my hands out. I'm not exactly light on my feet now, am I? I must have staggered or something and pulled the muscle then. It's not that bad.'

She was purposely missing the point. Of course it's that bad when your husband causes you to go over a chair.

'Pixie, you can't stay with him. If he's getting physical you've got to leave.' I went to put my arms around her solid shoulders. Because of her size, it was easy to forget sometimes how vulnerable she really was. She squeezed me back tightly.

'That's what I've been saying, love,' she nearly whispered. 'But I need to be able to support myself. I can't leave unless I do.' She straightened up. 'That's why I want to make a formal proposition for us to vote on tonight.' Her expression became closed again. 'About Fat Friends. Should we formally start the meeting? Who wants to be secretary?'

'I will,' I said, dreading Pixie's proposal. 'This meeting is called to order.'

Sometimes the formality of our board meetings seemed silly. After all it was just the four of us and Pete the bear.

'The accounts are looking great,' I said as I passed out the photocopy I'd prepared. 'Bookings are still going strong, as you can see, and we're getting over a thousand unique views a week on the website. Rob has calculated that that's nearly a thirty per cent conversion rate from views to bookings.'

'Does that mean if we doubled the number of people going on the website we'd double the number of bookings?' Ellie asked.

I shrugged. 'I'm not sure if it works like that but it would certainly boost them.'

'That's why *The Great British Makeover* is so important,' Jane said. 'It could make the club the hottest thing since . . .' she struggled to find the analogy '. . . salted caramel truffles.

182

Imagine doubling the number of people who can attend. That'd mean doubling the fees too.'

I nodded. 'And having to double the number of events we host, which means having to hire more people.'

'Actually, my idea might address that,' Pixie said, sounding uncharacteristically shy. 'Here, I've made some notes.' She smoothed out a few pages of lined paper covered in her loopy scrawl. 'I think we should expand by having a dating business within the club. It could be online-only, though that might be very expensive to set up. Someone would have to build a website for the profiles and such. So until we've got enough money we could run more speed-dating events. And singles nights too. They're almost pure profit since we don't usually have to hire the bar and can charge entry fees as well as the admin fee. We can accommodate up to around eighty people at each event, so that takes some of the pressure off Katie's event planning. The speed-dating night we ran last month netted us nearly a thousand quid. And we were over-subscribed, so people obviously like the idea.'

'I don't think we can judge based on one event,' I pointed out.

'I agree,' she said, suddenly less shy. 'We should have more and see how many people sign up.'

I knew I'd been out-manoeuvred. If I said yes, of course the events would fill up. Just look at how many people joined online dating sites in January after being trapped in the house over Christmas eating mince pies and bickering with family. Imagine what being single for months or years did to a person's psyche. Not that I was objecting to people finding love, but I had to lay my cards on the table.

'We could do that, but I have bigger concerns than whether people will come.'

'But it *is* a social club, sweetheart,' Jane said. 'The whole point of it is to have events that people want to come to.'

Was that the whole point though? I wasn't sure. Maybe the point was also to make our members feel good about themselves. Or, at least, not to make them feel bad. What was that medical saying? First, do no harm. That seemed like a good rule to live by.

'I'm sure that speed-dating will be very popular,' I said. 'I just worry about stigmatising our members even more than they already are. Something doesn't sit right with having a dating business where all the people joining are vulnerable.'

'So just because we're fat, we're vulnerable?' Pixie asked. 'Can we not make up our own minds? Do we need to be treated like we're feeble?'

'Don't twist my words, Pixie. All I'm saying is that our members don't always feel great about themselves. And that makes them vulnerable. I've told you about that study, about how men view themselves and women. Men underestimate their own size,' I explained to Jane and Ellie. 'And they see normal women as fat. So they walk around with flabby guts thinking they're God's gift, and they look down on women who are thinner than they are. That's not a recipe for success for our women members. You know how women think. If I get rejected, I assume it's because I'm not thin enough. Sure I might also be neurotic, or too gobby or whatever, but my size is the first thing I think of. I'm not the only one who thinks like that.'

Ellie nodded.

'I see your point,' Jane said. 'As empowering as the club is, it won't be enough for some of our members. And they might be very sensitive to rejection.'

'Exactly,' I said.

'On the other hand we had really good feedback from the speed-dating events,' she said. 'So it does seem to be what our members want.'

I crossed my arms. 'I just don't want to start something

184

that could do more harm than good. Not when the club has been so supportive for everyone. What if men start coming to the events looking for women who are just grateful for the attention? They could use it as a way to shag vulnerable women.'

'A lot of our members could use a good shag,' Pixie said. 'Speaking for myself anyway.'

She could be funny even when she was being a pain in the arse. 'Well, even so, that's the last thing they need.'

Pixie fixed me with the gaze she used on her children when they'd pushed her too far. 'I don't think you're the best person to judge what we need. Look at you. You're like a reformed alcoholic preaching to the drunks.'

I ignored her jibe. 'Well, the fact remains that I'm a co-founder of this club, just like you are, and Ellie and Jane. So I do have a say, just like everyone else. For me, it comes down to the fact that I don't want to be associated with a dating site for fat people. I think it's a bad idea that risks hurting our members. Just think how that will look if we became known as a chubby-chaser dating site. We could be completely crucified in the media. Think of our reputations.'

Pixie glared at me. 'Whose reputation, exactly? You mean *your* reputation, don't you, Katie? Is that it? Now that you're getting thin you don't want to be associated with fat people like us?'

Surely she must have known how much her words stung. We'd been friends for four years. These were my *best* friends.

'I can't believe you'd think that of me,' I said quietly. 'Is that what you all think?'

'No!' said Ellie. 'I don't think that at all.'

'Me neither,' said Jane. 'And nor does Pixie. Pixie, stop making Katie feel bad. You know she's only thinking of what's best. We're all emotional right now, what with Pixie's news about Trevor. I think you both have good points about the singles events.'

'We need to vote on it,' said Pixie.

'Maybe we should think about it for a while,' Ellie said.

'What's to think about?' Pixie asked. 'You've heard my argument. It's very profitable for the club. It was well-attended, and as Katie pointed out, dating sites are very popular these days, so we know our events will sell well. And you heard Katie's arguments against it. Let's vote. Okay? All in favour of starting a dating side for the club?'

Pixie's hand shot up. Slowly Jane's followed. I watched Ellie. She shook her head.

'All against?' Ellie and I put up our hands.

'Not passed.'

'All right,' Pixie said. 'I move to propose another speed-dating event and if it goes well, we can do more.'

She just wouldn't give up on her idea. This time Ellie put her hand up. 'It doesn't hurt to have one more and see how it goes. Maybe we can do a survey after to see how everyone feels?'

That did make sense and I knew Pixie wasn't being purposely difficult. She really thought that Fat Friends was a great business idea. If I were her I'd push just as hard. In fact I *was* pushing just as hard, in the opposite direction. I might resent her cutting comments, but I couldn't fault her for arguing for what she thought was right. Even if it was misguided. Plus, I hadn't forgotten how the meeting had started.

'I have one more motion to propose,' I said. 'I propose that Pixie should work for the club. I could cut the hours I work to one day. Pixie, could you work say, sixteen hours a week?' With our current bookings we could just about afford to pay for three days a week plus Rob, and the fifty quid a month we gave Rob's cousin to use the menagerie as our offices.

'Pixie,' Jane said. 'Why don't you let me take the children after school? Two more in the house won't make any difference, and they're really no trouble. I'd just need to be in the office on Fridays.'

Pixie nodded, smiling. 'You're all good friends,' she said.

'All in favour?' I said.

Four hands went into the air.

Pixie might not get her Fat Friends but at least she could start looking for a way out of her marriage.

CHAPTER TWENTY-FIVE

Mum always said that when one door closed, a window opened. In my case that usually meant a bathroom window too tiny to squeeze through. But to my surprise, giving up some of my hours to Pixie worked out for us both. Even though I was still doing just three days a week at Nutritious, mentally the balance shifted back to my day job.

Pixie and I didn't hold any grudges. Our friendship was too strong to stumble over one disagreement. I coached her on the event planning and she was ever-so keen to learn. As she sponged up all the information I threw at her, I realised how small and sad her Trevor-dominated world had become.

Within a few weeks, all the drama of the previous months faded away. Ellie and lovely Thomas were madly in love. Pixie was working her way out from under Trevor's thumb and I felt like I was once again firing on all pistons at Nutritious. Which was how I found myself dialling Jenny's number with newfound resolve one afternoon.

'Hi Jenny, it's Katie, from Nutritious.'

'Yes?' she snapped, effusing her usual milk of human kindness. 'I'm busy. I can't spend my entire day on the phone. Unlike you, apparently.'

'Yes, well Jenny, I *am* in sales. Which is why I'm on the phone a lot.' I took a deep breath. 'And today I've got a deal for you. We've got a new product that's getting a lot of good press—'

'The press are idiots.'

'And there are four clinical trials indicating its efficacy, and more than a hundred testimonials.'

'I've heard all this before.'

'And I've been authorised to give you a one hundred per cent free trial of the range. I could come see you to discuss it further, answer any questions you have and get you set up with the free products.'

'Give me one reason why I should say yes.'

For years this woman had cut me off at every turn. Not one phone call passed without an insult of some kind. Beelzebub had a cheerier disposition. I gave up.

'Do you know what, Jenny? I can't think of a reason that you'd accept, so I'm just going to say what I'm thinking. Maybe because, after six years of phone calls, I might be the longest relationship you've ever had. Perhaps because you've discovered one iota of courtesy in that bitter heart of yours. Or maybe because you like free stuff. Take your pick.'

Suddenly she laughed. It was much less wooden than I imagined someone without a soul would sound.

'Well, good on ya,' she said. 'That's the first honest response I've ever heard from you. It's nice to throw away the script, isn't it? I can meet next month. I'm making no promises. I still don't think your supplements are worth a damn. But I'll meet you.'

I wanted to whoop the walls down as I hung up, but yodelling wasn't popular in our office. I had to tell someone. Ellie was in the conference room taking notes for Clive. He wouldn't appreciate the interruption.

'Cressida?!' I called as I flew into her office. She was one person I knew wouldn't be on the phone. She never made calls these days. 'Oh, I'm sorry!'

Alex sat opposite her at the little round table tucked in the corner. 'I didn't realise you were in a meeting.' I was suddenly conscious of my too-big skirt and the scuffed, gum-soled black leather Mary Janes I used for commuting. I looked like an unstylish librarian in orthopaedic shoes.

Cressida shrugged and asked what I wanted.

'I've got a meeting with Jenny next month!'

'That's fantastic,' said Alex, grinning. 'Well done!' He answered Cressida's surprised look. 'What? Didn't you think I knew who Jenny was? I'm a man of the people you know, keeping it real with the staff and that. Innit.'

'You're a prat,' she said kindly. 'But you're a charming prat. Katie, that is wonderful news. Finally, the hard work pays off.'

'Thanks! I'll let you get back to your meeting. I just wanted to tell you that I'll be putting in for travel expenses.'

Actually, I just wanted to gloat to my boss, but that probably wasn't the shortest route to a Superior appraisal.

I was too excited to go straight back to my calls. I gave Ellie the news when she got out of the meeting, then went down to the park to call Rob.

'Can you talk?' I asked when he answered. It was a work day for him and I knew he'd be in his office with all the other IT programmers.

'I wouldn't have answered the phone otherwise. What's up?'

I told him about Jenny, embellishing for the sake of dramatic tension. When I got to the part about Jenny suggesting a visit, he said, 'Shut the front door, you did not get an appointment!'

'I did.' I felt suddenly flat. Already the excitement of winning Jenny over was smudging from constant handling.

That hadn't lasted long. No wonder adrenaline junkies were always looking for their next fix. 'So anyway, I just wanted to tell you. How's everything going with Pixie?'

'Fine. Good, actually,' he said. 'She's enthusiastic and flexible and she's a really good laugh.'

More than me? I wanted to ask.

'Listen, Katie, I've got to go, but that is really excellent news about your client. Congratulations.'

'Thanks, Rob,' I said as he hung up. Well, what did I expect? Heartfelt confessions of love at two in the afternoon, more than a month after our date? Plainly, he was my friend again, nothing more. At least there was no awkwardness when we spent time together at the events. If anything we were closer than ever. So why had he changed his mind about me? With the pounds coming off, you'd think that he'd have been more attracted to me, not less. Even if I now had rings under my eyes from lack of sleep, I was a size sixteen (just). For the first time in my life I could wear what everybody else wore. Cakey Katie wasn't quite ready to wake up from that lovely dream.

Was it worth it? I hadn't breathed a word of this to anyone, but it really was. It didn't matter that I was jittery and exhausted from my thyroid, or that my heart was still in overdrive. So what that I had to wear sweat pads to keep from ruining my clothes, which felt like having sanitary towels in my armpits. That was the price I was paying for being able to fit into Topshop's clothes.

The specialist's appointment had come around quickly and since everyone – from the consultant to the nurse to the receptionist out front – seemed completely unconcerned, by the time the GP gave me the biopsy results I was relaxed about it. And once I knew for sure that I wasn't terminal, it stopped feeling like a medical condition to be cured. It started to feel like the luckiest little nodule imaginable.

The GP had explained my options. Behind door number one: drugs that may or may not work and could cause nasty side effects. If they did work, I'd gain back all the weight I'd lost.

Behind door number two: radiotherapy, which the GP assured me was very effective. Over-effective, in fact. My thyroid could become underactive, which would mean I'd gain back all the weight and then some.

'What if I do nothing?' I'd asked him.

'You shouldn't do nothing,' he'd advised. 'Although your results are high–normal and there's no history of heart disease in your family—'

'And my heart is healthy, right?'

'Yes, it is. Even so, your thyroid is working abnormally. You need treatment.' His grey eyes bore into mine.

'I need time to decide.'

'Don't take too much time,' he'd warned.

That was a week ago. I hadn't yet made the follow-up appointment.

Alex's email was waiting for me when I got back upstairs to make my next call: *Well done again for turning Jenny around. That's got to be some kind of record for perseverance. This deserves dinner, don't you think?*

Dinner in an official capacity? Or dinner in an intimate who-knows-where-this-might-lead capacity? I searched my conscience for any Rob-shaped spiky bits. There were just a few twinges.

Effort counts in a budding romance and a month after he'd made any, I had to accept that whatever we'd had, and as nice as it was, it was clearly over. It served me right, I thought sadly as I emailed Alex to find a night when we were both free. I hadn't been wholly enthusiastic when Rob first kissed me, had I? That's what I get for not taking the chance when I had it.

CHAPTER TWENTY-SIX

Everyone was whispering at work. In the kitchen, in the lift, in the corridors, I stepped into furtive conversations all over the place. The bosses met more than usual in the big conference room, and they stopped having Ellie take minutes. Naturally we started monitoring the kitchen's fancy biscuit supply. They were the litmus test for strangers on the floor. Sometimes those strangers looked suspiciously like management consultants. We all knew they were the crows of the business world – harbingers of death.

It wasn't easy to train Smith, my *buddy*, with everyone around us worrying about their jobs. But I'd promised Alex I'd do it, so I found myself having to deflect his questions. I started to understand what mums went through when they didn't want their children to know there was no Santa Claus, or that Daddy and Aunt Clara had become more than just in-laws.

Smith had just finished shadowing me on a client call when he said, 'I've heard they're asking for voluntary redundancies.'

There it was. The word I dreaded. And certainly the word my mortgage provider would dread. My plan to drink the free office coffee hadn't yet amassed enough riches to offset that kind of income deficit.

'Who said that?' I kept my face impassive.

'You know Stacy in HR? She told me. Though not in an official capacity, you understand.' He smirked.

'You do get around,' I said, wondering why Racy Stacy would waste her hormones on a lowly trainee when there were bigger beds to hop into. I suppose Smith was a good-looking guy – dark, gelled hair made to look like bedhead, big brown eyes that crinkled when he laughed. But I found him just a smidge too slick. He always seemed to be half-listening to me and half-listening for a better opportunity.

He shrugged. 'I can't help it if the ladies love me. Stacy heard her boss talking about the list.'

I pulled my Nutritious work hat on. Stern Katie. 'Well, first of all, you said voluntary redundancies. If they're voluntary, then there can't be a list. And second of all, Stacy really shouldn't be eavesdropping on her boss. And she definitely shouldn't be spreading rumours that probably aren't even true.'

'I'm just telling you what she told me,' he said defensively.

'I'm not interested in your pillow talk, Smith.'

'Sofa talk, actually. And a bit of table talk, if you must know.' There was that smirk again.

'Spare me your smutty details, please. Now if you don't mind, I've got work to do before lunch. Why don't you run off and play with the other children.'

He saluted and went back to his desk, thick-skinned as ever. He'd make a fine salesman.

Normally I wouldn't talk that way to a colleague but Smith and I never really recovered from our first meeting. I'd be glad when the time came to wave good-bye to my *buddy*.

I told Ellie about the list at lunch.

'Should we worry?' I asked as we shared an order of chicken dumplings at the little Japanese restaurant I'd gone to with Alex. Had that really only been a few months ago?

She nodded as she dipped her gyoza. 'I think it's only a matter of time. Is your CV updated? It's a good idea to see what else is out there. You know, jump before we're pushed, if another opportunity came up.'

The waitress brought our salmon bento boxes and poured more green tea.

'But then we wouldn't get any redundancy payout.'

She snorted. 'What payout? Have you read your contract lately? One week per year. That won't go far.'

How depressing. When she first mentioned the company's finances I imagined taking a few months off before having to find another job.

'Have you been looking?'

'I have, a bit. Thomas thinks it's a good idea. Even if the company turns around, it's good to know your worth.'

'That's Thomas talking, isn't it?'

Ellie nodded. She was a literature graduate. She thought in couplets, not cost-benefits.

'There's not a lot to choose from though,' she added glumly as she stabbed another dumpling with her chopstick. The restaurant did offer forks but she wouldn't give up the chopsticks. She stabbed, scooped and slurped her way through Asia's cuisines.

'I'll have to spend some time on the weekend then,' I said. 'I'm out tonight hosting that cooking class with Rob.'

'That's right. Hey, guess what? I'm cooking tonight too!'

I choked on my pickled seaweed. 'You are?'

'I said I'd cook for Thomas. He's always doing the cooking.'

'For good reason, Ellie. You can't cook.'

'I don't cook. There's a difference. But we've spent so much time together since our weekend away that I feel guilty he's always the one cooking. I want to do something nice for him.'

'I'm not sure your cooking qualifies as nice. Why don't

195

you throw on something sleazy and take him to bed instead? At least you won't have to worry about poisoning him.'

'You underestimate me, darling. I've got it all under control.'

'You mean you're getting takeaway and hiding the containers.'

'Don't you ever tell him. I'll stop at M&S on the way home. You know they do that really nice lamb shank.'

'I s'pose that's safer. Remember to dirty a few pots for authenticity. And if you do ever want to learn how to cook for real, you could come to one of the classes you know. You won't be able to rely on M&S forever. Especially if you and Thomas get married one day.'

'Or if we moved in together. Maybe I'd better sign up for one.'

'You could have come tonight if you weren't already "cooking". I'm going straight after work. I'm sure we could squeeze you in and you might be able to bring the results home to feed Thomas. Could you do a later dinner?"

'Thanks, but no. M&S will give me all the instruction I need. *Remove outer packaging and place in oven at 180°C. Fool-proof.*' She snatched the last dumpling, then carefully sawed it in half with her chopstick and slid the biggest half to my plate.

By the time I arrived at the cooking school in Marylebone, I was worried. And not because someone was about to judge my chicken vol-au-vent.

I berated myself as I made my way to the kitchens. Oh, I'd been so smug, thinking my friendship with Rob had come through the kissing episode unscathed. Weren't we just the best of friends, able to snog without changing the dynamic?

But the dynamic had changed. There was nothing concrete I could point to, but he wasn't quite as enthusiastic around me these days. Why should he be? He now knew for sure that he didn't want to date me. Apropos of the evening ahead, he was the same old pot of water, with the ring turned down from high to medium. I kept watch, but it refused to boil.

The cooking school was housed in an old warehouse down a tiny alleyway. The kitchen we were using was enormous, with cream-painted Victorian iron beams supporting the ceiling high above us. Fifteen-foot-tall industrial windows ran all along one brick wall, letting in the early evening sun. Whenever the sun shone through my windows at home it just showed up all the dust. This room was spotlessly clean. A dozen workstations with hobs and ovens, gleaming knives and pristine chopping boards were spaced in two rows in front of the chef. Since it was a popular event we paired up in teams. Rob was just tying his chequered apron when I got to our station.

'You look like a celebrity chef!' I said, taking the apron he offered. He did look adorable, and ridiculously happy. 'Have you been on the sunbeds or something? Holidaying at the Suntastic in Costa del Hackney?'

'What do you take me for? No, I haven't been on the sunbeds. I was away sailing last weekend. In France. Some people at work invited me.'

'Oh. You didn't mention you were going away. Was it with Jim and, er, what's his name, your other friend with the beard?'

'No. It was with some different people. You don't know them.' He became keenly interested in the knife handles. 'What are these, Henkel? Very nice.'

Every instinct told me to leave it alone. It was none of my business who he frolicked with in France. If he wanted to waste his weekend quaffing rosé and feeding croissants to some woman, it was no business of mine. No good could come of knowing. I tacked my smile in place.

'Different, people, Rob? Female people, by chance? Was it a date, hmm?' Nosy Katie, never could leave well enough alone.

'I don't think it was a date,' he said. 'We all had a lot of fun though, and had perfect weather. Hence the tans.'

I just bet they had great tans. Probably sunbathed topless all weekend. They say curiosity killed the cat, but satisfaction brought him back. No, it didn't. It just made the cat wish she hadn't asked.

I seemed to be the only one in a sour mood by the time we'd checked everyone in and got started. Rob whistled and hummed, clucking to the tune of the Blue Danube Waltz as he danced our chicken into the roasting pan. He certainly was in a fine old mood. Why shouldn't he be? He'd probably had sex with some tan-all-over woman all weekend. I checked his expression for signs of sexual gratification. He definitely looked happy. But that could have been because we were about to cook and eat a two-course meal.

The chef was pleasant and unsweary, not a bit like the prima donna I'd feared. It probably wasn't in the school's best interest to set their grumpy chefs loose amongst the public. He explained everything slowly, and gave people a chance to ask questions. Still, I kept a careful eye on our clients, ready to step in if an extra pair of hands was needed. Rob was an adept cook, more than capable of making our meal.

'How's your day been?' he asked as we took a break to let the vol-au-vents cool. 'Were you able to book the meeting with Jenny?'

He remembered! He'd seemed so distracted when I called with the news, but maybe I was just being sensitive. Clearly he was listening to me. I was ridiculously happy for this tiny thing.

'Not yet,' I said. 'If I know Jenny, she hasn't finished toying with me. Just because she agreed to meet doesn't mean she'll make it easy. I'm ready for her though. Ever since Pixie took over some of my hours, I've had the energy for my day job. It couldn't have come at a better time actually, since I haven't been doing great there.' I took a deep breath and confessed about my review (it did feel like a confession), and about the company's money woes. 'So Jenny finally saying yes is a life-saver. Or hopefully a job-saver anyway.'

I was being dramatic. Even if the company had to make cuts, my job was probably safe. I was one of the longest-serving salespeople; they needed me.

'I'm glad Pixie has been doing well,' I told Rob magnanimously.

'She's really great,' he confirmed. 'Did you know she can write in shorthand? She did secretarial school before she met her husband. She can transcribe everything we say.' He laughed. 'You and I've probably lost dozens of brilliant ideas because we spend so much time faffing around and never write anything down.'

Yes, I thought, and I missed our faffing.

The roast chicken came out of the oven crisp and golden and oozing juices. 'Tent your birds!' the chef reminded us. 'Foil for ten minutes please.'

'God that smells amazing,' I said. 'There's no way this lot will be able to keep their mitts off the chickens. I can barely do it. I'm starving.'

'You're always starving these days,' Rob said. 'But that's because of your thyroid, right? You don't normally eat like a rugby player.'

I snapped my towel at him.

'Have you started the treatment yet?'

. . .

'Not yet.'

He stopped chopping the leeks we were using for the

chicken vol-au-vents, concern clouding his face. 'You know you can talk to my dad if you're not happy with your doctor. He really shouldn't be dragging his feet like this. You should be on the medicine by now. I know Dad's surgery is a bit far away from you, but he could have a look at your test results and get you started. Do you want me to call him?'

'No, no, that's okay, thanks. I like my doctor. He explained the options when I went in a few weeks ago. Do you know what the side effects are? Jesus, I'm starting to think it's better to have the condition.' I busied myself washing up the bowls we'd used.

'Katie.'

'Hmm?'

'Are you delaying this treatment?'

'What's that? I can't hear you over the water.' I turned the tap on full, spraying water about six feet in the air as it hit the ladle in the bottom of the sink. 'Oh shit!'

'That serves you right.' He threw me a dry towel. 'And I know you heard me. *Are* you delaying the treatment?'

I leaned against the counter, mopping my face. 'I'm not delaying, Rob. I'm deciding. This isn't easy, you know. The medicine might not even work. It takes months and can have awful side effects. The radiotherapy could make my thyroid slow right down, which means I'd end up fatter than I was before it went wonky. And then I'd be at risk of high blood pressure, heart problems, who knows what? I'm just taking my time, weighing the options.'

'Is one of your options to do nothing?' He watched me carefully. 'Because it sounds to me like it is. I've talked to my dad about an overactive thyroid and he said the treatments are effective. There aren't usually side effects.'

'You've got absolutely no right to talk to your father about my medical condition! That goes against the Hippocratic Oath!' I lowered my voice when several people looked over.

I could see he was losing his temper too. 'First of all, Katie, the Hippocratic Oath says nothing about a regular person talking to his father about his friend's condition. You're not even my dad's patient. Be as defensive as you like. You know I'm right. You're delaying because you don't want to gain the weight back. Putting your looks before your health is just stupid. You could be damaging your heart.'

'Oh, so now you're a doctor?'

'No, my dad is a doctor. That's why I talked to him and paid attention to what he said. You're not a doctor either, so you should pay attention to what your GP says . . . Are looks really so important to you?' He shook his head. 'I'd never have thought that of you, Katie. What happened to being happy as you are, huh? I guess that was all just empty talk. Well, congratulations. You sold it to the rest of us, hook, line and sinker.'

'I do believe that,' I said.

'Sure, it's easy to believe as long as you're not the one who's fat. You know, you've changed since you lost weight. You're vain now. Or maybe you've always been like that and it's just becoming apparent now. Looks aren't everything, you know.' Sadness clouded his face. 'Just because a person doesn't look perfect doesn't mean they're worth less. I thought you of all people knew that.' He threw his towel on the work surface. 'Why does everyone have to be so shallow? It shouldn't be all about looks.'

I was having a déjà vu moment. Where had I heard him say that before? Oh yes, it was when he'd ranted about his ex-girlfriend.

'It's not about looks! It's about . . . making the right decision given that the treatments have side effects.'

But I knew he didn't believe me. Why should he? I didn't really believe myself.

CHAPTER TWENTY-SEVEN

Rob's words bothered me all weekend but something stopped me from calling him. Maybe it was because he was furious with me. We were barely speaking by the end of the cooking class and instead of walking me to the Tube like he normally would have, he made an excuse to stay behind to talk to the chef. I might have believed he was looking for a few kitchen pointers but it was obvious he was avoiding me. I didn't blame him. Somehow everything had got muddled up. I hadn't meant for us to argue, or to make it sound like I was shallow. I really did have serious concerns about the side effects of the thyroid treatment. It just so happened that those side effects included gaining back all the weight I'd shed.

Even if he was just concerned for me, I wasn't sure he could really see my point of view. Sure, he was twenty pounds over his ideal weight, but he looked good in his clothes. And he hadn't lived with being fat his whole life. He wasn't the one who got called Katie Blubberbottom in school. He didn't look in the mirror every morning hoping to see a bit less of himself than he'd seen the night before, or pretend to be satisfied with accessories when shopping because shops didn't stock his size. He didn't feel the embarrassment when the dress he finally found and squeezed into in the dressing room wouldn't come off without help from the saleslady. He wasn't the one who always jammed himself against the window on the bus to keep his thigh from spilling over to the seat beside him. It was easy for Rob to judge. He should see how he felt after walking around in my size twenty clothes. Then he might understand why I'd hesitate to purposely reverse the weight loss that, for some reason, my body decided to give me. Instead of calling me shallow.

So when Alex came by my desk late Tuesday afternoon, whispered that I looked gorgeous and insisted on dinner that evening, I was more than ready to go out with him. If Rob wanted to believe that was shallow, so be it.

Of course now that Alex had seen me, the royal blue empire waist dress I'd worn to Cirque du Soleil would have to do. Rob had thought it looked pretty (get out of my head, Rob!).

'I've got us an early reservation at Les Trois Garcons,' Alex said as we left the office together. 'Have you been? It's just over in Shoreditch.' He stuck his arm out for a taxi and we bundled in before anyone from the office noticed us together.

I kept sneaking glances at Alex as we crept through the rush-hour traffic, hardly believing he was really there beside me. I half-expected him to get out when the cab stopped and thank me for the lift to the Tube.

He didn't. We stopped in front of a nondescript building that looked like it had once been a pub. Alex got out first to pay the driver.

'Here we are, madam,' he said, offering me his hand as I channelled Grace Kelly to help me exit the car with my knees together.

This was really happening.

He held the restaurant door open for me, ushering me

into the sumptuous interior. Just how many eccentric restaurants were there in London? First, the mad opera-house with Rob (I told you, Rob, go away!), now this. At first it had the look of an elegant 1920s salon . . . lived in by an insane auntie. Crystal waterfall chandeliers tumbled from the ceiling. Vintage leather handbags hung from wire above the diners' heads. Then there were the animals. A blonde ape wearing a crown and cross and smoking a cigar stood beside a tiger in a gorgeous 1920s crystal headdress. He was slightly outshone though by the surprisingly jaunty bulldog wearing a crown collar and fairy wings. Rob's cousin David could die happily after seeing such taxidermist's delights.

'You like?' Alex asked, grinning proudly. He knew how to make an impact.

'I'm not sure where to start,' I said. My head swivelled to take everything in. Everywhere I looked, something else surprised me. 'Oh, that's a bit . . . weird and creepy.' In the midst of a group of mounted herbivore heads was a giraffe. His regal, golden crowned head graced a six-foot-long neck, coming straight out of the wall.

'This isn't a restaurant for animal rights advocates,' he said. 'Or vegetarians. You're not either, are you?'

Was I? I didn't use cosmetics that were tested on animals, or eat veal or fois gras. But I wore leather shoes and happily tucked into a Sunday roast.

'Can one be a quasi animal rights advocate?'

'Do you want me to test you?' He waved for the waiter and ordered a bottle of red.

'Sure, go ahead.'

'Would you wear a coat made from polar bear?'

'Definitely not.'

'What about rabbit?'

I thought for a moment, then shook my head.

He leaned forward with his elbows on the table. 'What if the rabbit came from a farm where all the meat was eaten?'

'You mean like leather comes from cows, which we eat? I guess I might.'

'Then you're definitely not PETA material and we can continue this relationship.'

'Because I'd wear an animal if the meat gets eaten?'

'Nope. Because you didn't ask if the rabbits were mistreated. You're just as hard-hearted as I am. Let's drink to that.' He waited for the waiter to pour my wine. 'You like red, don't you?'

'Well, I usually drink white when I'm out, just because red stains my teeth. But I do like red, cheers!'

He nodded. 'Châteauneuf-du-Pape. Always nice. And red wine is better for your heart. Though your heart looks fine from where I'm sitting.'

'That's because you can't see it,' I started. 'It's actually beating like mad. I've got this thyroid thing you see— Oh, you meant you were looking at my . . . thank you.'

He shook his head, laughing. 'You really don't have any conceit at all, do you? That's so charming.'

Did you hear that, Rob? I thought. No conceit at all. Now leave me alone.

Alex continued, oblivious to my imaginary discussions. 'But you should learn to take a compliment. Here, let me help you get used to it.' He reached for my hand. 'Not only are you fun and nice, very sweet and always willing to bail my arse out, you're looking absolutely fantastic these days.'

I could feel my neck going blotchy from embarrassment. Oh yes, I'm sure I looked lovely just then. 'This is practice, right?'

When he let my hand go to open the menu, I wanted to snatch it back. Greedy Katie.

'Have you bought new clothes or something lately?' he

asked as he squinted at the starters. He used reading glasses when he was alone in his office, but he was too vain to wear them in front of people. I'd caught him bespectacled a few times when I bounded in unannounced. 'You look different, and I can't put my finger on it.'

He had to be joking. How could a man not notice an extra forty pounds?

'Er, I've lost a bit of weight.'

'Have you? That must be it, then. It really suits you. And that dress makes your eyes nearly violet.'

'Flattery will get you far,' I said. He topped up my wine glass as the waiter returned for our orders. Luckily there were posh-food-to-English translations beneath each option.

'I do hope so,' he said when the waiter had left. His eyes bored into mine. 'Because I would very much like to seduce you tonight.'

I felt faint. 'I think we should have our starters first, don't you?' There I was, engaging in witty repartee. I was normally tongue-tied when Alex asked me if my expenses were in on time.

'Can I take that as a maybe, then?'

'We'll see if you can compete with my smoked mackerel.'

'Oh, I do love a challenge.' He rubbed his hands together. 'And I guarantee I'm better than mackerel. More wine?'

I'd never been on a date like this before. I knew exactly where I stood with Alex. Going out with Rory had been a study in frustrated anticipation. I'd read his expressions like tarot cards, trying to glean meaning from them. Not that I'd waited for him to make an actual move. I cringed to think of how many times I'd manoeuvred to be alone with him. Sometimes I'd even faked sudden illnesses, knowing he'd stay behind to look after me (that sweet, guileless boy).

Even more recently, my date with Rob hadn't been a sure thing either. Yes, he'd said he liked me, and asked me out of his own free will – no faked stomach cramps necessary. He'd made sure we had a magical night. Sure, we'd kissed each other's faces off. But then, poof! Game over with no explanation and I was stuck second-guessing a man again.

I quite enjoyed the idea of someone besides me being the sure thing. Alex seemed more than happy to play his part.

The food lived up to the delectable décor, and thankfully wasn't too petite for French fare. I'd have concentrated more on my pork belly if Alex wasn't being so damn charming. He wanted to know all about me. I skimmed over the boring bits, aka most of my life, and told him about uni, and a bit about Mum and Dad.

'I'm an only child too now,' he said. 'I had an older sister, but she died on my eighth birthday.'

I didn't expect him to share something that personal with me.

'I'm so sorry. What happened?' I'd have loved a sister. I had Daphne for a few years, but she wasn't as good, since nobody could see her. Eventually we started fighting too much, so she packed her imaginary bags and left. Then I got a puppy and forgot all about her.

Alex ran his hand through his hair, making it stand on end for a few seconds before settling back into glossy disarray.

'Mum and Dad gave me my first BMX bike. An electric blue and white Raleigh with chopper handlebars. I couldn't believe my luck when Mum wheeled it into the kitchen during my birthday breakfast. They'd bought bike racks for the car and planned an entire birthday out on the trails. We drove to a big wood – it was a beautiful day, sunny even though it was November. My sister didn't want to be there. Being eleven she was too cool to spend the day with family. Her best friends went to a birthday party but she wasn't allowed to go because of me . . . Mum was trying to keep her entertained while we rode, playing I Spy.' He looked away for a moment. I fought the urge to pull him to my bosom for a cuddle. 'I was stoked to have my whole family with me. It was Claire's turn to play. She spied something beginning with T. Tree, trunk, tyre. We couldn't guess. There wasn't a level crossing, so no warning where Claire was standing ahead of us, on the track. The train killed her instantly.'

'Jesus Christ!' I hadn't expected to hear that over my petit fours. 'And you saw it? How awful. Oh, your poor parents!'

'I'm sorry, I didn't mean to bring the mood down,' he said. 'It was a horrible time. Mum had to go into the hospital for a while, but it was all a long time ago. I don't have the nightmares any more, but I don't generally talk about it.' He reached for my hand. 'With you though, I feel like I can.' He gently kissed my palm, staring into my eyes.

My heart fluttered. Hearing about his sister, I could understand why he was a private person. Despite our years together as colleagues I wouldn't have said we knew each other very well. Telling me something so personal leapfrogged him straight over the acquaintance label. We were friends. Well, hopefully more than friends.

He seemed to have the same idea. The waiter cleared our pudding plates and crept off. The restaurant was full and noisy but we seemed separate from the diners around us. Alex leaned over, his lips meeting mine. Slow, luxurious, this-could-go-on-all-night-type kisses.

'Well, that was nice,' I said when he pulled away.

'Nice?' He laughed. 'Then I didn't do it right.' This time he pulled my face close to his and kissed me hard, biting my bottom lip. 'Still only nice?' he murmured.

'The bill, please.'

'My thoughts exactly.'

We walked hand-in-hand to the Tube. I was surprised by the light outside, but then it was only just after nine thirty. I didn't ask where we were going. First of all, I had a pretty good idea. And second, if he confirmed what I suspected, I'd then have to agree or disagree. Better to arrive at the door with no advance knowledge (technically) and say, 'Well now, where are we?' as if I hadn't crept past his flat at least semi-annually.

'Well now, where are we?' I asked right on cue when we stopped outside the Victorian building.

'My flat, as it happens. I thought, what with it being late, we could have a drink here.'

I checked my watch. 'It's quarter past ten.'

'That's late for a farmer. My family are farmers. Drink?'

'I thought your family were doctors.'

'Rural doctors. With chickens. How about that drink?'

My phone rang just as we were walking up the narrow, Victorian, sisal-carpeted stairs to his flat on the second floor. 'It's Ellie. I can call her back later.'

'Does she know we're out together tonight?' he asked.

'No, I didn't mention it.'

'I'm hurt!' he said. 'Am I nothing more than your dirty little secret?'

Did that mean he was going to be dirty? I couldn't wait!

'But I suppose you were just being smart,' he continued. 'Since we could lose our jobs if anyone found out.'

'I didn't realise that. Though now you mention it, I guess I do remember something in my contract.' My phone rang again. Ellie. Did she have a sixth sense, feeling vibrations when I was about to shag? I let it go to voicemail.

I held my breath as we entered Alex's flat. How long had I dreamed of this?

He'd painted the walls a warm sandy yellow. Dark, wide-beamed wooden floors were scattered with colourful Kilim rugs, and a few African masks dotted the walls. There was little clutter though it wasn't sparse. I didn't spot any photos but recognised the souvenirs of a world-traveller. An earthen pot here, Tibetan prayer wheel there.

'You're probably right not to say anything,' he said, throwing himself beside me on the cream leather sofa with two crystal glasses of whiskey pinched between his fingers. He handed me one. 'Cheers. To our secret affair. I like the sound of that.'

The fumes alone made my eyes burn. I took a tiny sip. Yikes. Rocket fuel. That wouldn't mix well with the bottle of wine we'd shared. But since I didn't feel overly drunk, I assumed Alex had done the chivalrous thing and quaffed most of it.

'I can't get drunk tonight. Client meetings tomorrow you know.'

I said this like I had them all the time. Client meetings. Me! My shrinking waistline wasn't only giving me more wardrobe options.

'I'm really sorry,' I said as my phone pinged with a text. 'I'll just turn that off.'

But the text stopped me pushing the off button. *Call me as soon as you get msg. Ellie xx*

My first thought was for my parents. Someone had called the flat from the hospital. They'd had an accident. Or there'd been a build-up of radon gas in the house. Or Dad had a heart attack or they'd been hit by a train playing I Spy like Alex's sister. Trying not to sound like an orphan, I said, 'I've just got to give Ellie a quick call back.'

I let myself out into the stairwell. 'What's happened?' I said as soon as she picked up. I could hear voices in the background.

'Didn't you listen to your voicemail?'

She didn't want to tell me on the phone. My panic rose. 'No, I called straight back when I got your text. What is it?' Tears pinched my eyes.

'Jane's taking appetite suppressants, Katie. The ones like speed. She's lost five pounds this week. She got really defensive after she admitted she got them off the internet, and wouldn't give us any more detail, but I think she's taking more than she's supposed to. She's just stormed out of the restaurant. We've got to do something.'

I was so relieved that my parents hadn't been mown down by a locomotive that my next words were possibly less sensitive than they could have been. 'That's it? That's the emergency? Jane lost five pounds? Ellie, you scared the shit out of me. I thought it was something really serious.'

'This is serious! Didn't you hear me? Jane is taking speed to lose weight.'

'I'm sorry. I didn't mean that it's not serious. I just meant that it's not imminently serious. Can we talk about it tomorrow?'

'Pixie and I think we should confront Jane. Tomorrow, before this goes any further. We've got to talk sense into her.'

'But I can't tomorrow, I've got client meetings.'

'Jane's away Thursday and Friday in Paris for Andy's IT conference. Pixie is minding the children. What about Saturday? Oh, I nearly forgot! You don't know about Pixie! Should I pass the phone over to her?' I heard Pixie say something. 'No, okay. I'll tell you then. Pixie's got a place for her and the children! We're helping her move out on Saturday. See what you miss when you don't come out with us? Where are you anyway?'

'I'll explain later. Don't wait up, okay? I'll talk to you later.'

'Ah, I see, okay! Don't do anything I wouldn't do!' She rang off.

Given Ellie's sex life lately, that left a lot of options open.

What was Jane thinking? She knew how dangerous those stupid pills could be. I thought the club was making her see the world differently. Clearly it wasn't enough. We'd have to make her see sense on Saturday.

When I came back in to Alex, I found him slouched on the sofa, looking relaxed and happy, with his feet on the low carved wooden table. 'Everything all right?'

'Yes, fine, thanks. Our friend is moving out on Saturday and another friend . . . Well, we just need to help her move. May I use your loo please?'

'Sure, it's just down the corridor on the left. The light's on a pull string on the right, just inside the door.'

I stifled a guffaw when I clicked on the light. Alex's bathroom was my mum's dream – white-painted floorboards, antique French mirror and a double ended claw foot iron bath. I wanted to take my clothes off and have a long soak. Carefully I crept to the whitewashed armoire in the corner to peek inside. Mismatched threadbare towels were shoved in there, not one folded properly. Phew, Alex wasn't gay.

Stupidly I'd left my handbag in the living room, so had to resort to a remedial touch-up. I rubbed the smudged eyeliner from beneath my eyes and blotted my face with loo roll. I didn't look too bad, considering.

I scrutinised myself in the mirror. Come clean, Katie. Were there plans afoot to go to bed with Alex? I had to be honest with myself. Nothing about tonight had dimmed my feelings for him. If anything, they were stronger. When he told me about his sister, something melted inside me. I saw a man who'd been through hell, and I wanted to be close to him. Very, very close.

Alex hadn't stirred while I was in the loo. I moved to sit beside him. He drew me onto his lap instead.

'Katie, this has been an incredible evening . . . so far,' he whispered. He pulled me to him, kissing me urgently. As he held me, I slid beneath him. His hands moved slowly up my thigh. 'Such a beautiful figure,' he said between kisses.

'I don't want to wrinkle your dress. Perhaps you should hang it up?'

Cheeky sod. 'Not here,' I said, stopping his hand on the dress's zip.

He smiled, helped me up, and led me to his bedroom.

It was after three a.m. by the time my dress was back where it belonged. It might be several days before I stopped smiling. Alex was as amazing as I'd imagined. He was considerate, never making me feel the least bit uncomfortable. He lit a single candle and in that light I felt beautiful. He didn't rush us into intercourse. In fact he didn't hurry things along at all. I was the one who moved us to the next level, and then the next.

I'd have loved to cancel my client meetings and stay in bed with him all the next day but, typically thoughtful, he reminded me how important the meetings were for my career. So I let him call me a taxi and kiss me until we heard it pull up. It wasn't until I found myself back in my bed just before four a.m. that Rob barged back into my head. I had to figure out a way to lock that door so he didn't disturb Alex and me.

CHAPTER TWENTY-EIGHT

I got nearly three hours of fitful sleep so I was exhausted, but still happy, when I met Smith at the train station the next morning. Every time I thought of Alex a little flock of sparrows took flight in my tummy. Nothing was going to knock me off my cloud that day.

'All right, Smith?' I said when he ambled to our meeting spot just by the Costa Coffee.

'Just fine, Katie, thanks. Here, I got you one.' He handed me a glazed doughnut. 'I came from King's Cross. Home of the Krispy Kreme.' He chomped his doughnut in two bites. 'Careful, they're addictive.'

'Thanks, that's kind of you.' I had to remind myself that Smith probably didn't mean to annoy me. He just had a knack for it.

'Nah, it's a blatant attempt to kiss up. You are my boss, sort of. Have you got the tickets?' We walked toward the Departures board to see that our train was on time.

I liked the idea of being his boss-sort-of. I'd never been a boss before, unless I counted my brief career as a till clerk at our local supermarket. The manager put me in charge when he went to lunch, but I wouldn't call that an official role. Watching Smith, with his deliberately messed-up hair and slightly too-big suit, I felt more kindly disposed towards him. In taking him under my wing, I was nurturing his career. His future performance depended on how well I trained him. He was an all right kid, just a bit smarmy.

On the train I briefed him about our first client. Luckily she was nothing like Jenny (who still hadn't given me a firm date). I'd been talking to Afsaneh for nearly two years and she stocked lots of our products at her father's chain of chemists near Leeds. Once we'd finished talking business, we often then chatted about other things. So I knew all about how her family came to England from Iran after the Revolution and she knew all about the Curvy Girls Club. She was just the sort of woman I felt like I could be real-life friends with, and I couldn't wait to meet her.

'Do you think she's hot?' he asked when I'd finished briefing him.

As it happened, I did imagine she was hot. But I wasn't about to tell him that. 'Smith! Don't be a sexist arse.'

'That's not sexist. I just wondered what you think she looks like. I imagine Arab women as hot, because they wear those burkas. Makes me want to know what's underneath.'

'I'm sure that's not their intended purpose.'

'Well, you know – forbidden fruit and all that. How old is she?'

I wasn't about to feed his dirty little mind any titbits. 'I don't know.'

My phone bzzzed with a text. Alex?! 'Excuse me a sec.'

But it was Ellie, not Alex. *Good morning! I assume it was good, since you didn't come home last night :-) Did you have fun with ROB? :-)))) Ellie xx*

Of course she would think it was Rob I stayed out with. I kept my answer noncommittal. *On the train with Smith now.* (So she wouldn't try calling for details.) *Last night was fun. See you tonight after work. Should be home by six.*

I'd have to tell her about Alex, especially since we'd probably be seeing a lot more of each other. I might need her to cover for me at some point, if the company was serious about its non-fraternisation policy.

Afsaneh's office was easy to find from the train station. A rather uninspiring five-minute walk brought us to her pharmacy on a busy road that was chock-a-block with buses. We buzzed the intercom next door and the nondescript door clicked open. As I walked up the narrow stairs to the offices above the shop, I noted the sisal carpet, just like Alex's. I wondered if too much Alex could rot the brain and decided I'd take the chance.

Afsaneh was as beautiful as I expected her to be. She was clearly more beautiful than Smith expected. He was so smitten by her that he momentarily lost his bravado. Her gold jewellery and shoes looked expensive. She had very curly long black hair and huge almond-shaped green eyes. She wore more makeup than me, but then most twelve-year-olds wore more makeup than me.

By the time our meeting ended an hour later, Afsaneh and I were well and truly bonded. If I ever moved north I had a best friend in the making. Smith had stayed nice and quiet throughout, diligently taking notes. I handed her my card as the meeting wrapped up. To my surprise, Smith did the same. He shrugged. 'I just got them. I hope you don't mind.'

'Not at all,' said Afsaneh. 'It was a pleasure to meet you both.'

As we made our way downstairs, Smith found his tongue again. 'Just four hundred and ninety-nine cards left to give away.'

'You've got a crush on her,' I teased.

'Do not.' But he reddened and didn't joke any more about it.

At our second client visit, with a rather grumpy dietician not far from Afsaneh's office, Smith quietly took notes again. This time I couldn't put his silence down to infatuation. Middle-aged men with balding heads and beer bellies didn't normally turn him on. It must have been (dare I say it) professionalism. I liked this side of my protégée. He knew how to handle himself with clients. My training was paying off, I thought, as we boarded the train back to London.

As I watched the city recede I allowed myself a huge mental hug. Why shouldn't I be a tiny bit smug? Hadn't I completely turned my life around in the past few months? Coming up with that client visit plan to get around Cressida's objections was inspired. I was getting contracts renewed and Jenny was even going to give me a chance to meet. I was *so* on my way out of that Needs Improvement box. Examining my curvy silhouette in my new dove grey galaxy dress, I smirked. I was out of the Needs Improvement box there too.

Now I couldn't wait to start filming *The Great British Makeover*. Gok Wan was going to style *me*! I tried not to think about the naked part that would come first. There might have been less of me to fill a billboard recently but what was left had more dimples than the babies at a Huggies casting call. I could only hope for sympathetic lighting and a stronger constitution than I had last night.

When Alex had unzipped my dress, I'd panicked. Suddenly I could feel the little rolls of flesh on my back that I knew squeezed out below my bra strap. My slack thighs and wobbly upper arms screamed Fat Katie. Surely he'd be horrified. Sucking in my tummy only made creases appear across the rippling landscape. What had I been thinking? What must he be thinking?

But he didn't seem to notice. 'You're beautiful,' he'd

whispered. Those two little words calmed me. No man had ever told me that before. Life really couldn't be better.

As soon as I walked through our front door I knew that Ellie had been to M&S again. Delicious aromas infused the air.

'Ellie? What's the special occasion?' All the windows were open to let the warm breeze meander between the front of the flat and the back.

She popped through the kitchen doorway wearing the Kiss the Cook apron that Thomas had given her after their roasted lamb shank dinner. Kiss the ReHeater, more like.

'We're celebrating,' she said. 'Come sit down. Want a glass of wine? There's white open in the fridge.'

'I just need to check my emails and have a shower. I'm sticky from the train. I'll be right back. What are we celebrating?'

'I'll tell you when you come back in. Go shower.'

Just as I was scrolling through my emails a new one appeared, from Afsaneh. She'd beaten me to the draw, that thoughtful woman. We could definitely be best friends one day.

It was lovely to meet you as well, Smith, it read. *And yes, please do feel free to get in touch with any ideas you may have. Kindest regards, Afsaneh*

Smith? I scrolled down to the message beneath. Of course it was from Smith. Not cc:ing me in, I noted. Afsaneh must have added me manually to her reply.

There was nothing wrong with him emailing to thank a client for a visit. We were instructed to do that. But given that Afsaneh wasn't his client, it was a bit weird. And even weirder that he hadn't included me. And weirdest that he had asked to pitch products to her in future. I didn't like that one bit, but it wasn't something to mention to Cressida just yet. I'd be watching Smith closely.

I stepped out of my clothes in my bedroom and slipped on my dressing gown, popping my mobile in the pocket. Just in case Alex phoned.

It was the bathroom I'd fallen in love with when I first viewed the flat. Not only did it have room for a proper claw foot bath and a shower, there was a large sash window that overlooked the Tree of Heaven in the back garden. I'd spent many Saturday mornings soaking in that tub, staring out the open window. It was my favourite way to start a weekend. Then I'd set up for the day on the sofa, surrounded by the papers. It was a short walk to our eat-in kitchen (also light and airy) for regular caffeine top-ups.

Not that it had been a peaceful haven when I bought it. Dad had his doubts about whether the flat was even structurally sound when we first saw it. The previous resident had been there for nearly fifty years. He'd had a little hoarding habit. The family cleared the floor-to-ceiling rubbish after he died, and that's when they realised he'd also been very bad at DIY. Floorboards were torn up in the bedroom and living room and a leak in the kitchen meant the floor was rotten. The plaster had been pulled off the bedroom and bathroom walls, exposing the thin wood strips and struts beneath. The whole flat needed rewiring and plumbing.

But I was a tradesman's daughter. Dad agreed to call in favours from his builder friends, and did all the plastering himself. It took nearly two years to get the flat into decent condition, as Dad and his friends squeezed in a few hours at a time between other jobs. It felt like I'd forever be cooking on hotplates and shaking the builder's dust from my clothes. But eventually they finished, and Ellie moved in soon after.

I felt proud every time I walked up the road toward home. I saw the newly painted white stucco front and the waxflower shrubs that Mum and I had planted in the garden last year, and I knew I'd live there for a very long time.

My phone was ringing! I dashed the soap from my eyes and lunged for my robe, tracking wet footprints across the floor.

But it wasn't ringing. There were no missed calls. Just wishful thinking.

'What are we celebrating?' I asked Ellie when I went back into the kitchen.

'Love. Yours and mine,' she said, pouring my wine. 'Isn't it wonderful? Who'd have thought both of us would end up with such amazing men?'

'Well, *we're* amazing you know,' I pointed out. 'So we deserve amazing men. Has Thomas been extra-lovely today?' Thomas always seemed to be doing something thoughtful.

She sat opposite me on the rickety chair. We'd found them in a skip. Repainted cream and pale blue, they looked nice, but they protested every time someone tried sitting on one.

'No lovelier than usual. Cheers. To lovely men who deserve us, because we're so fabulous.' She took a big swig. 'So, tell me everything about last night!'

'Well,' I started, savouring her eager expression. 'I'll start by saying that it was probably one of the best nights of my life . . . even though it wasn't with who you think. I was with Alex, not Rob.'

She looked stunned. 'But I thought . . . but what about Rob?'

'What about him?' I snapped. 'I'm trying to tell you about the incredible night I had with Alex. If you recall, Rob never asked me out again after our date. There is no Rob.'

'Well, I'm sorry, Katie.' She crossed her arms. She always did that when she was prepared to argue her point. 'But there *is* a Rob. He's your friend. He's our friend, in fact, and you should talk to him before you go off sleeping with another man.'

'Conjecture. You don't know that I slept with Alex. And I don't need anyone's permission to go out with him. Least of all Rob's. Never mind. I'm sorry I mentioned anything.'

'Oh no. You're not getting off that easily. You think I don't know your tactics, Katie Winterbottom. You get all petulant when you don't want to have a grown-up conversation.'

That was the problem with arguing with your best friend. There were no unfamiliar manoeuvres.

'Ellie,' I said. 'You're twenty-five years old. What do you know about grown-ups?' I smirked.

'I know that you're not acting like one. Come clean, Katie. Did you get together with Alex just to spite Rob?'

'Spiteful sex? Not my style.'

She gasped. 'I didn't say sex. So you did have sex with Alex! How was it?'

'Oh, now suddenly you're interested in my night? Finished judging me?'

'No, not at all. I'll come back to the judgement. But I want to know all the details first.'

I knew she would judge me. I also knew she wouldn't do it until after I'd had the chance to revel in my news. She'd also be fair, and would act in my best interest. So I told her all about my night. My tummy fizzed recounting it. It really was perfect. And I couldn't wait to do it again. If only he'd call.

CHAPTER TWENTY-NINE

It was already humid on Saturday when we set off in the moving van toward Pixie's. Ellie was our nominated driver since Jane already had points on her licence and I'd never driven anything bigger than a VW Golf. Ellie coped well with the mix up in directions and unexpected one-way systems, and we pulled into Pixie's driveway only ten minutes late.

Pixie promised that we weren't moving her out under a shroud of secrecy. Trevor, she said, would be at the house when we arrived. That's what worried me. He hadn't been pleased with Pixie's new job or, by extension, those who gave it to her. If he pushed me over any chairs I was going straight to the police.

She said he'd been uncharacteristically subdued, all things considered, since she broke the news of her change of address. He even asked her to stay so they could go to counselling. She agreed to counselling but wasn't about to give up the place for her and the children.

I heard Pixie shouting as we knocked on the door. Worried looks shot between us.

'I told you no!' Pixie shouted over her shoulder as she yanked the door open. 'Hi, love. Come in.'

'Is everything all right?' Ellie asked, eyes darting down the hallway.

'Oh, fine. Trevor's just gone and promised Connor a puppy. His best friend got one when his parents split up. Connor thinks he's won the lottery. Believe it or not, it's been a relatively peaceful morning, considering. I've got a few more things to pack. Come upstairs and we can get it done quickly. Katie, will you please check on the children? They've gone quiet. I'd like to know that they're not killing each other.'

I went to the living room where Connor was face down, sobbing on the sofa. Kaitlin stood over him softly singing *You can't have a puppy*. Every time she said the word puppy he cried harder. Kaitlin watched me as she sang. I put my finger to my lips and shook my head. She stopped. Sometimes I was glad to be an only child.

'All right?' said Trevor behind me in the doorway. He looked unshaven and unhappy.

'Hi, Trevor. Yes, all right, thank you.' What was I to say to the man I was helping my friend leave? 'How are you?'

He rubbed his stubbly beard. 'As you'd expect. This came out of the blue. But Pixie says she needs to go. We're starting counselling you know.'

In all the years I'd known Trevor, the closest he'd got to a personal disclosure was when he admitted welling up when hearing 'Jerusalem' sung. This was not an emotionally sharing man. He must have taken Pixie seriously to tell me about the counselling.

'Well that's good. Very good.' I stopped myself from saying I hoped everything worked out, because I didn't. I thought Pixie could do much better than Trevor. I hoped she'd realise that too in the coming weeks, though I also understood why she'd agreed to counselling.

'Ready, love?' Pixie came down the stairs with a bin bag

in each hand. I noted she was talking to me, not Trevor. 'Just these bags for the van and we're ready to go.'

The mood became awkward as we realised we were about to witness Pixie's good-bye scene.

'I'll just take these out to the car,' I said, making a grab for the bags just as Jane did the same.

'I'll help,' Jane said. 'Come on, Ellie. Pixie, we'll meet you in the van.'

'Shall we take the children?' I asked, then realised Trevor was giving me a filthy look. 'Or, no, well, I guess you'll want to . . .'

'I'd like to say good-bye to my children, if that's all right,' said Trevor.

I felt like such a tit as we made our way to the van. As soon as we got there we saw the logistical problem. 'Where's Pixie going to fit?' Ellie asked.

Excellent question. Unless she wanted to ride in the back amongst the suitcases with the children, we needed another car.

Trevor seemed to realise the same thing. He trailed after Pixie from the house.

'We'll sort it out, don't worry,' Pixie was saying.

'Why do you have to be so damn stubborn, woman? Let me drive you and the children. You can't ride on the roof of the van you know.'

Pixie rounded on him. 'Trevor. I know I've messed up, okay? Yes, once again I've done it wrong. I should have thought about how we would get there before, but I didn't. So now I'll sort it myself.'

She looked at us, then back at the house. 'Give me the keys,' she said to Trevor. 'Our car keys. I'll drive it over with the children, come back to drop it off and take the train back.' She put her hand out. That woman was not going to take no for an answer.

* * *

224

The flat she'd found wasn't too far from the house. The children could stay in the same school and it would be easy for them to see their father.

It looked like any other 1950s block – brown brick and concrete with the flat doors facing external walkways along the front of the building.

'It doesn't look too bad,' I said to Jane and Ellie as we peered from the car park at the front. 'Is it special housing? You know, for women leaving abusive relationships?' I don't know what I expected; maybe haunted-eyed mothers with waifs grasping their skirts.

'No, it's a regular flat with a private landlord,' said Jane. 'Pixie doesn't qualify for sheltered accommodation because Trevor hasn't hit her.'

'Emotional abuse doesn't count?' Ellie asked.

'I guess with so many women getting beaten up, they have to prioritise,' I said.

I could only imagine what Pixie must be feeling, upending her life and leaving her husband. Excitement? Fear? She hadn't let on. In the past few days she'd kept conversations safely moored to the logistics of the move. I didn't blame her. She'd been thinking about her marriage for years. It was probably nice to leave the emotion out of it for a little while.

'Here we are!' she said to Connor and Kaitlin as she helped them from the car. 'What do you think?'

'We're living here?' Kaitlin asked quietly.

'Yes, for a while at least. Look, there are swings around the side. What do you think, love? Like it?'

'It's different from home,' Connor said, suspiciously eying the building.

'Well, yes. That's because this is a building and we live, lived, in a terraced house. But this will be nice. You'll see. We're on the third floor and there's a lift.'

'Our house has a lift?!' Connor's eyes went wide and his

round face broke into a grin. Promises of puppies and upheaval in his life were forgotten. 'Can I push the button?'

Pixie laughed. 'You'll have to take turns. We've got lots of button-pushing to do today. Are we ready?'

It took just a few hours to empty the van. Pixie had mostly taken clothes and kitchenware along with some of the children's toys. The first thing she did when we let ourselves in was to throw open all the windows. A nice breeze billowed the net curtains and soon cleared away the closed-off smell of the uninhabited flat. Their small one-bedroom home came furnished. The décor was a little tired but functional, with a brown leather sofa and two cream fabric reading chairs in the living room. A small table and four chairs stood against one wall in the kitchen. We put the toys away in a large wooden crate in the corner. Pixie set out a few of her favourite decorative pieces on the tables and shelves – the brightly painted earthenware vase she got on holiday in Majorca, some tall pillar candles in black iron holders, and her pride and joy: the red, green and yellow ceramic chicken that Connor and Kaitlin had made together for her birthday last year. It was very different from her house – more dated and clearly rented accommodation – but with their things in it, it would start to feel like home. It had everything she'd need. Mostly what she needed was time away from Trevor.

The bedroom walls were lined with white shelves and built-in cabinets for everyone's clothes and books. They made up the children's beds, shaking out Connor's *Shrek* duvet and Kaitlin's *Finding Nemo* coverlet (she was going to be an 'oceanographist' when she grew up), and the room became homely. Above the children's single beds was a mezzanine where Pixie would sleep.

'God, don't roll out of bed,' Ellie said, eying the circular metal staircase leading to the sleeping platform.

'I'd crush the children,' Pixie quipped. 'Go on up and have

a look. There's just enough room to stoop over beside the bed, but it's not so bad. All my clothes will fit with the children's into the cabinets. At least there's some privacy up there. And best of all, there's no Trevor.' She smiled.

'Does that mean you can retire your furry onesies?' I asked.

'Not a chance, love. I've grown to love them.'

'Even if you did throw them away,' Jane teased, 'you won't be bringing anyone back for a night of passion up there.'

'Love, for me a night of passion is watching *EastEnders* with a pint of ice cream. Ehem. Speaking of which . . . Katie? How was your night the other night? Did you enjoy your . . . ice cream?'

'What's this?' Jane asked.

'Erm, it was fine, thank you very much. Shall we see what the children are doing?'

Pixie ignored me. I knew she'd do that. 'Katie was out with Rob last week,' she said. 'She had a sleepover. Details, please. I have to live vicariously through my friends.'

'For the record, you've been misinformed. It wasn't Rob. It was my colleague, Alex, and it was fantastic!' I felt a twinge at the small fact that things weren't going quite to plan so far. But I pushed that aside. Just remembering the night tickled my tummy.

Pixie expression went funny. 'It wasn't Rob?' I shook my head. 'Oh, that is a shame.'

I laughed. 'Everyone wants me to go out with Rob.'

'No, that's not it,' Pixie said. 'The thing is . . . I may have been indiscreet.'

My heart dipped. Oh no. She hadn't.

'I thought it was Rob you'd been out with, so when we saw each other on Friday, I teased him about it. No wonder he looked confused. I'm so sorry, love. It was an innocent mistake. I hope you're not too embarrassed.'

I told Pixie it was no big deal. But I felt sick inside. What must Rob be thinking? Scratch that. I knew exactly what he was thinking. Slapper. I'd see him next Wednesday at the speed-dating event we were working at together. That gave me four days to think of something to say. Not that there was any way to make sleeping with Alex sound less sordid.

The children were desperate to go outside and play on the swings, so we took the lunch that we'd brought out to the picnic tables.

'This is nice!' Jane said, taking in the summer profusion of bushes and flowering shrubs that bordered the play area and separated it from the road. The grass was a little bare in patches but at least there was outside space for the children. 'I'm very happy for you, Pixie. It's the start of a new life. If that's what you want?'

Pixie considered the question. 'I feel like it's what I want, but I won't make any decisions lightly. Trevor's the father of my children. I have to consider that too. I'm just glad I'll have the space, physically and emotionally, to weigh up my decisions.' She tipped her face to the sun, looking more at peace than I'd seen her in a long time.

We spread a feast across the sturdy wooden table – quiches, sourdough bread and West Country cheese, enormous purple grapes and juicy red strawberries, low-fat hummus from the Turkish deli near Jane's house. I watched her pick at a piece of pitta. Then I caught Ellie's eye. We had to say something today. We'd agreed to do it after Pixie's move. There was probably a protocol or something, but we weren't exactly clued up when it came to interventions. How, exactly, did one tell a friend to stop their pill habit?

'Aren't you eating?' Pixie asked Jane, smoothly opening the way for our talk. I smiled gratefully at her. She gave me a tiny nod.

'Oh, I ate earlier,' Jane said. 'Isn't this weather lovely?'

'Earlier when?' I asked. 'We've been together since eight

o'clock this morning.' She looked pale, despite the sunshine and the exertions of the day so far.

'I'm just not hungry. You go ahead and eat. Everything looks delicious.'

'Jane, we know why you're not eating,' Pixie said. 'And we want to talk to you about it. We're worried about you, love. Those pills you're taking aren't good for you. You need to stop taking them.' Ellie and I nodded our agreement.

She looked at each of us. 'I appreciate your concern, but you really needn't worry. I feel better than I have in a very long time. I've got loads of energy, my clothes are starting to fit and most importantly, I'm beginning to feel like me again. They're just herbal supplements. They're not dangerous.'

'But they are, Jane,' Ellie said. 'And you've got loads of energy because you're taking speed. I've asked at work and those pills are associated with a higher risk of heart attack and stroke. They took a similar product off the market last year. These aren't just vitamins you've bought in Holland and Barrett or Boots. They're unregulated, off the internet . . . and I know you're taking more than you're supposed to be.'

Jane looked guilty. Then anger flashed across her face. 'They're the only thing that's worked in nearly a decade. I'm not giving them up. Don't I have a higher risk of heart attack or stroke from carrying around an extra three stone? At worst that means I've traded one risk factor for another, so I'm no worse off. Except that I'm getting slim, so that makes me better off, actually.' She crossed her arms.

I hadn't thought of it like that. Maybe she had a point. Being overweight *could* be dangerous. If she could get slim and have no higher risk than before—

'Bullshit!' said Pixie, blowing the trade-off argument out of the water 'Knowingly taking a drug that causes heart attacks is just stupid. Stop being stupid, Jane.'

'She's right, Jane,' I said. Of course she was right. As Ellie said, they were unregulated speed, no matter how natural the marketing made them sound. 'This isn't worth the weight loss. You've got to stop.'

'Katie, you of all people shouldn't be lecturing me about what's healthy! Look at you. Are you on that thyroid medicine the GP suggested? Or are you purposely not taking it so that you can stay thin? You might want to look at yourself before you start judging me.'

'That's unfair!' I said. 'I'm deciding what to do, Jane. I'm not purposely taking medication that could kill me.'

'No, instead you're purposely *not* taking medication that could keep you healthy. I can look on the internet too, you know. I've seen what an overactive thyroid can lead to – high blood pressure, osteoporosis, eye disease, heart attacks. So you ought to stop being a hypocrite. You're doing exactly the same as me, only you're not being honest about it.' She gathered up her handbag and stood. 'I'm tired now. I'd like to go, please.'

She waved away our objections. 'No. I'd like to go. Pixie, will you please take me back home? If not, I can take the train.'

Ellie and I watched Pixie drive off with Jane. I was sure that wasn't the way an intervention was supposed to go. We hadn't even told her we loved her.

'Do you think she'll see sense?' I asked Ellie as we cleared up our lunch.

She shrugged. 'I hope so. Otherwise . . . I don't know.'

CHAPTER THIRTY

I'd heard nothing from Alex all weekend, so I don't know what possessed me to walk past his office on Monday. It was no use trying to fool myself. It wasn't for a caffeine fix – I was already jittery from my morning cuppa. My diagnosis gave me the all-clear to indulge my caffeine habit again. Besides, the kitchen was on the other side of the floor. The loos were there too. Only the big conference room was down the hall past his office. So I had to pretend to be looking for my favourite pen (as of that minute, my very favourite standard issue blue biro), just in case. As an excuse it wouldn't stand up in court, but desperate people do desperate things.

I meandered past, walking as if contemplating something of deep importance. He looked up as he heard my footsteps (I walked extra-loud, just to be sure). I waved. He waved. He turned back to his computer screen. There was no way to take that as an invitation to stop for a chat. Luckily the conference room was empty, so at least I didn't have to stand in the corridor to wait the thirty seconds before starting back.

I peeked through his doorway, only to see him staring out

the window with his back to me. That wasn't the action of a man who wanted to talk. I was utterly depressed.

When Wednesday came around I still had no idea what to say to Rob. Pixie apologised again for dropping me in it, but I couldn't blame her for the gnawing angst with which I anticipated seeing him again. As I was the one who'd slept with Alex, I'd be the one to pay the price. I just hoped it wouldn't cost me a friendship. Not when the payoff seemed to be dateless nights and kicked-in self-esteem.

Rob was handing out name badges when I got to the already crowded bar. It was where Pixie and I hosted the first event. Her idea hadn't died the natural death I'd hoped. If anything, each speed-dating night was more popular than the last. Like it or not, Fat Friends was starting to look like a necessary eventuality. That didn't mean I had to be happy with the direction the club was taking.

After watching him from the bar, where I was ostensibly ensuring there was enough bar staff (actually avoiding him for just a few more minutes), I couldn't put it off any longer. It was time to face him.

'Hey,' he said, smiling as I approached. 'I'm glad you're here.' He handed me a badge he'd already made.

That sounded like his usual happy self. And he was glad to see me! The last few days of worry edged away a little.

'There are really too many people to do this alone. Great turnout, eh?'

So he was just glad to see me there as an employee. Crestfallen, I helped him label the rest of the would-be-daters. I kept a sneaky eye on him, alert for signs of anger, disappointment . . . judgement, disgust, hatred. The list of possibilities went on. We worked in silence until everyone was in place and it was time to start.

I recognised a few of the clients milling about. Even

pain-in-the-neck Arthur was there. 'Hello!' He waved when he saw me. 'Fancy meeting you here. Har har, get it? Meeting you here?'

I could see he'd made a big effort to look nice. His thinning hair was carefully combed to one side. He was neatly ironed from his checked shirt to his too-high trousers. I could smell a musky aftershave and see he'd nicked himself shaving. Something in my chest squeezed at his enthusiasm. I smiled. 'Very good, Arthur. Thanks for coming. I hope you'll have fun.'

'Oh, I know I will. Everybody is talking about these events, you know. I don't need to tell you that many a fair maiden has been won over here. I bet we'll have our first Curvy Girls Club wedding before long.' He patted his large tummy, something he often did in satisfaction.

I couldn't bear the hopeful look in his watery blue eyes. 'Just be . . . Just have fun, Arthur, and good luck. There'll be surveys at the end. Please do be sure to fill one out. We're interested in what everyone thinks.'

As he lumbered off I felt the stab of doubt again. More than eighty people had signed up. In return for their fifteen-quid fee was our implicit promise of the chance for love. How many of them would come away from tonight feeling worse about themselves? As I made a few last-minute checks I realised that I was asking as much for them as I was for myself.

Rob and I stood together while he kicked off the speed-dating, explaining that the women got to sit and the men had to hop tables when I rang the bell. He had just the right balance of friendliness and efficiency to put everyone at ease. Well, nearly everyone. I clicked the stopwatch and sat beside him, awkwardly casting about for something to say.

'Have you had a good week?' Lame.

'Yes, very good, thanks.' He fiddled with his pint.

'Good, good. Working?'

He nodded. 'Has your week been good?'

'Yes, fine.'

'I tried that new restaurant,' he said. 'Remember, the one in Clapham I mentioned?'

'Oh, yes. Was it good?' Clapham was miles away from his flat, and work. I wondered who he'd taken there.

'It was very good.' He smiled.

The watch beeped. *Ding a ling ling ling.* 'Gentlemen, please move to the next lady. Don't forget to write your notes first.'

'Good for you.' I nodded. 'Maybe I'll try it some time.'

. . .

'You could always go with your colleague,' he said.

Oh. Then we weren't avoiding this. I searched his impassive face. Two could play at that game.

'Is it romantic, for dates I mean?' I crossed my arms.

'Very. Candles everywhere. Nice little tucked-away tables.'

Nice to know that he wined and dined all his dates. Silly me; I'd thought he'd been imaginative. My mind flew back to our candle-lit restaurant with the tucked-away table. Despite getting angrier, my body tingled thinking about him touching my leg and stroking my hand that night. Traitorous body.

'I suppose it's easy to have a good time in surroundings like that,' I said. 'It wouldn't really matter who you were with.'

'Ah, but it does matter—'

Ding a ling ling ling . . .

'Sorry to interrupt. Must keep to the time,' I said. 'You were saying?'

'I was saying that it does matter who you're with. If, for example, you're with a very good friend, you'd definitely have a good time.'

'Or with a lover, I suppose, you're guaranteed a memorable night.'

234

'That depends on whether the lover is right for you,' he said. 'If not then it's just another date. It might be fun for that night, but you'd soon forget all about it and move on.'

So I'd been just another date. 'Still, it's sad when that happens,' I said truthfully. I didn't want to be awkward any more. 'Especially if you're perfect.'

'Yes, it's such a loss to the world when it doesn't work out for perfect people,' he said bitterly.

I'd never seen that hardness in him before. Had I missed part of the conversation? 'What?'

'Ring the bell.'

Ding a ling ling ling . . .

He continued. 'I suppose I shouldn't be surprised. Now that you're thin, naturally you can get men like Alex. I don't blame you, really. You've gone on about him for ages. Excuse me a minute. I'm going to get another drink. Do you want anything?'

'No, thanks.'

Rob stayed by the bar for the rest of the event. I didn't try to talk to him. No way. I didn't know what that was all about but if he wanted to believe I was that shallow, that I'd gone out with Alex because of his looks, then I didn't have anything to say to him.

We only made polite conversation when we had to speak. There was no reason for him to be so snappy. I was the one being unfairly judged. As I collected the surveys at the end, I resolved to work from home on Friday rather than cross paths with him.

Much as I hated to admit it as I looked over the surveys, most of our clients loved speed-dating. Even Arthur enjoyed himself, and he wasn't one to spare anyone's feelings by lying.

But the night hadn't gone well for everyone. My heart sank when I read the comments that two of the women had included on their forms. From one: *There was nobody here for me. Serves me right for thinking there would be.* And from another: *I feel worse than before I came. Speed-dating's not for me.* I thought about those women all the way back to the flat.

The idea of having to bare all for a national audience became real the following week when Channel 4 called Jane to arrange our meeting with all the head stylists. They didn't even give us enough notice for me to go to the gym every day to try to shore up some of the landslides my body had suffered from losing weight so quickly in the past few months.

Once again I had to call Cressida to excuse myself from the morning's work. But she didn't seem the least bit put out about it. She told me vaguely to have fun and rushed off the phone. Needs Improvement judgements aside, she really was the best kind of boss to have.

I dressed carefully for our TV meeting. Chocolate brown trousers with a lovely flowery sheer silk blouse from Topshop. I'd never get tired of saying that. Topshop Topshop Topshop. I was even wearing kitten heels, now that there was less of this cat to balance on pinpoints.

Jane seemed uncharacteristically nervous when we met outside the Tube. She smiled distractedly when I kissed her hello.

'All right?' I asked.

'Hmm? Oh, yes, yes. You look really lovely.' She stared at me.

'So do you!' She was wearing a pastel green summer dress, floaty and romantic, with jewelled flip-flops. She looked more like herself than she had in a long time.

Entering Rea's office, I could see that the TV producer had continued to embrace her inner hoarder. The sample piles were slowly enveloping the office furniture. New additions were heaped on top of old, teetering toward the ceiling. Four other people were already there, trying not to set off any handbag avalanches.

'Jane, Katie,' Rea began. 'I wanted you to meet the style directors who'll be coordinating everyone for the show. Tim Sparks is the creative director for *The Cutting Room* and he'll oversee your hair.'

Tim grasped my hand, enthusiastically kissing both cheeks. 'I can't wait to get my hands into that hair!' he exclaimed, his slender fifty-something frame quivering with excitement. Having not a strand of hair himself, he was free to unleash all his creativity on his clients. 'So rich and thick and dark, fabulicious, you're a dream!' Then he turned to Jane and made the same claim, only substituting blonde for dark. I bet nothing in his life was less than *fabulicious*.

'And this is Mary Weather, makeup artist extraordinaire.' The tiny young woman with thick trendy glasses inspected my face as she shook my hand. I could feel my pores widening under her scrutiny. Her fine light hair was gathered into an artfully messy bun and she didn't even look like she wore makeup. Do unto others what you wouldn't slap on yourself.

'And finally, our head stylists for the programme, Peony and Marigold.' The identical twins stared at each other before grasping our hands to say hello in stereo. If they'd dressed alike I'd have doubted their credentials. But one wore faded jeans with a pale pink vest and strings of long silver necklaces hung with bits of shell and feather. The other looked dainty in a pale grey shirt dress and ankle boots. Something stopped them from being pretty. There was nothing wrong with their features – pale eyes and lashes, pert noses and full lips; as a compilation they just didn't quite work.

'Sit, please, Jane and Katie.' Rea gestured to the only chairs in the room. 'So we wanted to meet today to run through the schedule for taping, answer any questions and resolve any issues. Have you got questions for us?'

Jane said, 'It's lovely to meet you all. Will you be the ones doing the styling, and cutting and makeup, or will it be someone else?'

'I've got a team,' said Tim. I'd bet it was a fabulicious one. 'And since we've got . . . how many?' He turned to Rea. 'Is it fifteen other girls to do, it could be any of us who does your hair. It depends on who's available when you're ready. Why, my darling, do you want me?' He flapped his hands like he'd been nominated for the Golden Scissors award.

'Well, it's just that I'd feel more comfortable knowing who it was so that I knew beforehand how you'd like to cut it. Since it's more permanent than makeup or clothes. Not that it's more important!' she rushed to assure the others.

'I understand, my pet. I'll be there for you, don't worry.' He looked immensely pleased to be so wanted.

Jane smiled gratefully.

'Katie, any questions?'

I shook my head.

'I have a question,' asked one of the botany twins as she stared at me. 'Where's the rest of you?'

The room was silent, except for the sound of the blood rushing to my face.

The other twin picked up her sibling's train of thought. 'It's just that the photos we had to work from showed you much bigger. We've put together an entire wardrobe, accessories, everything, based on those photos and your measurements. Now what are we supposed to do?'

They might try using smaller sizes. For superstar stylists they didn't seem to be very creative thinkers.

Rea intervened. 'I did mention that you shouldn't make any drastic changes, and Peony—'

'Marigold,' said one.

'Sorry, Marigold is right. Have you lost weight?'

'Well, yes,' I said. 'We both have.' Jane shot me a filthy look at being implicated in my transgression. 'But the show isn't about being fat. It's about the transformation that lets us be comfortable with our bodies. Right?'

Rea seemed to consider this. 'Yes . . . yes, of course that's the point. But we signed the contracts based on the bodies we thought we were working with. Now yours has changed. Please don't get me wrong, you look wonderful. But you are different from the concept we first agreed on.'

An uncomfortable silence surrounded us. There was nothing I could say to remedy the situation. Jane too, seemed at a loss. 'So what happens now?' she asked.

'I think I'll have to discuss it with the co-producers, and with Gok. We can talk again in a few days.' Her face was kindly but her voice stern.

'Sure, of course,' I said, standing. I shook everyone's hand, feeling very fabatrocious.

'It's not your fault,' Jane said as soon as we left the building. 'I know you, Katie. Do not blame yourself for this.' She put her arm around my shoulder and pulled me close as we walked toward the Tube. The sky began to spit fat drops, further darkening my mood.

I hadn't reckoned on these consequences of my happy thyroid. 'What if we lose the show, Jane? They could cancel it because I'm not what they want. Then there'll be no publicity for the club, and we won't grow, and you know we can't afford to give Pixie any more hours as it is. How is she supposed to support herself? She'll have to go back to Trevor.' I felt sick thinking that we were so close and I was ruining it for everyone.

'I hope we won't lose the show,' Jane said calmly. 'It's still a great idea, no matter what size you are. You were right in what you said to Rea. The programme is supposed to be about loving the body you've got. Not all of the women who've been on before were overweight. I'm sure that Rea and the team are discussing it right now and coming to the same conclusion. Even those twins will have to see reason. It's not like they can't find different sizes. They were a bit rude, weren't they?'

I laughed. 'It's not their fault. They're named after potted plants. Of course they're angry with the world.'

We hugged good-bye at the Tube, agreeing not to say anything to the others. There was no reason to worry them when everything might turn out fine. Besides, I was quite capable of worrying enough for everyone. I couldn't stop the sick feeling in the pit of my stomach. It felt like a lot of people's futures were sitting heavily in there.

CHAPTER THIRTY-ONE

That night I stepped on the scale in my beautiful bathroom and realised I'd reached my ideal weight for the first time in my adult life. My tummy might have more folds than an origami chicken but I fit into the dresses I liked. I should have felt excitement, elation, pride. But it seemed that stupid quip I'd made all those months ago was true. Being happy with yourself really wasn't simply a matter of pounds and ounces. So as I stood there, I tried to take stock of the things I liked about myself. To my surprise the list kept growing. When I finished my personal inventory my thoughts turned to my life, from big things like my friends and family to the little joys: opening the weekend papers and the takeaway sushi nights Ellie and I liked to indulge in. I thought about how I'd convinced Cressida to let me visit clients and won over Jennie. When I peered at the bathroom's wood floor, which I'd stripped and waxed myself one weekend, I remembered all the other ways I'd made my flat a home. Then I thought about the Curvy Girls Club and my heart swelled. I hadn't even known there was a hole to fill when we first thought of it. It ended up filling a chasm.

And finally I knew for a fact that there was a lot more to Katie Winterbottom than her dress size.

I was buoyant when I met my friends that night. Then talk turned to the Channel 4 meeting.

I was still sure that it was right to keep quiet about Rea's concerns, so gingerly I stepped from the frying pan to the edge of the hob, trying not to burn my toes. I described fabulicious Tim and the flower twins and the makeup artist who didn't practise what she preached.

'So it's all set then?' Ellie asked. She was counting the days till she got to meet Gok. It was to be the pinnacle of her celeb-stalking career so far. Just imagine what half-eaten morsel she'd snatch off his plate to hang on her bedroom wall.

I nodded, unwilling to actually voice a lie.

I could tell by the way Pixie narrowed her eyes that she didn't believe me. 'No problems at all?' she asked. 'They're happy with you and Jane doing the show?'

I couldn't look at Jane. I'd cave in if I did.

'Why wouldn't they be happy with us?' If the worst came to the worst, I'd have to claim the producers changed their minds at the very last minute.

'Well, you're supposed to be a role model for the Curvy Girls Club, right?' She laughed. 'And frankly, love, you haven't got enough rolls.'

I bit my tongue. She wasn't really upset about my weight . . . or not completely because of it anyway. She'd come to dinner straight from another counselling session with Trevor. It had taken him just a few weeks to go from contrite husband to arrogant prick. He probably realised she wasn't coming back, and wanted to punish her for everything that was wrong in his life. Luckily she only had to listen to him for an hour a week in the company of a neutral stranger. And even though she was happy with the children in their new flat, a tiny part of her must have wanted the Trevor she fell in love with to re-emerge from the counselling. After all, as she'd said, he was the father of her children.

So I kept quiet and hoped Rea would see sense.

Smith saw the first line of Alex's email just as I did the next afternoon at work, thanks to Outlook's alerts having absolutely no respect for privacy. It hung there in the corner of my screen for an eternity before fading away. *Hi Katie, I've been thinking about you. Want to get . . .* We sat at my desk in silence, watching the message fade.

'You know you can turn those off,' he finally said. 'In Settings. You just turn off the alerts.'

'Thanks. I'll do that . . .' My upper lip began to sweat. I wanted to push Smith off the chair so I could read the rest of the message. Of all the people to see that email, of course it had to be him, the conniving little fart. 'So, what was I saying?' I asked.

'Hmm, I'm not sure. Maybe you were going to tell me why our finance director is thinking about you?'

'No, I'm sure that wasn't it,' I said, squirming. One comment to Racy Stacy in HR and he could get me fired. Smith suddenly went from annoying to dangerous. 'I think we were going over the client capture system and I was telling you how to enter the notes.'

'Really? I think it was the other thing.'

'Listen, Smith. I'm not having this conversation. My personal life is absolutely none of your business. End of discussion.' I crossed my arms.

'Interesting approach, Katie. I'd probably have made up something about Alex thinking about me in relation to my money-saving idea on the stationery or something. Listen, I'll let you answer your email. Mustn't keep our bosses waiting, right? Thanks for the briefing.'

He swaggered off, probably to bed Stacy and whisper

sweet actionable offences in her ear. Of course I hadn't intimidated him.

As soon as the coast was clear I clicked on Alex's email.

Hi Katie, I've been thinking about you. Want to get together tonight? Sorry for the late notice but I'd love to see you if you're free. Let me know. Alex x

Any night but tonight! I was scheduled to work with Jane. Actually, it was disingenuous to call it work since we were taking everyone to see *The Book of Mormon*. People were auctioning off their infants for those seats. We'd booked tickets months ago. That was a lot of anticipation to give up for a date.

But this was Alex. All the excitement I'd managed to tuck away came tumbling back out when I let myself think about our night together.

This was also Alex, the man who'd literally turned his back on me (I hadn't forgotten that little humiliation). So which Alex was asking me out?

I sat back in my chair to take in the sudden turn of events. What with all the ignoring, you'd think he'd gone off me. Yet maybe that little bit of green that I found stuck between my teeth on our date hadn't been a deal-breaker. Perhaps he hadn't rethought his decision to ask me out when I accidentally snort-laughed on the Tube ride back to his place. And I wasn't so crap in bed that he'd been obliged to pretend the whole night never happened.

I could always ask Ellie to take my place at the theatre. She'd been properly put out when I told her we'd got the tickets. And it wasn't like Jane couldn't handle the event on her own anyway. It had been a bit selfish of me to book two tickets in the first place, considering how expensive they were.

As I stared at his email until the words blurred, I felt there must be a sensible strategy. Make him wait or tell him I wasn't free or something empowering like that. Someone savvier than me would have played it. My hands found the keys before I could think about it too much.

Hey Alex, I'd love to see you tonight. What did you have in mind? K x

I waited all of a hundred and twenty-seven seconds for a response, hardly breathing.

Let's go to my place. A xx

I'd love to. Are you cooking?

Ten long minutes passed before his next email.

I'd have to get some food in. Why don't we meet at our bar for a drink? We can grab a bite from there. Five thirty?

Work didn't even officially end till six. He was that keen.

Ellie wriggled with delight when I offered her my ticket. When she found out why, I almost had to clamp my hand over her mouth to keep her from telling the whole office about my evening plans.

'I'm so excited for you!' she whispered, still loud enough for heads to turn. 'And you look nice.'

'Yes . . .' That was true, at least on the surface. It wasn't my absolutely favourite outfit – I'd have preferred a dress to the black trousers and floaty top – but unless the Sainsbury Local around the corner did a line in sexy frocks, it was the best I would look. Unfortunately there were underlying structural issues. 'I'm wearing a terrible bra,' I confessed. 'It was white till I washed it with my jeans.' I hated that bra. On top of its dinginess, it was a minimiser. Without the sufficiently bounteous goods to subdue, I looked like I was wearing week-old helium balloons on my chest.

She grabbed the top of her blouse and stared down at her own chest. 'Mine's not too bad. It's pink. Do you want to wear it?'

Only a true friend would give you her bra. 'Thanks.' I grabbed her top for a look. 'Actually that matches my knickers a bit better too.'

'Good, because I'm not giving you my knickers.'

Friendship did have its limits.

We hurried to the loos to swap smalls. An old eyeliner was lodged in the pocket of my handbag so I swiped on some navy blue, and possibly a bit of conjunctivitis, and counted the minutes until I could slip out.

He was late. Inside the pub, patrons were even sparser than usual thanks to the sunny day. I didn't order a drink and vowed to stay no more than ten minutes. I did still have some pride, after all.

Assuming he showed up, this would be a momentous event. As I looked back over my romantic résumé I realised I'd never had a second date with a man I really *really* liked. I only put Rory, Rob and Alex in that category. The other men I'd gone out with were only Adequate.

He came through the door a few minutes later, full of smiles and apologies and offers to buy my wine. I told myself I'd definitely left when his time was up. I was very brave in theory.

'So, what have you been up to?' he asked, clinking my glass with his pint. 'Smith seems to be storming along. That's all down to you, I know.'

I blushed at the compliment. 'He's catching on fast.' I didn't mention that today he'd caught on to Alex and me. I hadn't said anything to Cressida about his emails to my clients either. It wasn't a good time to earn a reputation for not playing nicely with the other children. 'I've fixed a meeting with Jenny at the end of the month!' I told him instead.

Of course she claimed to have no recollection of agreeing to a meeting when I first called her. She only agreed when I lost my cool with her again. I worried that I was feeding some weird sado-masochistic fetish she had. If she met me wearing PVC, wanting to be spanked for being a naughty client, I was going to ask for overtime pay.

'I can't believe you've got Jenny to see you,' Alex said,

grinning. I was lost in that smile. 'Will Smith go with you?'
I shook my head. 'Oh. But I thought he was shadowing you
on all your client visits.'

'Is that a problem?'

'No, not at all. Hey, we're not here to talk about work
anyway.' He put his hand on my thigh. 'I want to hear all
about you. I'm really glad to see you. You have no idea how
glad.' He put his hand behind my neck and pulled me to his
lips. I felt a sensual flush course through me. 'You are such
an incredible kisser,' he said. 'So damn sexy. God, you have
no idea what you do to me.'

I glanced at his trousers. Actually I was getting a pretty
good idea. Seeing him so aroused made me weak-kneed, and
also a little powerful. I had the upper hand. I leaned in to
kiss him again, savouring his soft groans. The sound made
my belly clench.

'Let's go,' he whispered.

'I'm not hungry yet.'

'I'm not talking about food. Please. Let's go back to my
place. I have to get you into bed.' As he kissed me again I
gathered that his invitation hadn't been without ulterior
motives. An uncomfortable bit of grit settled into my conscience.
It wasn't too painful but it let me know it was there.

Still, I let him take my hand and lead me from the bar.
My motives weren't completely pure either.

Rush hour gave us a welcome excuse to jam our bodies
together in the packed Tube carriage. 'You'd best hold onto
me,' he murmured. I slid my arms around his waist as he
held the overhead rail with one hand, his other arm snaked
around my shoulders. Standing together like that, with my
breasts against his chest and his rather impressive erection
pushing against my tummy, it was easy to forget about the
commuters who surrounded us. By the time we got to Pimlico
I was nearly an orgasmic puddle.

He led me by the hand up the sisal stairs. 'Let's go to the bedroom,' he said, pushing me against the wall to kiss me. 'I want to be inside you.'

'What about dinner?' I teased.

'Sod dinner. Come on.' He walked down the hall. Then, 'Aren't you coming?'

A flicker of doubt crossed my mind again. I was too turned on to think straight but even so, something about the urgency of Alex's need made me hesitate. What about the romance, the slow seduction? Alex was racing to the finish line when I hadn't yet fired the starter pistol. Should I disqualify him?

He walked back to me and gently stroked my cheek. 'You are beautiful, Katie. I'm sorry, I've been rude. I'm just so turned on around you. But that's no excuse not to be a gentleman. That's what you deserve. Would you like something to drink?' He moved away from me, toward the kitchen. I wanted him close again.

His chivalry melted what little resolve I had. After all, I reasoned, didn't I want this too? 'Actually, I'd like you to take me to the bedroom.'

He smiled, kissed me roughly, and led the way.

We fumbled to strip each other's clothes, messily kissing in that way that's embarrassing in public, but so hot in the lead-up to sex. All decorum went out the window when we got into bed together. He knew exactly what he wanted and wasn't afraid to show me, or tell me. I did the same. It was liberating in every way possible. I wasn't just free from self-consciousness. I was, for those few hours, free from all the feelings that he usually stirred up. I simply enjoyed myself.

We'd barely finished when he pulled me to him again. 'I could fuck you forever,' he said.

'That's some stamina you've got.' The emotions came rushing back in, with hope in the lead.

'It's been a while,' he said. 'I'm so horny for you.' His movements became impatient. 'I'm ready again.'

I wasn't, really. Call me selfish, but I was a one-orgasm kind of girl. Besides, I wanted to cuddle and continue our date. It was still light outside. I laughed. 'You've tired me out!' I gently moved his hand from between my thighs.

'What about my needs?' he asked.

'I think you . . . didn't you just . . .?'

He nodded, grinning. 'And I could do it again. Look what you do to me. Come on.' He dove for my crotch again.

'No, really, I am tired. This was amazing.' He passionately returned my kisses. 'Now I've got an appetite.'

Something didn't feel right.

'Me too!'

'Pssh, not that kind. Should we get something to eat?' I wanted to get out of that bed. It felt too much like I was only there for one reason. I wanted to be there for many reasons.

'Are you serious?' He sat up. 'All right, if that's what you want.' He swung his legs to the floor with his back to me. It seemed more than a physical gesture.

Dressing again wasn't nearly as much fun as undressing had been. We were silent. Guiltily I put Ellie's bra back on. I couldn't shake the feeling I'd done something wrong.

'There's no food in the house,' Alex said, sounding more like my finance director than my lover. 'And I'm not really hungry anyway.' I followed him to the living room where he threw himself on the sofa without inviting me to join him. I became very aware that we were in his territory.

The message was loud and clear. I could have dinner if I wanted, but it wasn't going to be with him. With as much dignity as was humanly possible in the depths of humiliation, I said, 'I'll say good night then. Thanks for a . . . sexy night.' I kissed his lips, grabbed my handbag and fled down those sisal stairs before he could see my tears. Not that he'd have cared.

CHAPTER THIRTY-TWO

Ellie was acting weird when I got home. She didn't even ask how my date went. Ha, some date. That was the euphemism of the year. I was desperate to shower off the whole experience.

'I didn't expect you back this early,' she said from the sofa where she sat in her workout clothes with her bare feet tucked beneath her. The TV was on the twenty-four-hour rolling news with the sound turned down.

'Did something happen that I should know about?' I asked, suspending my urge to clean up to sit beside her.

She glanced up sharply. 'Why do you say that?'

'Just because the news is on. I didn't know if we were at war or something, that's all.'

'Oh, no, no, I don't think so. I wasn't really watching it.'

She didn't ask me where I was going when I got up to shower.

My head was crowded with thoughts of Alex. Unlike the previous six years of Alex-related mind clutter, this was unwelcome. I'd been a grade A, class one fool, thinking someone like Alex could ever want an actual relationship with someone like me. Of course he knew how pathetically desperate I was. It was the worst-kept secret in the western world.

The biggest disappointment about the whole sorry affair wasn't that Alex had obviously used me. It wasn't that, to him, I'd been nothing but a willing woman attached to a vagina. Or even that I'd been so deluded that I'd let him convince me otherwise. It was that, when the optimism ran out, self-loathing rushed in to fill the empty pools. Not strength, or thoughtful understanding or even anger at the man who'd used me. Just my own finger pointing back at me, telling me this was my fault. Despite all the evidence, I was the unworthy one.

It was easy to tell myself not to think that way. After all, I knew perfectly well it wasn't true. Alex had his own issues. He'd been a player for as long as I'd known him. He was the user, and the one who should feel bad. And still I blamed myself while he was probably watching *Celebrity Big Brother* with a beer in his hand and not a single regret in his heart.

I tried not to feel stupid for thinking that I'd been so stupid. Round and round I went as I tried to shower off the humiliation.

'Are you all right?' I asked Ellie when I returned to the living room. 'You seem upset. Is it Thomas?'

She shook her head. 'I have to tell you something, but I don't want to. You're going to be upset.'

I sat beside her. 'You couldn't make me feel any worse. Believe me.'

'Don't bet on that . . . Pixie has called a special meeting. Tomorrow. She wants a vote for Fat Friends.'

That wasn't a surprise. The speed-dating events had all been sell-outs and the survey feedback was generally good.

'You're sweet to worry for me, but I figured it was just a matter of time before she forced a vote. It's okay.'

She clicked off the telly, where images of the Prime Minister flickered. 'That's not the part that's going to upset you,' she said. 'Pixie also suggested that we should consider

251

whether . . . oh, I don't want to say it!' She covered her face with the throw pillow.

'Ellie, come on, don't get yourself worked up. Just tell me. It can't be that bad.'

She peered over the pillow's golden fringe. 'We need to think about whether you present the right image for the Curvy Girls Club any more. Now that you're no longer curvy.'

I was wrong. It was worse.

I went to the meeting the next night with a feeling of dread lodged firmly in my no-longer-curvy gut. At least Jane had made Ellie warn me, so that the coup d'état didn't come as a complete shock. I didn't call Jane. It had been my first instinct, but then I didn't want to put her in an even more uncomfortable situation. I'd argue my case in front of everyone.

She was already at the offices when Ellie and I arrived. 'I brought snacks,' she said, acting like this was just another girls' night out.

'Thanks, but I'm not hungry just now,' I said. I busied myself admiring David's newest furry works of art. Lately he'd gone down the fantastical route, creating the most improbable animals. I quite liked the mouse with sparrow wings, and the sparrow head on a mouse's body even had something interesting about it. But the turtle with a cat's head and feet was just creepy.

Pixie ambled in just as my continuing admiration of hybrid animals started to look conspicuously like avoidance.

'Sorry I'm late,' she said. 'I had to drop the children at home. Trevor's I mean. Everybody good?'

'All right, please stop right there,' I said, catching everyone's attention. 'Ellie told me what this meeting is about, so we can dispense with the chumminess. I'd prefer honesty, if you don't mind.'

All three friends stared at me. Pixie was the first to speak.

252

'Katie, love, what are you on about? There's no reason to get your knickers in a bunch when all we're doing is proposing board business.'

'Whatever,' I said crossly. 'Can we please just start?'

'What are these?' she asked Jane, pointing to the plastic box of baked goods. She was determined to do this on her terms.

'They're . . . whoo, it's hot in here, no?' Jane grabbed a bunch of papers off the desk to fan herself. 'They're choux pastry filled with gorgonzola. I thought it'd be nice to have something other than the usual M&S samosas.'

'Are you all right?' I asked, concerned at her sudden pallor. 'Your lips have gone blue.'

'I'm fine, really. Fine. Pixie's right, we should start before it gets too late. I told Andy I'd be home by nine.'

I hoped Pixie was proud of herself. Forcing this vote was making Jane feel ill.

'Whatever,' I said crossly. 'Can we please just start? Who's taking notes?'

Ellie waved her pen.

'Okay. Any new business?'

'Yes,' said Pixie. 'I'd like us to vote on whether Fat Friends should go ahead. We've had five more speed-dating nights since our last discussion, and they've all sold out. We've cleared over four thousand quid after expenses. They're our most profitable events. And the surveys show that they have a ninety-two per cent approval rating. Seventy-one per cent say they're excellent. We're on to something huge here. I think we should formalise this so we can decide on a strategy.'

'Aren't you worried about the eight per cent who give it a negative rating?' I asked. My objection sounded lame even to me. 'The comments show that it's not good for some of our clients.'

Pixie considered my question. 'You could make the same

253

argument about the tasting dinners we have. We're pushing double cream and butter on the overweight. That could contribute to heart attacks. We can't worry about everything that could be bad for every client. We're not the morality police, love. Besides, the speed-dating nights are our highest-rated events. If we cancelled anything with an eight per cent disapproval rating we wouldn't run any events.'

She waited for me to respond. I couldn't think of an objection to that.

'Does anyone have any other comments?' Pixie asked. Ellie shook her head. 'Then can we please vote? All in favour of Fat Friends becoming an official part of the club?' She raised her hand.

Jane's hand followed Pixie's into the air. 'I can't argue with ninety-two per cent of our members,' she said.

Poor Ellie. Her face was a study in anguish. I knew how much she wanted to be loyal to me. I also knew how she'd vote if emotions weren't part of the equation. She was eminently sensible and always weighed the pros and cons of her actions carefully – except sometimes when they involved her love life.

I put my hand in the air. Did I vote that way to silence my critics? Not really. I had to look at the facts, and they supported Pixie whether I liked it or not.

'Really, Katie?' asked Ellie. I nodded and she gratefully raised her hand.

'Unanimous,' Pixie said with less surprise than I'd hoped.

'I want to register a qualification though,' I said. 'I'm still worried about how these nights might impact our more—' I just stopped myself from saying vulnerable. 'Our less happy clients. Can we make sure we keep using the surveys to check that people aren't being alienated?'

Ellie diligently recorded my words.

'And I have a suggestion,' I continued. 'Can we *please* not call it Fat Friends? I feel very strongly about that. There's got to be a better name. We're clever. I'm sure we can think of something else.'

'Chubby Cherubs?' Pixie asked.

'Very funny.' The tension notably lifted in the room. 'Let's keep thinking.'

That wasn't as bad as I'd feared.

'Er, just one more thing, love. We should talk about your weight loss. Officially.'

So much for the light mood.

For the first time Pixie looked uncomfortable rather than bolshie. 'We started the club as a way to give overweight people a place where they felt comfortable as they are, right? Part of the reason they're happy to be with us is because they're in like-minded company. That's the whole point of the club. *We're* the norm in this world, not the size tens. So I wonder how they feel when you, the president, are now in that other world. You're not really one of us any more. Do you see what I mean?'

And just like that, I was cast back to my schooldays. Her delivery may have been a little less horrible. She didn't call me Cakey Katie, pour salt into my pudding or trip me on the stairs just to see the fat girl wobble. But she might as well have been speaking for the girls who'd taunted me. You're not one of us, and that makes you less than us. No matter what the scales said, I still carried all those extra pounds in inadequacies. Deep down, would I always be Fat Katie, no matter what the mirror showed me? That scared me more than anything.

Ellie looked like she might crawl under the table. Pixie held my gaze. The injustice of her statement washed over me in a bilious wave.

'Pixie, frankly, just . . . Just fuck you. I can't help the way I look, but you're acting like this is my fault.' I could hear my voice shaking. 'This has nothing to do with the amount of food I eat, you know.'

Her expression matched mine. 'So if it was just down to plain old eating, then it would be your fault? Does that mean being fat is our fault then?'

'That's not what I'm saying.'

'Oh, but it's exactly what you're saying. You said that it's not your fault because it has nothing to do with the amount you're eating. That means that if it did have to do with the amount you're eating, it would be your fault.'

'It's a medical condition, Pixie.'

'It's one that you're not getting treatment for! Don't you see that this is your choice? Don't get me wrong. I'd probably do the same thing in your shoes. But the fact is, you're choosing to be the size you are, and now you're different to us. That's all I'm saying. I'm not just trying to make you feel bad, you know.'

Then it was a remarkably lucky strike.

Jane stood up, swaying a little. 'Pixie, you're judging Katie and tearing her down like her weight loss is a personal affront to you.'

'She's right,' said Ellie. 'It's not fair to attack Katie, especially after all the support she's always given you. You're letting your personal feelings cloud your judgement.'

'But I'm not!' Pixie said. 'I seem to be the only one thinking about the club's members instead of our own feelings. I'm sorry but this is an issue and we're going to have to deal with it.'

'There's nothing more to say right now,' I said. 'We've had our vote about Fat Friends. I think we should adjourn this meeting now.'

Suddenly the colour drained from Jane's face. She sat back down, staring at the floor, then started to speak. Only a mangled sound emerged. Then her eyelids started to flutter.

'Jane? Are you all right?'

She didn't respond. Her eyelids were going crazy.

'Jane!'

She began to slip forward. I lunged forward to stop her toppling from the chair. Gently I lowered her to the floor.

'Jane! Jane, can you hear me?' She grunted faintly.

'Has she fainted?' Pixie asked. 'Her eyes are open. She's not epileptic or anything, is she?'

'No,' said Ellie. 'It doesn't look like a seizure. My parents' dog is epileptic. When Spike fits, his arms and legs jerk a lot more and he wets himself. I'm calling 999.'

'I'll get a cold cloth,' said Pixie. 'How long will the ambulance take?'

It seemed like hours, but was probably only a few minutes. We held and rubbed her hands, checking that she was still breathing. Her colour started to come back but she continued to twitch, oblivious to the three terrified women beside her.

When we heard the siren Ellie hurried outside to make sure the ambulance found us. Pixie and I stayed with Jane, gently telling her, and ourselves, that she'd be okay. Two female paramedics hurried in with bags and quickly took our places. All we could do was watch while they worked. They shone lights in her eyes, checked her throat and pulled open her blouse to stick patches to her chest and tummy, connected to a machine. All the while they spoke quietly to each other in acronyms and numbers. They asked us questions about her health and whether she'd had any earlier symptoms. When Ellie mentioned the diet pills, the paramedic swore under her breath. 'Bloody stuff.'

As the other paramedic watched the machine, she said, 'She's in arrhythmia. Tachycardia. Get the gurney, please.'

'What's happening?' Pixie asked. 'Is she going to be all right?'

The paramedic nodded. 'Her heart has gone out of rhythm and it's beating too fast. We'll just need to get her back into a rhythm.'

'She never could dance,' Pixie said. We smiled despite our fears.

Ellie rode in the ambulance with Jane, leaving Pixie and me to hurry to the Tube in silence. What was there to say? Speaking about Jane was too risky. If fate were to be tempted, that'd be just the excuse a bugger like him would look for. And whining because Pixie had said I didn't fit in with the other kids seemed rather petty given the circumstances.

Andy was already with Jane by the time we arrived to the busy A&E. 'What's going on?' I asked Ellie when she rushed to hug us in the waiting room.

'They think her heart is failing,' she cried. 'They've given her drugs to try to get it beating normally again and she's hooked up to a million machines. She looks so vulnerable in there!'

We clung together in the waiting room, attracting furtive glances from the walking wounded waiting to see a doctor. Of course everyone was curious about what the others were in for.

'Should we pray or something?' Ellie suggested. Pixie and I drew back to stare at our friend.

'Aren't you an atheist?' Pixie asked.

'Well yes, but Jane's not. She can't do it with a tube down her throat . . .' Her voice caught. 'And IV drips in her hands.'

I winced at the thought of her in there, surrounded by machines. Even if she wasn't awake she might have been aware that something was very wrong. Tears squeezed from my eyes at the idea that she might be terrified.

So we went to a corner and sat holding hands. 'Do we need to do it out loud?' I asked.

'I shouldn't think so,' Ellie said. 'He's supposed to be all-knowing, right?'

I contemplated what I wanted to say to the Big Man Upstairs. Not being on first-name terms, I felt I should start with an explanation about my lapsed membership status. My parents weren't natural churchgoers, though they did make me do my communion and confirmation. C of E only came up when it appeared on census forms and the like. We were Christians for bureaucratic purposes only.

'Are you done yet?' Pixie asked.

'Not yet,' I said, opening one eye. 'I'm covering all eventualities.'

'I used a blanket fix-what's-wrong prayer,' she said, opening her eye too. We sat there, watching each other from one eye until Ellie was finished. 'Feel better, love?'

She nodded just as a stocky middle-aged Asian doctor approached. 'Are you Jane's friends?' We nodded. At least he hadn't used the past tense. 'Her husband asked me to let you know that we seem to have Jane's heart episode under control. We've given her a medicine called adenosine and luckily it's worked.'

'It doesn't always?' I asked.

He shook his head. 'Sometimes we have to use cardioversion – the paddles you may have seen on TV.'

'Clear!' said Pixie.

'Exactly, yes, although it's not as dramatic as *Holby City* makes it look. The medication seems to have brought Jane's heart back into rhythm. She's resting now, sedated, and we'll keep her in for a day or so to make sure there aren't any more complications.'

'Do you know what caused this?' Ellie asked.

'Not definitively, no. We've run preliminary tests and she'll be under the treatment of a cardiologist who'll do a full assessment. Apparently she was taking diet supplements?' We nodded guiltily on her behalf. 'They can have side effects like this. My advice would be to stay away from them. Often we don't really know what they contain. That makes it very hard to treat when problems arise. She was also getting dangerously low on vitamins and minerals, so we're correcting that with a drip. You can go in to see her for a few minutes, although as I said, we've sedated her, so she won't be awake.'

My heart was in my mouth when we entered the cubicle where Jane lay in a hospital gown. Andy held the hand that wasn't trailing an IV drip. He smiled when he saw us.

'Hey,' he whispered. 'She's out of it, but they say her heart's beating okay again.' He gestured to the machine that blipped a red line across its screen just like in the films. 'Did you know about the pills?'

We nodded.

'Then why the hell didn't you tell me?' he hissed. 'I'd have made her stop them.'

'I'm sorry,' I said. 'We only just found out, and did try to make her stop. We confronted her about it the day we moved Pixie out. She got angry and left. I'm sorry, Andy. We should have talked to you about it.'

He blew out his cheeks, then gazed at his wife. 'I wish she could see herself the way I see her. Is it an illness, do you think? She can't see how beautiful she is. She only sees flaws.'

'I don't know if it's an illness, love,' said Pixie. 'But I do think you can't really understand how an overweight person feels unless you've been there yourself. It's hard to explain properly.'

Ellie spoke up. 'It's like there's a filter over you, and that's what your friends and family see. They're describing what they see through the filter. But you know what's beneath that filter. You can't believe that they won't see you without the filter one day. And then they'll be horrified. At least that's how I feel.'

I rubbed Ellie's arm. 'Can't you learn to like what's beneath the filter?'

'I don't know. I'm trying, I really am. I'm happier now than I was a year ago. The club has a lot to do with that. But sometimes it feels like a losing battle. Just look at Jane.'

CHAPTER THIRTY-THREE

Andy phoned in the morning to say that Jane was awake and feeling suitably stupid for nearly accidently killing herself. A diet aid would never again pass her lips, she promised. Just to be sure, he flushed her stash down the loo when he went home to change, and started looking into some therapy to help her. She wasn't so sure about the therapy but agreed to try.

I decided to go into the offices to clear up from last night. And I finally had something to say to Rob. It was early when I let myself in. The lights were still on from when we'd left with the ambulance. I picked up the scraps of medical packaging left on the floor and put the chairs back where they belonged. When I saw the cheese puffs Jane had made, with yellowing bits of gorgonzola where she'd filled the choux, the tears that had stayed thankfully lodged in their ducts in the heat of the crisis flowed. My friend had almost died last night, and for what? To fit into her old dresses. Anger swept through me. First she'd taken those Alli pills to crap out the calories, and now this. No wonder her body rebelled. What an incredibly stupid risk to take. There was no way that being thin was worth a possible heart attack.

As I sat alone under Pete the bear's watchful gaze I realised something. In a way, Pixie had been right, but for the wrong reasons. I didn't point the finger of blame for a person's size. How could I when I knew from a lifetime's experience just how complex the brain/food relationship really was?

I was simply saying that my overactive thyroid was a fact . . . and yet it *was* a fact that I'd chosen to accept. As much as I wanted to tell myself that I was simply taking the time to consider the options, that that was just responsible healthcare, it wasn't really true. I had the hammering heart and sweating palms to prove otherwise. I'd read the leaflet my GP gave me. My risk of an arrhythmia or heart attack was higher as long as my thyroid was overactive. Sure it was a smaller risk than for someone with heart disease in her family, but it was still a risk. I could spin it any way I liked. Pixie was right. When presented with the options, I'd chosen my figure.

Finally, I knew what I wanted to say to Rob.

He let himself in a few minutes after I'd cleaned up. 'Sorry, I didn't get an extra coffee,' he said. 'I didn't expect to see you here.'

I examined his statement like tea leaves, looking for their meaning. 'That's okay. I've got a cup here. Listen, something happened last night. Sit down.' We sat on opposite sides of his desk with the mouse menagerie between us. I told him about Jane, starting with the punch line – that she was okay.

'Those fucking pills!' he said, standing up to pace between his desk and Pete the bear. 'Why do people do this to themselves? And Jane is a smart woman. She had to know the risks.' He shook his head. 'You're sure she's okay? No long-term damage or anything?'

'The doctor says no. She's lucky. And she won't be taking any more diet pills.'

'What about you?'

'That's what I wanted to tell you. I'm going to make an appointment with the GP and get the treatment started.'

'Soon?'

'Yes, as soon as I can get an appointment. I'm sorry I've been such a bloody-minded arse lately.' A wave of sadness enveloped me. 'I haven't treated friends like you very well. I've been so wrapped up in my own crap, but that's no excuse for being a dick. Can you forgive me?'

'Come here.'

A hug never looked so inviting. When I slumped against his chest, sniffing his lemony aftershave, the floodgates opened. 'I'm sorry,' I sniffled. 'For everything. I'm not sure where we went wrong but I want to get back to the way we were.'

But that wouldn't be possible. At least, it wouldn't be possible to get back to the relationship I wanted.

'But we are friends like we were,' Rob said, missing the point. 'We've always been friends. You don't have to worry about that.' When he hugged me again I thought I felt something overly friendly. But I must have been mistaken.

'You wouldn't believe what an idiot this friend has been lately,' I murmured into his chest. I'd have given anything to know I'd always be welcome there.

'I'd probably believe it. I've known you for a while, remember?' He smiled, pulling away to look at me. Moment over. 'Are you talking about your colleague?' His jaw clenched.

'Amongst other things. I've been such a fool. You know how I've felt about Alex for ages. God, I blathered on enough about it. It always seemed like a completely unrealistic dream. And then . . . he started paying attention to me, and then we went out for drinks and one thing led to another. I saw a side of him I didn't expect, beyond the dreamworld Alex. He showed me a real sensitive side.' I hesitated, wondering if I should disclose something so personal about him. Then

263

I remembered how much loyalty he'd shown me. 'He had a sister who died on his birthday. The whole family was out together so that he could ride his new bike. They were playing I Spy, and she was hit by a train right in front of him. When he told me that, it struck a chord. And . . . well, I'll spare you all the gory details. But then he completely ignored me afterward.'

Rob's brow furrowed. 'She was hit by a train playing I Spy? He told you that?'

'I know.' I shook my head. 'I didn't expect anything that personal. But he seemed to feel close enough to me to say it. I was flattered. But then, as I said, he ignored me.'

'Boy, girl, mum, dad, on their bikes?'

'Yes, Rob. What's got into you?'

He rubbed his face. 'Oh Katie.' He quickly typed something into his computer. 'Come here. Look.'

In the video, a happy family of four pedalled along wooded tracks and over fields, pollen floating around them in the sunshine. The boy says, 'I spy with my little eye, something beginning with T.' Tractor, tree, train, teddy. No, no, no, no. The sister stops and says, 'Is it a track?' Train whistle, whoosh, fade to black.

'It was a Network Rail advert? I don't believe it!'

What kind of person makes up a dead sister? Maybe she wasn't even made up. For all I knew they had dinner together every week. She might have been the one who'd decorated his flat. I knew it was way too stylish for a man.

'That fucking lying wanker.'

'Katie, I've never heard you use such language.'

'I'm sorry but he deserves it. He used that story just to get me into bed.'

Rob winced. 'I suppose it's possible his father was the exec who came up with the advert from first-hand experience.'

'His father's a GP.'

'So you think. Sorry, that was insensitive. This guy's an arsehole. But anyone can be fooled once.'

My guilty face told him that wasn't the end of the story. I told him the rest as he slowly sipped his cooling coffee. He didn't interrupt.

'For a while I forgot that I was just Fat Katie,' I finished. 'It was kind of nice.'

'You're not just Fat Katie!' he said. 'Don't ever talk about yourself like that. Please. I'm sorry it didn't work out with Alex, if that's what you wanted. But you are not just Fat Katie. You're, well you're quite wonderful, actually. Any man should be over the moon to go out with you.'

I smiled my gratitude. Unfortunately Rob wasn't any man.

CHAPTER THIRTY-FOUR

The GP was able to fit me in on Monday morning. When I admitted he'd been right about needing treatment he was just the tiniest bit gloaty, but I suppose he needed to get his job satisfaction from somewhere. He gave me a prescription for something called Carbimazole, which he promised had nothing to do with carbs. Carbs or no carbs, in a couple of months I'd be back to my old self.

As I sat on the post-rush-hour Tube I tried to think about the bright side. It would be nice not to have my heart clattering in my chest like marbles going down the stairs. And I could stop wearing sweat-guards-cum-panty liners under my arms. It might take a month or two for the medicine to gradually start working, the doctor said, so at least my arse wouldn't balloon overnight.

I popped my head into Cressida's office when I got in. 'Hi there,' I said, standing in the doorway. Her expression froze when she saw me. 'Just to let you know, I'm back from my doctor's appointment. I'll have to go again in a few weeks to check the medication's working. But I can book the last appointment of the day so I shouldn't have to take much time off.'

'Oh, sure, okay, erm, yes fine. Excuse me, will you? I've got to run to a meeting.'

She must have been very late, and even more distracted than usual, because she didn't even have time to grab her BlackBerry off the desk.

Three meeting requests popped up when I turned on my computer. Clive wanted to see me. I seethed to think about how I'd helped Alex out of that vision board fix. Though I suppose that if the board bod wanted to meet me, I was at least getting some credit.

I'd already missed two of the proposed meetings. What a stellar show of company commitment, sure to impress him. He kept cancelling them and rescheduling at fifteen-minute intervals. I prepared my apology for making him wait.

When I walked past Alex's office on the way to the big conference room I gave him a shoulder cold enough to chill his beer on, and when I was sure he couldn't see me, the stink eye for good measure.

To my surprise, Clive wasn't alone in the conference room. 'Hi, Katie, thanks for coming. This is—'

'Stacy, yes I know. Hi Stacy.' Racy Stacy always managed to slink around the men in power so I shouldn't have been surprised to see her involved in the vision boards too. I'd bet her board was pasted with the Kama Sutra and 'after' photos of Katie Price.

'Hi, Katie, thanks for coming. Clive asked me to be here today because we're making some changes. He'll explain everything.'

I knew something was wrong by the way Clive cleared his throat.

'As you know, Katie, the company has been in some difficulty, and we've looked at ways to raise our revenue. Initiatives like the Try Before You Buy trials were very well-received. But we also had to look at our costs.' He kept looking at his notebook as he spoke and I realised he was reading a speech. 'After careful consideration we've decided that we'd be more effective as a smaller organisation. We're making several changes to the back office operations as well as some cost savings by combining office space where we have spare capacity.'

I really hoped this was about moving desks.

'But we've also had to look at some changes to the client-facing side and, unfortunately, that means a reduction in the workforce. We've asked for voluntary redundancies to minimise the disruption for people, and a number of staff have taken advantage of that. But it isn't enough.' He checked his notes. 'I'm afraid.'

Every last word was scripted, just like our sales pitches. Insert disbelieving laugh here.

Stacy slid a slender letter-headed envelope toward me. Those were the fancy envelopes that only got used in special circumstances. Despite the gravity of the situation I felt a stab of pride that my redundancy was deemed worthy of good stationery.

'This is your notice letter, explaining your termination date and redundancy package. Because of your years with us, you're eligible for several weeks!' She made this sound like I'd won the lottery. My hands shook as I opened the letter. Effective today, I was no longer employed by Nutritious, PLC. In appreciation for my years of service I was eligible for six weeks' pay.

'Only six weeks?' My bank was not going to be impressed with that.

'Plus the month of your notice period,' Stacy said. 'We don't expect you to work those four weeks so it's really like nearly three months' free money.'

'Why me?' I whispered to Clive.

He had the good grace to look uncomfortable as Stacy

answered for him. 'We had to assess each employee and unfortunately there were others with better performances.'

'It's because I was Needs Improvement in my last appraisal?'

'We assessed a number of factors. Your time with the company counted in your favour, for example.' She smiled sweetly through her lilo lips.

That was like being told you were the least ugly minger in the room.

'So what happens now, after this meeting?'

Stacy seemed relieved that I wasn't putting up a fight. I wondered if any of my colleagues would have to be carried out by security today.

'To minimise disruption on the floor, we suggest you go home after the meeting. We can arrange for your personal belongings to be brought round to you.'

I thought about that for a minute. Six years with a company and I wouldn't even get the chance to say good-bye to my colleagues. No leaving drinks, or good luck cake or forwarding email addresses. Just my belongings turning up in a box at my front door.

'Okay. You've already decided, so there's nothing I can do about that. There's just one person I need to talk to before I go.' I stood on shaking legs before I lost my nerve, and left the room. I was sure the floods would come later. Just then, shock and anger were running my machinery.

Alex was at his desk. I knocked on the side of the door before stomping in.

'You've just had the meeting?' he said.

So he wasn't going to feign ignorance. He looked haggard, I noticed. Despite knowing he was a complete dog turd, a little part of me – Hopeful Katie – wondered if it was because he was concerned about me.

'I'm leaving in a minute, but I wanted to ask you something first.' I paused, just in case he had any plans to try to make me feel better. He snapped his pen open and closed. Click-click, click-click, click-click. 'Did you know about the redundancies before we went out last time?'

His look could have given a polar bear frostbite. 'I'm the finance director. I signed the papers.'

My face burned and my voice rose. 'Before we went out, or after?'

'Katie, do you take me for a fool? You threw yourself at me. Of course I got in there one more time.' He shrugged. 'Come on, don't take it so hard. We both know you wanted it. Think of it as fulfilling your last wish. It's no big deal.' He glanced over my shoulder at the door, where Stacy stood.

'All right, I'm leaving,' I said to her. Then to him: 'You're a callous toadstool of a man.'

'Whatever makes you feel better. Drinks later, Stacy?' He winked at me. 'See you round, Katie. Sorry about the job.'

In a daze I stumbled to Ellie's desk. 'I've just been fired. I'm going home.'

'You've what?! I'm coming too.' She grabbed her bag, hooked her arm in mine and led me out of my office for the last time.

In the space of one Tube ride, the impact of what had happened hit home. People who've never been made redundant might envisage what it's like. They can imagine the sudden realisation that the income they rely on will stop, and the panic that sets in about trying to find another job. They've felt the universal reluctance that comes with having to update CVs and scrutinise job sites. All the what-ifs and worst-case scenarios play in their minds. But they can't know the overwhelming embarrassment of losing one's job. I felt physically ill every time I thought of my colleagues knowing I'd been made redundant. In fact, I only had to picture someone in the office and the humiliation welled up. They'd think I wasn't as good as they were. Would they remember some slip in performance and say, 'Well, I'm not really surprised'? I was the one chosen to go, not them. Eeenie, meenie, miney moe, catch a slacker by the toe.

'Do you want to get a drink?' Ellie asked as we let ourselves into the flat. 'It's nearly eleven.'

'What the hell, let's go to the pub. Do you mind?'

She dropped her laptop bag in the hall. 'Let's go.'

We were, understandably, nearly alone at our local. I ordered a bottle of wine but Ellie wouldn't let me pay for it. Already we were making allowances.

'Tell me everything,' she said as she poured generous glasses.

First I had to fill her in on recent bedroom events with he-of-the-incredible-shrinking-morality.

'Remember last week when I came home from seeing Alex? Well, I didn't come home early because nothing happened . . . we slept together again. I didn't tell you because I felt so stupid. I'm just sorry your bra had to be involved.' Now even my humiliation was humiliated.

'It's all right. It's probably not permanently traumatised . . . I wish you'd told me last week instead of keeping it all inside.'

'I just wanted to forget about it. And I didn't think it mattered, beyond my shattered self-esteem. But then this, today.'

'Do you think they're related?'

'They're definitely related. I got it straight from the jack-ass's mouth. Alex signed off on my redundancy . . . before we slept together. He knew they were going to make me redundant and wanted to get his end away one more time before the easy sex dried up. And I was stupid enough to let him.'

'You weren't stupid, Katie. You liked him. You did what any of us would. You trusted him.'

More fool me. Now I was screwed, in every sense of the word.

'What'll I do? I'll lose the flat if I don't find another job soon. I haven't got the savings to cover the mortgage for more than a month or two. I'll have to go live in my parents' spare room.' At the very idea the floods finally came. The bartender glanced at us. A lifetime of drunks had probably taught him not to get involved unless his personal property was involved.

'Have you thought about making a case for constructive dismissal? This sounds like it should be illegal. If Alex made you redundant because of the sex—'

That made me feel terrific. 'My sexual techniques are a fireable offence? Bit harsh, don't you think?'

She laughed. 'Maybe you didn't suck as much as you think you did. Ba dum bum. I mean that if he used you and then got rid of you, which he was able to do because of his position, then that might be illegal. Maybe you should talk to a solicitor about it. If there's a case, you could get your job back . . . Don't wrinkle your nose. You've got to be practical. You do like your job, and you're good at it. I bet lots of the employees have had at least one bad review. I think you've got a right to find out.'

My head told me she was right but my gut rebelled at the very idea. I'd probably feel differently if I were a man. They didn't usually get pinned with the Whinger label. I didn't want to be one of *those* women who sue their employers.

Then again, I didn't want to be one of those women who had no job, either.

'I'll think about it,' I said as Ellie went to the loo.

She called Thomas in the afternoon to find out if anyone else faced the axe. I felt slightly less conspicuous knowing four more heads had rolled – three boys and a girl and all senior staff like me. Thomas said everyone was jumpy by lunchtime as news filtered through the office, and that the bosses had called a meeting when it was over to congratulate the Chosen Ones who'd kept their jobs. That left everyone counting fingers and toes, and the minutes till they could get to the pub for a good old gossip.

'I really don't want to talk to a solicitor,' I told Ellie as we staggered back to the flat around dinnertime. 'The way I see it,' albeit blurrily at that point, 'I've got the club and we're expanding. Once the show airs we'll need the extra staff to run the thing. I'll call Jane and Pixie tonight and call an extraordinary meeting to ask for more hours. I only need three days a week, like I had with Nutritious, to cover my mortgage and expenses. Money'll be tight but it'll work for now.'

I was very pleased that so much alcohol had produced this elegant solution. Door closing, window opening and all that, I thought blearily. Everything would be fine.

CHAPTER THIRTY-FIVE

I woke the next morning with mood swings that made Naomi Campbell look like she just suffered a bit from PMT. One minute I convinced myself that redundancy was an opportunity. The Curvy Girls Club was my future, not nutritional supplements. Now I might have the chance to pursue that. Hurrah, elation! The next minute I saw looming mortgage payments carving great chunks out of my dwindling bank balance. Boo, paralysing fear and dejection.

Ellie reported back on events at the office. Jim, another of the Redundant Five, hadn't gone as quietly as hoped. He took the opportunity before they shut off his email to tell the company about every Christmas party snog, printer room grope and illicit affair he'd heard about in his six years with the company. Ellie forwarded me the email. It read like the Who's Who of shagging.

She also had it from Thomas that Smith took over all of my accounts with immediate effect. My days had been numbered from the time he started and Alex's *buddy* system had just been another cynical move. I'd trained my own replacement.

Naturally I spent most of the week wishing grievous bodily

harm on Alex and co but since I was a decent multi-tasker that still left a lot of time in the day to fill. No wonder bored housewives had affairs with their gardeners. It beat watching daytime telly.

By the time the club meeting came around on Thursday I'd cleaned under the sofa, the beds and inside the fridge, checked every tin, package and condiment for their expiration dates and ironed all my tee shirts (and Ellie's). I was contemplating alphabetising the spices. Much as I dreaded seeing Pixie again, I had to get out of the flat.

She and Rob were just finishing up when I got to the offices. A jealous jolt went through me as I watched them working companionably with their heads together.

'We're just agreeing on venues for the next speed-dating nights,' Pixie said. 'And looking at possibilities for a website. How are you, love? Did you have a relaxing day?'

We were technically on speaking terms again. She'd rung the day after our argument to apologise for making me feel bad, so I was trying to put my feelings aside for the good of the club, as she'd claimed to be doing. But if she thought she could bully me again she'd better think twice.

'I made snacks for tonight.' I showed her the turkey sausage rolls and cookies.

'Those look delicious. Give one here.'

'That's right, today's a day off for you, isn't it?' Rob said as he continued slamming away at the keyboard in fits and starts. He approached typing like a starving man assaulted a sandwich.

'Yes. Today and every day from now on.' I took a deep breath as the shame of saying it out loud hit me again. 'I was made redundant from Nutritious on Monday.'

Rob did a double-take. His clattering fingers stopped. 'Katie! I'm really sorry to hear that. Was it expected?'

'Not at all. The company made cuts. Five of us got the

chop. They called me into a conference room and handed me a termination letter. I think I'm still in shock.'

'I don't blame you,' he said. 'That's really troubling.'

Pixie didn't think anything of his comment but I knew he was talking about Alex.

'I know. I'm . . . weighing my options.'

'All right,' Pixie said. 'We're done here. Rob, take a sausage roll and get out. We've got club business to take care of tonight.'

'The convening of the Coven,' he said, grabbing a couple of rolls. Then he tipped a handful of cookies into his courier bag. 'I'll see you tomorrow, Katie.'

Ellie passed Rob on the way out, kissing him happily. She looked more excited than when we discovered that angel food cake had no fat.

'You'll never guess what happened today!' She wriggled, making shaky maraca hands.

'Alex's penis fell off in the kitchen and was trod on by Cressida?'

'Almost as good.' She beamed. 'Clive is having a thing with Racy Stacy.'

I didn't want to steal Ellie's thunder but, 'We knew that from Jim's email,' I reminded her.

'That's true. But apparently his wife didn't . . . at least not until Jim sent the email to her.' She was so excited I worried she'd leave a puddle on the floor. 'Apparently she's some bigwig in the City,' she continued. 'He found her email online and broke the bad news. Then, would you believe it? She came to the office looking for Clive. And Stacy. She stormed straight into the middle of the management meeting waving the email printout and asking Clive if it was true. Jim named dates and places and everything. When Clive denied it she punched him in the nose! I felt kind of bad for the little guy.'

Only Ellie would feel bad for a philanderer who got caught.

'Did she find Stacy?'

'No, someone tipped her off and she got away. And then when it was all over, Clive said, calm as you like, "I assume the last few minutes are not on the record." As if I'd need to write something like that down. I'll never forget it!'

It was a story to cheer my heart. I'd love to see Racy Stacy exposed for the Page Three model employee that she was. And so much the better if her lovers were outed in a Nutritious sting operation.

'How was your day?' Ellie asked me.

I gestured to the rolls and cookies.

'Very productive, I see. Did you update your CV or look on that website I wrote down?'

I mumbled something lame. I didn't have much time before my redundancy money ran out.

Ellie sighed. 'You have to do it this weekend. Tell her, Jane,' she said as Jane came in and threw herself into one of the chairs. 'Katie needs to get her CV out there. It takes time to find another job . . . Jane, is everything okay? Are you feeling ill?' She'd only been out of hospital for a week.

She shook her head. 'I feel fine, thanks. Rea from Channel 4 phoned just now.'

Ellie and Pixie made excited noises while I tried not to show my panic. Jane took out her knitting. She tore through yarn like highly strung actors popped Xanax. 'There's no easy way to say this, and I'm so sorry, Katie, but they don't feel you're right for the show.'

There it was, on the table for everyone to see.

'What do you mean?' Ellie asked. 'What's happened?'

'Katie's shrunk, that's what's happened,' Pixie said. 'That's it, isn't it? Your size is costing us our publicity.'

So much for our uneasy truce.

'What happens now, Jane? Are they cancelling the show?' Mentally, I begged her to say no.

But she nodded. 'If Gok hasn't got someone that fits their concept to make over on camera, there's no show.'

'Now what are we going to do?' Pixie demanded. 'Without the publicity we won't grow like we need to. This is a huge missed opportunity.' She glowered at me. Jane and Ellie looked more sympathetic.

I was surplus to requirement all over the place. Nutritious didn't want me. Gok didn't want me. Not even Alex the bastard wanted me. Though ironically, the problem wasn't really that I was surplus when it came to the show. The problem was that there wasn't enough of me.

'Is there any way to convince them to go ahead with the show?' I asked. Desperate Katie.

'I'm sorry, sweetheart. They're saying that because we signed contracts based on certain things—'

'My measurements, you mean.'

She nodded. 'They don't want to change the focus of the show. It's due to start recording in three weeks.'

'Do they still want you?' It hurt me to ask this question. She nodded. 'Then we've got to do something. The show can still go ahead. We just need Pixie or Ellie to do it.'

'Oh no,' said Pixie. 'No bloomin' way! You were the one who agreed to get your arse out for the nation.'

'But they don't want me, Pixie. That means someone else has to do it or we lose the chance. I'm sorry. I'd do it if I could. They've made it clear they don't want me.'

'You know, Katie, I could kill you for putting us in this position!' she cried. 'This was your responsibility, not ours. Now you're trying to make us feel like we're letting everyone down by not doing it. It's emotional blackmail. Friendship aside, from a business point of view, you're a real bitch for doing it.'

I winced. 'I don't think calling me a bitch is very business-like. *Friendship aside*, call me what you like; this is the situation we're in. Instead of cutting off your nose to spite your face, you might try thinking about what's best for everyone. I was willing to do it when we proposed the idea. Jane was willing to do it. You're the one being selfish, Pixie, not me.'

'Please,' Jane implored. 'Can we all calm down?'

Ellie mumbled something that got lost in the uproar.

'I'm selfish?!' Pixie said. 'I'm not the one who's been prancing around here with her new body and not a thought for what it means to the club.'

'That's not fair and you know it!' Jane shouted over the top of Pixie. 'Katie hasn't done anything on purpose. You're the one being the bitch here, not her. We all need to calm—'

'I said I could do it,' Ellie said more loudly. 'Will you please stop fighting if I do it?' I caught a glimpse into Ellie's childhood then. Her parents divorced when she went to secondary school. We'd probably just dredged up a few extra reasons to think about therapy.

'Really, sweetheart?' Jane asked. 'Are you positive you want to?'

'No, I'm not positive and I definitely don't want to. But I will if it means they'll go ahead with the show. Pixie is right. You two came up with an amazing idea. We can't let it slip away.'

'Do you want to talk to Thomas about it first?' Pixie asked. Her arms were still crossed, but her voice softened for Ellie.

'Why? It's my body, isn't it? I'm the one who gets to decide what happens to it. I'll do it,' she said with more conviction. 'Do you think they'd substitute me for Katie?'

Jane smiled. 'I'm sure they will – you'll be gorgeous on the show. Thank you. I've made myself sick thinking about telling you all afternoon. I'll call Rea first thing tomorrow. I'm sure they'll be happy with our solution. Now come on, we need a group hug. Katie, Pixie, please kiss and make up.

Things get said in the heat of the moment that we don't mean.'

She glared at me. I stared back.

'Sorry,' she mumbled as if she'd been caught stealing my ice lolly. She didn't look a bit sorry. 'We do still need to talk about this in the wider context though.'

'Why won't you let it drop, Pixie?' Ellie asked. 'Really, it's like you're out to get Katie. We're just here to decide whether we can afford to give her more hours.'

'But we also have to put that into context, love. I'm sorry if I'm the only one around here who's thinking of the club.'

'God, will you shut up with that?!' I said. 'You act like you're single-handedly running the thing. Up until a month ago it was me who booked all the events, and worked with Rob on the website, and worked with Jane on the Channel 4 opportunity . . . this club means everything to me. Implying that I don't care is just shitty. Wrong and shitty.'

'Fine, then if you've got its best interest in mind let's continue with the meeting.' Her voice was calm, friendly even. You'd never know she was instigating a rebellion. 'Ellie, you've got the notes from last time. Can you remind us where we left off?'

Ellie looked uncomfortable as she flipped through her pages. 'Pixie, you said that we started the club to give overweight people somewhere that's comfortable. We're in like-minded company . . . Then you asked how they feel seeing Katie, who's . . .' Her eyes darted to mine.

'It's okay, Ellie, I remember what she said. Go ahead.'

'You wondered how they feel to see Katie thin when she's supposed to be representing them. You said she's not one of us any more . . . for the record, I disagree with that. Katie will always be one of us, no matter what she looks like. She's our friend.'

'I know she is,' Pixie said. 'But we can't let our friendship

280

get in the way of what's best for the club. We're running a business. So we have to think about how we represent the Curvy Girls Club. That's all I've ever been saying. And given that even Channel 4 has now said she's not the right role model for us, I think we've got to talk honestly about that.'

'They didn't say that!' Jane said. 'They said she's not right for the programme. They didn't say anything about the club.'

Pixie considered this. 'But why isn't she right for the programme? Because they thought they were getting an over-weight woman to make over, and instead they've got a thin one. It doesn't fit with what they're trying to do on that programme. This is a segment for Love Your Body month. They want someone with enough body to love, to represent normal women in the UK. It's called *The Great British Makeover*, remember? Katie is meant to be representative of British women. Only she's not. And she's also not a repre-sentative for our members any more.'

I fought my instinct, which was to shout in her face. Gathering the kind of resolve that would have made Margaret Thatcher look like the Aluminium Lady, I said, 'I understand why Rea doesn't want me on the programme. But I don't think the same logic applies to the club. I'm not the president because of my size. I'm the president because I helped build it from nothing and, I think, because I've done a good job. My performance isn't dependent on my weight here any more than it is in the other parts of my life.'

'No,' Pixie said. 'And I'm not calling into question your ability to book the events. But as president, you represent the club, so in that role, how you look to our members does matter.' She sighed, as if considering something very important. 'I think we need to put friendship aside and be honest about whether Katie is the right person to be heading the Curvy Girls Club.'

'But Katie's right,' Ellie said. 'Her ability has nothing to do with her waistline. You're not being fair.'

'But I'm trying to be completely fair,' Pixie said smoothly. 'You're not listening to me. I haven't questioned her role as an employee. I'm asking what kind of image we're portraying with Katie at the head? You wouldn't have someone who looks totally unfit running a gym, would you? There's a reason everyone who works in those places looks like a gym bunny. Would anyone trust a breastfeeding or childbirth course run by a man? Probably not. A thin woman running a social club that's supposed to make fat people feel comfortable about themselves doesn't make sense either. You've got to put your feelings aside. If I'm wrong, then tell me why, logically.'

To my dismay, Jane and Ellie were silent. And actually, even I was having a hard time putting my finger on where her argument logically fell down. I could argue that she shouldn't be doing this after I'd supported her for so many years (emotional argument). I could say again that my ability to book events wasn't dependent on my weight (she hadn't said it was). But my job as president *was* to be the club's representative. And there was no getting around the fact that as far as the Curvy Girls Club was concerned, I no longer fit in.

'Is this how you all feel?'

There were tears in Jane's eyes. 'I can't think of a reason to argue against her. Except that we're friends and it's not fair.'

'Fair to whom?' Pixie asked. 'It's our job to do what's best for the club. If having the wrong image will stop people from joining then we need to address that.'

'Is there any evidence that this is the case?' Ellie asked. 'Because we can go on pure conjecture, but unless there's evidence that Katie is putting people off – sorry, Katie, you know what I mean – then I won't vote to remove her.'

I felt such love for my best friend in that moment that the sick feeling in my tummy subsided.

But Pixie was prepared. She pulled a small pile of papers from her desk drawer. 'These are some of the comments the clients have put on the speed-dating surveys.' She began reading from the sheets. '"Easy for people like Katie, but not for the rest of us."'

'Let me see that,' I said, snatching the paper. 'This doesn't prove anything. This comment could have been about anything, not just my weight.'

'And this,' she continued. '"Katie is looking great – are we still the *Curvy* Girls Club?" Or: "Great night but I'm a bit confused. Why is a thin person hosting an event for us?"'

Now Ellie looked as despondent as I felt. I was losing everything.

'Go ahead, then,' I said. 'You need to vote based on the evidence.'

'Do you want to say anything else?' Pixie asked.

I shook my head, watching the meeting as if I wasn't part of it. And in a way, I wasn't. Since the vote was directly about me, our club rules meant that I had to abstain anyway.

Pixie's hand went up, as I knew it would.

'I'm so sorry,' Ellie said, slowly raising her hand. Jane didn't need to raise hers.

So that was it. I was no longer president of the club I'd founded. Nearly a bloodless coup. Just a lot of internal bleeding.

'Who will be president then?' I asked.

'I guess we'll need to decide,' Jane said. 'But we don't have to do it now, do we? I'd rather not make any more major decisions tonight.'

Ellie caught my eye. 'We do have one more vote to take though,' Ellie reminded us. 'Katie wants more hours. That's still possible, right, now that she's . . . that her role has changed?'

'Anything's possible,' Pixie said. 'But we've got limited funds, as we know. Katie? Why do you want the extra hours?'

'You know why I want them, Pixie. I've lost my job and I need to pay my mortgage. Now that we're growing the dating business, I can work with Rob to create the website, and run all the extra events.' My heart pounded in my throat. Suddenly my simple solution didn't seem so simple. 'I need another two days a week, minimum.'

'Well, as it happens,' Pixie said. 'So do I. It looks like we're after the same thing.'

'You don't need those hours, Pixie. I know for a fact that Trevor is paying maintenance for you and the children. You might want them, but you don't need them.'

She ignored me. 'We need to look at who's better qualified to work for Fat Friends. Me, who proposed the idea to begin with and has championed it every step of the way? Or Katie, who did everything she could to stop it from happening? Who do you think, logically, would make a better representative for our new business venture?'

Subtly she gestured at her own belly, as if to declare: *Behold! I am wide of girth and fit to lead you.*

'Not again!' said Jane. 'I don't want to be caught between you two. I feel like we're taking sides personally, and I resent it. What has got into you lately? You've been on opposite sides for months now.'

I had my theories but wasn't about to accuse Pixie of being thinnist. There was a time and place for that. Tonight we had club business to get through.

'I'm sorry, Jane,' I said. 'But we are going to have to vote, because I need an answer.'

She nodded. 'You're right. Of course.'

I steeled myself for my last effort. 'You all know how devoted to the club I am, and have always been. You know how I've run it as president and I hope you know what a good job I can do with the dating business. Just because I didn't support it initially doesn't mean that I don't support it now. I voted for it too, remember? Pixie did a lot of work to persuade me that it was a good idea. So . . . vote for me.' I made a cheesy victory sign.

Pixie spoke up. 'Well, given that we've already established that Katie doesn't portray the right image for the club, I don't see how we can then turn around and say she's the right representative for its dating business. Okay, maybe she could help develop the website but we need someone who can also do the publicity and attend the events. Again, this isn't personal. It's a business and we've got to think about what the clients want. All the comments I read before came from speed-dating clients. Those were their words, not mine.'

I knew she'd go for the smear campaign.

'So,' I said. 'Your whole pitch is based on the fact that your waistline is bigger than mine?'

'No, Katie. First of all, it's based on the fact that I've done a good job for the club these past months. Are you implying that I haven't? That I'm only here as a fat charity case?'

'That's not what I'm saying.' The bullies in school used the same tactics, taunting me until I defended myself and then using my words against me.

'Good. Then you agree that I've done a good job. I'm also the one with the experience when it comes to the dating side. I've set it up, remember? Rob and I worked together on the flyers and other promotions. I'm also saying that I can be at the front of the business as a fitting representative.'

I couldn't argue with her experience. What did I bring to the dating side of the business? A six-year crush that ended in humiliation and a steadfast objection to Fat Friends. *I* wouldn't hire me.

So I wasn't surprised when Jane and Ellie had to vote in Pixie's favour. They had no choice based on the hard evidence, but they must have felt like jurors unable to convict a guilty man because of a technicality.

There wasn't much left to say after the vote, and nobody felt like eating turkey sausage rolls or cookies together. Ellie asked if I wanted her to come home with me but I waved her off to Thomas's. I wanted to be alone to lick my wounds.

CHAPTER THIRTY-SIX

I didn't feel much better the next morning as I stomped through horizontal rain on the way to the club's offices to work my paltry one day a week. Sleep hadn't put everything into proportion, or showed me that it was all for the best. It just stirred a big helping of pissed-off into my insomnia.

Who gets fired twice in a week? Sixteen-year-old slackers who steal from the till, maybe, or stoners caught sparking up in the storeroom. Not responsible adults who've worked years in their job and happen to be pretty damn good at it.

I pushed open the café door, pleased by the humid wall of heat that greeted me.

'Two cappuccinos to take away, please,' I said to the harried young waitress when the customers in front of me finished placing their order. Rob was always buying me coffee. Jobless or not, it was about time I repaid the favour.

'What are you doing here?' Rob said as he blew through the café door in a gust of windy rain. He looked like he'd swum over.

'Buying our coffees,' I said, holding up the small Styrofoam cups. I liked that our café hadn't gone over to paper cups. They reminded me of the Welcome Breaks Dad always

287

stopped at when we drove out to Cornwall to visit his sister in the school holidays. I still liked to leave teeth marks in the edge of the cup.

'Are you morally opposed to an umbrella?' I asked as we made our way to the offices. 'Or didn't you notice the hurricane when you left this morning?'

'This? This isn't rain. It's a fine mist at best.' His face began to drip.

'Here,' I said, trying to hold the umbrella over him. The wind whipped the canopy, nearly embedding a spoke in his temple.

He held the umbrella safely away from himself. 'I'm fine, really, though I don't know what I'm going to do with my hair.'

When he smiled like that, the cheeky bugger with his hair all wind-whipped, my heart did a little hop, skip, jump, and a backflip for good measure. That wasn't the thyroid.

'To what do I owe such a generous welcome?' he asked as we let ourselves into the offices.

'I have much to tell you and I don't want you nodding off.'

He held up David's latest creature – it looked like an iguana eating a mouse. 'At what point do we need to alert the authorities that my cousin may be a danger to neighbourhood pets?'

'I think that time has passed. As a family member, aren't you worried that one day you'll have ITV News camped in your front garden wanting to know if he was always a strange boy?'

'I'd like to think this is what keeps him sane. Anyway, what's happening that requires so much caffeine?'

'Last night we met to vote on me working a few more days for the club. And they ended up voting me out as president.'

I could see he was stunned. 'I didn't expect that. I thought you were going to go on about your love life.'

Ouch, that smarted. But why shouldn't he be utterly casual about the possibility? We were just friends after all.

'How can they do that? On what grounds?'

As I explained about Channel 4 and Pixie's views on our image, his expression darkened. 'You can't be removed because of your looks. It's illegal.'

'They're also not letting me work more on the dating side of the business. Same reason. That's not discriminating *against* me though. They're saying I'm too thin, not too fat. It's discriminating *for* me.' Even as I said it I knew it didn't sound right.

'Katie, they're discriminating based on your looks. It doesn't matter whether that's because you're too fat or too thin, too beautiful or because you'd scare small children. It must be illegal. You should talk to someone about this.'

I recoiled at the very idea. Sue my friends? No way. I couldn't bear the thought of Ellie and Jane being caught in the middle.

'I can't. If I sued anyone it would be Nutritious. I know Alex put me on the redundancy list when I don't have the worst employment record there. If they really did have to make cuts, there were others in the queue before me.'

'Why don't you let me call my brother? He's a solicitor and he's handled employment disputes before. I can call him right now. It doesn't hurt to talk to a professional.'

'I can't afford a solicitor. Made redundant, me, remember?' I was just making excuses. If I talked to a solicitor it would all become a bit too real.

'Katie, he's my brother. It won't cost anything just to talk to him. I'm calling now. Take the phone away if you don't want me to.'

I didn't move.

*   *   *

289

Rob's brother, Jeremy, was able to meet us on his lunch break so we hurried to Knightsbridge. I'd have known they were related even without the introductions. Jeremy too looked like he was about to tell you the best dirty joke ever – same friendly grin and lively eyes. He was a mere shadow of his little brother though, and I preferred Rob's burly frame to Jeremy's hardened one. Jeremy would be uncomfortable to fall asleep on, for one thing.

'I'm all yours till one, okay?' he said as we found a table at Pizza Express. 'It's so nice to finally meet you, Katie. Rob talks about you all the time.'

I smiled at Rob, who looked embarrassed.

'So I understand from Rob that you've had quite a lot of news this week, and you feel there might be a case for constructive dismissal.'

'Well, I don't know about that,' I said, blushing. I didn't like sounding so litigious. 'Rob just suggested I talk to you.' I wanted to set the record straight. This wasn't my idea.

'Okay. Can you tell me about your office job first? Then we can come on to the Curvy Girls Club.'

I really hadn't thought this through when Rob offered to call. Of course I'd have to tell him all about Alex. Which meant I'd have to tell Rob all about it again.

Rob seemed to realise the same thing. He set his menu down. 'Actually, I think I'd better leave you two alone to talk. Confidentiality and all that. I can grab something at the café next door. Katie, give me a call when you're done and we can take the Tube back together.' He rushed off before anyone could object.

Jeremy watched him go, shaking his head. 'I never know what's going on in his head.'

Join the club, I thought as I filled Jeremy in on the whole sordid situation. His sympathetic but professional countenance relaxed me. He probably learned that in law school.

Comforting Expressions 101. He took a lot of notes, occasionally interrupting to clarify points. 'Were you offered voluntary redundancy, or notified that it was an option for anyone?'

'Not officially,' I said, thinking of Smith's pillow talk with Racy Stacy. 'The first I heard of it was when they told me about my redundancy.'

He considered this for a moment. 'If they did offer it, but not to you, then combined with what you've told me about your relationship with the finance director, and your acceptable appraisals bar the last one, you may have a case for constructive dismissal. We'd need to find out whether any other employees had a worse appraisal record than you. Generally the way this works is that we notify the company that you've retained us as solicitors, and are exploring your legal options. If they know they've illegally dismissed you then that's often enough to make them reconsider. This isn't a clear-cut case but I think you've got reason to approach them anyway.' He stared at me and for a second I saw Rob's eyes. I had to ignore the tickle in my belly. Wrong man, Katie. 'What's your ideal outcome here? Do you want your job back? Or do you want compensation?'

I thought about his question. I'd liked Nutritious well enough when I'd worked there, but I had no burning desire to make supplements my career. It was different in the early days. Once I realised I could do it, I was proud of my work. I even spent valuable weekend brain power thinking of the best way to get ahead. But that desire waned when the Curvy Girls Club started up. *That* felt more like a calling.

'I'm not sure I want my job back. Alex is still there, which would be awkward. And all my colleagues know I've been made redundant. If I came back they'd all know management didn't want me there. I had another plan, which would have been perfect if it had worked out. If I could work at least three days a week for the club then I can pay my mortgage and have a little left over for the occasional Friday night takeaway.'

'You measure success in Friday night takeaways? I can see why you and Rob are such good friends.' He laughed Rob's laugh.

'But it's a moot point since Pixie brought up the issue of my weight and got the others to vote against me as president, so now I don't even get that little payment. I think Rob mentioned that on the phone.' He nodded. 'Then they agreed not to give me the extra days. Basically I'm stuffed unless I get another job within a month.'

At the thought, financial panic made it hard to breathe. I was happy to rehash the insults of the last week but unless this was leading somewhere, it was just another lunch I couldn't afford.

Jeremy sighed. 'Unfortunately there's no law against employment discrimination based on appearance. There are a few cases in the American courts and the law may change, but so far there's no movement here. However, unless there's a clear reason for removing you as president – for example if you haven't done your job properly – then you may have been unfairly dismissed. You should think about making a case.'

The thought of becoming one of those people who sued everyone sat uncomfortably on my conscience. *I'm writing to inform you that the party of the first part, Mr John Smith, will seek damages from you, the party of the second part, for the following incident. It has been established that on the fifth of the tenth of this year, you cut your granddaughter Jemima's carrots rather big, causing her some distress. The party of the first part, hereafter known as your son, seeks damages of . . .* It was all a bit icky to contemplate.

We finished our pizzas talking about more entertaining topics, like what a pain in the arse Rob was as a little brother.

'So? Will we see you on *Judge Judy*?' Rob asked as we made our way back to the Tube station. 'You could do worse than having my brother on your side. He can be a real barracuda. You should have seen him negotiating terms for our holidays with Dad when we were young – we stayed up past nine o'clock, had no chores and lots of pocket money.'

'Funny, those are exactly the terms I'd want at Nutritious . . . No, I don't think I'll go after them. My heart's not in it. It'd be nice to get some more money out of them but what if they offer to have me back? Then I'd have a job that I didn't really want, and a position at the club that I really want but don't have.'

'You're going after the girls then?'

'I don't want to think of it as going after them. It's nothing personal—'

'Said the SS Commander.'

'Rob, please don't make this any harder than it already is. Do you think I want to threaten to sue them? I hate the thought. These are my best friends. I'm going to try to talk to them first.'

He looked properly contrite. 'I'm sorry. I know this is hard for you, and the fact that it's completely unfair makes it even worse. I'm here for you, okay?'

'Thanks, that's nice to know . . . I'm glad we're friends again.'

'We were always friends, Katie.'

'Can I ask you something?' I asked, just as the Tube pulled into the station. I was about to be living proof that humans enjoyed kicking themselves when they were down. 'What really happened? I mean I know it doesn't matter now,' I rushed to assure him. 'I just wondered.'

The carriage was crowded with summer tourists. We squeezed in between the rows of seats where at least a feeble breeze played through the carriage. I took heart that the people jammed up against us were too excited about their recent visit to Harrods to pay any attention to our conversation.

Rob looked like he wasn't going to answer me. Then he said, 'You changed. When you started losing weight, you changed.'

I wasn't sure if that was better or worse than I expected. I thought he'd cite a personal habit or, god, *technique* that wasn't to his liking, something that happened on our date that put him off. Well of course I'd changed. I'd lost a quarter of my body weight.

'So you went off me because I lost weight? Are you saying you like chunky monkeys?'

'Why do you have to be rude about it?'

'Be rude about what?'

'Overweight people. See? That's what I mean. You get thin and all of a sudden everyone else is a chunky monkey. Chunky monkeys are people too, you know.'

'I can't take you seriously when you keep saying chunky monkey. You sound like a Ben & Jerry's advert.' I tried a smile. He didn't return it. 'You're serious? You think I'm prejudiced against fat people? Rob, I am a fat person. Maybe I've lost weight but my image of myself is in here.' I tapped my head.

He blew out his cheeks. 'There are women who constantly run down other women, and blacks who are prejudiced against other blacks. An overweight person can be prejudiced against others. We don't have the corner on morality you know . . . You've become vain, Katie. For the last few months you've done nothing but try to get me to give you compliments on your looks. I don't really care about your looks, you know. But you clearly do. Your constant jokes about fat people just got old.'

He was being oversensitive.

'This was never a problem before I started losing weight. Was it? You didn't mind my jokes when we were all in the same big fat boat.'

'See? There you go again with the jokes. I don't need to be reminded of my size all the time. Believe me, I'm aware of it.'

'How did this suddenly become about you? Rob, what's going on inside your head? Because this isn't about me being vain or making jokes, is it?'

'It is, Katie. That's exactly what it's about. You talk about people as if they're only the outer shell of skin and bones and fat that you can see. You even do it to yourself when you call yourself Fat Katie. We're more than just what you see. I always thought you knew that. I was sad to be proven wrong, that's all.'

I felt my throat constrict. So that's what he thought of me.

'Rob, I'm sorry that I've come across that way. Maybe I got caught up in the weight loss, but I am exactly the same person underneath. And you, you are so much more than meets the eye. I've always known that. That's why we're friends.'

He scoffed. 'Friends. Thanks for being my *friend*. Nice to know that when it came to more than that, you went for Alex with the six-pack abs.'

He was right in a way. But mostly he was very wrong.

'Rob, you know I'd had a crush on Alex for six years. Yes, I was flattered when he started paying attention to me. I'm sorry about that, but first of all you'd already made it clear that there wouldn't be another date. If you think I only went for him because of his body, or that I didn't want to go out with you because of yours, then you don't know me as well as I thought you did.' I shook with anger at being misjudged. Again.

'How could I get involved with you knowing I wasn't what you wanted? Thank you, but I had that with my ex.'

'Do you think I wanted you to be different? Thinner?' I asked quietly. 'Christ, you're an idiot! Rob, I don't know how many ways I can tell you that I like you exactly the way you are. You're one of my best friends. You're smart and funny. I think you're gorgeous and our date was one of the best I've ever had. But then you had to go and ruin everything by ignoring me.'

'I didn't ignore you.'

'But you didn't say anything about going out again. You put us right back into the friend zone. This was your doing, Rob, not mine. Why would you do that?'

He didn't answer right away.

'Do you remember you texted me after our date? Remember what you said? Here, I'll read it to you.' He pulled his phone from his pocket. '"I've lost 23lbs, woo hoo! Could be the start of a whole new me – roll on Thin Katie!" How was I supposed to answer that? "Gee, thanks for telling me about your weight, Katie. By the way, I had the most incredible night. I'm just sorry you didn't think to mention it?"'

Hadn't I mentioned it? I'd certainly thought it. Why hadn't I just texted what I really wanted to say?

'That's it? Because of that text you didn't want to see me again?'

'No. Even on our date there were warning signs, when you were talking about Fat Friends being bad for your image. Suddenly it was all about your image.'

'Not too many warning signs to kiss me, I noticed.'

'I liked you, Katie, a lot. But then every time I saw you

296

after that, you just fished for compliments. That's what I mean. You changed.'

'Believe me, the one thing I've learned in the past few weeks is how little looks really matter in the scheme of things. Everyone seems to be telling me otherwise, but I know it's not true. It's in there.' I thumped him, perhaps a little too hard, in the chest. 'In there is what counts. Of course, by the time I realised it, it was too late. You'd already had your romantic date at that restaurant in Clapham.'

He thought for a moment. 'I went with my colleague. He lives around the corner and wanted to try it. God, maybe that makes me gay. D'you think?'

'Shut up.' We stared at each other. 'So what happens now that I know you weren't purposely cruel, or gay, and you know that my vanity was a temporary madness?'

He stared at the Tube map over my shoulder. Finally he said, 'I'm sorry if I misjudged you. Can we please start over?' he asked. 'I mean go back to where we were before we went out. I'd be happy with that.'

I nodded, feeling the disappointment wash over me. I may no longer be shallow and prejudiced in his eyes, but I wasn't someone he wanted to go out with either. Sad Katie.

CHAPTER THIRTY-SEVEN

I thought a lot about my friends after meeting with Rob's brother. That probably spiked the share price of Kleenex.

Dozens of scenes played like extra-soppy Saturday afternoon romcoms – in soft-focus and untrue to reality. By the end of the week my mind had Pixie and me running across poppy-strewn fields to embrace against a vivid sunset.

In actual fact Pixie didn't run and grass gave me hay fever. We were more likely to hug over crème slices at Patisserie Valerie. That's the problem with memories when you're hurting over somebody. They're completely untrustworthy.

And I was hurting, as much as if she'd broken up with me. Which, in a way, she had. It wasn't a clean break though, since we were still technically friends and the Curvy Girls Club co-founders, which was about as comfortable as sleeping in the spare room in the marital home for the sake of the children.

Being realistic, Pixie and I were unlikely to recover from this. I'd have to be a magnanimous person on the scale of the Dalai Lama. That wasn't likely. I still resented being passed over for the netball team in sixth form.

That was my problem. In one ear, resentment told me not

to bother talking to her again except through solicitors. In the other, love whispered that we had a history together. I couldn't discard that without at least trying to make her see sense. So I called another meeting, wondering if it would be my last.

Ellie still felt like she'd given me the kiss of Judas. I could have won her over at home in the week running up to the meeting, but it was unfair to do that just because we shared a bathroom. In the same way, she didn't ask me why I'd called the meeting. What happened in meetings stayed in meetings. I promised her that I wasn't holding a grudge because of her vote, and I meant it. She and Jane were caught between two bull-headed women.

Besides, she had enough to worry about. Having thrown herself on the naked grenade for the sake of the club, it didn't take long for her to realise that she was, in fact, going to have to bare her body to the nation. Jane called Rea at Channel 4 and arranged for them to meet our new representative. Of course they loved her, and the programme would go ahead as scheduled. Taping began in two weeks and we should have a flood of new members when it aired next month.

So no matter how things ended for me, the future of the Curvy Girls Club was bright. We'd get the new clients we needed to pay for expansion. That, at least, made me feel better. That, and the fact that it wasn't going to be my arse on the billboard.

I didn't bother to make any snacks for the meeting. No one expected you to cater for your own funeral. Jeremy had briefed me on how best to tell my friends I'd see them in court, but I doubted I'd use his notes. He didn't know them like I hoped I did.

A wave of nostalgia overcame me when I let myself into the darkened offices. Pete the bear looked sympathetic, if a bit more mangy than usual. The summer's heat hadn't agreed with him. There was no sign of David's latest efforts. Either he'd run out of roadkill or he'd been on holiday, maybe snorkelling in the Med. I'd never seen him stuff a fish. I'd have to get Rob to remind him that he had an entire class of animal yet to mould into unsettling tableaus.

Ellie and Jane came in together. They stopped talking when they saw me.

'Hello, sweetheart,' said Jane.

'You were talking about me,' I said. 'That's okay, carry on.'

'We were only saying we hoped tonight would be more comfortable than last time,' Ellie said. 'You haven't told us why you've called the meeting.'

Pixie came in behind them, out of breath and red in the face. 'I'm not late, am I? I got caught up talking to Trevor.' She rolled her eyes.

On the one hand I was grateful for the air of normality. But really, she could have been a *little* uncomfortable about ousting me.

'We can get started if that's okay.' I sat in Rob's chair and the others settled around me. 'So, you're wondering why I called you all here . . .'

Poor attempt at a joke. Nobody got it.

'Erm, well, I wanted to talk to you about your decision to remove me as president.' My statement hung there like a whiffy fart.

'Is there anything left to say?' asked Pixie, crossing her arms.

I nodded. 'I want you all to recall a few things. Pixie, do you remember that time we went to Stratford-upon-Avon and the rude little boy next to us asked his mum why you were so fat? Or telling me that you always get cakes for takeaway so nobody sees you eat them?'

'That reminds me,' Pixie said. 'Nearly forgot about this.'

She pulled a squashed chocolate muffin from her handbag. 'We can share.'

'And Jane,' I continued as Pixie enjoyed her illicit muffin safely amongst friends. 'You felt like your colleagues were talking behind your back when you gained weight. Remember?' She winced, giving me a stab of guilt for bringing it up, even for good reason.

'Ellie?'

'Oh, you don't need to remind me of how many times I've felt like shite because of my weight.' She laughed nervously. 'I've got them all catalogued up here.' She tapped her temple.

I shrugged. 'So why is it okay for you to single me out because of my weight when it's not okay for others to do it to you?'

'That's different, Katie, and you know it,' Pixie said. 'We're stigmatised for being overweight. As were you before your thyroid gave you the helping hand. We're prejudiced against and made to feel like crap about ourselves. I'm sorry that you feel bad about being thin but excuse me if I don't cry tears for you. *Don't hate me because I'm so beautiful,*' she mocked.

'Pixie, can't you see that it's the same thing? You're saying I can't do my job as president or work more on the dating business because I don't look like everybody else around here. I'm sorry but that's just as wrong as a thin person doing it to you.'

I looked at each of them, challenging them to argue.

'It does feel like this is different though, Katie,' Jane murmured. 'You're one of the normal ones now. It's like men complaining that they're being reverse-discriminated against when companies look to put more women on their boards. When you've got all the advantages it seems a bit, I don't know, unreasonable to complain.'

'Thanks, Jane,' said Pixie. 'That's exactly what I meant.'

I shook my head in frustration. I didn't want to hit the nuclear button and tell them what Jeremy said about unfair dismissal. A scorched earth policy definitely had to be the last resort.

'And frankly I'm surprised that you'd even want to stay here,' Pixie continued. 'It's not like you need us any more. Face it, Katie, you've outgrown us. Excuse the backwards pun. Jane is right. You're in the regular world now.'

I couldn't keep the tears of lost friendship from leaking out. Within seconds I was a snivelling mess.

'Pixie, you don't get to decide where I fit in the world. I do. I've got news for you. You throw words like normal around, but I'm not the normal one. You are. You and Jane and Ellie and the other sixty per cent of the population that's overweight. Where I fit is decided by what's in here.' I pointed to my heart. 'Not what's out here. I cannot believe you're being so obtuse. You're doing to me exactly what's been done to us all our lives. But because you're not the one being made to feel like shite, the one being excluded and rejected by every one of your best friends, it's okay. That's no way to treat a person. Fat or thin, prejudice is prejudice. And it's wrong. Justify it any way you like but it will always be wrong.' I hiccupped. 'And another thing. This isn't a business, Pixie, where we have to make hard-headed decisions like some maniacal Sir Alan Sugar. This is us, together because we love each other and wanted to be together. It's grown into the club, but that's not the point of it. We're here to support each other, as friends first. So to turn on me now, after everything I've done for you over the years, isn't being a good businesswoman. It's called being a bad friend.'

'We have to think of what's right for the club,' she said.

'Pixie, listen to yourself!' Ellie said. 'We are here because we're friends. Our size is incidental to that.'

Pixie narrowed her eyes. 'So you're going to be emotional

302

about this too? Well, I'm sorry about that.' Pixie said. 'Jane? Surely you can see that we have to think about the future of the club?'

'I do see that,' she said. 'But I also see that Katie is our best friend. There has to be room for both here.'

'This is unbelievable! You're acting like I've got some vendetta against Katie. Can't you see what an opportunity we have here? You've all agreed that I'm the best person to grow Fat Friends, remember? And I'm committed to doing that. She doesn't want the dating business. She would have held us back. It's nothing personal.'

She might as well have waved a red rag at a bull with that phrase. *It's nothing personal.* How many times had I heard that in my life? Well, it bloody was personal.

'As long as we're not being personal, Pixie, then I've got a proposal to make myself. I don't think you fit the ethos of the Curvy Girls Club. You've proven yourself unwilling to give the support that this club was founded on. You're putting profit before friendship. That's not what we're about. So yes, maybe you're technically the best person to run the dating business, but the fact is, I don't want this club to be about business. I want it to be about friendship. I want us to remember why we started it, and I want it to be a place where everyone is welcome, because we're not just a microcosm of the bigger world. We're a refuge from it. It's not about business, Pixie. It is about emotion and friendship. At least that's what I want it to be.'

I was shaking as I stared at them. Those seconds seemed to stretch to years. My friends were slipping away. And my job, the club, Rob, all gone. I had no idea where I fit in the world any more, but I knew where I no longer fit. In the space of six months I'd lost fifty pounds and everything that was important to me. Some weight loss plan.

'I propose a vote,' said Ellie. 'Our ethos should be made

official, since it's the whole basis of the club. We need to agree on that. Personally, I don't want to put business over friendship either, or profit over support. That's what the world out there is like. It doesn't have to be the one in here.'

'I agree,' said Jane.

'Me too,' I said.

'Pixie?'

'So you're going to let your emotions cloud your judgement?' she said.

'I'm going to let my friendship guide my judgement,' Jane said. 'Because that's what will make me happy. So, friendship and support over business and profit. All in favour?'

Three hands went in the air.

'Passed,' said Ellie. She stepped forward and put her arms around me. 'I'm so sorry I've made you feel bad,' she said. 'I didn't mean to. When I voted against you as president it had nothing to do with our friendship. You'll always be my best friend. Even if you got thinner than Kate Moss while eating ice cream every day I'd still love you.'

I never really doubted her friendship, but it was nice to hear her assurances anyway.

Then Jane spoke up. 'I owe you an apology too, sweetheart. I was wrong to vote you out of the presidency because you're thin. You're right, it's still discrimination and it's no better than the people who sneer at us for being fat. Can you forgive me?'

I nodded, not trusting my voice. I noticed that Pixie stood apart from us now. It had been coming for weeks, but I was sad to see it happening.

'Well, given the circumstances I have a proposal too,' she said. 'The club shouldn't continue with the dating business. Clearly your hearts aren't in it if you're willing to turn your backs on such an opportunity when you could grow it here and expand to other cities.'

'Why would we want to do that?'

'You may not want to, but I do.' She took a deep breath. 'I was going to tell you tonight anyway. I'm taking the children to Manchester. I've been thinking about it since I left Trevor. I'm not going back to him. I know that for sure, and he does too now. I told him just now, before coming here. I'll need to make a new life for myself, and London is just too expensive. I've talked to my parents and they want me and the children up there with them. They've got the extra bedroom. It'll be a bit crowded, but they can look after the children while I work, and that'll bring in money to help them and support us too. It's what's best for the children. And now, given what's happened here, I think it's right for me too.'

Now Pixie's intransigence about the dating business and her moves to keep me from blocking her made sense. Her self-preservation was selfish, yes, and hurtful in the way she went about it, but somehow a bit more understandable than plain old mean-spiritedness. Pixie wasn't only being a bad friend. She was doing everything she felt she had to do to be a good mother.

'So I'm going to have to quit the club. But I want to take the dating business to Manchester. You don't really want it anyway, and I think I can make it a success. I want the chance to try. If you'll let me.'

'Pixie, despite these last few weeks,' Jane said, 'I'll be sad to see you go.'

I was surprised to feel the same way. I knew we'd never get our old friendship back, but I did want her to be okay.

'You know my feelings about the dating business,' I said. 'I don't want it, so you're welcome to it as far as I'm concerned. All in favour?'

Four hands went up.

'I still don't want it to be called Fat Friends though, whether the club is involved or not,' I said.

'Well, I've been thinking about that,' said Pixie. 'And you're right.'

'I'm what?' I said. 'Can you say that again please?'

'You're right, Katie. So what do you think of the Big Beautiful Dating Club instead?'

'The Big Beautiful . . . I like it! In fact I love it! The Big Beautiful Dating Club. It has a nice healthy ring to it, don't you think?'

'Finally we agree on something,' she said, smiling as her eyes locked with mine. I took a deep breath, and smiled back. She didn't apologise. That wouldn't be her style. But we understood each other a little better, and that was something at least.

CHAPTER THIRTY-EIGHT

Two weeks later, Ellie and I got to the studios early for the programme filming. With so much excitement (me) and nervousness (her), neither of us had any chance of a lie-in anyway.

The whole crew was friendly and I even found myself warming to the botany twins when I saw how much care and attention they took over Ellie's wardrobe. Mary Weather gave her a flawless complexion and the photographer spent most of the morning joking with her to get her comfortable with her national television debut. Gok was a consummate professional and within minutes of meeting we were dying to be his best friend. I caught Ellie pocketing one of the makeup sponges he'd used for her box frame celebrity collection and it all started to seem like a bit of a laugh.

But then, as Ellie stood under the lights with the camera clicking away, I saw the look of fear in her eyes when Rea asked her to take off the robe. Guilt punched me in the gut. It should have been me standing there terrified, not her.

'It's all right, Ellie, you are beautiful,' I said from beside the photographer. She looked uncertain, her limbs stiff and unmoving. Then she took a deep breath, shrugged and let the robe drop to the floor. She stood there in her bra and pants for the photographer, and his camera caught the grin that lit up her face. I wouldn't have missed that for the world.

When she was clothed again, I asked her how she felt.

She thought for a moment. 'Like I've grown a few inches taller,' she said. 'I feel bigger, in the best possible way.'

During the lunch break we hurried over to the studio next door to see how Jane was doing. Fabulicious Tim had given her a long bob that framed her lovely face. It reminded me of a photo on her side table, of her at the beach on her honeymoon. Her smile was the same, happy and confident.

'Are you sad that you're not involved?' she asked as we chose our sandwiches and drinks from the catering table.

'A little bit,' I said. 'You look like you're having so much fun.'

'I'm surprised, but I am,' she said. 'I really am. All the therapy is helping. It's pretty intensive, three times a week, but I knew it wouldn't be easy to break a decade-long habit of feeling crappy. My therapist has me talking to myself in the mirror every morning like a lunatic, telling my reflection all the things I like about myself.'

'Is it working?' I asked.

She nodded. 'Whenever I think about my size I counter it with something positive about me. Between the counselling, Andy and being with everyone at the club, it really is working. I can hardly believe it, but it is. I'm actually getting happy.' She looked stunned at this admission.

Ellie squeezed her arm. 'That's wonderful!'

'Finally you're seeing what we've seen all along,' I said. 'You're beautiful.'

She smiled. 'Thanks, sweetheart. And I've been thinking about going back into presenting.'

'Oh, Jane, that's great!' I said.

'I know. Just making the decision feels pretty great. And actually, I've been talking to Rea about it. She thinks there are a couple of programmes that might suit me. I'm sure they won't be big segments but that's okay with me. It's been a long time since I was in front of a camera. Until today.'

My phone buzzed with a text. *How's it going?* Pixie wanted to know. *Probably more fun than emptying boxes, but then I'm doing it with my clothes on, which is more than you lot can say. Have fun! Call me tonight. xo*

I showed it to my friends. 'It was the right thing,' I said, thinking both of Pixie's move and her exit from the club. 'But we do owe her a lot. All this started because of her, when she quit Slimming Zone.'

'And it'll continue because of us and our members,' Ellie said. 'Cheers to the Curvy Girls Club.'

'And to our futures,' Jane added.

We raised our glasses to that.

Rob was waiting outside when we left the studios.

'Hi, Rob,' Ellie said. 'We'll see you later, Katie, okay?'

'But I thought we were having dinner now?'

'Uh, nah, I'm not really hungry.'

'Me neither,' said Jane. 'I couldn't eat a bite after that lunch.'

Rob smiled as my friends walked off together. 'Hi. How'd it go?'

'What are you doing here?' He still texted me the weekly website stats, but hadn't been to any of the events. I tried not to mind, but of course I did. As much as I'd willed my feelings to return to the comfortable platonic relationship we started out with, they just weren't budging.

'Jane told me you were here. I hope you don't mind. Katie, I need to apologise for being such an arse. You were right about what you said on the Tube. I've been unfair, pushing my own issues on you. That makes me the self-centred one, not you. You did get a little wrapped up in your new figure but I'd probably do the same thing in your shoes. I don't know what it's like to lose fifty pounds.'

'Not nearly as good as you'd probably imagine.'

'Well, thin or fat, you're still you. And I like you, very much.' He took my hand in his. 'I'd like to start over please, if we can. But from after our date, where we should have left off.'

I thought about that. Then I shook my head. 'That won't work for me. I'm sorry.' I hated to do it to him but it was time to be true to myself. I was tired of half-measures and compromises. I didn't want to start from our date, because that held all the baggage from before. Alex, Rob's ex-girlfriend, his feelings . . . mine.

His face fell. 'I'm sorry. But I guess I can understand why.'

'Hmm. Maybe not.' I dropped his hand. Then I took it again in a firm handshake. 'Hi. I'm Katie. Not Fat Katie. Not Thin Katie. Just Katie. It's very nice to meet you.' I smiled, hoping he'd return the sentiment. But whether he did or not, I knew that finally, after everything, we were friends again.

As I held his gaze, willing him to understand, I realised that it was our own misconceptions that had so easily snuffed out our relationship. If we were going to be more than friends, we'd have to start fresh, to see each other as we really were, clearly and without prejudice, not reflected in other people's expectations.

Rob grasped my hand. 'It's nice to meet you, Katie. I'm Rob. But not just Rob. Hung-like-a-donkey Rob. Would you like to have dinner with me? I know a very romantic restaurant in Clapham.'

[THE END]

310

Every time you write a review, an author gets a cupcake, so if you enjoyed *The Curvy Girls Club*, please take a minute to share your thoughts on your favourite Book websites.

The *real* Curvy Girls Club

You can also be part of the real Curvy Girls Club – a friendly, supportive community where everyone is welcome, a fun place for people who want to love themselves. Think of it as the most flattering fitting room in the world – perfect lighting and mirrors that make you feel fantastic.

Club members are treated to a daily dose of loveliness – empowering reminders that you're pretty great just the way you are. Chat with one another, get involved in the book club and, once there are enough members, check out the real life social events. We've all got one thing in common: We want to live in a world where everyone is welcome no matter where they tip the scales.

Join the club, the Facebook group, or say hi
on Twitter or Pinterest
www.thecurvygirlsclub.blogspot.co.uk

The Curvy Girls Club
Book Club Questions

1. The message of the book is about being happy in your own skin – no matter what that skin may look like. It's something that Katie talks about near the beginning of the book, yet when the TV presenter makes fun of a skinny intern, Katie laughs. Is teasing a woman for being too thin the same as teasing a woman for being too fat? Do you feel more empathy for one group than the other?

2. Which character did you most identify with? Why?

3. Once you understand Pixie's motives, is she justified in her actions involving the club and Katie? Do her arguments stand up from a business point of view (as opposed to an emotional one)?

4. Thinking about Jane's obsession with weight loss, how far is too far when it comes to losing weight? Where do you draw the line?

5. Who do you think was the stronger character, Katie or Pixie?

6. Ellie snoops on her boyfriend's phone and finds something she doesn't like. Have you ever snooped where you shouldn't have? Do the ends justify the means?

7. Katie experiences prejudice from her employers. Are there any situations in which an employer is justified in wanting a person to look a certain way (let's exclude modelling)?

8. Katie, Pixie, Jane and Ellie all struggle with self-esteem in different ways. What's the biggest thing that gives a woman her self-esteem? How can someone improve her own self-esteem?

9. What were your first impressions of the main characters? Did those change by the end of the book?

10. Would you go on How to Look Good Naked?